# 12

# MYSTERY
STORIES

JACK ADRIAN is a leading authority on all aspects of popular fiction of the late nineteenth and twentieth centuries. He has edited numerous single-author collections by writers as diverse as E. F. Benson, Edgar Wallace, and Rafael Sabatini. His general anthologies include two collections of short stories from *The Strand Magazine* (*Detective Stories* and *Strange Tales*, both 1991), as well as *The Oxford Book of Historical Stories* (with Michael Cox, 1994), *Hard-Boiled: An Anthology of American Crime Stories* (with Bill Pronzini, 1995), and *Twelve Tales of Murder* (1998).

## Oxford Twelves

*Twelve Mystery Stories*
JACK ADRIAN

*Twelve Tales of Murder*
JACK ADRIAN

*Twelve Tales of the Supernatural*
MICHAEL COX

*Twelve Victorian Ghost Stories*
MICHAEL COX

*Twelve Irish Ghost Stories*
PATRICIA CRAIG

*Twelve American Crime Stories*
ROSEMARY HERBERT

*Twelve American Detective Stories*
EDWARD D. HOCH

*Twelve Women Detective Stories*
LAURA MARCUS

## Forthcoming:

*Twelve English Detective Stories*
MICHAEL COX

*Twelve Gothic Tales*
RICHARD DALBY

# 12
# MYSTERY
# STORIES

*Selected and introduced by*

JACK ADRIAN

Oxford   New York

OXFORD UNIVERSITY PRESS

1998

Oxford University Press, Great Clarendon Street, Oxford OX2 6DP

Oxford New York
Athens Auckland Bangkok Bogota Bombay
Buenos Aires Calcutta Cape Town Dar es Salaam
Delhi Florence Hong Kong Istanbul Karachi
Kuala Lumpur Madras Madrid Melbourne
Mexico City Nairobi Paris Singapore
Taipei Tokyo Toronto Warsaw

and associated companies in
Berlin Ibadan

Oxford is a trade mark of Oxford University Press

Introduction, selection, and notes © Jack Adrian 1998
First published as an Oxford University Press paperback 1998.

British Library Cataloguing in Publication Data

Data available

Library of Congress Cataloging in Publication Data
12 Mystery stories/selected and introduced by Jack Adrian.
Contents: A night in an old castle/G. P. R. James—Sir Dominick's bargain/
J. Sheridan le Fanu—The Knightsbridge mystery/Charles Reade—Paul Vargas/
Hugh Conway—Gerald/Stanley J. Weyman—My first patient/Mabel E. Wotton—
A fatal affinity/Roy Horniman and C. E. Morland—The story of the man with the watches/
Arthur Conan Doyle—The third figure/Frank Aubrey—The yellow box/J. B. Harris-Burland—
The man with the ebony crutches/Ward Muir—The horror of the automaton/Guy Thorne.
1. Detective and mystery stories, English.   I. Adrian, Jack.
PR1309.D4A14 1998     823'.087208—dc21     97–42975
ISBN 0–19–288074–8 (pbk.)

1 3 5 7 9 10 8 6 4 2

Typeset by Jayvee, Trivandrum, India
Printed in Great Britain by
Cox & Wyman
Reading, England

# ACKNOWLEDGEMENTS

In the preparation of this volume of stories, I am (as ever) grateful for the help given and the interest shown by the following friends and colleagues: Bob Adey, Mike Ashley, Richard Dalby, Owen Dudley Edwards, Professor Douglas Greene, and John C. Moran, as well as the staff of the Bodleian Library, Oxford (in particular Richard Bell, Head of Reader Services, Christine Mason, Jackie Dean, Rosemary McCarthy, and John Slatter of the Nuneham Courtney out-station).

# CONTENTS

*Acknowledgements* v

*Introduction* ix

## 1
G. P. R. JAMES (1799–1860)
*A Night in an Old Castle* (1843)
1

## 2
J. SHERIDAN LE FANU (1814–73)
*Sir Dominick's Bargain* (1872)
16

## 3
CHARLES READE (1814–84)
*The Knightsbridge Mystery* (1884)
31

## 4
HUGH CONWAY (1847–85)
*Paul Vargas: A Mystery* (1884)
68

## 5
STANLEY J. WEYMAN (1855–1928)
*Gerald* (1887)
90

# Contents

**6**

MABEL E. WOTTON (*fl.* 1855–1912)
*My First Patient* (1890)
105

**7**

ROY HORNIMAN (1874–1930) and C. E. MORLAND (*fl.* 1890–1905)
*A Fatal Affinity* (1894)
116

**8**

ARTHUR CONAN DOYLE (1859–1930)
*The Story of the Man with the Watches* (1898)
142

**9**

FRANK AUBREY (1840–1927)
*The Third Figure* (1899)
158

**10**

J. B. HARRIS-BURLAND (1870–1926)
*The Yellow Box* (1899)
171

**11**

WARD MUIR (1878–1927)
*The Man with the Ebony Crutches* (1908)
190

**12**

GUY THORNE (1876–1923)
*The Horror of the Automaton* (1913)
211

*Biographical Notes and Sources*   225

*Source Acknowledgements*   233

# INTRODUCTION

The mystery story, in this collection of tales, is by no means the mystery story of the 1920s and 1930s. During that so-called 'Golden Age' of crime fiction (and despite the vigorous efforts of Dorothy L. Sayers, G. K. Chesterton, and the rest of their Detection Club cohorts to highlight pure ratiocination at the expense of brute force) 'mystery' and 'detection' were almost invariably conjoined, Siamese twin-like, and the phrase 'mystery and detection' itself was more often than not short-hand for tramp-steamers, say, hooting mournfully on a fog-enshrouded Thames somewhere below Wapping Old Stairs, the sound not quite concealing the muffled cries of the heroine, bound and partially gagged, in the bilges; or cowled figures sporting long-barrelled Browning .45 automatics and lurking in the dripping shrubberies of Byzantinely passagewayed country houses; or Chicago gunmen transported from the suburbs of Cicero to Piccadilly Circus. And naturally there was an inexhaustible supply of more or less eccentric sleuths (far more action-than deduction-oriented) to cope with all of the above and any of the other preposterous paraphernalia of the inter-war mystery thriller.

Here is quite different paraphernalia. Here is a world that is smokier, foggier, less effulgent. An umbrous world where electricity has not yet banished the candle, where flame gutters uneasily in the hint of a draught, where gaslight rises and sinks, inexplicably. A world of choking black bombazine, of taffeta and old lace, of thick, hooped skirts sweeping the floorboards in the empty room above. A world where sounds seem altogether crisper: the creak of leather in a black barouche, the trumpet of a terrified horse, the cries of the carters and the echoing crack of whips, the crunching grind of iron on straw, where the dead lie. A world where much of what is seen is seen in the sharpest relief, life is lived at the fullest pelt, and emotions are for the most part explicit, unequivocal, not to be misunderstood.

To be sure, strong emotions have always been the stock-in-trade of the concocter of popular fictions, whether from the 1840s or the 1990s. In the late-nineteenth-century mystery story, however, they can be experienced at their rawest. Writ large, as it were, within the fabric of each tale are generous helpings of (not necessarily in this order, and only very rarely all at once) shock, bafflement, exhilaration, rapture, rage, frenzy, despair, hopelessness, horror, terror, hate.

In this sense in particular the tale of mystery is closely allied to the tale of sensation—a phenomenon of the 1860s, yet one whose influence stretches into the twentieth-century and, ceaselessly revised, renewed and updated, doubtless well beyond. Both genres depend heavily upon raw emotion, quivering passions, a turmoil of the senses. Both, to a greater or lesser degree, deal in melodrama—'fiction with biceps' as the novelist Charles Reade once remarked. Both (and especially the tale of mystery) rely on the narrative structures of the Irish Gothicist Sheridan Le Fanu and the American fantasist Edgar Allan Poe, with more than a hint of Dickens for good measure, as well as the intricate plotting techniques of Wilkie Collins (very useful as a basis for making sense of labyrinthine familial connections often revealed in the final chapters).

Where the mystery story begins to edge away from pure sensation—away from fictionalizing a scandal of the day (chimney-sweep children, magdalenes thronging city centres, lunatic asylum abuses) and using it as a platform upon which to thump the tub—is in the sense of mood or atmosphere certain writers were able effectively to summon up during the course of their narratives.

Sensation writers, too, made use of 'atmosphere' (emotional, physical, climatic), but the best—or worst—tended to deploy it immoderately; indeed, extravagantly: piling it on and cramming it in. Especially emotional atmosphere (although the average sensation writer was never so happy as when he or she was busy reworking the first chapter of *Bleak House*).

Few writers of the popular nineteenth-century mystery tale were subtle in their general approach to the task (but then no one could accuse Poe or Le Fanu, at their most culminatory, of being that—though both could be if the need arose, and the exigencies of the plot demanded it). But the best are able to practise a certain restraint at times when restraint and not intemperance is required. Even, as here, such literary rip-roarers as G. P. R. James and Charles Reade.

'Mystery' in this collection takes in far more than its twentieth-century equivalent. Most of the stories have some extra ingredient, however slight, however mild, that lifts them out of the general run. And many are remarkably modern in both mood and tone.

In Conan Doyle's 'The Man with the Watches' (in which, it is argued by experts, Holmes makes an anonymous appearance) the puzzle is relatively simple; here the 'extra ingredient' is a secondary, perhaps rather more baffling, conundrum: did Doyle unconsciously draw, or deliberately set out to describe (and the 'Mary Jane' taunt here is highly suggestive), a homosexual relationship at the story's heart? Charles Reade's 'The Knightsbridge Mystery' features a clever piece of plotting (a disguise) as well as an authentic end-of-penultimate-chapter shock in the modern manner. Ward Muir's 'The Man with the Ebony Crutches', too, contains a by no means telegraphed surprise. Stanley Weyman's 'Gerald' is a fine example of the inexplicable situation which in the end (though engineered a touch, and dependent upon the old 'look-alike' dodge) makes perfect sense.

In one or two instances madness is the rationale behind ghastly events and baffling circumstances. The Victorian mystery writer was fond of madness since, paradoxically, it explained, or at any rate made some kind of sense out of, a generally disordered universe. The super-natural plays its part—obviously in Le Fanu's 'Sir Dominick's Bargain', Frank Aubrey's 'The Third Figure', and Guy Thorne's 'The Horror of the Automaton'; less obviously in Hugh Conway's relent-lessly mysterious 'Paul Vargas' and Roy Horniman's and C. E. Morland's 'A Fatal Affinity', both of which feature another favourite Victorian plot obsession: the psychic link.

There are (even for the compiler) a few real surprises. G. P. R. James's 'A Night in an Old Castle' (written around 150 years ago, when fustian was the norm in the language of popular fiction) is fresh and alive and immensely readable. Mabel Wotton's 'My First Patient' glides effortlessly up to a stunning shock, then goes even further, cli-maxing with a scene of madness and horror. 'The Yellow Box' by John Harris-Burland (an erstwhile Newdigate Prizewinner who eschewed high art for low literature) is the perfect fusion of sensation and mys-tery: is the story of the ravings of a madman, the grotesque fancy of an unhinged mind—or can it be the sober narrative of one beset by an abhuman agency intent upon his destruction?

## Introduction

The range of stories here is deliberately wide, the span above 70 years. Yet all would be recognized by the founding fathers of the 'tale of mystery' Poe and Le Fanu, Dickens and Collins, since all feature to a greater or lesser extent the best and most enticing elements of the genre—madness and revenge, terror and obsession, the grotesque and the arabesque, dark and tantalizing secrets; above all, a lurking sense of unease.

JACK ADRIAN
*August 1997*

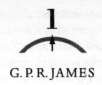

## 1

### G. P. R. JAMES

# A Night in an Old Castle

It was one of the most awful nights I ever remember having seen. We had set out from St Goar in a carriage which we hired at Cologne, drawn by two black horses, which proved as stubborn and strange a pair of brutes as man could undertake to drive.

Not that I undertook it, for I wanted to see the Rhine from the land route, and not to weary my arms and occupy my attention with an unprofitable pair of dirty reins; but my friend, Mr Lawrence, was rather fond of pulling at horses' mouths and he preferred driving himself, and me too, to being troubled—bored he called it—with a coachman. The landlord of the 'Adler' knew me well, and had no fear of trusting his horses with me, though, to say sooth, I had some fear of trusting myself with them.

I got in, however, beside my friend, and away we went. As far as Bonn all was well enough; but there the horses insisted upon stopping to eat. Lawrence tried to persuade them it would be better to go on; but it was of no use: they had been accustomed to stop at the Star, and stop they would. We made the best of it, fed the horses, and got some dinner ourselves, and then we set out again.

Thus we were at length going along the high and proper road, at a speed dangerous to market men and women, and to our own necks; but even that at length was quieted down, and our further journey only suffered interruption from an occasional dart which both the horses would make at any diverging road that led away from the river, as if they had a presentiment that their course up the stream would lead to something strange and horrible.

About three o'clock we saw a large heavy cloud begin to rise before us, overtopping the mountains, overshadowing the Rhine. It was only in hue that it bore the look of a thundercloud. It had no knobs, or pillars, or writhing twists about it; but it was inky black, and kept advancing like a wall of marble, dark as night at the lower part, and leaden-grey at the superior edge.

A light wind at length fluttered in our faces, hot and unrefreshing, like the breath of fever.

'Put up the hood!' said Lawrence, 'we are going to have it!'

Hardly had he spoken when a bright flash burst from the cloud, and I could see a serpent-like line of fire dart across the Rhine. Then came a clap of thunder which I thought would bring the rocks and mountains on our heads.

There were two or three more such flashes, and two or three other roars, and then the giant began to weep. Down came the rain like fury: it seemed as if we had got into the middle of a waterspout; and the sky, too, grew so dark that an unnatural shadow filled the whole valley of the Rhine, lately so bright and smiling.

At length, to complete our discomforts, night fell; and one so black and murky I have never seen. It was in vain whipping; neither horse would go the least out of his determined pace; and, besides, the whip had become so soaked and limp that it was of little service, moving as unwillingly as the brutes themselves, and curling itself up into a thousand knots.

I got as far back in the carriage as I could, and said nothing. As for my companion he seemed at his wits' end, and I could hear muttered curses which might have well been spared, but which I was in no mood to reprove.

At length he said, 'This will never do! I cannot see a step before me. We shall meet with some accident. Let us get into the first place of shelter we can find. Any cottage, any roadside public-house or beer-house, is better than this.'

'I do not think you will find anything of the kind,' I answered gloomily; 'if you do, I can be contented with any place to get out of this pelting—a cave in the rock if nothing better.'

He drove on nearly at a walk for about two miles further, and then suddenly pulled up. I could hardly see anything but a great black point of rock sticking out, as it seemed to me, right across the road. But

Lawrence declared that he perceived a shed under the rock, and a building on the top of it, and asked me to get out and reconnoitre.

I was as glad to catch at straws as he could be, and I alighted as well as I could, stumbling upon a large stone over which he had nearly driven us, and sinking deep in mud and mire. I now found that the rock which had seemed to block the way was only one of those many little points round which the river turns in its course through the mountains, and on approaching near it I discovered the shed he had seen. It was an old dilapidated timber-built hut, which might have belonged at some former period to a boatman, or perhaps a vine-dresser, but it was open at two sides, and we might as well have been in the carriage as there.

By the side, however, I found a path with a step or two cut in the rock, and I judged rightly that it must lead to the building Lawrence had seen above. On returning to the side of the carriage, I clearly perceived the building too, and made it out to be one of the old castles of which such multitudes stud the banks of the frontier river. Some of these, as we all know, are in a very ruinous, some in a more perfect, state; and I proposed to my companion to draw the horses and carriage under the shed, climb the path, and take our chance of what we should find above.

Phaethon himself could not have been more sick of charioteering than Lawrence was: he jumped at the proposal. We secured our vehicle and its brutes as well as we could, and I began to climb. Lawrence stayed a minute behind to get the portmanteau out from under the seat where we had stowed it to keep it dry; and then came hallooing after me with it upon his shoulder.

'Do you think there is a chance of finding anyone up there?' he asked, as he overtook me.

'A chance, certainly; but a poor one,' I answered. 'Marxburg and one or two other old castles are inhabited; but not many. However, we shall soon know; for this one is low down, thank Heaven! and here we are at some gate or barbican.'

I cannot say that it was very promising to the feel—for sight aided us but little—and the multitude of stones we tumbled over gave no idea of the castle itself being in a high state of repair. Lawrence thought fit to give a loud halloo; but the whistling wind drowned it—

and would have drowned it if he had shouted like Achilles from the trenches.

We next had to pick our way across what had probably been a court of the castle; that was an easy matter, for the stones in the open space were few, and the inequalities not many. The moon, I suppose, had risen by this time, for there seemed more light, though the rain ceased not; but we could now perceive several towers and walls quite plainly; and at length I found myself under a deep archway, on one side of which the drifting deluge did not reach me.

As soon as I got under shelter, I extracted my large box of matches and lighted one easily enough. It burned while one might count twenty, but that sufficed to show us that we were under a great gateway between two high towers. A second which I lighted Lawrence carried out into an inner court, but it was extinguished in a moment.

I had perceived, however, a doorway on either side of this arch, and the spikes of a portcullis protruding through the arch above, which showed that the castle had some woodwork left about it; and as soon as he came back we lighted another match, and set out to explore what was behind the two doorways, which we managed easily by getting a new light as soon as the old one was burned out.

On the right there was nothing but one small room, with no exit but the entrance, and with a roof broken in and rank weeds rising from the encumbered floor. On the left was a room of the same size, equally dilapidated, but with a second door and two steps leading to a larger room or hall, the roof of which was perfect except at one end. There were two old lozenge-shaped windows likewise, minus a few panes; but the sills were raised nearly a man's height from the floor, and thus, when one was seated on the ground, one's head was out of the draught.

Comparison is a wonderful thing, and the place looked quite comfortable. Lawrence threw down the portmanteau, and while he held a lighted match, I undid it and got out a wax candle. We had now the means of light till morning, and it remained to get some dry clothing, if it could be found. We had each a dress-suit and a couple of shirts in the portmanteau; and though the rain in one spot had contrived to penetrate the solid leather and wet the shoulder of my coat and the knee of his pantaloons, it was certainly better to have but one damp place of a few inches about one than to be wet all over.

We therefore dressed ourselves in what the apprentice boys would call our best clothes, and a little brandy from the flask made us feel still more comfortable. The taste for luxuries increases with marvellous rapidity under indulgence. An hour before, we should have thought a dry coat and a place of shelter formed the height of human felicity, but now we began to long for a fire on the broad stone hearth at the end of the room.

Lawrence was fertile in resources and keen-sighted enough. He had remarked a quantity of fallen rafters in the first little room we had entered, and he now made sundry pilgrimages thither in the dark—for we dared not take out the candle—till he had accumulated enough wood to keep us dry all night. Some of it was wet and would not burn, but other pieces were quite dry, and we soon had a roaring fire, by which we sat down on the ground, hoping to make ourselves comfortable.

Oh the vanity of human expectations! As long as we had been busy in repairing our previous disasters we had been well enough; but as soon as we were still—no, not quite so soon as that, but by the time we had stared into the fire for ten minutes, and made out half a dozen pictures on the firebrands, miseries began to press upon us.

'I wish to heaven I had something to sit upon!' said Lawrence, 'if it were but a three-legged stool. My knees get quite cramped.'

'How the wind howls and mourns,' said I, listening. 'It would not surprise me if one half of this old crazy place were to come down upon our heads.'

'The rain is pouring on as heavily as ever,' said Lawrence. 'I should not wonder if that puddle at the other end were to swell into a lake and wash us out at the door.'

'Those poor brutes of horses,' said I, 'must have a bad time of it, and the chaise will be like a full sponge.'

'Come, come!' said Lawrence, 'this will never do. We shall croak ourselves into a fit of the horrors. Let us forget the storm, and the horses, and the old tumbledown place, and fancy ourselves in a middling sort of inn, with a good fire, but little to eat. It is the best policy to laugh at petty evils. Come, can not you tell us a story beginning "Once upon a time"?'

I was in no fit mood for story-telling, but there was some philosophy in his plan, and I accordingly agreed, upon the condition that when I had concluded my narrative he would tell another story.

'Once upon a time,' I said, 'when the late Duke of Hamilton was a young man, and travelling in Italy—making the grand tour, as it was called in those days—he came one night to a solitary inn in the mountains, where he was forced to take refuge from a storm something like that which we have met with today——'

'Oh, I know that story,' cried Lawrence, interrupting me; 'I have heard it a hundred times; and besides, you do not tell it right—My God, what is that?'

As he spoke, he sprang up on his feet with a look of consternation and a face turning suddenly pale.

'What? what?' I cried, 'I heard nothing.'

'Listen!' he said, 'it was certainly a shriek.'

We were silent as death for the next minute, and then again, rising above the moaning wind and pattering rain, came one of the most piercing, agonizing shrieks I ever heard. It seemed quite close to where we sat—driven in, as it were, through the broken panes of the casement.

'There must have been some accident,' I said, anxiously. 'Let us go down and see.'

We had contrived to fix our candle between two pieces of firewood, and, leaving it burning, we hurried out through the little ante-room to the old dark archway. The night seemed blacker than ever, and the storm no less severe.

'Stay, stay!' said Lawrence; 'let us listen. We hear nothing to direct us where to search.'

I stopped, and we bent our ears in vain for another sound. We heard the wind sigh, and the rustling patter of the rain, and the roaring of the mighty river as, swollen tremendously, it went roaring along through its rocky channel, but nothing like a human voice made itself heard.

No answer was returned, and again and again he called without obtaining a reply. It was evident that the lips which had uttered those sounds of pain or terror were either far away or still in death; and having nothing to guide us further, we returned to our place of shelter.

At length, quite tired out, I proposed that we should try to sleep.

Lawrence ensconced himself behind the door; I took up a position in the other corner, sitting on the floor with my back supported by the two walls, and at a sufficient distance from the window.

I should have said we had piled more wood on the fire, in such a way as we hoped would keep it in at least till we woke; and it flickered and flared and cast strange lights upon the walls and old windows, and upon a door at the other end of the room which we had never particularly examined, on account of the wet and decayed state of the floor in that part.

It was a very common door—a great mass of planks placed perpendicularly and bound together by two great horizontal bars—but as the firelight played upon it, there was something unpleasant to me in its aspect. I kept my eyes fixed upon it, and wondered what was beyond; and, in the sort of unpleasant fancifulness which besets one sometimes when dreary, I began to imagine all sorts of things. It seemed to me to move as if about to be opened; but it was only the shaking of the wind.

It looked like a prison door, I thought—the entrance to some unhappy wretch's cell; and when I was half asleep, I asked myself if there could be anyone there still—could the shrieks we heard issue thence—or could the spirit of the tortured captive still come back to mourn over the sorrows endured in life? I shut my eyes to get rid of the sight of it; but when I opened them again, there it was staring me full in the face.

Sometimes when the flame subsided indeed, I lost sight of it; but that was as bad or worse than the full view, for then I could not tell whether it was open or shut. But at length, calling myself a fool, I turned away from it, and soon after dozed off to sleep.

I could not have been really in slumber more than a hour, and was dreaming that I had just been carried off a road into a river, and just heard all the roaring and rushing of a torrent in my ears, when Lawrence woke me by shaking me violently by the shoulder, and exclaiming: 'Listen, listen! What in the fiend's name can all that be?'

I started up bewildered; but in a moment I heard sounds such as I never heard before in my life; frantic yells and cries, and groans even—all very different from the shrieks we had heard before. Then, suddenly, there was a wild peal of laughter ringing all through the room, more terrible than the rest.

I cannot bear to be wakened suddenly out of sleep; but to be roused by such sounds as that quite overcame me, and I shook like a leaf. Still, my eyes turned towards the door at the other end of the room. The fire had sunk low; the rays of our solitary candle did not reach it, but there was now another light upon it, fitful as the flickering of the flame, but paler and colder. It seemed blue almost to me. But as soon as I could recall my senses I perceived that the moon was breaking the clouds, and from time to time shining through the casement as the scattered vapours were hurried over her by the wind.

'What in Heaven's name can it be?' I exclaimed, quite aghast.

'I don't know, but we must see,' answered my companion, who had been awake longer and recovered his presence of mind. 'Light the other candle, and bring the one that is alight. We must find out what this is. Some poor creature may be wanting help.'

'The sound comes from beyond that door,' I said: 'let us see what is behind it.'

I acknowledge I had some trepidation in making the proposal, but my peculiar temperament urged me forward in spite of myself towards scenes which I could not doubt were fearful; and I can boldly say that if Lawrence had hesitated to go I would have gone alone.

Taking the candle in my hand, then, I advanced at once towards the door. Lawrence stopped a moment to examine by the light I had left behind a pair of pistols which he had brought in his pockets.

Thus I had reached the door before he came up, and had opened it, for all the ironwork but a latch had been carried off.

The moment it was thrown back, the cries and groans were heard more distinctly than before; but I could see nothing before me but darkness, and it required a moment or two for the light to penetrate the darkness beyond. I had not taken two steps beyond the threshold ere Lawrence was by my side, and we found ourselves in a stone passage without windows, appearing to lead round the building. Ten paces on, however, we came to the top of a flight of steps, broken and mouldy, with grass and weeds growing up between the crevices. It was a work of some danger to descend those steps, for they rocked and tottered under the foot.

When we were about half-way down, the sounds, which had been growing louder and louder, suddenly ceased, and a death-like stillness succeeded.

'Stay a bit,' said my companion: 'let us reconnoitre. We may as well look before we leap. Hold up the light.'

I did as he asked, but the faint rays of the candle showed us nothing but the black irregular faces of the rock on either side, a small rill of water percolating through a crevice, and flowing over, down upon the steps, along which it poured in miniature cascades, and beyond, a black chasm where we could see nothing.

'Come on,' said Lawrence, advancing; 'we must see the end of it.'

Forward we went—down, down, some two-and-thirty steps more, without hearing another sound; but just as we reached the bottom step something gave a wild sort of yell, and I could hear a scrambling and tumbling at a good distance in advance.

My heart beat terribly, and Lawrence stopped short. I was far more agitated than he was, but he showed what he felt more, and anyone who had seen us would have said that he was frightened, I perfectly cool. He had passed me on the stairs; I now passed him, and holding the light high up gazed around.

It was very difficult to see anything distinctly, but here and there the beams caught upon rough points of rock, and low arches rudely hewn in the dark stone, and I made out that we were in a series of vaults excavated below the castle, with massive partitions between them, and here and there a doorway or passage from one to the other.

It seemed a perfect labyrinth at first sight, and now that all was silent again, we had nothing to guide us. I listened, but all was still as death; and I was advancing again, when my companion asked me to stop, and proposed that we should examine the ground on each side as we went on, marking the spot from which we started. It seemed a good plan, and I was stooping down to pile up some of the loose stones with which the ground or floor was plentifully encumbered, when a large black snake glided away, and at the same moment a bat or a small owl flitted by, and extinguished the light with its wings.

'Good Heaven, how unlucky!' cried Lawrence; 'have you got the matchbox?'

'No,' I answered; 'I left it on the floor near where I was sleeping.

Feel your way up the steps, my good friend, and bring it and the other candle. I will remain here till you come. Be quick!'

'You go; let me stay,' said Lawrence. But I was ashamed to accept his offer; and there was a something, I knew not what, that urged me to remain. 'No, no,' I said, 'go quickly; but give me one of your pistols,' and I repeated the last words in German, lest anyone who understood that language should be within earshot.

We were so near the foot of the steps that Lawrence could make no mistake, and I soon heard his feet ascending at a rapid rate, tripping and stumbling, it is true, but still going on. As I listened, I thought I heard a light sound also from the other side, but I concluded that it was but the echo of his steps through the hollow passages, and I stood quite still, hardly breathing. I could hear my heart beat, and the arteries of the throat were very unpleasant—throb, throb, throbbing.

After a moment or two I heard Lawrence's feet as it seemed to me almost above me, and I know not what impression of having some other being near me, made me resolve to cock the pistol. I tried to do it with my thumb as I held it in my right hand, but the lock went hard, and I found it would be necessary to lay down the candle to effect it.

Just as I was stooping to do so, I became suddenly conscious of having some living creature close by me; and the next instant I felt cold fingers at my throat, and an arm thrown round me. Not a word was spoken, but the grasp became tight upon my neck, and I struggled violently for breath and life. But the strength of the being that grasped me seemed gigantic, and his hand felt like a hand of iron.

Oh what a moment was that! Never, except in a terrible dream, have I felt anything like it. I tried to cry, to shout, but I could not, his hold of my throat was so tight; power of muscle seemed to fail me; my head turned giddy; my heart felt as if stopping; flashes of light shone from my eyes.

My right hand, however, was free, and by a violent effort I forced back the cock of the pistol nearly to the click; but then I lost all power. The hammer fell; the weapon went off with a loud echoing report, and for an instant, by the flash, I saw a hideous face with a grey beard close gazing into mine.

The sound of Lawrence's footsteps running rapidly overhead were the most joyful I had ever heard; but the next instant I felt myself cast violently backward, and I fell half stunned and bewildered to the ground.

Before I could rise the light of the candle began to appear, as Lawrence came down the stairs, first faint, and then brighter; and I heard his voice exclaiming, 'What has happened? what has happened?'

'Take care!' I cried faintly; 'there is some man or some devil here, and he has half killed me!'

Looking carefully around, Lawrence helped me to rise, and then we picked up the candle I had let fall and lighted it again, he gazing in my face from time to time, but seeming hardly to like to take his eyes off the vaults, or to enter into any conversation, for fear of some sudden attack. Nothing was to be seen, however; my savage assailant was gone, leaving no trace behind him but a cut upon the back of my head, received as he cast me backward.

'What has happened?' said Lawrence at length, in a very low voice. 'Why, your face looks quite blue, and you are bleeding!'

'No wonder,' I answered; 'for I have been half strangled, and have nearly had my brains dashed out.'

From time to time he asked a question, and I answered, till he had heard all that had happened, and then, after a minute's thought, he said, 'Do you know, I think we had better give this up, and barricade ourselves into the room upstairs. There may be more of these ruffians than one.'

'No, no,' I answered; 'I am resolved to see the end of it. There is only one, depend upon it, or I should have had both upon me. We are two, and can deal with him at all events. I have a great notion that some crime has been committed here this night, and we ought to ascertain the facts. Those first shrieks were from a woman's voice.'

'Well, well,' answered my companion, 'I am with you, if you are ready. Here, take one light and one pistol, and you examine the right-hand vaults while I take the left. We are now on our guard, and can help each other.'

We walked on accordingly, very slowly and carefully, taking care to look around us at every step, for the vaults were very rugged and irregular, and there was many a point and angle which might have concealed an assailant, but we met with no living creature. At length

I thought I perceived a glimmer of light before me, but a little to the left, and calling up Lawrence, who was at some yards' distance, I pointed it out to him.

'To be sure I see it,' he answered; 'it is the moon shining. We must be near the entrance of the vaults. But what is that? There seems to be someone lying down there.'

He laid his hand upon my arm as he spoke, and we both stood still and gazed forward. The object towards which his eyes were directed certainly looked like a human figure, but it moved not in the least, and I slowly advanced towards it. Gradually I discerned what it was. There was the dress of a woman, gay coloured and considerably ornamented, and a neat little foot and shoe, with a small buckle in it, resting on a piece of fallen rock. The head was away from us, and she lay perfectly still.

My spirit felt chilled; but I went on, quickening my pace, and Lawrence and I soon stood beside her, holding the lights over her.

She was a young girl of nineteen or twenty, dressed in gala costume, with some touch of the city garb, some of the peasant attire. Her hair, which was all loose, wet, and dishevelled, was exceedingly rich and beautiful, and her face must have been very pretty in the sweet happy colouring of health and life. Now it was deathly pale, and the windows of the soul were closed. It was a sad, sad sight to see!

Her garments were all wet, and there was some froth about the mouth, but the fingers of the hands were limp and natural, as if there had been no struggle, and the features of the face were not distorted. There was, however, a wound upon her temple, from which some blood had flowed, and some scratches upon her cheek, and upon the small fair ears.

How came she by her death? How came she there? Was she slain by accident, or had she met with violence? were the questions that pressed upon our thoughts. But we said little then, and after a time left her where we found her. It mattered not to her that the bed was hard or the air cold.

We searched every corner of the vaults, however, for him I could not help believing her murderer, but without success; and on going to the mouth of the vault, where there had once been a door, long gone to warm some peasant's winter hearth, we found that it led out upon the road close by the side of the Rhine, and hardly a dozen paces from the river.

It was clear how he had escaped; and we sadly took our way back to the chamber above, where we passed the rest of the night in melancholy talk over the sad events that must have happened.

We slept no more, nor tried to sleep; but as soon as the east was grey went down to the shed where we had left the horses, and resumed our journey, to give information at the next village of what we had discovered.

The horses were very stiff, and at first could hardly drag us along, for the road was in a horrible state, but they soon warmed to the work, and in little more than three-quarters of an hour we reached a small village, where we got some refreshment, while the landlord of the little Gasthaus ran at my request for the Polizei.

When the only officer in the place came, I told him every thing that had happened in the best German I could muster, and willingly agreed to go back with him to the spot, and show him where the body lay. The rumour spread like wildfire in the village; a crowd of the good peasantry collected round the door; and when we set out, taking a torch or two with us, as I described the vaults as very dark, we had at least a hundred persons in our train, among whom were a number of youths and young girls.

As nothing but one old chaise was to be procured in the village, and it did not look as if it would rain, we pursued our way on foot, but we certainly accomplished the distance faster than we had done with two horses in the morning. All the way the officer—I really do not know his right German title—continued conversing with Lawrence, who did not understand a word of German, and with myself, for whom his German was a world too fast.

I gave him, however, all the information I could, and as his language has the strange peculiarity of being easier to speak than to understand, I made him master, I believe, of every little incident of the last eventful night.

My description of the face of the man who had first nearly strangled me and then nearly dashed my brains out, and of whom I had caught a glimpse by the flash of the pistol, seemed to interest him more than all the rest. He stopped when I gave it to him, called several of the girls and young men about him, and conversed with them for a moment or two with a good deal of eagerness.

The greater part of what they said escaped me, but I heard a proper name frequently repeated, sounding like Herr Katzenberger, and the whole ended with a sad and gloomy shake of the head.

Soon after we resumed our advance we came to the mouth of the vault. It required no torches, however, to let us see what we sought for. The sun, still low, was shining slantingly beneath the heavy brows of the rocky arch, and the rays receded to the spot where the body of the poor girl lay.

They made a little bier of vine poles and branches, and laid the fair corpse upon it. Then they sought for various green leaves and some of the long-lingering autumn flowers, and strewed them tastefully over the body; and then four stout men raised the death-litter on their shoulders and bore it away towards the village.

I had the policeman for my companion; and beseeching him to speak slowly, I asked if he could give me any explanation of the strange and terrible events which must have happened.

'We know very little as yet,' he answered; 'but we shall probably know more soon. This young lady, poor thing! was the only daughter of a rich but cross-grained man, living at a village a short way further down the Rhine, on the other side. Her mother, who died three years ago, was from our own village. She was dancing away gaily last evening with our young folks, just before the storm came on; for her father had brought her up in his boat, and left her at her aunt's.

'When it came on with thunder and lightning, they all went into the house, and, as misfortune would have it, that young lad who is carrying the head of the bier sat down by her in a corner, and they could not part soon enough. He was a lover of hers, everyone knew; but her father was hard against the match, and before they had been in the house an hour the old man came in and found them chatting in their corner. Perhaps he would have stayed all night had it not been for that; but he got very angry, and made her go away with him in his boat in the very midst of the storm.

'He said he had been on the Rhine many a worse night than that— though few of us had ever seen one. But he was obstinate as a bull, and away they went, though she cried terribly, both from fear and vexation. What happened after, none of us can tell, but old Herr Katzenberger has a grey beard, just such as you speak of.'

They carried the body to the little old church, and laid it in the aisle; and then they sent for the village doctor to examine into the mode of her death. I was not present when he came, but I heard afterward that he pronounced her to have died from drowning, and declared that the wound on the temple must have occurred by a blow against some rock when life was quite or nearly extinct. 'Otherwise,' he said, 'it would have bled much more, for the artery itself was torn.'

For my part, I was marched up with Lawrence to the Ampthaus, and there subjected to manifold interrogatories, the answers to which were all carefully taken down.

In the midst of these we were interrupted by the inroad of a dozen of peasants, dragging along a man who struggled violently with them, but in whom every one present recognized the father of the poor girl whose body we had found. The peasants said they had found him some six miles off, tearing his flesh with his teeth, and evidently in a state of furious insanity. They had found it very difficult to master him, they declared, for his strength was prodigious.

He was the only witness of what had taken place during that terrible night upon the river, and he could give no sane account. He often accused himself of murdering his child; but the good people charitably concluded that he merely meant he had been the cause of her death by taking her upon the treacherous waters on such a night as that; and the fact of his boat having drifted ashore some miles further down, broken and bottom upward, seemed to confirm that opinion.

I made some enquiries regarding the unfortunate man during a subsequent tour; but I only learned that he continued hopelessly insane, without a glimmer of returning reason.

J. SHERIDAN LE FANU

# Sir Dominick's Bargain

In the early autumn of the year 1838, business called me to the south of Ireland. The weather was delightful, the scenery and people were new to me, and sending my luggage on by the mail-coach route in charge of a servant, I hired a serviceable nag at a posting-house, and, full of the curiosity of an explorer, I commenced a leisurely journey of five-and-twenty miles on horseback, by sequestered crossroads, to my place of destination. By bog and hill, by plain and ruined castle, and many a winding stream, my picturesque road led me.

I had started late, and having made little more than half my journey, I was thinking of making a short halt at the next convenient place, and letting my horse have a rest and a feed, and making some provision also for the comforts of his rider.

It was about four o'clock when the road, ascending a gradual steep, found a passage through a rocky gorge between the abrupt termination of a range of mountains to my left and a rocky hill that rose dark and sudden at my right. Below me lay a little thatched village, under a long line of gigantic beech trees, through the boughs of which the lowly chimneys sent up their thin turf-smoke. To my left, stretched away for miles, ascending the mountain range I have mentioned, a wild park, through whose sward and ferns the rock broke, time-worn and lichen-stained. This park was studded with straggling wood, which thickened to something like a forest, behind and beyond the little village I was approaching, clothing the irregular ascent of the hillsides with beautiful, and in some places, discoloured foliage.

As you descend, the road winds slightly, with the grey park-wall, built of loose stone, and mantled here and there with ivy, at its left, and crosses a shallow ford; and as I approached the village, through breaks in the woodlands, I caught glimpses of the long front of an old ruined house, placed among the trees, about half-way up the picturesque mountainside.

The solitude and melancholy of this ruin piqued my curiosity, and when I had reached the rude thatched public house, with the sign of St Columbkill, with robes, mitre, and crozier displayed over its lintel, having seen to my horse and made a good meal myself on a rasher and eggs, I began to think again of the wooded park and the ruinous house, and resolved on a ramble of half an hour among its sylvan solitudes.

The name of the place, I found, was Dunoran; and beside the gate a stile admitted to the grounds, through which, with a pensive enjoyment, I began to saunter towards the dilapidated mansion.

A long grass-grown road, with many turns and windings, led up to the old house, under the shadow of the wood.

The road as it approached the house skirted the edge of a precipitous glen, clothed with hazel, dwarf-oak, and thorn, and the silent house stood with its wide-open hall-door facing this dark ravine, the further edge of which was crowned with towering forest; and great trees stood about the house and its deserted courtyard and stables.

I walked in and looked about me, through passages overgrown with nettles and weeds; from room to room with ceilings rotted, and here and there a great beam dark and worn, with tendrils of ivy trailing over it. The tall walls with rotten plaster were stained and mouldy, and in some rooms the remains of decayed wainscoting crazily swung to and fro. The almost sashless windows were darkened also with ivy, and about the tall chimneys the jackdaws were wheeling, while from the huge trees that overhung the glen in sombre masses at the other side, the rooks kept up a ceaseless cawing.

As I walked through these melancholy passages—peeping only into some of the rooms, for the flooring was quite gone in the middle, and bowed down towards the centre, and the house was very nearly unroofed, a state of things which made the exploration a little critical—I began to wonder why so grand a house, in the midst of scenery so picturesque, had been permitted to go to decay; I dreamed of the hospitalities of which it had long ago been the rallying place, and I thought what a scene of Redgauntlet revelries it might disclose at midnight.

The great staircase was of oak, which had stood the weather wonderfully, and I sat down upon its steps, musing vaguely on the transitoriness of all things under the sun.

Except for the hoarse and distant clamour of the rooks, hardly aud-ible where I sat, no sound broke the profound stillness of the spot. Such a sense of solitude I have seldom experienced before. The air was stirless, there was not even the rustle of a withered leaf along the passage. It was oppressive. The tall trees that stood close about the building darkened it, and added something of awe to the melancholy of the scene.

In this mood I heard, with an unpleasant surprise, close to me, a voice that was drawling, and, I fancied, sneering, repeat the words: 'Food for worms, dead and rotten; God over all.'

There was a small window in the wall, here very thick, which had been built up, and in the dark recess of this, deep in the shadow, I now saw a sharp-featured man, sitting with his feet dangling. His keen eyes were fixed on me, and he was smiling cynically, and before I had well recovered my surprise, he repeated the distich:

> *'If death was a thing that money could buy,*
> *The rich they would live, and the poor they would die.'*

'It was a grand house in its day, sir,' he continued, 'Dunoran House, and the Sarsfields. Sir Dominick Sarsfield was the last of the old stock. He lost his life not six foot away from where you are sitting.'

As he thus spoke he let himself down, with a little jump, on to the ground.

He was a dark-faced, sharp-featured, little hunchback, and had a walking-stick in his hand, with the end of which he pointed to a rusty stain in the plaster of the wall.

'Do you mind that mark, sir?' he asked.

'Yes,' I said, standing up, and looking at it, with a curious anticipa-tion of something worth hearing.

'That's about seven or eight feet from the ground, sir, and you'll not guess what it is.'

'I dare say not,' said I, 'unless it is a stain from the weather.'

' 'Tis nothing so lucky, sir,' he answered, with the same cynical
smile and a wag of his head, still pointing at the mark with his stick.
'That's a splash of brains and blood. It's there this hundhred years; and
it will never leave it while the wall stands.'

'He was murdered, then?'

'Worse than that, sir,' he answered.

'He killed himself, perhaps?'

'Worse than that, itself, this cross between us and harm! I'm oulder
than I look, sir; you wouldn't guess my years.'

He became silent, and looked at me, evidently inviting a guess.

'Well, I should guess you to be about five-and-fifty.'

He laughed, and took a pinch of snuff, and said:

'I'm that, your honour, and something to the back of it. I was seventy last Candlemas. You would not a' thought that, to look at me.'

'Upon my word, I should not; I can hardly believe it even now. Still,
you don't remember Sir Dominick Sarsfield's death?' I said, glancing
up at the ominous stain on the wall.

'No, sir, that was a long while before I was born. But my grandfather was butler here long ago, and many a time I heard tell how
Sir Dominick came by his death. There was no masther in the great
house ever since that happened. But there was two sarvants in care of
it, and my aunt was one o' them; and she kep' me here wid her till I
was nine year old, and she was lavin' the place to go to Dublin; and
from that time it was let to go down. The wind sthript the roof, and
the rain rotted the timber, and little by little, in sixty years' time, it
kem to what you see. But I have a likin' for it still, for the sake of ould
times; and I never come this way but I take a look in. I don't think it's
many more times I'll be turnin' to see the ould place, for I'll be undher
the sod myself before long.'

'You'll outlive younger people,' I said.

And, quitting that trite subject, I ran on:

'I don't wonder that you like this old place; it is a beautiful spot,
such noble trees.'

'I wish ye seen the glin when the nuts is ripe; they're the sweetest
nuts in all Ireland, I think,' he rejoined, with a practical sense of the
picturesque. 'You'd fill your pockets while you'd be lookin' about
you.'

'These are very fine old woods,' I remarked. 'I have not seen any in Ireland I thought so beautiful.'

'Eiah! your honour, the woods about here is nothing to what they wor. All the mountains along here was wood when my father was a gossoon, and Murroa Wood was the grandest of them all. All oak mostly, and all cut down as bare as the road. Not one left here that's fit to compare with them. Which way did your honour come hither—from Limerick?'

'No. Killaloe.'

'Well, then, you passed the ground where Murroa Wood was in former times. You kem undher Lisnavourra, the steep knob of a hill about a mile above the village here. 'Twas near that Murroa Wood was, and 'twas there Sir Dominick Sarsfield first met the devil, the Lord between us and harm, and a bad meeting it was for him and his.'

I had become interested in the adventure which had occurred in the very scenery which had so greatly attracted me, and my new acquaintance, the little hunchback, was easily entreated to tell me the story, and spoke thus, so soon as we had each resumed his seat:

It was a fine estate when Sir Dominick came into it; and grand doings there was entirely, feasting and fiddling, free quarters for all the pipes in the counthry round, and a welcome for every one that liked to come. There was wine, by the hogshead, for the quality; and potteen enough to set a town a-fire, and beer and cidher enough to float a navy, for the boys and girls, and the likes o' me. It was kep' up the best part of a month, till the weather broke, and the rain spoilt the sod for the moneen jigs, and the fair of Allybally Killudeen comin' on they wor obliged to give over their divarsion, and attind to the pigs.

But Sir Dominick was only beginnin' when they wor lavin' off. There was no way of gettin' rid of his money and estates he did not try—what with drinkin', dicin', racin', cards, and all soarts, it was not many years before the estates wor in debt, and Sir Dominick a distressed man. He showed a bold front to the world as long as he could; and then he sould his dogs, and most of his horses, and gev out he was going to thravel in France, and the like; and so off with him for a while; and no one in these parts heard tale or tidings of him for two or three years. Till at last quite unexpected, one night there comes a rapping at the big kitchen window. It was past ten o'clock, and old Connor Hanlon, the butler, my grandfather, was sittin' by the fire alone, warming his shins over it. There was keen east wind blowing along the mountains that night, and whistling cowld enough through the tops of the trees and soundin' lonesome through the long chimneys.

(And the storyteller glanced up at the nearest stack visible from his seat.)

So he wasn't quite sure of the knockin' at the window, and up he gets, and sees his master's face.

My grandfather was glad to see him safe, for it was a long time since there was any news of him; but he was sorry, too, for it was a changed place and only himself and old Juggy Broadrick in charge of the house, and a man in the stables, and it was a poor thing to see him comin' back to his own like that.

He shook Con by the hand, and says he:

'I came here to say a word to you. I left my horse with Dick in the stable; I may want him again before morning, or I may never want him.'

And with that he turns into the big kitchen, and draws a stool, and sits down to take an air of the fire.

'Sit down, Connor, opposite me, and listen to what I tell you, and don't be afeard to say what you think.'

He spoke all the time lookin' into the fire, with his hands stretched over it, and a tired man he looked.

'An' why should I be afeard, Masther Dominick?' says my grandfather. 'Yourself was a good masther to me, and so was your father, rest his sould, before you, and I'll say the truth, and dar' the devil, and more than that, for any Sarsfield of Dunoran, much less yourself, and a good right I'd have.'

'It's all over with me, Con,' said Sir Dominick.

'Heaven forbid!' says my grandfather.

' 'Tis past praying for,' says Sir Dominick. 'The last guinea's gone; the ould place will follow it. It must be sold, and I'm come here, I don't know why, like a ghost to have a last look round me, and go off in the dark again.'

And with that he tould him to be sure, in case he should hear of his death, to give the oak box, in the closet off his room, to his

21

cousin, Pat Sarsfield, in Dublin, and the sword and pistols his grand-father carried in Aughrim, and two or three thrifling things of the kind.

And says he, 'Con, they say if the divil gives you money overnight, you'll find nothing but a bagful of pebbles, and chips, and nutshells, in the morning. If I thought he played fair, I'm in the humour to make a bargain with him tonight.'

'Lord forbid!' says my grandfather, standing up, with a start, and crossing himself.

'They say the country's full of men, listin' sogers for the King o' France. If I light on one o' them, I'll not refuse his offer. How contrary things goes! How long is it since me and Captain Waller fought the jewel at New Castle?'

'Six years, Masther Dominick, and ye broke his thigh with the bullet the first shot.'

'I did, Con,' says he, 'and I wish, instead, he had shot me through the heart. Have you any whisky?'

My grandfather took it out of the buffer, and the masther pours out some into a bowl, and drank it off.

'I'll go out and have a look at my horse,' says he, standing up. There was a sort of a stare in his eyes, as he pulled his riding-cloak about him, as if there was something bad in his thoughts.

'Sure, I won't be a minute running out myself to the stable, and looking after the horse for you myself,' says my grandfather.

'I'm not goin' to the stable,' says Sir Dominick; 'I may as well tell you, for I see you found it out already—I'm goin' across the deer-park; if I come back you'll see me in an hour's time. But, anyhow, you'd better not follow me, for if you do, I'll shoot you, and that 'id be a bad ending to our friendship.'

And with that he walks down this passage here, and turns the key in the side door at that end of it, and out wid him on the sod into the moonlight and the cowld wind; and my grandfather seen him walkin' hard towards the park-wall, and then he comes in and closes the door with a heavy heart.

Sir Dominick stopped to think when he got to the middle of the deer-park, for he had not made up his mind, when he left the house and the whisky did not clear his head, only it gev him courage.

He did not feel the cowld wind now, nor fear death, nor think much of anything but the name and fall of the old family.

And he made up his mind, if no better thought came to him between that and there, so soon as he came to Murroa Wood, he'd hang himself from one of the oak branches with his cravat.

It was a bright moonlight night, there was just a bit of a cloud driving across the moon now and then, but, only for that, as light a'most as day.

Down he goes, right for the wood of Murroa. It seemed to him every step he took was as long as three, and it was no time till he was among the big oak-threes with their roots spreading from one to another, and their branches stretching overhead like the timbers of a naked roof, and the moon shining down through them, and casting their shadows thick and twist abroad on the ground as black as my shoe.

He was sobering a bit by this time, and he slacked his pace, and he thought 'twould be better to list in the French king's army, and thry what that might do for him, for he knew a man might take his own life any time, but it would puzzle him to take it back again when he liked.

Just as he made up his mind not to make away with him himself, what should he hear but a step clinkin' along the dry ground under the trees, and soon he sees a grand gentleman right before him comin' up to meet him.

He was a handsome young man like himself, and he wore a cocked hat with gold lace round it, such as officers wear on their coats, and he had on a dress the same as French officers wore in them times.

He stopped opposite Sir Dominick, and he cum to a standstill also.

The two gentlemen took off their hats to one another, and says the stranger:

'I am recruiting, sir,' says he, 'for my sovereign, and you'll find my money won't turn into pebbles, chips, and nutshells, by tomorrow.'

At the same time he pulls out a big purse full of gold.

The minute he set eyes on that gentleman, Sir Dominick had his own opinion of him; and at those words he felt the very hair standing up on his head.

'Don't be afraid,' says he, 'the money won't burn you. If it proves honest gold, and if it prospers with you, I'm willing to make a bargain.

23

This is the last day of February,' says he; 'I'll serve you seven years, and at the end of that time you shall serve me, and I'll come for you when the seven years is over, when the clock turns the minute between February and March; and the first of March ye'll come away with me, or never. You'll not find me a bad master, any more than a bad servant. I love my own; and I command all the pleasure and the glory of the world. The bargain dates from this day, and the lease is out at midnight on the last day I told you; and in the year'—he told him the year, it was easy reckoned, but I forget it—'and if you'd rather wait,' he says, 'for eight months and twenty-eight days, before you sign the writin', you may, if you meet me here. But I can't do a great deal for you in the meantime; and if you don't sign then, all you get from me, up to that time, will vanish away, and you'll be just as you are tonight, and ready to hang yourself on the first tree you meet.'

Well, the end of it was, Sir Dominick chose to wait, and he came back to the house with a big bag full of money, as round as your hat a'most.

My grandfather was glad enough, you may be sure, to see the master safe and sound again so soon. Into the kitchen he bangs again, and swings the bag o' money on the table; and he stands up straight, and heaves up his shoulders like a man that has just got shut of a load; and he looks at the bag, and my grandfather looks at him, and from him to it, and back again. Sir Dominick looked as white as a sheet, and says he:

'I don't know, Con, what's in it; it's the heaviest load I ever carried.'

He seemed shy of openin' the bag; and he made my grandfather heap up a roaring fire of turf and wood, and then, at last, he opens it, and, sure enough, 'twas stuffed full o' golden guineas, bright and new, as if they were only that minute out o' the mint.

Sir Dominick made my grandfather sit at his elbow while he counted every guinea in the bag.

When he was done countin', and it wasn't far from daylight when that time came, Sir Dominick made my grandfather swear not to tell a word about it. And a close secret it was for many a day after.

When the eight months and twenty-eight days were pretty near spent and ended, Sir Dominick returned to the house here with a troubled mind, in doubt what was best to be done, and no one alive but my grandfather knew anything about the matter, and he not half what had happened.

As the day drew near, towards the end of October, Sir Dominick grew only more and more troubled in mind.

One time he made up his mind to have no more to say to such things, nor to speak again with the like of them he met with in the wood of Murroa. Then, again, his heart failed him when he thought of his debts, and he not knowing where to turn. Then, only a week before the day, everything began to go wrong with him. One man wrote from London to say that Sir Dominick paid three thousand pounds to the wrong man, and must pay it over again; another demanded a debt he never heard of before; and another, in Dublin, denied the payment of a thundherin' big bill, and Sir Dominick could nowhere find the receipt, and so on, wid fifty other things as bad.

Well, by the time the night of the 28th of October came round, he was a'most ready to lose his senses with all the demands that was risin' up again him on all sides, and nothing to meet them but the help of the one dhreadful friend he had to depind on at night in the oak-wood down there below.

So there was nothing for it but to go through with the business that was begun already, and about the same hour as he went last, he takes off the little Crucifix he wore round his neck, for he was a Catholic, and his gospel, and his bit o' the thrue cross that he had in a locket, for since he took the money from the Evil One he was growin' frightful in himself, and got all he could to guard him from the power of the devil. But tonight, for his life, he daren't take them with him. So he gives them into my grandfather's hands without a word, only he looked as white as a sheet o' paper; and he takes his hat and sword, and telling my grandfather to watch for him, away he goes, to try what would come of it.

It was a fine still night, and the moon—not so bright, though, now as the first time—was shinin' over heath and rock, and down on the lonesome oak-wood below him.

His heart beat thick as he drew near it. There was not a sound, not even the distant bark of a dog from the village behind him. There was not a lonesomer spot in the country round, and if it wasn't for his debts and losses that was drivin' him on half mad, in spite of his fears for his soul and his hopes of paradise, and all his good angel was whis-perin' in his ear, he would a' turned back, and sent for his clargy, and made his confession and his penance, and changed his ways, and led a good life, for he was frightened enough to have done a great dale.

Softer and slower he stept as he got, once more, in undher the big branches of the oak-threes; and when he got in a bit, near where he met with the bad spirit before, he stopped and looked round him, and felt himself, every bit, turning as cowld as a dead man, and you may be sure he did not feel much betther when he seen the same man steppin' from behind the big tree that was touchin' his elbow a'most.

'You found the money good,' says he, 'but it was not enough. No matter, you shall have enough and to spare. I'll see after your luck, and I'll give you a hint whenever it can serve you; and any time you want to see me you have only to come down here, and call my face to mind, and wish me present. You shan't owe a shilling by the end of the year, and you shall never miss the right card, the best throw, and the win-ning horse. Are you willing?'

The young gentleman's voice almost stuck in his throat, and his hair was rising on his head, but he did get out a word or two to signify that he consented; and with that the Evil One handed him a needle, and bid him give him three drops of blood from his arm; and he took them in the cup of an acorn, and gave him a pen, and bid him write some words that he repeated, and Sir Dominick did not understand, on two thin slips of parchment. He took one himself and the other he sunk in Sir Dominick's arm at the place where he drew the blood, and he closed the flesh over it. And that's as true as you're sittin' there!

Well, Sir Dominick went home. He was a frightened man, and well he might be. But in a little time he began to grow aisier in his mind. Anyhow, he got out of debt very quick, and money came tumbling in to make him richer, and everything he took in hand prospered, and he never made a wager, or played a game, but he won; and for all that, there was not a poor man on the estate that was not happier than Sir Dominick.

So he took again to his old ways; for, when the money came back, all came back, and there were hounds and horses, and wine galore, and no end of company, and grand doin's, and divarsion, up here at the great house. And some said Sir Dominick was thinkin' of gettin' married; and more said he wasn't. But, anyhow, there was somethin' troublin' him more than common, and so one night, unknownst to all, away he goes to the lonesome oak-wood. It was something, maybe, my grandfather thought was troublin' him about a beautiful young lady he was jealous of, and mad in love with her. But that was only guess.

Well, when Sir Dominick got into the wood this time, he grew more in dread than ever; and he was on the point of turnin' and lavin' the place, when who should he see, close beside him, but my gentleman, seated on a big stone undher one of the trees. In place of looking the fine young gentleman in gold lace and grand clothes he appeared before, he was now in rags, he looked twice the size he had been, and his face smutted with soot, and he had a murtherin' big steel hammer, as heavy as a half-hundhred, with a handle a yard long, across his knees. It was so dark under the tree, he did not see him quite clear for some time.

He stood up, and he looked awful tall entirely. And what passed between them in that discourse my grandfather never heered. But Sir Dominick was as black as night afterwards, and hadn't a laugh for anything nor a word a'most for anyone, and he only grew worse and worse, and darker and darker. And now this thing, whatever it was, used to come to him of its own accord, whether he wanted it or no; sometimes in one shape, and sometimes in another, in lonesome places, and sometimes at his side by night when he'd be ridin' home alone, until at last he lost heart altogether and sent for the priest.

The priest was with him a long time, and when he heered the whole story, he rode off all the way for the bishop, and the bishop came here to the great house next day, and he gev Sir Dominick a good advice. He toult him he must give over dicin', and swearin', and drinkin', and all bad company, and live a vartuous steady life until the seven years bargain was out, and if the divil didn't come for him the minute afther the stroke of twelve the first morning of the month of March, he was safe out of the bargain. There was not more than eight or ten months to run now before the seven years wor out, and he lived all the time according to the bishop's advice, as strict as if he was 'in retreat'.

Well, you may guess he felt quare enough when the mornin' of the 28th of February came.

The priest came up by appointment, and Sir Dominick and his raverence wor together in the room you see there, and kep' up their prayers together till the clock struck twelve, and a good hour after, and not a sign of a disturbance, nor nothing came near them, and the priest slep' that night in the house in the room next Sir Dominick's, and all went over as comfortable as could be, and they shook hands, and kissed like two comrades after winning a battle.

So, now, Sir Dominick thought he might as well have a pleasant evening, after all his fastin' and praying; and he sent round to half a dozen of the neighbouring gentlemen to come and dine with him, and his raverance stayed and dined also, and a roarin' bowl o' punch they had, and no end o' wine, and the swearin' and dice, and cards and guineas changing hands, and songs and stories, that wouldn't do anyone good to hear, and the priest slipped away, when he seen the turn things was takin', and it was not far from the stroke of twelve when Sir Dominick, sitting at the head of his table, swears, 'this is the best first of March I ever sat down with my friends'.

'It ain't the first o' March,' says Mr Hiffernan of Ballyvoreen. He was a scholard, and always kep' an almanack.

'What is it, then?' says Sir Dominick, startin' up, and dhroppin' the ladle into the bowl, and starin' at him as if he had two heads.

' 'Tis the twenty-ninth of February, leap year,' says he. And just as they were talkin' the clock strikes twelve; and my grandfather, who was half asleep in a chair by the fire in the hall, openin' his eyes, sees a short square fellow with a cloak on, and long, black hair bushin' out from under his hat, standin' just there where you see the bit o' light shinin' again' the wall.

(My hunchbacked friend pointed with his stick to a little patch of red sunset light that relieved the deepening shadow of the passage.)

'Tell your master,' says he, in an awful voice, like the growl of a baist, 'that I'm here by appointment, and expect him downstairs this minute.'

Up goes my grandfather, by these very steps you are sittin' on.

'Tell him I can't come down yet,' says Sir Dominick, and he turns to the company in the room, and says he with a cold sweat shinin' on his face, 'For God's sake, gentlemen, will any of you jump from the window and bring the priest here?' One looked at another and no one knew what to make of it, and in the meantime, up comes my grandfather again, and says he, tremblin', 'He says, sir, unless you go down to him, he'll come up to you.'

'I don't understand this, gentlemen, I'll see what it means,' says Sir Dominick, trying to put a face on it, and walkin' out o' the room like a man through the press-room, with the hangman waitin' for him outside. Down the stairs he comes, and two or three of the gentlemen peeping over the banisters, to see. My grandfather was walking six or eight steps behind him, and he seen the stranger take a stride out to meet Sir Dominick, and catch him up in his arms, and whirl his head against the wall, and wi' that the hall-doore flies open, and out goes the candles, and the turf and wood-ashes flyin' with the wind out o' the hall-fire, ran in a drift o' sparks along the floore by his feet.

Down runs the gintlemen. Bang goes the hall-doore. Some comes runnin' up, and more runnin' down, with lights. It was all over with Sir Dominick. They lifted up the corpse, and put its shoulders again' the wall; but there was not a gasp left in him. He was cowld and stiffenin' already.

Pat Donovan was comin' up to the great house late that night and after he passed the little brook, that the carriage track up to the house crosses, and about fifty steps to this side of it, his dog, that was by his side, makes a sudden wheel, and springs over the wall and sets up a yowlin' inside you'd hear a mile away; and that minute two men passed him by in silence, goin' down from the house, one of them short and square, and the other like Sir Dominick in shape, but there was little light under the trees where he was, and they looked only like shadows; and as they passed him by he could not hear the sound of their feet and he drew back to the wall frightened; and when he got up to the great house, he found all in confusion, and the master's body, with the head smashed to pieces, lying just on *that spot*.

The narrator stood up and indicated with the point of his stick the exact site of the body, and, as I looked, the shadow deepened, the red stain of sunlight vanished from the wall, and the sun had gone down behind the distant hill of New Castle, leaving the haunted scene in the deep grey of darkening twilight.

So I and the storyteller parted, not without good wishes on both sides, and a little 'tip' which seemed not unwelcome, from me.

It was dusk and the moon up by the time I reached the village, remounted my nag, and looked my last on the scene of the terrible legend of Dunoran.

# 3

## CHARLES READE

# The Knightsbridge Mystery

In Charles the Second's day the 'Swan' was denounced by the dramatists as a house where unfaithful wives and mistresses met their gallants.

But in the next century, when John Clarke was the Freeholder, no special imputation of that sort rested on it; it was a country inn with large stables, horsed the Brentford coach, and entertained man and beast on journeys long or short. It had also permanent visitors, especially in summer, for it was near London, and yet a rural retreat; meadows on each side, Hyde Park at back, Knightsbridge Green in front.

Amongst the permanent lodgers was Mr Gardiner, a substantial man; and Captain Cowen, a retired officer of moderate means, had lately taken two rooms for himself and his son. Mr Gardiner often joined the company in the public room, but the Cowens kept to themselves upstairs.

This was soon noticed and resented, in that age of few books and free converse. Some said, 'Oh, we are not good enough for him!' others enquired what a half-pay Captain had to give himself airs about. Candour interposed and supplied the climax: 'Nay, my masters, the Captain may be in hiding from duns, or from the runners; now I think on't, the York mail was robbed scarce a se'nnight before his worship came a hiding here.'

But the landlady's tongue ran the other way. Her weight was sixteen stone, her sentiments were her interests, and her tongue her tomahawk. ' 'Tis pity,' said she one day, 'some folk can't keep their tongues from blackening of their betters. The Captain is a civil-spoken gentleman—Lord send there were more of them in these parts!—as takes his hat off to me whenever he meets me, and pays his reckoning weekly. If he has a mind to be private, what business is that of yours, or yours? But curs must bark at their betters.'

Detraction, thus roughly quelled for certain seconds, revived at intervals whenever Dame Cust's broad back was turned. It was mildly encountered one evening by Gardiner. 'Nay, good sirs,' said he, 'you mistake the worthy Captain. To have fought at Blenheim and Malplaquet, no man hath less vanity. 'Tis for his son he holds aloof. He guards the youth like a mother, and will not have him hear our taproom jests. He worships the boy—a sullen lout, sirs; but paternal love is blind. He told me once he had loved his wife dearly, and lost her young, and this was all he had of her. "And," said he, "I'd spill blood like water for him, my own the first." "Then, sir," says I, "I fear he will give you a sore heart, one day." "And welcome," says my Captain, and his face like iron.'

Somebody remarked that no man keeps out of company who is good company; but Mr Gardiner parried that dogma. 'When young master is abed, my neighbour does sometimes invite me to share a bottle; and a sprightlier companion I would not desire. Such stories of battles, and duels, and love intrigues!'

'Now there's an old fox for you,' said one approvingly. It reconciled him to the Captain's decency to find that it was only hypocrisy.

'I like not—a man—who wears—a mask,' hiccoughed a hitherto silent personage, revealing his clandestine drunkenness and unsuspected wisdom at one blow.

These various theories were still fermenting in the bosom of the 'Swan', when one day there rode up to the door a gorgeous officer, hot from the minister's levée, in scarlet and gold, with an order like a starfish glittering on his breast. His servant, a private soldier, rode behind him, and slipping hastily from his saddle held his master's horse while he dismounted. Just then Captain Cowen came out for his afternoon walk. He started, and cried out, 'Colonel Barrington!'

'Ay, brother,' cried the other, and instantly the two officers embraced, and even kissed each other, for that feminine custom had not yet retired across the Channel; and these were soldiers who had fought and bled side by side, and nursed each other in turn; and your true soldier does not nurse by halves; his vigilance and tenderness are an example to women, and he rustleth not.

Captain Cowen invited Colonel Barrington to his room, and that warrior marched down the passage after him, single file, with long brass spurs and sabre clinking at his heels; and the establishment ducked and smiled, and respected Captain Cowen for the reason we admire the moon.

Seated in Cowen's room, the newcomer said heartily: 'Well, Ned, I come not empty-handed. Here is thy pension at last'; and handed him a parchment with a seal like a poached egg.

Cowen changed colour, and thanked him with an emotion he rarely betrayed, and gloated over the precious document. His cast-iron features relaxed, and he said: 'It comes in the nick of time, for now I can send my dear Jack to college.'

This led somehow to an exposure of his affairs. He had just £110 a year, derived from the sale of his commission, which he had invested, at fifteen per cent, with a well-known mercantile house in the City. 'So now,' said he, 'I shall divide it all in three; Jack will want two parts to live at Oxford, and I can do well enough here on one.' The rest of the conversation does not matter, so I dismiss it and Colonel Barrington for the time. A few days afterward Jack went to college, and Captain Cowen reduced his expenses, and dined at the shilling ordinary, and indeed took all his moderate repasts in public.

Instead of the severe and reserved character he had worn while his son was with him, he now shone out a boon companion, and sometimes kept the table in a roar with his marvellous mimicries of all the characters, male or female, that lived in the inn or frequented it, and sometimes held them breathless with adventures, dangers, intrigues, in which a leading part had been played by himself or his friends.

He became quite a popular character, except with one or two envious bodies, whom he eclipsed; they revenged themselves by saying it was all braggadocio—his battles had been fought over a bottle, and by the fireside.

The district east and west of Knightsbridge had long been infested with footpads; they robbed passengers in the country lanes, which then abounded, and sometimes on the King's highway, from which those lanes offered an easy escape.

One moonlight night Captain Cowen was returning home alone from an entertainment at Fulham, when suddenly the air seemed to fill with a woman's screams and cries. They issued from a lane on his right hand. He whipped out his sword and dashed down the lane. It took a sudden turn, and in a moment he came upon three footpads, robbing and maltreating an old gentleman and his wife. The old man's sword lay at a distance, struck from his feeble hand; the woman's tongue proved the better weapon, for at least it brought an ally.

The nearest robber, seeing the Captain come at him with his drawn sword glittering in the moonshine, fired hastily, and grazed his cheek, and was skewered like a frog the next moment; his cry of agony mingled with two shouts of dismay, and the other footpads fled; but even as they turned Captain Cowen's nimble blade entered the shoulder of one, and pierced the fleshy part. He escaped, however, but howling and bleeding.

Captain Cowen handed over the lady and gentleman to the people who flocked to the place, now the work was done, and the disabled robber to the guardians of the public peace, who arrived last of all. He himself withdrew apart and wiped his sword very carefully and minutely with a white pocket-handkerchief, and then retired.

He was so far from parading his exploit that he went round by the park and let himself into the 'Swan' with his private key, and was going quietly to bed, when the chambermaid met him, and up flew her arms with cries of dismay. 'Oh, Captain! Captain! Look at you—smothered in blood! I shall faint.'

'Tush! Silly wench!' said Captain Cowen. 'I am not hurt.'

'Not hurt, sir! And bleeding like a pig! Your cheek—your poor cheek!'

Captain Cowen put up his hand, and found that blood was really welling from his cheek and ear.

He looked grave for a moment, then assured her it was but a scratch, and offered to convince her of that. 'Bring me some luke-warm water, and thou shalt be my doctor. But, Barbara, prithee publish it not.'

Next morning an officer of justice enquired after him at the 'Swan', and demanded his attendance at Bow Street at two that afternoon, to give evidence against the footpads. This was the very thing he wished to avoid; but there was no evading the summons.

The officer was invited into the bar by the landlady, and sang the gallant Captain's exploit, with his own variations. The inn began to ring with Cowen's praises. Indeed, there was now but one detractor left—the hostler, Daniel Cox, a drunken fellow of sinister aspect, who had for some time stared and lowered at Captain Cowen, and muttered mysterious things, doubts as to his being a real Captain, etc., etc. Which incoherent murmurs of a muddle-headed drunkard were not treated as oracular by any human creature, though the stable-boy once went so far as to say, 'I sometimes almost thinks as how our Dan do know summut; only he don't rightly know what 'tis, along o' being always muddled in liquor.'

Cowen, who seemed to notice little, but noticed everything, had observed the lowering looks of this fellow, and felt he had an enemy; it even made him a little uneasy, though he was too proud and self-possessed to show it.

With this exception, then, everybody greeted him with hearty compliments, and he was cheered out of the inn, marching to Bow Street.

Daniel Cox, who—as accidents will happen—was sober that morning, saw him out, and then put on his own coat.

'Take thou charge of the stable, Sam,' said he.

'Why, where be'st going at this time o' day?'

'I be going to Bow Street,' said Daniel doggedly.

At Bow Street Captain Cowen was received with great respect, and a seat given him by the sitting magistrate while some minor cases were disposed of.

In due course the highway robbery was called and proved by the parties who, unluckily for the accused, had been actually robbed before Cowen interfered.

Then the oath was tendered to Cowen; he stood up by the magistrate's side and deposed, with military brevity and exactness to the facts I have related, but refused to swear to the identity of the individual culprit who stood pale and trembling at the dock.

The Attorney for the Crown, after pressing in vain, said, 'Quite right, Captain Cowen; a witness cannot be too scrupulous.'

He then called an officer who had found the robber leaning against a railing fainting from loss of blood, scarce a furlong from the scene of the robbery, and wounded in the shoulder. That let in Captain Cowen's evidence, and the culprit was committed for trial, and soon after peached upon his only comrade at large. The other lay in the hospital at Newgate.

The magistrate complimented Captain Cowen on his conduct and his evidence, and he went away universally admired. Yet he was not elated nor indeed content. Sitting by the magistrate's side, after he had given his evidence, he happened to look all round the Court, and in a distant corner he saw the enormous mottled nose and sinister eyes of Daniel Cox glaring at him with a strange but puzzled expression.

Cowen had learned to read faces, and he said to himself: 'What is there in that ruffian's mind about me? Did he know me years ago? I cannot remember him. Curse the beast—one would almost—think—he is cudgelling his drunken memory. I'll keep an eye on *you*.'

He went home thoughtful and discomposed, because this drunkard glowered at him so. The reception he met with at the 'Swan' effaced the impression. He was received with acclamations, and now that publicity was forced on him he accepted it, and revelled in popularity.

About this time he received a letter from his son, enclosing a notice from the college tutor, speaking highly of his ability, good conduct, devotion to study.

This made the father swell with loving pride.

Jack hinted modestly that there were unavoidable expenses and his funds were dwindling. He enclosed an account that showed how the money went.

The father wrote back and bade him be easy; he should have every farthing required and speedily. 'For,' said he, 'my half-year's interest is due now.'

Two days after he had a letter from his man of business begging him to call. He went with alacrity, making sure his money was waiting for him as usual.

His lawyer received him very gravely, and begged him to be seated. He then broke to him some appalling news. The great house of

Brown, Molyneux & Co. had suspended payments at noon the day before, and were not expected to pay a shilling in the pound. Captain Cowen's little fortune was gone—all but his pension of £80 a year.

He sat like a man turned to stone; then he clasped his hands with agony, and uttered two words—no more: 'My son!'

He rose and left the place like one in a dream. He got down to Knightsbridge, he hardly knew how. At the very door of the inn he fell down in a fit. The people of the inn were round him in a moment, and restoratives freely supplied. His sturdy nature soon revived; but with the moral and physical shock, his lips were slightly distorted over his clenched teeth. His face, too, was ashy pale.

When he came to himself the first face he noticed was that of Daniel Cox, eyeing him, not with pity, but with puzzled curiosity. Cowen shuddered and closed his own eyes to avoid this blighting glare. Then, without opening them, he muttered: 'What has befallen me? I feel no wound.'

'Laws forbid, sir!' said the landlady, leaning over him. 'Your honour did but swoon for once, to show you was born of a woman, and not made of naught but steel. Here, you gaping loons and sluts, help the Captain to his room amongst ye, and then go about your business.'

This order was promptly executed, so far as assisting Captain Cowen to rise; but he was no sooner on his feet than he waved them all from him haughtily, and said: 'Let me be. It is the mind—it is the mind'; and he smote his forehead in despair, for now it all came back on him.

Then he rushed into the inn and locked himself into his room. Female curiosity buzzed about the doors, but was not admitted until he had recovered his fortitude, and formed a bitter resolution to defend himself and his son against all mankind.

At last there came a timid tap, and a mellow voice said: 'It is only me, Captain. Prithee let me in.'

He opened to her, and there was Barbara with a large tray and a snow-white cloth. She spread a table deftly, and uncovered a roast capon, and uncorked a bottle of white port, talking all the time. 'The mistress says you must eat a bit, and drink this good wine, for her sake. Indeed, sir, 'twill do you good after your swoon.' With many such encouraging words she got him to sit down and eat, and then filled his glass and put it to his lips. He could not eat much, but he drank the white port—a wine much prized, and purer than the purple vintage of our day.

At last came Barbara's post-diet. 'But alack! to think of your fainting dead away! Oh, Captain, what is the trouble?'

The tear was in Barbara's eye, though she was the emissary of Dame Cust's curiosity, and all curiosity herself.

Captain Cowen, who had been expecting this question for some time, replied doggedly: 'I have lost the best friend I had in the world.'

'Dear heart!' said Barbara, and a big tear of sympathy, that had been gathering ever since she entered the room, rolled down her cheeks.

She put up a corner of her apron to her eyes. 'Alas, poor soul!' said she. 'Ay, I do know how hard it is to love and lose; but bethink you, sir, 'tis the lot of man. Our own turn must come. And you have your son left to thank God for, and a warm friend or two in this place, thof they be but humble.'

'Ay, good wench,' said the soldier, his iron nature touched for a moment by her goodness and simplicity, 'and none I value more than thee. But leave me awhile.'

The young woman's honest cheeks reddened at the praise of such a man. 'Your will's my pleasure, sir,' said she, and retired, leaving the capon and the wine.

Any little compunction he might have at refusing his confidence to this humble friend did not trouble him long. He looked on women as leaky vessels; and he had firmly resolved not to make his situation worse by telling the base world that he was poor. Many a hard rub had put a fine point on this man of steel.

He glozed the matter, too, in his own mind. 'I told her no lie. I *have* lost my best friend, for I've lost my money.'

From that day Captain Cowen visited the taproom no more, and indeed seldom went out by daylight. He was all alone now, for Mr Gardiner was gone to Wiltshire to collect his rents. In his solitary chamber Cowen ruminated his loss and the villainy of mankind, and his busy brain resolved scheme after scheme to repair the impending ruin of his son's prospects. It was there the iron entered his soul. The example of the very footpads he had baffled occurred to him in his more desperate moments, but he fought the temptation down; and in due course one of them was transported, and one hung, the other languished in Newgate.

By-and-by he began to be mysteriously busy, and the door always locked. No clue was ever found to his labours but bits of melted wax in the fender and a tuft or two of grey hair, and it was never discovered in Knightsbridge that he often begged in the City at dusk, in a disguise so perfect that a frequenter of the 'Swan' once gave him a groat. Thus did he levy his tax upon the stony place that had undone him.

Instead of taking his afternoon walk as heretofore, he would sit disconsolate on the seat of a staircase window that looked into the yard, and so take the air and sun; and it was owing to this new habit he overheard, one day, a dialogue, in which the foggy voice of the hostler predominated at first. He was running down Captain Cowen to a pot-boy. The pot-boy stood up for him. That annoyed Cox. He spoke louder and louder the more he was opposed, till at last he bawled out: 'I tell ye I've seen him a-sitting by the judge, and I've seen him in the dock.'

At these words Captain Cowen recoiled, though he was already out of sight, and his eye glittered like a basilisk's.

But immediately a new voice broke upon the scene, a woman's. 'Thou foul-mouthed knave. Is it for thee to slander men of worship, and give the inn a bad name? Remember I have but to lift my finger to hang thee, so drive me not to't. Begone to thy horses this moment; thou art not fit to be among Christians. Begone, I say, or it shall be the worse for thee'; and she drove him across the yard, and followed him up with a current of invectives eloquent even at a distance, though the words were no longer distinct; and who should this be but the housemaid, Barbara Lamb, so gentle, mellow, and melodious before the gentlefolk, and especially her hero, Captain Cowen!

As for Daniel Cox, he cowered, writhed, and wriggled away before her, and slipped into the stable.

Captain Cowen was now soured by trouble, and this persistent enmity of that fellow roused at last a fixed and deadly hatred in his mind, all the more intense that fear mingled with it.

He sounded Barbara; asked her what nonsense that ruffian had been talking, and what he had done that she could hang him for. But

Barbara would not say a malicious word against a fellow-servant in cold blood. 'I can keep a secret,' said she. 'If he keeps his tongue off you, I'll keep mine.'

'So be it,' said Cowen. 'Then I warn you I am sick of his insolence; and drunkards must be taught not to make enemies of sober men nor fools of wise men.' He said this so bitterly that, to soothe him, she begged him not to trouble about the ravings of a sot. 'Dear heart,' said she, 'nobody heeds Dan Cox.'

Some days afterwards she told him that Dan had been drinking harder than ever, and wouldn't trouble honest folk long, for he had the delusions that go before a drunkard's end; why, he had told the stable-boy he had seen a vision of himself climb over the garden wall, and enter the house by the back door. 'The poor wretch says he knew himself by his *bottle nose* and his cow-skin waistcoat; and, to be sure, there is no such nose in the parish—thank Heaven for 't!—and not many such waistcoats.' She laughed heartily, but Cowen's lip curled in a venomous sneer. He said: 'More likely 'twas the knave himself. Look to your spoons, if such a face as that walks by night.' Barbara turned grave directly; he eyed her askant, and saw the random shot had gone home.

Captain Cowen now often slept in the City, alleging business.

Mr Gardiner wrote from Salisbury, ordering his room to be ready and his sheets well aired.

One afternoon he returned with a bag and a small valise, prodigiously heavy. He had a fire lighted, though it was a fine autumn, for he was chilled with his journey, and invited Captain Cowen to sup with him. The latter consented, but begged it might be an early supper, as he must sleep in the City.

'I am sorry for that,' said Gardiner. 'I have a hundred and eighty guineas there in that bag, and a man could get into my room from yours.'

'Not if you lock the middle door,' said Cowen. 'But I can leave you the key of my outer door, for that matter.'

This offer was accepted; but still Mr Gardiner felt uneasy. There had been several robberies at inns, and it was a rainy, gusty night. He was depressed and ill at ease. Then Captain Cowen offered him his pistols, and helped him load them—two bullets in each. He also went and fetched him a bottle of the best port, and after drinking one glass with him, hurried away, and left his key with him for further security.

Mr Gardiner, left to himself, made up a great fire and drank a glass or two of the wine; it seemed remarkably heady, and raised his spirits. After all, it was only for one night; tomorrow he would deposit his gold in the bank. He began to unpack his things and put his night-dress to the fire; but by and by he felt so drowsy that he did but take his coat off, put his pistols under the pillow, and lay down on the bed and fell fast asleep.

That night Barbara Lamb awoke twice, thinking each time she heard doors open and shut on the floor below her.

But it was a gusty night, and she concluded it was most likely the wind. Still a residue of uneasiness made her rise at five instead of six, and she lighted her tinder and came down with a rush-light. She found Captain Cowen's door wide open; it had been locked when she went to bed. That alarmed her greatly. She looked in. A glance was enough. She cried, 'Thieves! thieves!' and in a moment uttered scream upon scream.

In an incredibly short time pale and eager faces of men and women filled the passage.

Cowen's room, being open, was entered first. On the floor lay what Barbara had seen at a glance—his portmanteau rifled and the clothes scattered about. The door of communication was ajar; they opened it, and an appalling sight met their eyes: Mr Gardiner was lying in a pool of blood and moaning feebly. There was little hope of saving him; no human body could long survive such a loss of the vital fluid. But it so happened there was a country surgeon in the house. He staunched the wounds—there were three—and somebody or other had the sense to beg the victim to make a statement. He was unable at first; but under powerful stimulants revived at last, and showed a strong wish to aid justice in avenging him. By this time they had got a magistrate to attend, and he put his ear to the dying man's lips; but others heard, so hushed was the room and so keen the awe and curiosity of each panting heart.

'I had gold in my portmanteau, and was afraid. I drank a bottle of wine with Captain Cowen, and he left me. He lent me his key and his pistols. I locked both doors. I felt very sleepy, and lay down. When I woke a man was leaning over my portmanteau. His back was towards

me. I took a pistol, and aimed steadily. It missed fire. The man turned
and sprang on me. I had caught up a knife, one we had for supper. I
stabbed him with all my force. He wrested it from me, and I felt piercing blows. I am slain. Ay, I am slain.'

'But the man, sir. Did you not see his face at all?'

'Not till he fell on me. But then, very plainly. The moon shone.'

'Pray describe him.'

'Broken hat.'

'Yes.'

'Hairy waistcoat.'

'Yes.'

'Enormous nose.'

'Do you know him?'

'Ay. The hostler, Cox.'

There was a groan of horror and a cry for vengeance.

'Silence,' said the magistrate. 'Mr Gardiner, you are a dying man.
Words may kill. Be careful. Have you any doubts?'

'About what?'

'That the villain was Daniel Cox.'

'None whatever.'

At these words the men and women, who were glaring with pale
faces and all their senses strained at the dying man and his faint yet terrible denunciation, broke into two bands; some remained rooted to
the place, the rest hurried with cries of vengeance in search of Daniel
Cox. They were met in the yard by two constables, and rushed first to
the stables, not that they hoped to find him there. Of course he had
absconded with his booty.

The stable door was ajar. They tore it open.

The grey dawn revealed Cox fast asleep on the straw in the first
empty stall, and his bottle in the manger. His clothes were bloody, and
the man was drunk. They pulled him, cursed him, struck him, and
would have torn him in pieces, but the constables interfered, set him
up against the rail, like timber, and searched his bosom, and found—
a wound; then turned all his pockets inside out, amidst great expectations, and found—three half-pence and the key of the stable door.

They ransacked the straw, and all the premises, and found—nothing.

Then, to make him sober and get something out of him, they pumped upon his head till he was very nearly choked. However, it told on him. He gasped for breath awhile, and rolled his eyes, and then coolly asked them had they found the villain.

They shook their fists at him. 'Ay, we have found the villain, red-handed.'

'I mean him as prowls about these parts in my waistcoat, and drove his knife into me last night—wonder a didn't kill me out of hand. Have ye found *him* amongst ye?'

This question met with a volley of jeers and execrations, and the constables pinioned him, and bundled him off in a cart to Bow Street, to wait examination.

Meantime two Bow Street runners came down with a warrant, and made a careful examination of the premises. The two keys were on the table. Mr Gardiner's outer door was locked. There was no money either in his portmanteau or Captain Cowen's. Both pistols were found loaded, but no priming in the pan of the one that lay on the bed; the other was primed, but the bullets were above the powder.

Bradbury, one of the runners, took particular notice of all.

Outside, blood was traced from the stable to the garden wall, and under this wall, in the grass, a bloody knife was found belonging to the 'Swan' Inn. There was one knife less in Mr Gardiner's room than had been carried up to his supper.

Mr Gardiner lingered till noon, but never spoke again.

The news spread swiftly, and Captain Cowen came home in the afternoon, very pale and shocked.

He had heard of a robbery and murder at the 'Swan', and came to know more. The landlady told him all that had transpired, and that the villain Cox was in prison.

Cowen listened thoughtfully, and said: 'Cox! No doubt he is a knave; but murder!—I should never have suspected him of that.'

The landlady pooh-poohed his doubts. 'Why, sir, the poor gentleman knew him, and wounded him in self-defence, and the rogue was found a-bleeding from that very wound, and my knife as done the murder not a stone's-throw from him as done it, which it was that Dan Cox, and he'll swing for't, please God.' Then, changing her tone, she said solemnly, 'You'll come and see him, sir?'

'Yes,' said Cowen resolutely, with scarce a moment's hesitation.

The landlady led the way, and took the keys out of her pocket and opened Cowen's door. 'We keep all locked,' said she, half apologetically; 'the magistrate bade us; and everything as we found it—God help us! There—look at your portmanteau. I wish you may not have been robbed as well.'

'No matter,' said he.

'But it matters to *me*,' said she, 'for the credit of the house.' Then she gave him the key of the inner door, and waved her hand towards it, and sat down and began to cry.

Cowen went in and saw the appalling sight. He returned quickly, looking like a ghost, and muttered, 'This is a terrible business.'

'It is a bad business for me and all,' said she. 'He have robbed you too, I'll go bail.'

Captain Cowen examined his trunk carefully. 'Nothing to speak of,' said he. 'I've lost eight guineas and my gold watch.'

'There!—there!—there!' cried the landlady.

'What does that matter, dame? *He* has lost his life.'

'Ay, poor soul. But 'twon't bring him back, you being robbed and all. Was ever such an unfortunate woman? Murder and robbery in *my* house! Travellers will shun it like a pest-house. And the new landlord, he only wanted a good excuse to take it down altogether.'

This was followed by more sobbing and crying. Cowen took her downstairs into the bar, and comforted her. They had a glass of spirits together, and he encouraged the flow of her egotism, till at last she fully persuaded herself it was *her* calamity that one man was robbed and another murdered in *her* house.

Cowen, always a favourite, quite won her heart by falling into this view of the matter, and when he told her he must go back to the City again, for he had important business, and besides had no money left, either in his pockets or his rifled valise, she encouraged him to go, and said kindly, indeed it was no place for him now; it was very good of him to come back at all—but both apartments should be scoured and made decent in a very few days; and a new carpet down in Mr Gardiner's room.

So Cowen went back to the City, and left this notable woman to mop up *her* murder.

At Bow Street, next morning, in answer to the evidence of his guilt, Cox told a tale which the magistrate said was even more ridiculous than most of the stories uneducated criminals get up on such occasions: with this single comment he committed Cox for trial.

Everybody was of the magistrate's opinion, except a single Bow Street runner, the same who had already examined the premises. This man suspected Cox, but had one qualm of doubt founded on the place where he had discovered the knife, and the circumstance of the blood being traced from that place to the stable, and not from the inn to the stable, and on a remark Cox had made to him in the cart. 'I don't belong to the house. I haan't got no keys to go in and out o' nights. And if I took a hatful of gold, I'd be off with it into another country—wouldn't *you?* Him as took the gentleman's money, he knew where 'twas, and he have got it; I didn't, and I haan't.'

Bradbury came down to the 'Swan', and asked the landlady a question or two. She gave him short answers. He then told her that he wished to examine the wine that had come down from Mr Gardiner's room.

The landlady looked him in the face, and said it had been drunk by the servants or thrown away long ago.

'I have my doubts of that,' said he.

'And welcome,' said she.

Then he wished to examine the keyholes.

'No,' said she; 'there has been prying enough into my house.'

Said he angrily: 'You are obstructing justice. It is very suspicious.'

'It is you that is suspicious, and a mischief-maker into the bargain,' said she. 'How do I know what you might put into my wine and my keyholes, and say you found it? You are well known, you Bow Street runners, for your hanky-panky tricks. Have *you* got a search-warrant, to throw more discredit upon my house? No? Then pack! and learn the law before you teach it me.'

Bradbury retired, bitterly indignant, and his indignation strengthened his faint doubt of Cox's guilt.

He set a friend to watch the 'Swan', and he himself gave his mind to the whole case, and visited Cox in Newgate three times before his trial.

The next novelty was that legal assistance was provided for Cox by a person who expressed compassion for his poverty and inability to defend himself, guilty or not guilty; and that benevolent person was— Captain Cowen.

In due course Daniel Cox was arraigned at the bar of the Old Bailey for robbery and murder.

The deposition of the murdered man was put in by the Crown and the witnesses sworn who heard it, and Captain Cowen was called to support a portion of it. He swore that he supped with the deceased and loaded one pistol for him, while Mr Gardiner loaded the other; lent him the key of his own door for further security, and himself slept in the City.

The judge asked him where, and he said, '13 Farringdon Street'.

It was elicited from him that he had provided counsel for the prisoner.

His evidence was very short and to the point. It did not directly touch the accused, and the defendant's counsel—in spite of his client's eager desire—declined to cross-examine Captain Cowen. He thought a hostile examination of so respectable a witness, who brought nothing home to the accused, would only raise more indignation against his client.

The prosecution was strengthened by the reluctant evidence of Barbara Lamb. She deposed that three years ago Cox had been detected by her stealing money from a gentleman's table in the 'Swan' Inn, and she gave the details.

The judge asked her whether this was at night.

'No, my lord; at about four of the clock. He is never in the house at night; the mistress can't abide him.'

'Has he any key of the house?'

'Oh dear no, my lord.'

The rest of the evidence for the Crown is virtually before the reader.

For the defence it was proved that the man was found drunk, with no money nor keys upon him, and that the knife was found under the wall, and the blood was traceable from the wall to the stable. Bradbury, who proved this, tried to get in about the wine; but this was stopped as irrelevant. 'There is only one person under suspicion,' said the judge, rather sternly.

As counsel were not allowed in that day to make speeches to the jury, but only to examine and cross-examine and discuss points of law, Daniel Cox had to speak in his own defence.

'My lord,' said he, 'it was my double done it.'

'Your what?' asked my lord, a little peevishly.

'My double. There's a rogue prowls about the "Swan" at nights, which you couldn't tell him from me. (*Laughter*.) You needn't to laugh me to the gallows. I tell ye he have got a nose like mine.' (*Laughter*.)

*Clerk of Arraigns*. Keep silence in the court, on pain of imprisonment.

'And he have got a waistcoat the very spit of mine, and a tumble-down hat such as I do wear. I saw him go by and let hisself into the "Swan" with a key, and I told Sam Pott next morning.'

*Judge*. Who is Sam Pott?

*Culprit*. Why, my stable-boy, to be sure.

*Judge*. Is he in court?

*Culprit*. I don't know. Ay, there he is.

*Judge*. Then you'd better call him.

*Culprit* (*shouting*). Hy! Sam!

*Sam*. Here be I. (*Loud laughter*.)

The judge explained calmly that to call a witness meant to put him in the box and swear him, and that although it was irregular, yet he should allow Pott to be sworn, if it would do the prisoner any good.

Prisoner's counsel said he had no wish to swear Mr Pott.

'Well, Mr Gurney,' said the judge, 'I don't think he can do you any harm.' Meaning in so desperate a case.

Thereupon Sam Pott was sworn, and deposed that Cox had told him about this double.

'When?'

'Often and often.'

'Before the murder?'

'Long afore that.'

*Counsel for the Crown*. Did you ever see this double?

'Not I.'

*Counsel*. I thought not.

Daniel Cox went on to say that on the night of the murder he was up with a sick horse, and he saw his double let himself out of the inn the back way, and then turn round and close the door softly; so he slipped out to meet him. But the double saw him, and made for the garden wall. He ran up and caught him with one leg over the wall, and seized a black bag he was carrying off; the figure dropped it, and he heard a lot of money chink: that thereupon he cried 'Thieves!' and seized the man; but immediately received a blow, and lost his senses for a time. When he came to the man and the bag were both gone, and he felt so sick that he staggered to the stable and drank a pint of neat brandy, and he remembered no more till they jumped on him, and told him he had robbed and murdered a gentleman inside the 'Swan' Inn. 'What they can't tell me,' said Daniel, beginning to shout, 'is how I could know who has got money, and who haan't, inside the "Swan" Inn. I keeps the stables, not the inn; and where be my keys to open and shut the "Swan"? I never had none. And where's the gentleman's money? 'Twas somebody in the inn as done it, for to have the money, and when you find the money, you'll find the man.'

The prosecuting counsel ridiculed this defence, and *inter alia* asked the jury whether they thought it was a double the witness Lamb had caught robbing in the inn three years ago.

The judge summed up very closely, giving the evidence of every witness. What follows is a mere synopsis of his charge.

He showed it was beyond doubt that Mr Gardiner returned to the inn with money, having collected his rents in Wiltshire; and this was known in the inn, and proved by several, and might have transpired in the yard or the taproom. The unfortunate gentleman took Captain Cowen, a respectable person, his neighbour in the inn, into his confidence, and revealed his uneasiness. Captain Cowen swore that he supped with him, but could not stay all night, most unfortunately. But he encouraged him, left him his pistols, and helped him load them.

Then his lordship read the dying man's deposition.

The person thus solemnly denounced was found in the stable, bleeding from a recent wound, which seems to connect him at once with the deed as described by the dying man.

'But here,' said my lord, 'the chain is no longer perfect. A knife, taken from the "Swan", was found under the garden wall, and the first traces of blood commenced there, and continued to the stable, and were abundant on the straw and on the person of the accused. This was proved by the constable and others. No money was found on him, and no keys that could have opened any outer doors of the "Swan" Inn. The accused had, however, three years before, been guilty of a theft from a gentleman in the inn, which negatives his pretence that he always confined himself to the stables. It did not, however, appear that on the occasion of the theft he had unlocked any doors, or possessed the means. The witness for the Crown, Barbara Lamb, was clear on that.

'The prisoner's own solution of the mystery was not very credible. He said he had a double—or a person wearing his clothes and appearance; and he had seen this person prowling about long before the murder, and had spoken of the double to one Pott. Pott deposed that Cox had spoken of this double more than once; but admitted he never saw the double with his own eyes.

'This double, says the accused, on the fatal night let himself out of the "Swan" Inn and escaped to the garden wall. There he (Cox) came up with this mysterious person, and a scuffle ensued in which a bag was dropped and gave the sound of coin; and then Cox held the man and cried, "Thieves!" but presently received a wound and fainted, and on recovering himself, staggered to the stables and drank a pint of brandy.

'The story sounds ridiculous, and there is no direct evidence to back it; but there is a circumstance that lends some colour to it. There was one bloodstained instrument, and no more, found on the premises, and that knife answers to the description given by the dying man, and, indeed, may be taken to be the very knife missing from his room; and this knife was found under the garden wall, and there the blood commenced and was traced to the stable.

'Here,' said my lord, 'to my mind, lies the defence. Look at the case on all sides, gentlemen—an undoubted murder done by hands; no suspicion resting on any known person but the prisoner—a man who had already robbed in the inn; a confident recognition by one whose deposition is legal evidence, but evidence we cannot cross-examine; and a recognition by moonlight only and in the heat of a struggle.

'If on this evidence, weakened not a little by the position of the knife and the traces of blood, and met by the prisoner's declaration, which accords with that single branch of the evidence, you have a doubt, it is your duty to give the prisoner the full benefit of that doubt, as I have endeavoured to do; and if you have no doubt, why then you have only to support the law and protect the lives of peaceful citizens. Whoever has committed this crime, it certainly is an alarming circumstance that, in a public inn, surrounded by honest people, guarded by locked doors, and armed with pistols, a peaceful citizen can be robbed like this of his money and his life.'

The jury saw a murder at an inn; an accused, who had already robbed in that inn, and was denounced as his murderer by the victim. The verdict seemed to them to be Cox, or impunity. They all slept at inns; a double they had never seen; undetected accomplices they had all heard of. They waited twenty minutes, and brought in their verdict—Guilty.

The judge put on his black cap, and condemned Daniel Cox to be hanged by the neck till he was dead.

After the trial was over, and the condemned man led back to prison to await his execution, Bradbury went straight to 13 Farringdon Street and enquired for Captain Cowen.

'No such name here,' said the good woman of the house.

'But you keep lodgers?'

'Nay, we keep but one; and he is no Captain—he is a City clerk.'

'Well, madam, it is not idle curiosity, I assure you, but was not the lodger before him Captain Cowen?'

'Laws, no! it was a parson. Your rakehelly Captains wouldn't suit the like of us. 'Twas a reverend clerk; a grave old gentleman. He wasn't very well to do, I think; his cassock was worn, but he paid his way.'

'Keep late hours?'

'Not when he was in town; but he had a country cure.'

'Then you have let him in after midnight.'

'Nay, I keep no such hours. I lent him a pass-key. He came in and out from the country when he chose. I would have you to know he was an old man, and a sober man, and an honest man; I'd wager my life on that. And excuse me, sir, but who be you, that do catechise me so about my lodgers?'

'I am an officer, madam.'

The simple woman turned pale and clasped her hands. 'An officer!' she cried. 'Alack! what have I done *now?*'

'Why, nothing, madam,' said the wily Bradbury. 'An officer's business is to protect such as you, not to trouble you, for all the world. There, now, I'll tell you where the shoe pinches. This Captain Cowen has just sworn in a court of justice that he slept here on the 15th of last October.'

'He never did, then. Our good parson had no acquaintances in the town. Not a soul ever visited him.'

'Mother,' said a young girl, peeping in, 'I think he knew somebody of that very name. He did ask me once to post a letter for him, and it was to some man of worship, and the name was Cowen, yes—Cowen 'twas. I'm sure of it. By the same token, he never gave me another letter, and that made me pay the more attention.'

'Jane, you are too curious,' said the mother.

'And I am very much obliged to you, my little maid,' said the officer, 'and also to you, madam,' and so took his leave.

One evening, all of a sudden, Captain Cowen ordered a prime horse at the 'Swan', strapped his valise on before him, and rode out of the yard post-haste; he went without drawing bridle to Clapham, and then looked round him, and seeing no other horseman near trotted gently round into the Borough, then into the City, and slept at an inn in Holborn. He had bespoken a particular room beforehand, a little room he frequented. He entered it with an air of anxiety. But this soon vanished after he had examined the floor carefully. His horse was ordered at five o'clock next morning. He took a glass of strong waters at the door to fortify his stomach, but breakfasted at Uxbridge and fed his good horse. He dined at Beaconsfield, baited at Thame, and supped with his son at Oxford; next day paid all the young man's debts, and spent a week with him.

His conduct was strange: boisterously gay and sullenly despondent by turns. During the week came an unexpected visitor, General Sir Robert Barrington. This officer was going out to America to fill an important office. He had something in view for young Cowen, and came to judge quietly of his capacity. But he did not say anything at that time, for fear of exciting hopes he might possibly disappoint.

51

However, he was much taken with the young man. Oxford had polished him. His modest reticence, until invited to speak, recommended him to older men, especially as his answers were judicious, when invited to give his opinion. The tutors also spoke very highly of him.

'You may well love that boy,' said General Barrington to the father.

'God bless you for praising him!' said the other. 'Ay, I love him too well.'

Soon after the General left Cowen changed some gold for notes, and took his departure for London, having first sent word of his return. He meant to start after breakfast and make one day of it; but he lingered with his son, and did not cross Magdalen Bridge till one o'clock.

This time he rode through Dorchester, Benson, and Henley, and as it grew dark resolved to sleep at Maidenhead.

Just after Hurley Bottom, at four cross-roads, three highwaymen spurred on him from right and left. 'Your money or your life!'

He whipped a pistol out of his holster and pulled at the nearest head in a moment.

The pistol missed fire. The next moment a blow from the butt-end of a horse-pistol dazed him, and he was dragged off his horse and his valise emptied in a minute.

Before they had done with him, however, there was a clatter of hoofs, and the robbers sprang to their nags and galloped away for the bare life as a troop of yeomanry rode up. The thing was so common the newcomers read the situation at a glance, and some of the best mounted gave chase; the others attended to Captain Cowen, caught his horse, strapped on his valise, and took him with them into Maidenhead, his head aching, his heart sickening and raging by turns. All his gold gone, nothing left but a few £1 notes that he had sewed into the lining of his coat.

He reached the 'Swan' next day in a state of sullen despair. 'A curse is on me,' he said. '*My* pistol miss fire; *my* gold gone.'

He was welcomed warmly. He stared with surprise. Barbara led the way to his old room and opened it. He started back. 'Not there,' he said, with a shudder.

'Alack! Captain, we have kept it for you. Sure *you* are not afear'd.'

'No,' said he doggedly; 'no hope, no fear.'

She stared, but said nothing.

He had hardly got into the room when, click, a key was turned in the door of communication. 'A traveller there!' said he. Then, bitterly, 'Things are soon forgotten in an inn.'

'Not by me,' said Barbara solemnly. 'But you know our dame, she can't let money go by her. 'Tis our best room, mostly, and nobody would use it that knows the place. He is a stranger. He is from the wars; will have it he is English, but talks foreign. He is civil enough when he is sober, but when he has got a drop he does maunder away, to be sure, and sings such songs I never.'

'How long has he been here?' asked Cowen.

'Five days, and the mistress hopes he will stay as many more, just to break the spell.'

'He can stay or go,' said Cowen. 'I am in no humour for company. I have been robbed, girl.'

'You robbed, sir? Not openly, I am sure.'

'Openly—but by numbers—three of them. I should soon have sped one, but my pistol snapped fire just like his. There, leave me, girl; fate is against me, and a curse upon me. Bubbled out of my fortune in the City, robbed of my gold upon the road. To be honest is to be a fool.'

He flung himself on the bed with a groan of anguish, and the ready tears ran down soft Barbara's cheeks. She had tact, however, in her humble way, and did not prattle to a strong man in a moment of wild distress. She just turned and cast a lingering glance of pity on him, and went to fetch him food and wine. She had often seen an unhappy man the better for eating and drinking.

When she was gone he cursed himself for his weakness in letting her know his misfortunes. They would be all over the house soon. 'Why, that fellow next door must have heard me bawl them out. I have lost my head,' said he, 'and I never needed it more.'

Barbara returned with the cold powdered beef and carrots, and a bottle of wine she had paid for herself. She found him sullen, but composed. He made her solemnly promise not to mention his losses. She consented readily, and said, 'You know I can hold my tongue.'

When he had eaten and drunk and felt stronger he resolved to put a question to her. 'How about that poor fellow?'

She looked puzzled a moment, then turned pale, and said, solemnly: ' 'Tis for this day week I hear. 'Twas to be last week, but the King did respite him for a fortnight.'

'Ah! indeed! Do you know why?'

'No, indeed. In his place, I'd rather have been put out of the way at once; for they will surely hang him.'

Now in our day the respite is very rare: a criminal is hanged or reprieved. But at the period of our story men were often respited for short or long periods, yet suffered at last. One poor wretch was respited for two years, yet executed. This respite, therefore, was nothing unusual, and Cowen, though he looked thoughtful, had no downright suspicion of anything so serious to himself as really lay beneath the surface of this not unusual occurrence.

I shall, however, let the reader know more about it. The judge in reporting the case notified to the proper authority that he desired his Majesty to know he was not entirely at ease about the verdict. There was a lacuna in the evidence against this prisoner. He stated the flaw in a very few words. But he did not suggest any remedy.

Now the public clamoured for the man's execution, that travellers might be safe. The King's adviser thought that if the judge had serious doubts, it was his business to tell the jury so. The order for execution issued.

Three days after this the judge received a letter from Bradbury, which I give verbatim.

### The King v. Cox.

MY LORD,—Forgive my writing to you in a case of blood. There is no other way. Daniel Cox was not defended. Counsel went against his wish, and would not throw suspicion on any other. That made it Cox or nobody. But there was a man in the inn whose conduct was suspicious. He furnished the wine that made the victim sleepy—and I must tell you the landlady would not let me see the remnant of the wine. She did everything to baffle me and defeat justice—he loaded two pistols so that neither could go off. He has got a pass-key, and goes in and out of the 'Swan' at all hours. He provided counsel for Daniel Cox. That could only be through compunction.

He swore in court that he slept that night at 13 Farringdon Street. Your lordship will find it on your notes. For 'twas you put the question, and methinks heaven inspired you. An hour after the trial I was at 13 Farringdon

Street. No Cowen and no Captain had ever lodged there nor slept there. Present lodger, a City clerk; lodger at date of murder, an old clergyman that said he had a country cure, and got the simple body to trust him with a pass-key; so he came in and out at all hours of the night. This man was no clerk, but, as I believe, the cracksman that did the job at the 'Swan'.

My lord, there is always two in a job of this sort—the professional man and the confederate. Cowen was the confederate, hocussed the wine, loaded the pistols, and lent his pass-key to the cracksman. The cracksman opened the other door with his tools, unless Cowen made him duplicate keys. Neither of them intended violence, or they would have used their own weapons. The wine was drugged expressly to make that needless. The cracksman, instead of a black mask, put on a calf-skin waistcoat and a bottle-nose, and that passed muster for Cox by moonlight; it puzzled Cox by moonlight, and deceived Gardiner by moonlight.

For the love of God get me a respite for the innocent man, and I will undertake to bring the crime home to the cracksman and to his confederate Cowen.

Bradbury signed this with his name and quality.

The judge was not sorry to see the doubt his own wariness had raised so powerfully confirmed. He sent this missive on to the minister, with the remark that he had received a letter which ought not to have been sent to him, but to those in whose hands the prisoner's fate rested. He thought it his duty, however, to transcribe from his notes the question he had put to Captain Cowen, and his reply that he had slept at 13 Farringdon Street on the night of the murder, and also the substance of the prisoner's defence, with the remark that, as stated by that uneducated person, it had appeared ridiculous; but that after studying this Bow Street officer's statements, and assuming them to be in the main correct, it did not appear ridiculous, but only remarkable, and it reconciled all the undisputed facts, whereas that Cox was the murderer was and ever must remain irreconcilable with the position of the knife and the track of the blood.

Bradbury's letter and the above comment found their way to the King, and he granted what was asked—a respite.

Bradbury and his fellows went to work to find the old clergyman, *alias* cracksman. But he had melted away without a trace, and they got no other clue. But during Cowen's absence they got a traveller, i.e. a disguised agent, into the inn, who found relics of wax in the keyholes of Cowen's outer door and of the door of communication.

Bradbury sent this information in two letters, one to the judge, and one to the minister.

But this did not advance him much. He had long been sure that Cowen was in it. It was the professional hand, the actual robber and murderer, he wanted.

The days succeeded one another—nothing was done. He lamented, too late, he had not applied for a reprieve, or even a pardon. He deplored his own presumption in assuming that he could unravel such a mystery entirely. His busy brain schemed night and day; he lost his sleep, and even his appetite. At last, in sheer despair, he proposed to himself a new solution, and acted upon it in the dark and with consummate subtlety; for he said to himself: 'I am in deeper water than I thought. Lord, how they skim a case at the Old Bailey! They take a pond for a puddle, and go to fathom it with a forefinger.'

Captain Cowen sank into a settled gloom, but he no longer courted solitude; it gave him the horrors. He preferred to be in company, though he no longer shone in it. He made acquaintance with his neighbour, and rather liked him. The man had been in the Commissariat Department, and seemed half surprised at the honour a Captain did him in conversing with him. But he was well versed in all the incidents of the late wars, and Cowen was glad to go with him into the past; for the present was dead, and the future horrible.

This Mr Cutler, so deferential when sober, was inclined to be more familiar when in his cups, and that generally ended in his singing and talking to himself in his own room in the absurdest way. He never went out without a black leather case strapped across his back like a dispatch box. When joked and asked as to the contents, he used to say, 'Papers, papers,' curtly.

One evening, being rather the worse for liquor, he dropped it, and there was a metallic sound. This was immediately commented on by the wags of the company.

'That fell heavy for paper,' said one.

'And there was a ring,' said another.

'Come, unload thy pack, comrade, and show us thy papers.'

Cutler was sobered in a moment, and looked scared. Cowen observed this, and quietly left the room. He went upstairs to his own room, and mounting on a chair he found a thin place in the partition and made an eyelet-hole.

That very night he made use of this with good effect. Cutler came up to bed, singing and whistling, but presently threw down something heavy, and was silent. Cowen spied, and saw him kneel down, draw from his bosom a key suspended round his neck by a ribbon, and open the dispatch box. There were papers in it, but only to deaden the sound of a great many new guineas that glittered in the light of the candle, and seemed to fire, and fill the receptacle.

Cutler looked furtively round, plunged his hands in them, took them out by handfuls, admired them, kissed them, and seemed to worship them, locked them up again, and put the black case under his pillow.

While they were glaring in the light, Cowen's eyes flashed with unholy fire. He clutched his hands at them where he stood, but they were inaccessible. He sat down despondent, and cursed the injustice of fate. Bubbled out of money in the City; robbed on the road; but when another had money, it was safe: he left his keys in the locks of both doors, and his gold never quitted him.

Not long after this discovery he got a letter from his son, telling him that the college bill for battels, or commons, had come in, and he was unable to pay it; he begged his father to disburse it, or he should lose credit.

This tormented the unhappy father, and the proximity of gold tantalized him so that he bought a phial of laudanum and secreted it about his person.

'Better die,' said he, 'and leave my boy to Barrington. Such a legacy from his dead comrade will be sacred, and he has the world at his feet.'

He even ordered a bottle of red port and kept it by him to swill the laudanum in, and so get drunk and die.

But when it came to the point he faltered.

Meantime the day drew near for the execution of Daniel Cox. Bradbury had undertaken too much; his cracksman seemed to the King's advisers as shadowy as the double of Daniel Cox.

The evening before that fatal day Cowen came to a wild resolution; he would go to Tyburn at noon, which was the hour fixed, and would die under that man's gibbet—so was this powerful mind unhinged.

This desperate idea was uppermost in his mind when he went up to his bedroom.

But he resisted. No, he would never play the coward while there was a chance left on the cards; while there is life there is hope. He seized the bottle, uncorked it, and tossed off a glass. It was potent, and tingled through his veins and warmed his heart.

He set the bottle down before him. He filled another glass; but before he put it to his lips jocund noises were heard coming up the stairs, and noisy, drunken voices, and two boon companions of his neighbour Cutler—who had a double-bedded room opposite him—parted with him for the night. He was not drunk enough, it seems, for he kept demanding 't'other bottle'. His friends, however, were of a different opinion; they bundled him into his room and locked him in from the other side, and shortly after burst into their own room, and were more garrulous than articulate.

Cutler, thus disposed of, kept saying and shouting and whining that he must have 't'other bottle'. In short, any one at a distance would have thought he was announcing sixteen different propositions, so various were the accents of anger, grief, expostulation, deprecation, supplication, imprecation, and whining tenderness in which he declared he must have 't'other bo'l'.

At last he came bump against the door of communication. 'Neighbour,' said he, 'your wuship, I mean, great man of war.'

'Well, sir?'

'Let's have t'other bo'l.'

Cowen's eyes flashed; he took out his phial of laudanum and emptied about a fifth part of it into the bottle.

Cutler whined at the door: 'Do open the door, your wuship, and let's have t'other (hic).'

'Why, the key is on your side.'

A feeble-minded laugh at the discovery, a fumbling with the key, and the door opened and Cutler stood in the doorway, with his cravat disgracefully loose, and his visage wreathed in foolish smiles. His eyes goggled; he pointed with a mixture of surprise and low cunning at the table. 'Why, there *is* t'other bo'l! Let's have'm.'

'Nay,' said Cowen, 'I drain no bottles at this time; one glass suffices me. I drink your health.' He raised his glass.

Cutler grabbed the bottle and said brutally: 'And I'll drink yours!' and shut the door with a slam, but was too intent on his prize to lock it.

Cowen sat and listened.

He heard the wine gurgle, and the drunkard draw a long breath of delight.

Then there was a pause; then a snatch of song, rather melodious and more articulate than Mr Cutler's recent attempts at discourse.

Then another gurgle and another loud 'Ah!'

Then a vocal attempt, which broke down by degrees.

Then a snore.

Then a somnolent remark—'All right!'

Then a staggering on to his feet. Then a swaying to and fro, and a subsiding against the door.

Then by and by a little reel at the bed and a fall flat on the floor.

Then stertorous breathing.

Cowen sat still at the keyhole some time, then took off his boots and softly mounted his chair, and applied his eye to the peephole.

Cutler was lying on his stomach between the table and the bed.

Cowen came to the door on tiptoe and turned the handle gently; the door yielded.

He lost nerve for the first time in his life. What horrible shame, should the man come to his senses and see him!

He stepped back into his own room, ripped up his portmanteau, and took out, from between the leather and the lining, a disguise and a mask. He put them on.

Then he took his loaded cane; for he thought to himself, 'No more stabbing in that room,' and he crept through the door like a cat.

The man lay breathing stertorously, and his lips blowing out at every exhalation like lifeless lips urged by a strong wind, so that Cowen began to fear, not that he might wake, but that he might die.

It flashed across him he should have to leave England.

What he came to do seemed now wonderfully easy; he took the key by its ribbon carefully off the sleeper's neck, unlocked the dispatch box, took off his hat, put the gold into it, locked the dispatch box, replaced the key, took up his hatful of money, and retired slowly on tiptoe as he came.

He had but deposited his stick and the booty on the bed, when the sham drunkard pinned him from behind, and uttered a shrill whistle. With a fierce snarl Cowen whirled his captor round like a feather, and dashed with him against the post of his own door, stunning the man so that he relaxed his hold, and Cowen whirled him round again, and kicked him in the stomach so felly that he was doubled up out of the way, and contributed nothing more to the struggle except his last meal. At this very moment two Bow Street runners rushed madly upon Cowen through the door of communication. He met one in full career with a blow so tremendous that it sounded through the house, and drove him all across the room against the window, where he fell down senseless; the other he struck rather short, and though the blood spurted and the man staggered, he was on him again in a moment, and pinned him. Cowen, a master of pugilism, got his head under his left shoulder, and pommelled him cruelly; but the fellow managed to hold on, till a powerful foot kicked in the door at a blow, and Bradbury himself sprang on Captain Cowen with all the fury of a tiger; he seized him by the throat from behind, and throttled him, and set his knee to his back; the other, though mauled and bleeding, whipped out a short rope, and pinioned him in a turn of the hand. Then all stood panting but the disabled men, and once more the passage and the room were filled with pale faces and panting bosoms.

Lights flashed on the scene, and instantly loud screams from the landlady and her maids, and as they screamed they pointed with trembling fingers.

And well they might. There—caught red-handed in an act of robbery and violence, a few steps from the place of the mysterious murder, stood the stately figure of Captain Cowen and the mottled face and bottle nose of Daniel Cox, condemned to die in just twelve hours' time.

'Ay, scream, ye fools,' roared Bradbury, 'that couldn't see a church by daylight.' Then, shaking his fist at Cowen: 'Thou villain! 'Tisn't one man you have murdered, 'tis two. But please God I'll save one of them yet, and hang you in his place. Way, there! not a moment to lose.'

In another minute they were all in the yard, and a hackney-coach sent for.

Captain Cowen said to Bradbury, 'This thing on my face is choking me.'

'Oh, better than you have been choked—at Tyburn and all.'

'Hang me. Don't pillory me. I've served my country.'

Bradbury removed the wax mask. He said afterwards he had no power to refuse the villain, he was so grand and gentle.

'Thank you, sir. Now, what can I do for you? Save Daniel Cox?'

'Ay, do that and I'll forgive you.'

'Give me a sheet of paper.'

Bradbury, impressed by the man's tone of sincerity, took him into the bar, and getting all his men round him, placed paper and ink before him.

He addressed to General Barrington, in attendance on his Majesty, these:

GENERAL,—See his Majesty betimes, tell him from me that Daniel Cox, condemned to die at noon, is innocent, and get him a reprieve. Oh, Barrington, come to your lost comrade. The bearer will tell you where I am. I cannot.

EDWARD COWEN.

'Send a man you can trust to Windsor with that, and take me to my most welcome death.'

A trusty officer was dispatched to Windsor, and in about an hour Cowen was lodged in Newgate.

All that night Bradbury laboured to save the man that was condemned to die. He knocked up the sheriff of Middlesex, and told him all.

'Don't come to me,' said the sheriff; 'go to the minister.'

He rode to the minister's house. The minister was up. His wife gave a ball—windows blazing, shadows dancing—music—lights. Night turned into day. Bradbury knocked. The door flew open, and revealed a line of bedizened footmen, dotted at intervals up the stairs.

'I must see my lord. Life or death. I'm an officer from Bow Street.'

'You can't see my lord. He is entertaining the Proosian Ambassador and his sweet.'

'I must see him, or an innocent man will die tomorrow. Tell him so. Here's a guinea.'

'Is there? Step aside here.'

He waited in torments till the message went through the gamut of lackeys, and got, more or less mutilated, to the minister.

He detached a buffer, who proposed to Mr Bradbury to call at the Do-little office in Westminster next morning.

'No,' said Bradbury, 'I don't leave the house till I see him. Innocent blood shall not be spilled for want of a word in time.'

The buffer retired, and in came a duffer, who said the occasion was not convenient.

'Ay, but it is,' said Bradbury, 'and if my lord is not here in five minutes, I'll go upstairs and tell my tale before them all, and see if they are all hairdressers' dummies, without heart, or conscience, or sense.'

In five minutes in came a gentleman, with an order on his breast, and said, 'You are a Bow Street officer?'

'Yes, my lord.'

'Name?'

'Bradbury.'

'You say the man condemned to die tomorrow is innocent?'

'Yes, my lord.'

'How do you know?'

'Just taken the real culprit.'

'When is the other to suffer?'

'Twelve tomorrow.'

'Seems short time. Humph! Will you be good enough to take a line to the sheriff? Formal message tomorrow.'

The actual message ran:

Delay execution of Cox till we hear from Windsor. Bearer will give reasons.

With this Bradbury hurried away, not to the sheriff, but the prison: and infected the gaoler and the chaplain and all the turnkeys with pity for the condemned, and the spirit of delay.

Bradbury breakfasted, and washed his face, and off to the sheriff. Sheriff was gone out. Bradbury hunted him from pillar to post, and could find him nowhere. He was at last obliged to go and wait for him at Newgate.

He arrived at the stroke of twelve to superintend the execution. Bradbury put the minister's note into his hand.

'This is no use,' said he. 'I want an order from his Majesty, or the Privy Council at least.'

'Not to delay,' suggested the chaplain. 'You have all the day for it.'

'All the day! I can't be all the day hanging a single man. My time is precious, gentlemen.' Then, his bark being worse than his bite, he said, 'I shall come again at four o'clock, and then, if there is no news from Windsor, the law must take its course.'

He never came again, though, for even as he turned his back to retire, there was a faint cry from the furthest part of the crowd, a paper raised on a hussar's lance, and as the mob fell back on every side, a royal aide-de-camp rode up, followed closely by the mounted runner, and delivered to the sheriff a reprieve under the sign-manual of his Majesty, George the First.

At 2 p.m. of the same day General Sir Robert Barrington reached Newgate, and saw Captain Cowen in private. That unhappy man fell on his knees and made a confession.

Barrington was horrified, and turned as cold as ice to him. He stood erect as a statue. 'A soldier to rob,' said he. 'Murder was bad enough—but to rob!'

Cowen, with his head and hands all hanging down, could only say faintly: 'I have been robbed and ruined, and it was for my boy. Ah me! what will become of him? I have lost my soul for him, and now he will be ruined and disgraced—by me, who would have died for him.' The strong man shook with agony, and his head and hands almost touched the ground.

Sir Robert Barrington looked at him and pondered.

'No,' said he, relenting a little, 'that is the one thing I can do for you. I had made up my mind to take your son to Canada as my secretary, and I will take him. But he must change his name. I sail next Thursday.'

The broken man stared wildly; then started up and blessed him; and from that moment the wild hope entered his breast that he might keep his son unstained by his crime, and even ignorant of it.

Barrington said that was impossible; but yielded to the father's prayers, and consented to act as if it was possible. He would send a messenger to Oxford, with money and instructions to bring the young man up and put him on board the ship at Gravesend.

This difficult scheme once conceived, there was not a moment to be lost. Barrington sent down a mounted messenger to Oxford, with money and instructions.

Cowen sent for Bradbury, and asked him when he was to appear at Bow Street.

'Tomorrow, I suppose.'

'Do me a favour. Get all your witnesses; make the case complete, and show me only once to the public before I am tried.'

'Well, Captain,' said Bradbury, 'you were square with me about poor Cox. I don't see as it matters much to you; but I'll not say you nay.' He saw the solicitor for the Crown, and asked a few days to collect all his evidence. The functionary named Friday.

This was conveyed next day to Cowen, and put him in a fever; it gave him a chance of keeping his son ignorant, but no certainty. Ships were eternally detained at Gravesend waiting for a wind; there were no steam-tugs then to draw them into blue water. Even going down the Channel letters boarded them if the wind slacked. He walked his room to and fro, like a caged tiger, day and night.

Wednesday evening Barrington came with the news that his son was at the 'Star' in Cornhill. 'I have got him to bed,' said he, 'and, Lord forgive me, I have let him think he will see you before we go down to Gravesend tomorrow.'

'Then let me see him,' said the miserable father. 'He shall know naught from me.'

They applied to the gaoler, and urged that he could be a prisoner all the time, surrounded by constables in disguise. No; the gaoler would not risk his place and an indictment. Bradbury was sent for, and made light of the responsibility. 'I brought him here,' said he, 'and I will take him to the "Star", I and my fellows. Indeed, he will give us no trouble this time. Why, that would blow the gaff, and make the young gentleman fly to the whole thing.'

'It can only be done by authority,' was the gaoler's reply.

'Then by authority it shall be done,' said Sir Robert. 'Mr Bradbury, have three men here with a coach at one o'clock, and a regiment, if you like, to watch the "Star".'

Punctually at one came Barrington with an authority. It was a request from the queen. The gaoler took it respectfully. It was an authority not worth a button; but he knew he could not lose his place, with this writing to brandish at need.

The father and son dined with the General at the 'Star'. Bradbury and one of his fellows waited as private servants; other officers, in plain clothes, watched back and front.

At three o'clock father and son parted; the son with many tears, the father with dry eyes, but a voice that trembled as he blessed him.

Young Cowen, now Morris, went down to Gravesend with his chief; the criminal back to Newgate, respectfully bowed from the door of the 'Star' by landlord and waiters.

At first he was comparatively calm, but as the night advanced became restless, and by and by began to pace his cell again like a caged lion.

At twenty minutes past eleven a turnkey brought him a line; a horseman had galloped in with it from Gravesend.

A fair wind—we weigh anchor at the full tide. It is a merchant vessel, and the Captain under my orders to keep off shore and take no messages. Farewell. Turn to the God you have forgotten. He alone can pardon you.

On receiving this note, Cowen betook him to his knees.

In this attitude the gaoler found him when he went his round.

He waited till the Captain rose, and then let him know that an able lawyer was in waiting, instructed to defend him at Bow Street next morning. The truth is, the females of the 'Swan' had clubbed money for this purpose.

Cowen declined to see him. 'I thank you, sir,' said he, 'I will defend myself.'

He said, however, he had a little favour to ask.

'I have been,' said he, 'of late much agitated and fatigued, and a sore trial awaits me in the morning. A few hours of unbroken sleep would be a boon to me.'

'The turnkeys must come in to see you are all right.'

'It is their duty; but I will lie in sight of the door if they will be good enough not to wake me.'

'There can be no objection to that, Captain, and I am glad to see you calmer.'

'Thank you; never calmer in my life.'

He got his pillow, set two chairs, and composed himself to sleep. He put the candle on the table, that the turnkeys might peep through the door and see him.

Once or twice they peeped in very softly, and saw him sleeping in the full light of the candle, to moderate which, apparently, he had thrown a white handkerchief over his face.

At nine in the morning they brought him his breakfast, as he must be at Bow Street between ten and eleven.

When they came so near him it struck them he lay too still.

They took off the handkerchief.

He had been dead some hours.

Yes, there, calm, grave, and noble, incapable, as it seemed, either of the passions that had destroyed him, or the tender affection which redeemed, yet inspired his crimes, lay the corpse of Edward Cowen.

Thus miserably perished a man in whom were many elements of greatness.

He left what little money he had to Bradbury, in a note imploring him to keep particulars out of the journals, for his son's sake, and such was the influence on Bradbury of the scene at the 'Star', the man's dead face, and his dying words, that, though public detail was his interest, nothing transpired but that the gentleman who had been arrested on suspicion of being concerned in the murder at the 'Swan Inn' had committed suicide; to which was added, by another hand, 'Cox, however, has the King's pardon, and the affair still remains shrouded with mystery.'

Cox was permitted to see the body of Cowen, and whether the features had gone back to youth, or his own brain, long sobered in earnest, had enlightened his memory, recognized him as a man he had seen committed for horse stealing at Ipswich, when he himself was the mayor's groom; but some girl lent the accused a file, and he cut his way out of the cage.

Cox's calamity was his greatest blessing. He went into Newgate scarcely knowing there was a God; he came out thoroughly enlightened in that respect by the teaching of the chaplain and the death of Cowen. He went in a drunkard; the noose that dangled over his head so long terrified him into lifelong sobriety—for he laid all the blame on liquor—and he came out as bitter a foe to drink as drink had been to him.

His case excited sympathy; a considerable sum was subscribed to set him up in trade. He became a horse-dealer on a small scale; but he was really a most excellent judge of horses, and being sober, enlarged his business; horsed a coach or two; attended fairs, and eventually made a fortune by dealing in cavalry horses under Government contracts.

As his money increased, his nose diminished, and when he died, old and regretted, only a pink tinge revealed the habits of his earlier life.

Mrs Martha Cust and Barbara Lamb were no longer sure, but they doubted to their dying day the innocence of the ugly fellow, and the guilt of the handsome, civil-spoken gentleman.

But they converted nobody to their opinion.

# 4

HUGH CONWAY

# Paul Vargas: A Mystery

During the course of my professional career I have met with many strange things. The strangest, the most incomprehensible of all, I am about to narrate.

Its effect upon me was such, that, without pausing for investigation or enquiry, I turned and fled from the town—even from the country in which I witnessed it. It was only when I was some thousands of miles away that I recovered from my terror sufficiently to think calmly over what had happened. Then I vowed a self-imposed vow that for many many years I would mention the matter to no one. My reasons for secrecy were these:

In the first place I was, as I am now, a doctor. Now I am fairly well-to-do, and have little anxiety about the future. Then I was struggling hard to make a living. Such being the case, I argued that the telling of an incredible, monstrous tale—the truth of which, however, I should be bound to uphold in spite of everything and everybody—would do little towards enhancing my reputation for common sense, or improving my professional prospects.

In the second place I determined to wait, in the hope that, some time or another, matters might be explained to my satisfaction.

So it is that for twenty years I have kept my own counsel. My first reason for silence no longer exists; whilst, as to the second, I have now given up hoping for an elucidation. The one person who might make things clear I have never seen since.

Although nearly a third of a man's allotted years has passed, there need be no fear of my magnifying or mystifying anything. The circumstances are still fresh in my mind; moreover, in the fear that memory should play me false, I wrote down at the time all that happened—wrote it with a minuteness and technical detail which would be out of place here.

My story concerns a man whom I saw but thrice in my lifetime; or, I should rather say, saw during three brief periods of my lifetime. We were medical students together. His name—I do not change it—was Paul Vargas.

He was a tall, dark-haired, pale-faced young man: strikingly handsome in his own peculiar style. His nose was aquiline and well-formed: the broad forehead betokened great intellectual power, and the mouth, chin, and strong square jaw all spoke of strength of will and resolution. But had all these features been irregular and unpleasing, the eyes alone would have redeemed the face from plainness. More luminous, eloquent, expressive eyes I have never seen. Their dark beauty was enhanced by a distension of the pupil, seldom met with when the sight is perfect as was Vargas's. They possessed in a remarkable degree the power of reflecting the owner's emotions. Bright as they always were, they sparkled with his mirth, they glittered with his scorn, and when he seemed trying to read the very soul of the man he looked at, their concentrated gaze was such as few could bear with perfect ease.

This is a description of Paul Vargas as I remember him when first we met. I may add that in age he was two years my senior; in intellect a hundred.

Of Vargas's family and antecedents his fellow-students knew nothing. That he was of foreign extraction was clearly shown by his name and general appearance. It was supposed that Jewish blood ran in his veins, but this was pure conjecture; for the young man was as reticent concerning his religious opinions as he was about everything else connected with his private history.

I cannot say he was my friend. Indeed, I believe he had no friends, and I think may add, no enemies. He was too polite and obliging to make foes; although there was usually a calm air of superiority about all he said and did, which at times rather nettled such an unlicked lot of cubs as most of us were in those days.

Yet, if we were not bosom friends, for some months I saw a great deal of Paul Vargas. He was an indefatigable student, and, as if the prescribed course of study was not enough for him, was engaged during his leisure hours on some original and delicate experiments, conducted simply for his own pleasure. Wanting someone to assist him he was good enough to choose me. Why, I never knew. I flattered myself it was because he thought me cleverer than my fellows; but it may have been that he thought me duller and less likely to anticipate or forestall his discoveries.

Under this arrangement I found myself two or three nights in every week at his rooms. From his lavish expenditure in furniture and scientific apparatus, it was clear that Vargas had means of his own. His surroundings were very different from those with which the ordinary medical student must be contented.

All our fraternity looked upon Paul Vargas as abnormally clever; and when the closer intercourse began between us, I found at first no reason to differ from the general opinion. He seemed to have all the works of medical and surgical authorities at his finger ends. He acquired fresh knowledge without effort. He was an accomplished linguist. Let the book or pamphlet be English, French, or German, he read it with equal ease, and, moreover, had the valuable knack of extracting the gist of the matter, whilst throwing aside any worthless lumber which surrounded it. From my average intellectual station I could but admire and envy his rapid and brilliant flights.

He made my visits to him pleasant ones. Our work over for the evening, it was his custom to keep me for an hour or two smoking and chatting; but our talk was not the confidences between two friends. Indeed, it was little more than scientific gossip, and the occasional airing of certain theories: for Vargas, if silent about himself and his private affairs, at least, expressed his opinions on the world in general openly and freely.

He had resolved to become a specialist. He poured out the vials of his scorn on the ordinary general practitioner—the marvellous being who, with equal confidence, is ready to grapple with fever, gout, consumption, blindness, deafness, broken bones, and all the other ills and accidents which afflict mankind.

'It is absurd!' he said. 'As well expect the man who made the lenses for that microscope to make the brasswork also—as well ask the author of this treatise to print and bind it! I tell you one organ, one bit of the microcosm called man, demands a life's study before the cleverest dare to say he understands it.'

Certainly the organ selected by Vargas for his special study was the most complex and unsatisfactory of all—the brain. Any work, new or obsolete, which treated upon it—anything which seemed to demonstrate the connection between mind and body, he examined with intense eagerness. The writings and speculations of the veriest old charlatans were not beneath his notice. The series of experiments we were conducting were to the same end. I need not describe them, but something of their nature may be guessed at, when I say it was long before the time when certain persons endeavoured to persuade the world that scientists were fiends in human shape, who inflicted unheard-of tortures on the lower orders of animals, solely to gratify a lust for cruelty.

We had been engaged on our researches for some weeks—Vargas's researches I should call them, as by this time my conjectures as to what he aimed at had come to an end. I grew tired of groping in the dark, and was making up my mind to tell him he must enlighten me or seek other assistance. Besides, I began to think that, after all, my first estimate of his ability was not quite correct.

He certainly talked at times in the strangest and most erratic way. Some of his speculations and theories were enough, if true, to upset all the recognized canons of science. So wild, indeed, that at times I wondered if, like many others, his genius was allied to madness.

At this time a wave of superstition crossed the country—one of those periodical waves, which, whether called mesmerism, clairvoyance, electro-biology, spiritualism, or thought-reading, rise, culminate, and fall in precisely the same manner.

Paul Vargas, although ridiculing the new craze, read everything that touched upon it, even down to the penny-a-liner's accounts of mysterious occurrences.

'The truth may be found anywhere,' he said; 'if there is a diamond in the ground the most ignorant boor may, unwittingly, dig it out.'

One night I found him in a strange preoccupied mood. He did his work mechanically, and I could see that his thoughts kept straying away. We finished earlier than usual, and for a while he sat opposite to me in silence. Then he raised his eyes and asked me a question.

What that question was I have never been able to remember. I have racked my brain again and again, but have never recalled the purport of it. All I know is, it was, from a scientific point of view, so supremely ridiculous that I burst into a peal of laughter.

For a moment Paul Vargas's eyes positively flamed. Feeling that our relations were not friendly enough to excuse the indiscretion on my part, I hastened to apologize. He was himself again directly, and, with his calm superior smile on his lips, assured me I had done nothing which demanded an apology. He then changed the conversation, and during the remainder of my stay talked as rationally and instructively as the most methodical old lecturer in the schools.

He bade me goodnight with his usual politeness, and sent me away glad that my ill-timed mirth had not offended him. Yet the next morning I received a note saying he had decided to discontinue that particular series of researches in which I had given him such invaluable assistance.

I was somewhat nettled at this summary dismissal. Vargas asked me to his rooms no more, and he was not the man to call upon uninvited. So, except in the schools and in the streets, I saw nothing more of him.

It was predicted by those who should know best that Paul Vargas would be the scholar of the year. I alone dared to doubt it. In spite of his great talents and capacity for work, I fancied there was that in his nature which would defeat these high hopes. There was something wrong—something eccentric about him. In plain English, I believed, if not mad now, Vargas would end his days in a madhouse.

However, he never went up for his last examination. He had a surprise in store for us. Just before the final trial in which he was to reap such laurels he vanished. He went without a word of warning—went bag and baggage. He left no debts behind him. He defrauded no one. He simply, without giving a reason for his departure, went away and left no trace behind him. Some time afterwards it was reported that he had come into a large fortune. This explanation of his conduct was a plausible one, and was generally accepted as correct.

After the nine days' wonder had died away I, like others, ceased to think about the missing man. The years went by, I passed my examination creditably, and was very proud and hopeful when duly authorized to place MD after my name.

I have narrated how I first met Paul Vargas. I had no expectation of again seeing him, nor any great wish to do so. But we met a second time. It was in this wise.

When I took my medical degree I was far from being the staid, sober man I now am. Having a little money of my own I resolved to see something of the world before I settled down. I was not rich enough to be quite idle, so I began by making one or two voyages as doctor to an emigrant ship. I soon grew tired of this occupation, and being in England, but not yet cured of roving, I cast about for something professional to take me abroad. I had not long to wait. Cholera was raging in the East. A fund had been raised to send out a few English doctors: I tendered my services which were accepted.

At Constantinople I was detained several days waiting instructions. One day, whilst idly strolling through the streets, I came face to face with Paul Vargas.

Although he wore the fez and was in appearance more Turkish than English, I knew him at once and accosted him by his name. Surprised as he looked at my salutation, he had evidently no wish to deny his identity. As soon as he recognized me he greeted me cordially, and having learnt what brought me to Constantinople, insisted that I should pay him a visit. I willingly consented to do so. I was most curious to ascertain why he had thrown up the profession so suddenly. The day being still young I started then and there with him for his home.

Naturally, almost my first question was why he left us so mysteriously.

'I had my reasons,' he said.

'They must have been powerful ones.'

He turned his dark eyes full upon me.

'They were,' he said. 'I grew sick of the life. After all, what did it mean? Work, work, work, only to find out how little one really knew or ever could know by study. Why, in one half-hour I learned more by pure chance than anyone else has yet dreamed of.'

I questioned him as to the meaning of his arrogant assertion, but he evaded me with all his old adroitness; then we reached his house, and I forgot all save admiration.

His house was just outside the city. House! it might be called a small palace. Here he lived in true Oriental luxury. Judging from the profusion which surrounded him, and from the lavish scale on which his establishment was conducted, I felt sure that the report of his having inherited a fortune was quite correct. All that money could buy, all that an intellectual Sybarite could desire, seemed to be his. Books, paintings, statuary, costly furniture, rich tapestries, the choicest dishes, and the rarest wines. Only a man in the enjoyment of a princely income could live in such style and splendour.

He led me from room to room, until he opened the door of one more beautifully garnished than any of the others. A girl was sitting at the window. As we entered she sprang forward with a cry of joy, and threw her arms round Vargas.

He returned her passionate embrace; kissed her, whispered some words of love in a strange, musical language, then gently disengaging himself, said—

'Myrrha, welcome an old friend of mine, an Englishman.'

She turned towards me. Her beauty absolutely dazzled me. She was tall and majestic; coil upon coil of jet black hair crowned her well-poised queenly head. Her cheek had the clear brown tinge of the south. Her eyes were glorious. Never before had I seen such a splendid creature. The perfection of her form, the look of splendid health and glowing vitality would have been enough to make her an object of the greatest interest to any one of my own profession.

The bright colours of her rich dress well became her. Although in years she was but a girl, the gold and jewels which covered her hands, arms, and neck, seemed quite in keeping with her beauty. As I looked at her I felt that Paul Vargas's earthly paradise ought to be complete.

She came forward with unembarrassed grace, smiled a bright smile, and giving me her hand, bade me welcome in English, correct enough, although tempered by a slight foreign accent.

After a little while Vargas suggested that I should walk round the gardens with him. As we left the room, the look which passed between him and the girl was quite enough to show the complete love they bore one another.

'Your wife, I suppose?' I said, when we were alone. 'She is very beautiful.'

'My love, my life, my very soul!' he exclaimed passionately. 'But not my wife in your sense of the word.'

I said no more, feeling the subject was a delicate one to handle. Who Myrrha was, or why she should live, unmarried, with him was none of my business.

I had not been long in his society before I discovered that Paul Vargas was, in some ways, much changed—I may say improved. He seemed altogether a better sort of fellow than the man I had known of old. No less polite, but more natural. His invariably charming manners were enhanced by the addition of something like friendliness. In an hour's time I felt that I had made more progress with him than I had in the whole of our previous intercourse. I attributed this change to the power of love, for, wife or no wife, it was plain that the man loved his beautiful companion with all the force of his strong nature.

Yet it shocked me to discover that all the old ambition was dead. I mourned that such a highly gifted man could at his age withdraw completely from the battlefield, and seem only to strive to make life as soft and sensuous as it might be possible for wealth to make it. I spoke once or twice to this effect, but the darkness of his brow and the shortness of his answers told me I trod on forbidden ground. For his own sake I hoped that the day would come when he would weary of his voluptuous existence and long for the bracing tonics of hard work and the struggle for success.

I was detained in Constantinople three days longer. Vargas pressed me to take up my abode with him. It was not worth while to do this, as at any moment I might be ordered away. But I spent several hours of each day with him. He was always glad to see me. Perhaps the sweetness of his seclusion was already beginning to pall upon him, and the occasional sight of a commonplace work-a-day face was a welcome one.

The route came at last. I bade my friend goodbye, and sighed as I thought how grimly the scenes of death and misery to which I was about to pass would contrast with the Elysium I was quitting. Vargas accompanied me to the steamer by which the first part of the journey was to be made.

'Do you mean to live here all your life?' I asked.

'No, I shall grow weary of it—very soon, I expect.'

'And then?'

'Then I shall sell everything and try another land.'

'You must be rich to live as you do.'

'I was rich. I had sixty thousand pounds—but in the last year or two I have spent two-thirds of my fortune.'

'Two-thirds of your capital! What folly!'

He shrugged his shoulders, and smiled that old superior smile. Then a deep gloom settled on his handsome face.

'I have plenty left—plenty to last my time,' he said.

'What nonsense you talk! What do you mean by your time?'

He leaned towards me, placed his hand on my arm, and looked at me with an expression in his eyes which thrilled me.

'I mean this,' he said, slowly. 'I could, if I chose, tell you the exact day—if not the exact hour at which I shall die. You see how I live, so can understand that if I have money to last my time, that time is short.'

'My dear fellow!' I exclaimed, 'have you any complaint—any secret malady?'

'None—I am hale and sound as you. Nevertheless I shall die as I have said.'

His absolute conviction impressed me more than I cared to show. 'A man must die of something specific,' I said. 'If you can predict your illness, can you not take steps to prolong your life?'

'Prolong my life!' he echoed as one in a dream. 'Yes, I can prolong my life—but I will not.'

I could only conclude that Paul Vargas meditated self-destruction.

'Why should you not care to live?' I urged.

'Care to live?' he cried bitterly. 'Man, I revel in life! I have youth, strength, love—fame I could have if I wished for it. Yet it is because I may have fewer temptations to prolong my life that I am squandering my wealth—that I let ambition beckon in vain—that, when the moment draws near, I shall forsake the woman I love.'

It was as I guessed years ago, Paul Vargas was mad!

He sank into moody silence, broken only when the moment of my departure came. Then he roused himself, shook hands with me and bade me good speed.

'We shall meet again some day,' I said cheerfully.

His dark eyes gleamed with all the old scorn they were wont to express when any one, whose words were not worth listening to, opposed him in argument.

'We shall meet no more,' he said, curtly and coldly, turning away and retracing his steps.

He was wrong. We met again!

I worked through the cholera: saw many awful sights: gained much experience and a certain amount of praise. On my way home I enquired for Vargas, and found he had disposed of his house and its entire contents, departing no one knew whither.

Two years went by: I was still unsettled: still holding roving commissions. I blush to say that I had been attacked by the gold fever, and in my haste to grow rich had lost, in mining, nearly all I possessed. I cured myself before the disease grew chronic, but ashamed to return all but penniless to England, I sojourned for a while in one of those mushroom towns of America—towns which spring up almost in a night, wherever there is a chance of making money.

I rather liked the life. It was rough but full of interest. The town held several thousand inhabitants, so there was plenty of work for me and another doctor. If our patients were in luck we were well paid for our services; if, as was usually the case, they were out of luck we received nothing and were not so foolish as to expect more. Still, taking one with another, I found the healing art paid me much better than mining. My studies of human nature were certainly extended at New Durham. I met with all sorts of characters, from the educated gentleman who had come out to win wealth by the sweat of his brow down to the lowest ruffian who lived by plundering his own kind, and my experiences were such that when I did return to England I was competent to write as an authority on the proper treatment of gunshot wounds.

One evening I met the other doctor. We were the best of friends. As our community was at present constituted there was no occasion for professional rivalry. Our hands were always full of work. Indeed, if we manoeuvred at all against each other, it was with the view of shunting off a troublesome patient.

'I wish you'd look in at Webber's when you pass,' said Dr Jones. 'There's a patient of mine there. He's going to die, but for the life of me I can't tell what ails him.'

I promised to call and give my opinion on the case.

Webber's was a mixture of drinking bar, gambling hell, and

lodging-house. Its patrons were not of the most select class, and the scuffles and rows that went on there made the house a disgrace even to New Durham. By this time I was too well known to fear insult even in the lowest den of infamy, so I entered boldly and asked to be conducted to Dr Jones's patient.

A blowsy, sodden-faced, vicious-looking woman led me upstairs and turned the handle of a door.

'He ought to be dead by now,' she said. 'If the doctor can't cure him, or he don't die in two days, out he bundles.'

I walked into the room, taking no notice of the brutal threat. There, on a wretched apology for a bed—with a look of heart-rending despair in his large dark eyes, lay Paul Vargas!

I thought I must be dreaming. The man I had seen little more than two years ago, lapped in absurd luxury—spending money like water to gratify every taste, every desire—now lying in this wretched den, and if Jones's view of the case was correct, dying like a dog! I shuddered with horror and hastened to his side.

He knew me. He was conscious. I could tell that much by the light which leapt into his eyes as I approached.

'Vargas, my poor fellow,' I said, 'what does this mean?'

As I spoke I remembered how he had predicted his own death. He must have remembered it too, for although he made no reply, and lay still as a log, there was a look in his eyes which might express the satisfaction felt by a successful prophet, when one who has laughed at his forecast is bound, at last, to realize its correctness.

I addressed him again and again. Not a word did he answer; so at last I was compelled to think that his power of speech was gone. Then I went to work to thoroughly inspect him and ascertain the nature of his complaint.

I sounded him, tested every organ, examined every limb; but like my colleague was utterly unable to find the cause of his illness. Of course I laboured under the great disadvantage of being unable to get a word of description of his pains from the patient himself. I satisfied myself that he had absolutely lost the power of moving his limbs. This utter helplessness made me fancy the spine might be broken, but it was not so. Paralysis suggested itself, but the obviously clear state of the mind as shown by those eloquent eyes was sufficient to send this idea to the background. At last I gave up, fairly baffled. I could give no name to his ailment—could fix no seat for it. His bodily weakness was great; but weakness must be caused by something. What was that something? So far as my knowledge went there was no specific disease; yet I was as certain as Dr Jones that Paul Vargas, if not dying, was about to die.

And underneath us was the din of drunken men and unsexed women. Ribaldry and blasphemy, oaths and shrieks, laughter and shouts, rose and penetrated the frail planks which bounded the small, dirty room in which the sufferer lay. At all cost he must be moved to more comfortable quarters.

I went downstairs and questioned the Webbers as to how he came there. All they knew was that late one night the man entered the house and asked for a bed. He was accommodated with one, and for two days no one troubled about him. Then someone looked him up and found him in his present deplorable state. One of the inmates who had a grain of kindness left fetched Dr Jones. That was all they knew of the affair.

I managed to secure the assistance of four strong and almost sober men. I paid what reckoning was due at Webber's, then set about removing the poor fellow. He was carried carefully downstairs, laid on an extemporized stretcher, and borne to my house, which, fortunately, was only a few hundred yards away. During the transit he was perfectly conscious, but he spoke no word, nor, by any act of his own, moved hand or foot. I saw him safely installed in my own bed, and having satisfied myself that no immediate evil was likely to result from the removal, went out to look for someone to nurse him.

I was obliged to seek extraneous aid as my household consisted of an old negro who came of a morning to cook my breakfast and tidy up the place. Except for this I was my own servant.

Decent women in a place like New Durham are few and far between, but at last I found one to whom I thought I might venture to entrust my patient, and who, for a handsome consideration, consented to act as sick-nurse. I took her back with me and instructed her to do what seemed to me best for the poor fellow. She was to give him, as often as he would take them, brandy and water and some nourishing spoon meat.

Vargas was now lying with his eyes shut. Except that he undoubtedly breathed he might be dead. I watched him for more than an hour, yet found his state a greater puzzle than ever. So utterly at sea I was that I dared not prescribe for him, fearing I might do more harm than good.

It was growing late. I had a long hard day before me on the morrow. I had to ride many miles, and doubted whether I could get back the same day. Yet, late as it was, I did not retire to rest before I had thoroughly examined the clothes and other personal matters which I had brought from Webber's with the sick man. I hoped to come across the name of some friend to whom I could write and make his state known. Money or articles of value I had little expectation of finding—such things would soon disappear from the person of anyone who lay dying at Webber's!

The only scrap of writing I met with was a letter in a woman's hand. It was short, and although every word showed passionate love, it ended in a manner which told me that a separation had taken place.

'You may leave me,' it ran; 'you may hide yourself in the furthest corner of the world: yet when the moment you know of comes and you need me, I shall find you. Till then, farewell.'

On the flyleaf was pencilled, in Vargas's peculiar handwriting, 'If I can find the strength of will to leave her, my beloved, surely I can die in secret and in silence.'

There was no envelope, no date; no address; no signature to the letter. All it showed me was that Paul Vargas still clung to his morbid prophecy—that he had made up his mind he was to die, and it may be had been driven into his present state by his strange monomania. The mystery was—why should he leave the woman he loved and come here to die alone and uncared for. It was, of course, just possible that in some way he had learnt that I was in New Durham, and when illness overtook him was making his way to me.

This could only be explained by the man himself, and he was without power of speech.

After giving the nurse strict instructions to call me if her charge's condition showed any change, I went to the bed I had rigged up in my sitting room, and in a minute was fast asleep. After I had slept for about three hours a knocking at my door aroused me. I opened it and found the nurse standing outside. Her bonnet and cloak were on, and by the light of the lamp she carried with a tremulous hand I saw that her face was ghastly pale, but nevertheless, wearing a defiant, injured look.

'What's the matter?' I asked.

'I'm going home,' she said, sullenly.

'Going home! Nonsense! Go back to the sick room. Is the man worse?'

'I wouldn't go back for a hundred pounds—I'm going home.'

Thinking some sudden whim had seized her I expostulated, commanded, and entreated. She was inflexible. Then I insisted upon knowing the meaning of such extraordinary conduct. For a while she refused to give me any explanation. At last, she said she had been frightened to death. It was the man's eyes, she added, with a shiver. He had opened them and stared at her. The moment I heard this I ran to his room, fearing the worst. I found nothing to excite alarm; Vargas was quiet, apparently sleeping. So I returned to the stupid woman, rated her soundly, and bade her go back and resume her duties.

Not she! Horses would not drag her into that room again—money would not bribe her to re-enter it. The man had looked at her with those fearful eyes of his until she felt that in another moment she must go mad or die. Why did she not move out of the range of his vision? She had done so; but it was all the same, she knew he was still looking at her—he was looking at her even now—she would never get away from that look until she was out of the house.

By this time the foolish creature was trembling like a leaf; and, moreover, had worked herself up to a pitch bordering on hysteria. Even if I could have convinced her of her folly, she would have been useless for nursing purposes, so I told her to get out of the house as soon as she liked; then, sulkily drawing on my clothes, went to spend the rest of the night by Vargas's bed.

His pulse still beat with feeble regularity. He seemed in want of nothing; so I placed a low chair near the bed and sat down. As I sat there my head was just on a level with his pillow. I watched the pale still face for some time, then I fell into a doze. I woke, looked once more at Vargas, then again closed my eyes, and this time really slept, feeling sure that the slightest movement of his head on the pillow would arouse me, I did not struggle against drowsiness.

Presently I began to dream—a dream so incoherent that I can give no clear description of it. Something or some one was trying to over-power me, whether mentally or physically I cannot say. I was resisting to the best of my ability, the final struggle for mastery was just immi-nent, when, of course, I awoke—awoke to find Paul Vargas's lumi-nous eyes, with strangely dilated pupils, gazing fully into mine. The whole strength of his mind, his very soul, seemed to be thrown into that fixed gaze.

I seemed to shrivel up and grow small beneath it. Those dark, mas-terful eyes, held me spellbound; fascinated me; deprived me of volition or power of motion; fettered me; forbade me even to blink an eyelid. With a strong steady stroke they pierced me through and through, and I felt they meant to subjugate my mind even as they had already subjugated my body, and as their gaze grew more and more intense, I knew that in another moment I must be their slave!

With this thought my own thoughts faded. For a while all seemed dim, misty, and inexplicable, but even through the mist I see those two points glowing with dark sustained fire. I can resist no longer, I am conquered, my will has quitted me and is another's!

Then thought came quickly enough. I am ill—dying in a strange place. There is one I love. She is miles and miles away; but not too far to reach me in time. A burning desire to write to her comes over me. I must and will write before it is too late! Yet I curse myself for the wish as in some dim way I know that some fearful thing must happen if she finds me alive.

Then all consciousness leaves me, except that I have the impression I am out of doors and can feel the night air on my brow. Suddenly I come to myself. I am standing, bareheaded, close to the post-office, with a kind of idea in my bewildered brain that I have just posted a let-ter. I feel battered and shaken, large beads of perspiration are on my forehead. In a dazed way I walk back to my house, the door of which I find left wide open—an act of trustfulness scarcely due to New Durham. I enter, throw myself into a chair, and shudder at what has taken place.

No—not at what has taken place, but at what might have taken place. For I know that Paul Vargas, although speechless and more helpless than an infant, has by the exercise of some strange weird mental power so influenced me that I have identified myself with him, and done as he would have done. His unspoken commands may have worked no evil, but I shudder as I feel sure that had he ordered me, whilst in that mesmeric state, to murder my best friend, I should have done so.

It was only when annoyance and anger succeeded fear, I found myself able to return to him. I felt much mortified that I, in the full vigour of manhood had been conquered and enslaved by the act of a stronger will than my own. I went back to the sickroom, and found Vargas lying with closed eyes. I laid my hand on his shoulder, bent down to his ear and said—

'When you recover I will have a full explanation of the jugglery you have practised upon me.'

I resumed my seat, fearing his strange power no longer. Now that I knew he wielded it I was armed against it. I flattered myself that only by attacking me unawares could he influence me in so mysterious a manner. When next he opened his eyes I did not shun them. I might well have done so—their expression was one of anguish and horror— the expression one might imagine would lurk in the eyes of a conscience-stricken man to whom had just come the knowledge that he had committed some awful crime. Every now and then they turned to me in wild beseeching terror, but they bore no trace of that strange mesmeric power.

Paul Vargas, if he was to die, seemed doomed to die a lingering death. For some ten days longer he lay in that curious state—his symptoms, or rather absence of symptoms, driving Jones and myself to our wits' end. We tried all we could think of without beneficial results. Every day he grew a little weaker—every day his pulse was rather feebler, than on the preceding day. Such stimulant and nutriment as I could force down his throat seemed to do no good. Slowly— very slowly—his life was ebbing away, but so surely that I was fain to come to the sad conclusion that in spite of all our efforts he would slip through our fingers. By this time he had grown frightfully emaciated, and although I am convinced he suffered little or no bodily pain; the look of anguish in his staring dark eyes was positively painful to encounter.

I had obtained the services of another nurse, and was thankful to find that, to her, the dying man was not an object of dread; although, after my own experiences, I could not blame her predecessor.

Hour after hour, day after day, Paul Vargas lay, unable to move or speak; yet I felt sure in full possession of his mental faculties. Several times I noticed, when the door was opened, a look of dread come into his eyes. He breathed freer when he saw that the newcomer was the nurse or myself. This puzzled me, for if, as I suspected, he had willed that I should write a letter and send it to the proper place, his look should have been one of hope and expectancy, instead of its displaying unmistakable signs of fear.

Although Vargas often gave me the impression that he was trying to subject me again to that strange influence, it was only once more that he attained anything like success. One day, grown bold at finding I had as yet avoided a repetition of my thraldom, and, perhaps egged on by curiosity, I met his strange fixed gaze half-way and defied him to conquer me. In a moment or two I found I had miscalculated my powers, and—although I blush to say it—I felt that in another second I must yield to him, and as before, do all he wished. At that critical moment the nurse entered the room and spoke to me. Her voice and presence broke the spell. Thank God, it was so! Vargas was sending an impulse into my mind—urging me in some way which I knew would be irresistible—to perform, not some harmless task, but to go to my medicine chest and fetch a dose of laudanum heavy enough to send him to sleep for ever. And I say, without hesitation, that had the woman not entered the room at that very moment, I should have been forced to do the man's bidding.

Yet I had no wish to cut his few last days short! If I had given him that poison it would have been suicide, not murder!

Although he had predicted his own death, why was Paul Vargas so anxious to die, that he had endeavoured to make me kill him? Unless their tortures are unbearable, few dying persons seek to precipitate matters; and this one, I am sure, suffered little or no pain. His death was lingering and tedious, but not painful.

After this fresh attempt to coerce me, I was almost afraid to leave him alone with the nurse. I even took the precaution of being present when Dr Jones, out of professional curiosity, paid him an occasional visit.

The tension on my nerves grew unbearable. I prayed fervently for the man's recovery, or, if recovery was out of the question, for his death. At last the time came when the latter seemed to be drawing very, very near—so near that Jones, whose interest in the case was unabated, said, as he left me in the evening—

'He will die tonight or before tomorrow is over. I believe he has only kept himself alive the last few days by sheer force of will and determination not to die.'

I assented gloomily, wished my colleague goodnight, and went to rest.

Next morning, just after breakfast, I heard a rap at my door. I opened it and found myself face to face with a woman. She was tall, and even the long black cloak she wore did not hide the grace and symmetry of her figure. A thick veil covered her face. Thinking she had come for advice I begged her to enter the house.

I led her to my sitting-room. She raised her veil and looked at me. I knew her in a moment. She was the lovely girl who had shared with Vargas that luxurious eastern paradise—the girl whom he called Myrrha.

She looked pale and weary, but still very beautiful. Her sombre attire could not diminish her charms. My one thought, as I gazed at her was, how any man, of his own free will, could tear himself from such a creature? Yet, for some unknown reason, Paul Vargas had done so.

It was clear that I was entirely forgotten. No start of recognition showed that my face was anything but that of a stranger. I did not wonder at this, I was much changed; bronzed and bearded; was, in fact, as rough looking a customer as many of my own patients.

For a moment she seemed unable to speak. Her eyes looked at mine as though they would anticipate what I had to tell her. Her lips trembled, but no words came from them.

At last she spoke. 'There is a gentleman here—dying.'

'Yes,' I replied. 'Mr Vargas is here.'

'Am I in time?—is he still alive?'

'He is very, very ill, but still alive.'

A wretch reprieved on the scaffold could not have displayed more delight than did Myrrha when she heard my words. A look of indescribable joy flashed into her face. She clasped her hands in passionate thankfulness and tears of rapture filled her eyes. Poor girl, she had little enough to rejoice at! She was in time—in time for what? To see her lover die. That was all!

'Take me to him at once,' she said, moving towards the door.

I suggested a little rest and refreshment first. She declined both, peremptorily.

'Not a moment must be wasted. I have travelled night and day since I received his letter. Quick, take me to him, or it may be too late!'

I asked her to follow me. She threw off her long cloak, and I saw that her dress beneath it was plain black. No ribbon, jewel, or ornament broke its sable lines. With a look of ineffable joy on her face she followed me to Vargas's room.

'Let me go first and prepare him,' I said.

'No,' she replied, sternly. 'Let me pass.'

She laid her hand on the door, opened it, and preceded me into the room.

Paul Vargas's eyes were turned—as, indeed, they had for the last few days been mostly turned—towards the door; yet the look which leapt into them was not one of joy and welcome. It was a look of woe—of supreme agony. A convulsive shudder ran across his face, and I expected his next breath would be the last.

Why should the advent of his beautiful visitor so affect him? Had he treated this woman so evilly, that he dreaded lest she came to his deathbed to heap reproaches on his head. Yet, he himself had summoned her—brought her from afar—by the letter which he had willed me to write.

Injured or not, Myrrha came to console, not reproach. My doubts on this point were at once set at rest. With a cry of passionate grief she threw herself on her knees beside the bed: clasped the poor wasted hand in hers, and covered it with tears and kisses. In a strange tongue—one unknown to me—she spoke words which I knew were words of fervent love. The musical voice, the thrilling accent, the gestures she used, were interpreters sufficient to make me understand that she was rejoicing that death had spared her lover long enough for her to see him once more.

A soft look, a look that echoed her own, came over the sufferer's face—a look of infinite tenderness and deathless love. But it was transient. His eyes grew stern. I fancied they tried to drive her away; then, as she heeded not his commands, they besought and appealed to her. In vain—the strange girl laughed joyfully as a bride who welcomes her bridegroom. She kissed her lover again and again. Then, with a weary sigh, Paul Vargas closed his eyes—never, I thought, to reopen them. I went to his side.

He was not dead; but he bore infallible signs of approaching dissolution. Practically, it was of little moment whether he died now or in an hour's time. Nothing could save him. Still, the wish one always feels to prolong the faintest flicker of life prompted me to speak to Myrrha.

'The excitement will kill him,' I whispered.

She sprang to her feet as if stung. She threw me a glance so full of horror that I started. Then, bending over Vargas, she satisfied herself that he still breathed.

'Go,' she whispered, fiercely. 'Leave me alone with my love. Take that woman with you.'

I hesitated. I wanted to see the end. But I could not dispute the sacred claims of love and grief, or help sympathizing with the girl in her desire to be alone with the dying man. My duties were ended. I had done all I could; but death in his present mysterious garb had conquered me. The man must die. How could he die better than in the arms of the woman he loved?

I motioned to the nurse to leave the room. I followed her through the door; then turned to take my last look at Paul Vargas.

He was lying apparently unconscious. Myrrha had thrown herself on the bed by his side. His poor pale face was drawn close to her full red lips. Her bosom beat against his. Her arms were wreathed around him, holding him to her. The contrast between life and death— between the rich, strong glowing life of the young girl, and that of the man now ebbed away to its last few sands, was startling. I closed the door reverently. My eyes filled with tears and I sighed for the sorrow which was about to fall on the devoted, passionate creature. How would she bear it! Then I went about my duties, knowing that when I returned home, I should have a patient the less.

I rode some miles into the country, to see a miner who had met with an accident which would most likely prove fatal. Just as I reached his cabin my horse fell suddenly lame. I led him the rest of the way and, having done all I could for the injured man, started to return home. There was nothing for it but to leave my horse to be fetched the next day, and walk back to New Durham.

I strode on as briskly as the nature of the track would allow. As I trudged along I thought of Myrrha and Paul Vargas, and wondered if by any chance I should find him alive on my return. I was so preoccupied with these thoughts that, not until I was close to him, did I notice a man lying on the side of the track.

At first I thought it was one of the common sights of the neighbourhood; a man dead-drunk, but as I stood over him I found, for a wonder, it was not so. The man's back was towards me; his face was buried in the herbage; but I could hear him sobbing as if his heart was about to burst. As he lay there he threw his arms out with wild gestures of despair—he dug his fingers into the ground and tore at it as one racked by unbearable torture. He was evidently a prey to some fearful bodily or mental distress. Whichever it might be, I could not pass without proffering my assistance.

His agitation was so great that he had no idea of my proximity. I spoke, but my words fell unheeded. Sob after sob burst forth from him.

I stooped and placed my hand on his arm. 'My poor fellow,' I said, 'what is the matter?'

At my touch he sprang to his feet. God of Heaven! shall I ever forget that moment. Before me stood Paul Vargas, well and strong, as when we parted some years ago in Constantinople!

What saved me from fainting I cannot tell. The man stood there before me—the very man I had left an hour or two ago at his last gasp! He stood there and cast a shadow. He did not fade away or disappear as a vision or hallucination should do. There was life and strength in every limb. His face was pale but it was with the pallor of grief: for, even now the tears were running from his eyes, and he was wringing his hands in agony.

Speak! I could not have fashioned a word. My tongue clave to my palate. My lips were parched and dry. All I could do was to stare at him, with chattering teeth, bristling hair and ice-cold blood.

He came to my side. He grasped my arm. He was still flesh and blood. Even in that supreme moment his strong convulsive clutch told me that. He spoke. His voice was as the voice of a living man—yet as the voice of one from whom all joy of life has departed.

'Go home,' he said. 'Go home and learn how the strongest may tremble at death—at what a cost he will buy life—how the selfish desire to live can conquer love. You asked me once if I could not prolong life. You are answered. You brought her to me—you yielded then, but not the second time when I would have undone the deed. Go home, before I kill you.'

Something in his whole bearing struck me with deadly terror—a natural human terror. I turned and fled for my life, until my limbs refused to bear me further. Then I sank on the ground and, I believe, lost consciousness.

When I recovered I made the best of my way home, telling myself as I walked along that overwork and want of sleep were acting on me. I had dreamed an absurd horrible dream. Nevertheless I trembled in every limb as I opened the door of the room in which I had left Paul Vargas, dying in the arms of the woman who loved him.

Death had been there during my absence. I knew the meaning of that long shapeless form stretched out on the bed, covered by the white sheet. Yet I trembled more and more. The words I had heard in my supposed dream came to me clear and distinct. It was some time before I could summon courage enough to move the covering from the dead face. I did so at last and I believe shrieked aloud.

Lying there in her black funereal dress, her fair hands crossed on her breast, her waxen face still bearing a smile, lay the girl whom I knew only by the name of Myrrha—dead!

# 5

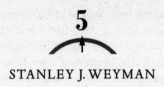

## STANLEY J. WEYMAN

# Gerald

I have friends who tell me that they seldom walk the streets of London without wondering what is passing behind the house-fronts; without picturing a comedy here, a love-scene there, and behind the dingy cane blinds a something ill-defined, a something odd and *bizarre*. They experience—if you believe them—a sense of loneliness out in the street, an impatience of the sameness of all these many houses, their dull bricks and discreet windows, and a longing that someone would step out and ask them to enter and see the play.

Well, I have never felt any of these things; but as I was passing through Fitzhardinge Square about half-past ten o'clock one evening in last July, after dining, if I remember rightly, in Baker Street, something happened to me which I fancy may be of interest to such people.

I was passing through the square from north to south, and to avoid a small crowd, which some reception had drawn together, I left the pavement and struck across the road to the path round the oval garden; which, by the way, contains a few of the finest trees in London. This part was in deep shadow, so that when I presently emerged from it and recrossed the road to the pavement near the top of Fitzhardinge Street, I had an advantage over any persons on the pavement. They were under the lamps, while I, coming from beneath the trees, was almost invisible.

The door of the house immediately in front of me as I crossed was open, and an elderly man-servant out of livery was standing at it, looking up and down the pavement by turns. It was his air of furtive anxiety that drew my attention to him. He was not like a man looking for a cab, or waiting for his sweetheart; and I had my eye upon him as

I stepped upon the pavement before him. But my surprise was great when he uttered a low exclamation of dismay at sight of me, and made as if he would escape; while his face, in the full glare of the light, grew so pale and terror-stricken that he might before have been completely at his ease. I was astonished and instinctively stood still returning his gaze; for perhaps twenty seconds we remained so, he speechless, and his hands fallen by his side. Then, before I could move on, as I was in the act of doing, he cried, 'Oh! Mr George! Oh! Mr George!' in a tone that rang out in the stillness rather as a wail than an ordinary cry.

My name, my surname I mean, is George. For a moment I took the address to myself, forgetting that the man was a stranger, and my heart began to beat more quickly with fear of what might have happened. 'What is it?' I exclaimed. 'What is it?' and I shook back from the lower part of my face the silk muffler I was wearing. The evening was close, but I had been suffering from a sore throat.

He came nearer and peered more closely at me, and I dismissed my fear; for I thought that I could see the discovery of his mistake dawning upon him. His pallid face, on which the pallor was the more noticeable as his plump features were those of a man with whom the world as a rule went well, regained some of its lost colour, and a sigh of relief passed his lips. But this feeling was only momentary. The joy of escape from whatever blow he had thought imminent gave place at once to his previous state of miserable expectancy of something or other.

'You took me for another person,' I said, preparing to pass on. At that moment I could have sworn—I would have given one hundred to one twice over—that he was going to say Yes. To my intense astonishment, he did not. With a very visible effort he said, 'No!'

'Eh! What?' I exclaimed. I had taken a step or two.

'No, sir.'

'Then what is it?' I said. 'What do you want, my good fellow?'

Watching his shuffling indeterminate manner I wondered if he were sane. His next answer reassured me on that point. There was an almost desperate deliberation about its manner. 'My master wishes to see you, sir, if you will kindly walk in for five minutes,' was what he said.

I should have replied, 'Who is your master?' if I had been wise; or cried, 'Nonsense!' and gone my way. But the mind when it is spurred

91

*Stanley J. Weyman*

by a sudden emergency often overruns the more obvious course to adopt a worse. It was possible that one of my intimates had taken the house, and said in his butler's presence that he wished to see me. Thinking of that I answered, 'Are you sure of this? Have you not made a mistake, my man?'

With an obstinate sullenness that was new in him, he said, No, he had not. Would I please to walk in? He stepped briskly forward as he spoke, and induced me by a kind of gentle urgency to enter the house, taking from me with the ease of a trained servant my hat, coat, and muffler. Finding himself in the course of his duties he gained more composure; while I, being thus treated, lost my sense of the strangeness of the proceeding, and only awoke to a full consciousness of my position when he had softly shut the door behind us and was in the act of putting up the chain.

Then I confess I looked round a little alarmed at my precipitancy. But I found the hall spacious, lofty, and dark-panelled, the ordinary hall of an old London house. The big fireplace was filled with plants in flower. There were rugs on the floor and a number of chairs with painted crests on the backs, and in a corner was an old sedan chair, its poles upright against the wall.

No other servants were visible, it is true. But apart from this all was in order, all was quiet, and any idea of violence was manifestly absurd.

At the same time the affair seemed of the strangest. Why should the butler in charge of a well-arranged and handsome house—the house of an ordinary wealthy gentleman—why should he loiter about the open doorway as if anxious to feel the presence of his kind? Why should he show such nervous excitement and terror as I had witnessed? Why should he introduce a stranger?

I had reached this point when he led the way upstairs. The staircase was wide, the steps were low and broad. On either side at the head of the flight stood a beautiful Venus of white Parian marble. They were not common reproductions, and I paused. I could see beyond them a Hercules and a Meleager of bronze, and delicately tinted draperies and ottomans that under the light of a silver hanging-lamp—a gem from Malta—changed a mere lobby to a fairies' nook. The sight filled me with a certain suspicion; which was dispelled, however, when my hand rested for an instant upon the reddish pedestal that supported one of the statues. The cold touch of the marble was enough for me. The pillars were not of composite; of which they certainly would have consisted in a gaming-house, or worse.

Three steps carried me across the lobby to a curtained doorway by which the servant was waiting. I saw that the 'shakes' were upon him again. His impatience was so ill-concealed that I was not surprised— though I was taken aback—when he dropped the mask altogether, and as I passed him—it being now too late for me to retreat undiscovered, if the room were occupied—laid a trembling hand upon my arm and thrust his face close to mine. 'Ask how he is! Say anything,' he whispered trembling, 'no matter what, sir! Only, for the love of heaven, stay five minutes!'

He gave me a gentle push forward as he spoke—pleasant all this!— and announced in a loud quavering voice, 'Mr George!'—which was true enough. I found myself walking round a screen at the same time that something in the room, a long dimly lighted room, fell with a brisk rattling sound, and there was the scuffling noise of a person, still hidden from me by the screen, rising to his feet in haste.

Next moment I was face to face with two men. One, a handsome elderly gentleman, who wore grey moustaches and would have seemed in place at a service club, was still in his chair regarding me with a perfectly calm unmoved face, as if my entrance at that hour were the commonest incident of his life. The other had risen and stood looking at me askance. He was five-and-twenty years younger than his companion and as goodlooking in a different way. But now his face was white and drawn, distorted by the same expression of terror—aye, and a darker and fiercer terror than that which I had already seen upon the servant's features; it was the face of one in a desperate strait. He looked as a man looks who has put all he has in the world upon an outsider—and done it twice. In that quiet drawing-room by the side of his placid companion, with nothing whatever in their surroundings to account for his emotion, his panic-stricken face shocked me inexpressibly.

They were in evening dress; and between them was a chess-table, its men in disorder: almost touching this was another small table bearing a tray of Apollinaris water and spirits. On this the young man was resting one hand as if but for its support he would have fallen.

To add one more fact, I had never seen either of them in my life.

Or wait; could that be true? If so, it must be indeed a nightmare I was suffering. For the elder man broke the silence by addressing me in a quiet ordinary tone that exactly matched his face. 'Sit down, George,' he said, 'don't stand there. I did not expect you this evening.' He held out his hand, without rising from his chair, and I advanced and shook it in silence. 'I thought you were in Liverpool. How are you?' he continued.

'Very well, I thank you,' I muttered mechanically.

'Not very well, I should say,' he retorted. 'You are as hoarse as a raven. You have a bad cold at best. It is nothing worse, my boy, is it?' with anxiety.

'No, a throat cough; nothing else,' I murmured, resigning myself to this astonishing reception—this evident concern for my welfare on the part of a man whom I had never seen in my life.

'That is well!' he answered cheerily. Not only did my presence cause him no surprise. It gave him, without doubt, actual pleasure!

It was otherwise with his companion; grimly and painfully so indeed. He had made no advances to me, spoken no word, scarcely altered his position. His eyes he had never taken from me. Yet in him there was a change. He had discovered, exactly as had the butler before him, his mistake. The sickly terror was gone from his face, and a half-frightened malevolence not much more pleasant to witness had taken its place. Why this did not break out in any active form was part of the general mystery given to me to solve. I could only surmise from glances which he later cast from time to time towards the door, and from the occasional faint creaking of a board in that direction, that his self-restraint had to do with my friend the butler. The inconsequences of dreamland ran through it all: why the elder man remained in error; why the younger with that passion on his face was tongue-tied; why the great house was so still; why the servant should have mixed me up with this business at all—these were questions as unanswerable, one as the other.

And the fog in my mind grew denser when the old gentleman turned from me as if my presence were a usual thing, and rapped the table before him impatiently. 'Now, Gerald!' cried he in sharp tones, 'have you put those pieces back? Good heavens! I am glad that I have not nerves like yours! Don't remember the squares, boy? Here, give them to me!' With a hasty gesture of his hand, something like a mesmeric pass over the board, he set down the half-dozen pieces with a rapid tap! tap! tap! which made it abundantly clear that he, at any rate, had no doubt of their former positions.

'You will not mind sitting by until we have finished the game?' he continued, speaking to me, and in a voice I fancied more genial than that which he had used to Gerald. 'You are anxious to talk to me about your letter, George?' he went on when I did not answer. 'The fact is that I have not read the inclosure. Barnes, as usual, read the outer letter to me, in which you said the matter was private and of grave importance; and I intended to go to Laura tomorrow, as you suggested, and get her to read the news to me. Now you have returned so soon, I am glad that I did not trouble her.'

'Just so, sir,' I said, listening with all my ears; and wondering.

'Well I hope there is nothing very bad the matter, my boy?' he replied. 'However—Gerald! it is your move!—ten minutes more of such play as your brother's, and I shall be at your service.'

Gerald made a hurried move. The piece rattled upon the board as if he had been playing the castanets. His father made him take it back. I sat watching the two in wonder and silence. What did it all mean? Why should Barnes—doubtless behind the screen listening—read the outer letter? Why must Laura be employed to read the inner? Why could not this cultivated and refined gentleman before me read his— Ah! That much was disclosed to me. A mere turn of the hand did it. He had made another of those passes over the board, and I learned from it what an ordinary examination would not have detected. He, the old soldier with the placid face and light-blue eyes, was blind! Quite blind!

I began to see more clearly now, and from this moment I took up, at any rate in my own mind, a different position. Possibly the servant who had impelled me into the middle of this had had his own good reasons for doing so, as I now began to discern. But with a clue to the labyrinth in my hand I could no longer move passively at any other's impulse. I must act for myself. For a while I sat still and made no sign. My suspicions were presently confirmed. The elder man more than once scolded his opponent for playing slowly; in one of these intervals he took from an inside pocket of his dress waistcoat a small packet.

'You had better take your letter, George,' he said. 'If there are, as you mentioned, originals in it, they will be more safe with you than with me. You can tell me all about it, *viva voce*, now you are here. Gerald will leave us alone presently.'

He held the papers towards me. To take them would be to take an active part in the imposture, and I hesitated, my own hand half out-stretched. But my eyes fell at the critical instant upon Master Gerald's face, and my scruples took themselves off. He was eying the packet with an intense greed, and a trembling longing—a very itching of the fingers and toes, to fall upon the prey—that put an end to my doubts. I rose and took the papers. With a quiet, but I think significant, look in his direction, I placed them in the breast-pocket of my evening coat. I had no safer receptacle about me, or into that they would have gone.

'Very well, sir,' I said. 'There is no particular hurry. I think the matter will keep, as things now are, until tomorrow.'

'To be sure. You ought not to be out with such a cold at night, my boy,' he answered. 'You will find a decanter of the Scotch whisky you gave me last Christmas on the tray. Will you have some with hot water and a lemon, George? The servants are all at the theatre—Gerald begged a holiday for them—but Barnes will get you the things in a minute.'

'Thank you; I won't trouble him. I will take some with cold water,' I replied, thinking I should gain in this way what I wanted—time to think: five minutes to myself, while they played.

But I was out in my reckoning. 'I will have mine now too,' he said. 'Will you mix it, Gerald?'

Gerald jumped up to do it with tolerable alacrity. I sat still, prefer-ring to help myself, when he should have attended to his father—if his father it was. I felt more easy now that I had those papers in my pocket. The more I thought of it, the more certain I became that they were the object aimed at by whatever devilry was on foot; and that possession of them gave me the whip-hand. My young gentleman might snarl and show his teeth, but the prize had escaped him.

Perhaps I was a little too confident: a little too contemptuous of my opponent; a little too proud of the firmness with which I had taken at one and the same time the responsibility and the post of vantage. A creak of the board behind the screen roused me from my thoughts.

It fell upon my ear trumpet-tongued: a sudden note of warning. I glanced up with a start, and a conviction that I was being caught napping, and looked instinctively towards the young man. He was busy at the tray, his back to me. Relieved of my fear of I did not know what—perhaps a desperate attack upon my pocket, I was removing my eyes, when, in doing so, I caught sight of his reflection in a small mirror beyond him. Ah!

What was he busy about? Nothing. Absolutely nothing, at the moment. He was standing motionless—I could fancy him breathless also—a strange listening expression on his face; which seemed to me to have faded to a greyish tinge. His left-hand was clasping a half-filled tumbler: the other was at his waistcoat pocket. So he stood during perhaps a second or two, a small lamp upon the tray before him illumining his handsome figure; and then his eyes, glancing up, met the reflection of mine in the mirror. Swiftly as the thought itself could pass from brain to limb, the hand which had been resting in the pocket flashed with a clatter among the glasses; and turning almost as quickly, he brought one of the latter to the chess-table, and set it down unsteadily.

What had I seen! Nothing; actually nothing. Just what Gerald had been doing. Yet my heart was going as many strokes to the minute as a losing crew. I rose abruptly.

'Wait a moment, sir,' I said, as the elder man laid his hand upon the glass, 'I don't think that Gerald has mixed this quite as you like it.'

He had already lifted it to his lips. I looked from him to Gerald. That young gentleman's colour, though he faced me hardily, shifted more than once, and he seemed to be swallowing a succession of over-sized fives-balls; but his eyes met mine in a vicious kind of smile that was not without its gleam of triumph. I was persuaded that all was right even before his father said so.

'Perhaps you have mixed for me, Gerald?' I suggested pleasantly.

'No!' he answered in sullen defiance. He filled a glass with something—perhaps it was water—and drank it, his back towards me. He had not spoken so much as a single word to me before.

The blind man's ear recognized the tone now. 'I wish you boys would agree better,' he said wearily. 'Gerald, go to bed. I would as soon play chess with an idiot from Earlswood. Generally you can play the game if you are good for nothing else; but since your brother came in, you have not made a move which any one not an imbecile would make. Go to bed, boy! Go to bed!'

I had stepped to the table while he was speaking. One of the glasses was full. I lifted it with seeming unconcern to my nose. There was whisky in it as well as water. Then *had* Gerald mixed for me? At any rate, I put the tumbler aside, and helped myself afresh. When I set the glass down empty, my mind was made up.

'Gerald does not seem inclined to move, sir, so I will,' I said quietly. 'I will call in the morning and discuss that matter, if it will suit you. But tonight I feel inclined to get to bed early.'

'Quite right, my boy. I would ask you to take a bed here instead of turning out, but I suppose that Laura will be expecting you. Come in any time tomorrow morning. Shall Barnes call a cab for you?'

'I think I will walk,' I answered, shaking the proffered hand. 'By the way, sir,' I added, 'have you heard who is the new Home Secretary?'

'Yes, Henry Matthews,' he replied. 'Gerald told me. He had heard it at the club.'

'It is to be hoped that he will have no womanish scruples about capital punishment,' I said as if I were incidentally considering the appointment. And with that last shot at Mr Gerald—he turned green, I thought, a colour which does not go well with a black moustache— I walked out of the room, so peaceful, so cosy, so softly lighted as it looked, I remember; and downstairs. I hoped that I had paralysed the young fellow, and might leave the house without molestation.

But as I gained the foot of the stairs he tapped me on the shoulder. I saw then, looking at him, that I had mistaken my man. Every trace of the sullen defiance which had marked his manner throughout the interview upstairs was gone. His face was still pale, but it wore a gentle smile as we confronted one another under the hall lamp. 'I have not the pleasure of knowing you, but let me thank you for your help,' he said in a low voice, yet with a kind of frank spontaneity. 'Barnes's idea of bringing you in was a splendid one, and I am immensely obliged to you.'

'Don't mention it,' I answered stiffly, proceeding with my preparations for going out, as if he were not there; although I must confess that this complete change in him exercised my mind no little.

'I feel so sure that we may rely upon your discretion,' he went on, ignoring my tone, 'that I need say nothing about that. Of course, we owe you an explanation, but as your cold is really yours and not my brother's, you will not mind if I read you the riddle tomorrow instead of keeping you from your bed tonight?'

'It will do equally well—indeed better,' I said, putting on my overcoat, and buttoning it carefully across my chest, while I affected to be looking with curiosity at the sedan chair.

He pointed lightly to the place where the packet lay. 'You are forgetting the papers,' he reminded me. His tone almost compelled the answer, 'To be sure.'

But I had pretty well made up my mind, and I answered instead, 'Not at all. They are quite safe, thank you.'

'But you don't—I beg your pardon——' he said, opening his eyes very wide, as if some new light were beginning to shine upon his mind and he could scarcely believe its revelations. 'You don't really mean that you are going to take those papers away with you?'

'Certainly.'

'My dear sir!' he remonstrated earnestly. 'This is preposterous. Pray forgive me the reminder, but those papers, as my father gave you to understand, are private papers, which he supposed himself to be handing to my brother George.'

'Just so!' was all I said. And I took a step towards the door.

'You really mean to take them?' he asked, seriously.

'I do; unless you can satisfactorily explain the part I have played this evening. And also make it clear to me that you have a right to the possession of the papers.'

'Confound it! If I must do so tonight, I must!' he said reluctantly. 'I trust to your honour, sir, to keep the explanation secret.' I bowed, and he resumed. 'My elder brother and I are in business together. Lately we have had losses which have crippled us so severely that we decided to disclose them to Sir Charles and ask his help. George did so yesterday by letter, giving certain notes of our liabilities. You ask why he did not make such a statement by word of mouth? Because he had to go to Liverpool at a moment's notice to make a last effort to arrange the matter. And as for me,' with a curious grimace, 'my father would as soon discuss business with his dog! Sooner!'

*Stanley J. Weyman*

'Well?' I said. He had paused, and was absently flicking the blossoms off the geraniums in the fireplace with his pocket-handkerchief, looking moodily at his work the while. I cannot remember noticing the handkerchief, yet I seem to be able to see it now. It had a red border, and was heavily scented with white rose. 'Well?'

'Well,' he continued, with a visible effort, 'my father has been ailing lately, and this morning his usual doctor made him see Bristowe. He is an authority on heart-disease, as you doubtless know; and his opinion is,' he added in a lower voice and with some emotion, 'that even a slight shock may prove fatal.'

I began to feel hot and uncomfortable. What was I to think? The packet was becoming as lead in my pocket.

'Of course,' he resumed more briskly, 'that threw our difficulties into the shade at once; and my first impulse was to get these papers from him. Don't you see that? All day I have been trying in vain to effect it. I took Barnes, who is an old servant, partially into my confidence, but we could think of no plan. My father, like many people who have lost their sight, is jealous, and I was at my wits' end, when Barnes brought you up. Your likeness,' he added in a parenthesis, looking at me reflectively, 'to George put the idea into his head, I fancy? Yes, it must have been so. When I heard you announced, for a moment I thought that you were George.'

'And you called up a look of the warmest welcome,' I put in dryly.

He coloured, but answered almost immediately, 'I was afraid that he would assume that the governor had read his letter, and blurt out something about it. Good lord! if you knew the funk in which I have been all the evening lest my father should ask either of us to read the letter!' and he gathered up his handkerchief with a sigh of relief, and wiped his forehead.

'I could see it very plainly,' I answered, going slowly in my mind over what he had told me. If the truth must be confessed, I was in no slight quandary what I should do, or what I should believe. Was this really the key to it all? Dared I doubt it? or that that which I had constructed was a mare's nest—the mere framework of a mare's nest. For the life of me I could not tell!

'Well?' he said presently, looking up with an offended air. 'Is there anything else I can explain? or will you have the kindness to return my property to me now?'

'There is one thing, about which I should like to ask a question,' I said.

'Ask on,' he replied; and I wondered whether there was not a little too much of bravado in the tone of sufferance he assumed.

'Why do you carry——' I went on, raising my eyes to his, and pausing on the word an instant—'that little medicament—you know what I mean—in your waistcoat pocket, my friend?'

He perceptibly flinched. 'I don't quite—quite understand,' he began to stammer. Then he changed his tone and went on rapidly, 'No! I will be frank with you, Mr—Mr——'

'George,' I said, calmly.

'Ah, indeed?' a trifle surprised, 'Mr George! Well, it is something Bristowe gave me this morning to be administered to my father—without his knowledge, if possible—whenever he grows excited. I did not think that you had seen it.'

Nor had I. I had only inferred its presence. But having inferred rightly once, I was inclined to trust my inference further. Moreover, while he gave this explanation, his breath came and went so quickly that my former suspicions returned. I was ready for him when he said, 'Now I will trouble you, if you please, for those papers?' and held out his hand.

'I cannot give them to you,' I replied, point blank.

'You cannot give them to me now?' he repeated.

'No. Moreover, the packet is sealed. I do not see, on second thoughts, what harm I can do you—now that it is out of your father's hands—by keeping it until tomorrow, when I will return it to your brother, from whom it came.'

'He will not be in London,' he answered doggedly. He stepped between me and the door with looks which I did not like. At the same time I felt that some allowance must be made for a man treated in this way.

'I am sorry,' I said, 'but I cannot do what you ask. I will do this, however. If you think the delay of importance, and will give me your brother's address in Liverpool, I will undertake to post the letters to him at once.'

He considered the offer, eying me the while with the same dis-favour which he had exhibited in the drawing-room. At last he said slowly, 'If you will do that?'

'I will,' I repeated. 'I will do it immediately.'

He gave me the direction—'George Ritherdon, at the London and North-Western Hotel, Liverpool,' and in return I gave him my own name and address. Then I parted from him, with a civil goodnight on either side—and little liking I fancy—the clocks striking midnight, and the servants coming in as I passed out into the cool darkness of the square.

Late as it was, I went straight to my club, determined that as I had assumed the responsibility there should be no laches on my part. There I placed the packet, together with a short note explaining how it came into my possession, in an outer envelope, and dropped the whole duly directed and stamped into the nearest pillar box. I could not register it at that hour, and rather than wait until next morning, I omitted the precaution, merely requesting Mr Ritherdon to acknow-ledge its receipt.

Well, some days passed during which it may be imagined that I thought no little about my odd experience. It was the story of the Lady and the Tiger over again. I had the choice of two alternatives at least. I might either believe the young fellow's story, which certainly had the merit of explaining in a fairly probable manner an occurrence of so odd a character as not to lend itself freely to explanation. Or I might disbelieve his story, plausible in its very strangeness as it was, in favour of my own vague suspicions. Which was I to do?

Well, I set out by preferring the former alternative. This, notwith-standing that I had to some extent committed myself against it by withholding the papers. But with each day that passed without bring-ing me an answer from Liverpool, I leaned more and more to the other side. I began to pin my faith to the tiger, adding each morning a point to the odds in the animal's favour. So it went on until ten days had passed.

Then a little out of curiosity, but more, I gravely declare, because I thought it the right thing to do, I resolved to seek out George Rither-don. I had no difficulty in learning where he might be found. I turned up the firm of Ritherdon Brothers (George and Gerald), cotton-spinners and India merchants, in the first directory I consulted. And about noon the next day I called at their place of business, and sent in my card to the senior partner. I waited five minutes—curiously scanned by the porter, who no doubt saw a likeness between me and his employer—and then I was admitted to the latter's room.

He was a tall man with a fair beard, not one whit like Gerald, and yet tolerably good looking; if I say more I shall seem to be describing myself. I fancied him to be balder about the temples, however, and greyer and more careworn than the man I am in the habit of seeing in my shaving-glass. His eyes, too, had a hard look, and he seemed in ill-health. All these things I took in later. At the time I only noticed his clothes. 'So the old gentleman is dead,' I thought, 'and the young one's tale is true after all!' George Ritherdon was in deep mourning.

'I wrote to you,' I began, taking the seat to which he pointed, 'about a fortnight ago.'

He looked at my card, which he held in his hand. 'I think not,' he said slowly.

'Yes,' I repeated. 'You were then at the London and North-Western Hotel, at Liverpool.'

He was stepping to his writing-table, but he stopped abruptly. 'I was in Liverpool,' he answered in a different tone, 'but I was not at that hotel. You are thinking of my brother, are you not?'

'No,' I said. 'It was your brother who told me you were there.'

'Perhaps you had better explain what was the subject of your letter,' he suggested, speaking in the weary tone of one returning to a painful matter. 'I have been through a great trouble lately, and this may well have been overlooked.'

I said I would, and as briefly as possible I told the main facts of my strange visit in Fitzhardinge Square. He was much moved, walking up and down the room as he listened, and giving vent to exclamations from time to time, until I came to the arrangement I had finally made with his brother. Then he raised his hand as one might do in pain.

'Enough!' he said abruptly. 'Barnes told me a rambling tale of some stranger. I understand it all now.'

'So do I, I think!' I replied dryly. 'Your brother went to Liverpool, and received the papers in your name?'

He murmured what I took for 'Yes.' But he did not utter a single word of acknowledgement to me, or of reprobation of his brother's deceit. I thought some such word should have been spoken; and I let my feelings carry me away. 'Let me tell you,' I said, warmly, 'that your brother is a ——'

'Hush!' he said, holding up his hand again. 'He is dead.'

'Dead!' I repeated, shocked and amazed.

'Have you not read of it in the papers? It is in all the papers,' he said wearily. 'He committed suicide—God forgive me for it!—at Liverpool, at the hotel you have mentioned, and the day after you saw him.'

And so it was. He had committed some serious forgery—he had always been wild, though his father, slow to see it, had only lately closed his purse to him—and the forged signatures had come into his brother's power. He had cheated his brother before. There had long been bad blood between them, the one being as coldly business-like and masterful as the other was idle and jealous.

'I told him,' the elder said to me, shading his eyes with his hand 'that I should let him be prosecuted, that I would not protect or shelter him. The threat nearly drove him mad; and while it was hanging over him, I wrote to disclose the matter to Sir Charles. Gerald thought his last chance lay in recovering this letter unread. The proofs against him destroyed, he might laugh at me. His first attempts failed; and then he planned with Barnes' cognizance to get possession of the packet by drugging my father's whisky. Barnes' courage deserted him; he called you in, and—and you know the rest.'

'But,' I said softly, 'your brother did get the letter—at Liverpool.'

George Ritherdon groaned. 'Yes,' he said, 'he did. But the proofs were not enclosed. After writing the outside letter I changed my mind, and withheld them, explaining my reasons within. He found his plot laid in vain; and it was under the shock of this disappointment—the packet lay before him, resealed and directed to me—that he—that he did it. Poor Gerald!'

'Poor Gerald!' I said. What else remained to be said?

It may be a survival of superstition, yet, when I dine in Baker Street now, I take some care to go home by any other route than that through Fitzhardinge Square.

# 6

# My First Patient

. . . and may I beg you to visit us in your private rather than in your professional capacity? Since my dear wife has been failing thus sadly, she has evinced a great dread of medical men; and were she to guess you other than an ordinary guest, I tremble for the consequences. The carriage will meet you at Blackburne Station at whatever hour you name.

Yours very truly,
ARTHUR CRAWFORD.

This is an extract from a letter that I received on the 10th of June 1870, and being but a young fellow of twenty-six, I was very much elated thereby. The great drawback to being what is called a specialist is that the generality of people—for what reason I have never been able to discover—are afraid to employ you until you are well on in years, and consequently this Mrs Crawford for whom my services had been enlisted was my first private patient. My speciality was madness; and tiring equally of hospital-work and of idling in my own rooms, I was heartily thankful for the good luck that had befallen me. In a previous letter, Mr Crawford had given a detailed account of his wife's symptoms; and now all arrangements were completed, and I was due at his Berkshire home on the following day.

When the train steamed into the little country station, I found a carriage and pair ready to meet me. Evidently, to judge by the general get-up of the whole thing, the Crawfords were wealthy folk; and this impression was confirmed when we reached the house, which was standing in the midst of a lovely park. The hall-doors were standing open, and my host met me on the threshold with outstretched hands.

'This is exceedingly kind of you,' he said genially, 'for I know you have come at your very earliest convenience. Journey from town pleasant? Yes? That's right. James, take Mr Lennox's things to his room. Lunch in the morning-room, hey? Come along, my dear sir; you must be half famished.' So saying, he preceded me down a long corridor, whence I caught distant glimpses of a beautiful garden at the back of the house, and into a snug little room where luncheon was laid. While I discussed a cold chicken, Mr Crawford went on chatting; and ere I went to my room for a wash and brush up before presenting myself to his wife, we were excellent friends.

I do not think I ever met a man who so much charmed me at first sight; nay, he more than charmed, he captivated me. He was about thirty, and exceedingly handsome, with fair curly hair, and bright blue eyes. He had a bronzed complexion and a hearty laugh, and was altogether a most attractive specimen of a young Englishman. When I had finished luncheon, his manner changed abruptly as he began speaking of his young wife.

'I did not like to enter upon the subject before you were rested,' he began courteously; 'but I am intensely anxious you should see her. For some months past she has been suffering from intense melancholia, and lately she has taken a deep distrust of those around her, more particularly of me.' He stopped abruptly and bit his lips. 'Doctor, I simply worship her,' he went on passionately. 'When I married her five years ago, she was the blithest, merriest girl in all the shire; and now, to see her like this—why, it breaks my heart!' and he dropped into a chair and buried his face in his hands.

There was an awkward pause, for in those days I was too inexperienced to be much of a hand at consolation, and then I stepped nearer to him and laid my hand upon his shoulder. 'Come, come,' I said cheerily, 'there is no need to despair like this. We must hope for the best. How does she show her distrust of you?'

He raised his head to answer me. 'By keeping the boy from me, for one thing. She will hardly let me touch him.'

'The boy? A son of yours?'

'Our only child,' he answered—'a dear little fellow of nearly four; and she betrays a terrible fear whenever I have him with me.'

'Does she eat well?'

'Hardly at all.'

'Sleep at night?'

He shook his head; and then followed a string of various professional questions. Our conversation at an end, I requested to be shown to my room, promising to be in the drawing-room for five-o'clock tea, when I should be introduced to Mrs Crawford.

'As *Mr* Lennox, if you please,' suggested her husband as we crossed the hall. 'You remember that I asked you to drop the doctor, and seem an ordinary visitor?'

Of course I agreed; and then he told me he had spoken to her of me as an old college friend; and finally he left me to myself.

When I descended to the drawing-room, I found both Crawford and his wife waiting for me. He was standing by the open window playing with the climbing roses that were nodding by its sill: he was talking merrily as I entered, and looked the personification of life and good spirits. A girl was standing by the mantelshelf with her back towards me, and I had barely time to admire the slight figure and graceful pose, before Crawford's voice rang out in hearty cordiality.

'Ah! there you are at last! Let me introduce you to my wife. Beatrice, this is Mr John Lennox.'

She had half turned when he began speaking; but as he said my name, she gave a sudden gasp and confronted me with large startled eyes. I have seen the eyes of a snared bird and those of a hunted stag, but I have never seen such a look of piteous fear as dwelt in hers then. For one moment she seemed half mad with terror; but the next it fled as quickly as it came, and she held out her hand in greeting. As she did so, an ugly scar on the smooth white wrist caught my eye. It looked to me like an unskilful cut from a knife, and while we were exchanging commonplaces as to my journey, etc., I was wondering as to whether she had ever attempted her own life. She was in the first flush of her womanhood, and her glorious blue eyes and coil of auburn hair would alone have sufficed to stamp her as a beautiful woman, had it not been that the curious expression of her face outweighed every other fascination. She gave me the impression of being literally consumed by a terrible dread, to the nature of which I of course as yet held no clue; and with this dread, an equally strong desire to suppress all outward indication of it. Add to this, the fact that her face was entirely colourless, and that the hand she had given me, in spite of the June sunshine, was as cold as ice, and it will be seen that my first case promised to be full of interest.

She poured out the tea silently, while her husband and I went on chatting, and she did not speak again until he proposed to ring the nursery bell.

'We have not seen Bertie all day,' he added, 'and I know you would like to show him off to Lennox.'

'He is having his tea,' she rejoined quickly. 'Show him off in the morning, Arthur; I don't think we want him now.'

'Oh fie! There is an unkind mamma! I wonder what Bertie would say to you? He can finish his tea here, dear. I'll fetch him.'

'No, no; I'll go.' She ran out of the room as she spoke; and Crawford turned to me with a weary-looking smile.

'You see, Lennox? I generally give way; but I am afraid of it growing upon her, if I never see the child. He is such a splendid fellow!' As he spoke, his wife returned with the boy in her arms.

'I met him in the hall,' she explained; 'he was just coming in from his walk. No, Arthur, don't take him: he is not at all heavy.' This last to her husband, who had advanced with outstretched hands. 'Look here, Bertie, darling. Who likes cake?' She seated herself on a low chair, still keeping a jealous arm around the child, and went on talking, this time to me. 'Arthur and I quarrel over this small boy.' She laughed a little, but it sounded very mirthless. 'The last cause of dissension is his health. I think he is growing delicate and wants change, and papa doesn't agree. Does he, my beauty?'

The boy laughed as she held him yet more closely to her; and looking at his rosy cheeks and bright eyes, it seemed to me that there could not be a healthier youngster.

'I am afraid I must take papa's side,' I said. 'You must not alarm yourself unnecessarily, dear Mrs Crawford, for I think——'

I stopped abruptly, alarmed by the expression on her face. I was new at my work, be it remembered; but I think that older men than I would have been frightened. Bertie had rebelled against the detaining arm; and sliding on to the floor, had run to his father and climbed into his arms.

A fine game of romps now ensued, and the mother sat and watched them. Sitting there facing her, I too was watching. In my student days, I had kept a tame lizard, and by whistling to it, had been able to direct its movements at will, and now I was reminded of my whilom pet by watching Beatrice Crawford's eyes. Every motion of her husband's, as he ran round the room tossing the laughing boy in his arms, appeared to hold a fascination for her, and her gaze never left him but once. That once was when she walked swiftly to a further table and possessed herself of a paperknife, which she handed to me, commenting on its curious make. It was of steel and sharply pointed; and I handed it back again with the remark that it would make a nasty weapon if needed. She took it without glancing at me again; but her husband had caught her words, and now came up to us breathless and laughing, with Bertie clinging round his neck.

'Don't hold that thing, my darling,' he said tenderly. 'I hate to see such an ugly knife in your dear little hands.'

'Give it to Bertie, mamma,' cried the child, stretching dimpled hands for the coveted treasure; and his father, with an injunction to be careful, was taking it from her to give to him, when, with a muffled cry, she snatched the knife back and dashed it through the open window into the garden beyond.

'You shan't have it!—you shan't have it!' she cried excitedly, while a bright red spot burned on either cheek. 'You would——' With marvellous self-control, she stopped dead short; and after an almost imperceptible pause, she added in her usual quiet tones: 'Pray, forgive me, Arthur; I am so afraid of Bertie hurting himself. Go up to the nursery, dear. Mamma will come to you.'

Awestruck at her late passion, the child went gently out of the room, and his mother following him, I was left alone with Crawford. It went to my heart to see the pained, drawn look on his face, but the scene had at all events put one thing beyond a doubt; Mrs Crawford was not merely failing in brain-power—she was mad.

A couple of days went by, and I became fairly puzzled. All the ordinary verbal tests when applied to my patient proved complete failures. Her memory was excellent, and indeed in this respect she was far better than her husband, who was constantly forgetting things. As to her judgement, it struck me as above the average, for she was a widely read woman, and we had a stiff argument one night as to the merits of our favourite authors. She managed her own housekeeping, and capitally she did it too; and, in fact—not to exhaust the reader's patience by entering into details—the only visible outcome of her mental aberration was this extreme terror in which she lived, and for which I could find no reason. (I may remark parenthetically that the mad undoubtedly have rules of their own by which they are influenced. Experience thus teaching me that Mrs Crawford had some reason for this, to us, inexplicable dread—even though it might be but a fear of her own shadow—it became my business to solve this reason.) What baffled me most was the fact that while it was Crawford himself who primarily excited this terror, she was undeniably fond of him. Indeed, the word 'fond' is hardly suitable, for she simply adored him. I never heard him express the slightest wish as to the household arrangements but it was instantly fulfilled, while every whim—and he was the most whimsical of men—was implicitly obeyed. In fact, at the end of a week I was precisely in the same state as when I first entered the house. But that my *amour propre* was piqued, and I felt angry at my non-success, I should have been paying a very enjoyable visit. Arthur Crawford made a capital host, and although, as I have already said, he was a very whimsical man, and was subject to unaccountable fits of depression, he and I got on excellently together.

At the end of the week, something happened which had the double effect of lowering me several inches in my own estimation, and of placing matters in a totally different light. It was an exceedingly hot night; and after we had all gone to bed, I was tempted to leave my room, and, seating myself by the open window in the corridor, to indulge in an extra cigar. The fact that it was a fine moonlight night, and that while the corridor window boasted a lovely view, that of my own room looked into the stables, amply justified my choice of a seat. I had been there for perhaps an hour, when I heard the Crawfords talking in their room, which was on a level with my own. The tones were excited and eager; and fearing that Mrs Crawford might be lashing herself into a fury, and that her husband might be ignorantly increasing it, I stole down to their door and stood listening.

'Arthur, dear, give it to me. You don't want it tonight. Why not wait until the morning?'

These were the first words that I caught, spoken in Mrs Crawford's usually gentle tones.

'Give it to you? No; not I! I know a trick worth two of that. Ah, you think I don't know that you and that confounded mealy mouthed doctor are in league against me.'

Crawford's voice, shrill and mocking, but undoubtedly his. Good Heavens! was the man drunk? There was a moment's pause, and then he began again, this time more gently.

'Come, come, Beatrice. Drop this stupid joking. I only want to have a little cut at Bertie, just a little cut; and look! the knife is so bright and sharp, it cannot hurt him much.'

The wall seemed to reel around me as I leaned against it for support. In a flash of revelation that nearly blinded me, as I realized the full horror of the situation, I understood for the first time how matters actually stood. Crawford himself was the madman, and the devoted wife, whom I had been taught to look upon as insane, had known the truth all this time; and knowing it, for some inscrutable woman's reason, had shielded him, perhaps at the cost of her very life. In a moment the meaning of his many whims, his loss of memory, his fits of depression, were made clear to me, and as I thought of the martyrdom through which his girl-wife had passed, I cursed myself for the readiness with which I had been duped.

While these thoughts were rushing through my brain, I had noiselessly opened the outer door, and now stood in the dressing-room, peering into the bedroom beyond. The door between the two was standing open, but a heavy curtain hung in the aperture, and by making a little slit in it by means of my penknife, I was enabled to command a view of the interior. At the further end of the apartment lay Bertie asleep in his cot. Standing before him, clad in a long white wrapper, and with her auburn hair flowing over her shoulders, was the young mother herself, while at some paces from her stood Crawford, still in evening dress, and balancing in his fingers a long glittering dagger, that I recognized as one that usually hung in the library below. By this time he had dropped his angry tones, and was speaking in his accustomed pleasant fashion.

'You know, dear,' he was saying, 'it really is necessary that we both drink some. Half a glassful of young and innocent blood, and we both shall keep young and happy for ever.'

111

'Won't my blood do?' asked the girl desperately. She stretched her bare arms towards him and forced a smile to her poor quivering lips. 'You are much fonder of me, aren't you, dear? I shall do much better.'

He laughed softly. 'No, no, my darling; not you. I wouldn't hurt you for all the gold of all the Indies.' He stopped suddenly, as if struck by his own words. 'Gold?' he repeated. 'Ah! yes, of course, I must have gold. Where did I put it now?'

He retreated a few steps, looking uneasily from side to side.

'Perhaps you left it in the library. Ring for James. Or go to Mr Lennox, Arthur; he will help you to find it.'

He laughed again—a low monotonous laugh, to which my hospital-work had but too well accustomed me, and then he moved nearer her, still balancing the dagger in his long nervous fingers. That terrible knife! If he had only put it down for a moment, I could have rushed in and secured it before turning to him, but as matters were, cruel experience taught me that the instant he caught sight of me, he would rush to the child, to carry his dreadful purpose into effect, and that the mother in all probability would fall the victim. On the other hand, I dared not quit my post to summon assistance, and so leave Beatrice entirely at his mercy. I glanced round the dressing-room, and the window-cord caught my eye. It was new and strong. I cut it as high as I could reach, and crept back to my hole at the curtain. Crawford was growing rapidly angry.

'Give me that boy!' he cried roughly. 'Get out of the way, Beatrice, and let me have him'; and he caught her by the arm and dragged her from the cot.

'Arthur, Arthur! husband, sweetheart!' She clasped both arms around his neck, and raised imploring eyes to his; but the sight of the thin white face only moved him to greater wrath.

'It is all your fault I have not made you strong long ago,' he exclaimed irritably. 'You never laugh now, and you can't sing, and you won't dance.'

'Dance? Oh yes, I can. Look, Arthur!' She drew rapidly back towards the cot, speaking in her ordinary quiet voice. 'You shall do what you like with Bertie; I was only joking. Only we must have our dance first, you know.'

With a sudden movement, she stooped and lifted the sleeping child from the bed, talking all the time in an arch merry voice, that still retained its old power over the poor madman. He nodded approvingly as she began rocking to and fro with the boy in her arms, and he moved a chair or two, to give her more space.

'Dance, Beatrice!' He began whistling a then fashionable valse, beating time to the air with the dagger, of which he never relinquished his hold.

'Very well,' she responded cheerily. 'Stand by the mantelpiece and give us plenty of room. Now, then, my baby boy; one, two, and off we go.'

My life has shown me instances of self-devotion in plenty, I have seen proofs of ready wit, and more of indomitable pluck, but I have never seen them so marvellously combined as on that terrible June night. Instinct taught me what she meant to do. She had persuaded her husband to stand at the end of the room furthest from the curtain that hid her one means of escape, and now she intended to hazard her only chance, dash through it, lock the door on the other side, and then go for help. Backwards and forwards, round and round, she circled, a weird enough figure in her white draperies. The little white feet were bare, and it taxed her utmost strength to hold the heavy boy in her arms, but with a sublime heroism of which I should never have believed her capable, she never once paused for breath. A miracle alone kept the child asleep, but when I saw the poor mother's lips move dumbly between the snatches of the gay valse she was humming, I felt that she was praying God he might not waken. Nearer and nearer the curtain she came; but, to my horror, I perceived that Crawford was growing uneasy and advancing slowly in the rear.

'Mrs Crawford! Quick!'

There was not a minute to be lost. I tore the curtain aside, and she rushed towards me; but ere I could fasten the heavy door, her husband was upon us. With a yell of baffled rage, he was tearing after her through the open doorway, and in another moment would have reached her with uplifted knife, when I tripped him up, and he fell headlong to the floor. He was stunned by his fall, and while I fastened his hands and feet by means of the cut window-cord, his wife went back to the inner room and rang loudly for assistance.

Ere he came to himself, Arthur Crawford was safely secured in my own room. Leaving him there under charge of the menservants, I went back to seek Mrs Crawford. She was lying on the bedroom floor with her nervous fingers still tightly interlaced, and by her side sat her little son, warm and rosy from his broken sleep. He was kissing the paling lips as I came hastily into the room, and now held up a warning finger as I knelt beside them.

'Poor mamma is fast asleep,' he whispered. 'And she is so cold!'

She was not dead. The long and frightful mental strain through which she had passed brought on brain-fever, and for some days we despaired of her life, but she came through it bravely, and ere the summer waned, I had the satisfaction of installing both mother and son in a seaside cottage, far enough away from her Berkshire home.

Crawford, poor fellow, only lived a few months, for a dangerous fall in the asylum grounds put a merciful termination to his confinement. During those few months, I visited him occasionally, and he always spoke most tenderly of his wife, whom he imagined was dead.

When he died, I went to break the news to his young widow; and while staying in her pretty Devonshire cottage, I solved much that had puzzled me. Her terror at my first introduction to her had been occasioned by the fact that she had at once recognized me as Lennox, the mad doctor. I had been pointed out to her in the Park the season before. She dreaded Arthur's incipient madness being known to anyone, for she had a blind terror of a lunatic asylum in connection with her idolized husband, and hoped that a quiet country life, free from trouble and contradiction, might in time restore him. But had he never broken out before? I asked, for it seemed to me incomprehensible that so slight a frame should be capable of such courage. Once, she said, only once, and then he had been bent on killing himself. In struggling with him for the possession of the knife, he had accidentally cut her wrist, and so occasioned the ugly scar that disfigured it. As for Bertie's presence on that fatal night, she told me he had always been accustomed to sleep in their room, and as I had refused to second her theory that the child wanted change of air, and so aid in sending him out of the house, she could devise no other means of getting rid of him.

And then I took my leave, and I have never seen Mrs Crawford from that day to this; but still, in spite of a certain pair of sweet brown eyes which make the sunshine of my home, I am forced to admit that there is no woman on earth for whom I have such a boundless admiration as for that unfortunate lady of whom I at one time thought as my first patient.

# 7

## ROY HORNIMAN and C. E. MORLAND

# A Fatal Affinity

In those days I was only a journalist. Do not cavil at the word *only*, you successful 'writers of leading articles', 'special correspondents', or 'one of the crowd', to influential Dailies. Journalism does not always mean the position you have attained. I wrote for the papers, indeed, but with faint heart that never knew my writings were accepted till I received the hardly earned shillings that cost me so many hours' work. Still, even in a dingy, depressing second-floor back room my ambition was never dormant. I longed to give the world something it could applaud before life and its hardships had quite 'frozen me up within', and when an introduction was offered me to the editor of the *Hyde Park Magazine*, a well-established monthly much thought of in literary as well as in fashionable circles, I was intensely grateful. To my great gratification, after one or two articles published in its pages, I was promoted to the staff, and then, in the intervals of my work for Mr Kerr, I had leisure to think out and write the sketch of a novel. I submitted the idea to the editor, who was much struck by it and encouraged me to fill in and complete, assuring me that if it turned out as brilliantly as it promised, he would accept it for his periodical, whose serials were written by the best-known authors of the day. This conversation was intensely stimulating; and, full of enthusiasm, I set to work.

Night had fallen. My first chapter, that stumbling-block over which so many of us fall, had been finished for some time, and I had felt like a beginner on a bicycle, once the wheels had begun to go round I could ride on in triumph, and I had written chapter after chapter easily.

I am often chaffed on my method of working. Solitude, except for the physical labour with pen in hand, is of no use to me—I must have air and companionship, even of the unknown, to help me think, and in a crowd my brain is at its best—overflowing with ideas, some more useful than others.

Tonight I must go out—must start off in search of thought. My work should be equal, and what I had done, even to my critical mind, was strong and full of hope.

To the left of Westminster Bridge there is a flight of steps, near to which the river boats arrive and depart, and over the parapet of these steps, surrounded, but always alone, I loved to linger, watching the dark waters below, the changing skies above; listening to the distant hum of the never quiet city and the vague murmurings of countless passers-by. This evening of a sultry August day the wind had risen and was wailing softly, while, with many a pause, large drops of rain fell on the dry, dusty pavement, and people hurried past, anxious to get to their homes before the storm burst from the heavy clouds o'erhead.

Big Ben was striking nine.

The weather had no effect on me—I was too full of my heroine, whom I had already brought on to the scene—my heroine with the red hair and emerald eyes, with skin of vivid white, and lips of coral still gleaming with the moisture of its ocean bed. Lifelike she stood in my brain, appealing to my heart and senses as a living mistress might have done. Suddenly the creation of my mind took form—with my heart beating wildly, I saw before me my ideal in the flesh.

No other living soul was near, as, in the fitful yellow gleam, she stood under the gas lamp not half a dozen yards away; and as a stifled exclamation burst from me, she turned her eyes upon me, made a step forward, then paused, and, with a startled look in which were mingled reproach and disappointment, she glided away up the incline leading to the Embankment.

Full of excitement, but keeping carefully in the shadows of the opposite trees, I followed her. She paused at a shabby looking house in Cecil Street, and, after a furtive look round which passed my presence over, she rang an iron hanging bell gently. The old servant who answered it must have been waiting on the other side, for he opened the door immediately, the street lamp lighting up his anxious face and white hair distinctly.

'Ah, Miss Ruth, how glad I am——' he began eagerly, but she put her finger on her lip, and whispering 'Hush!' passed in quickly.

The windows were all dark, and the house had an uninhabited look that struck coldly on me. With a shiver and a strange, nervous feeling of dread, I moved away and walked home to Jermyn Street, pondering deeply on the curious coincidence.

The sight of a well-lighted, comfortable room soon dispelled my gloom, but not my mental excitement. Had I been the victim of hallucination? Was it in a dream I had seen and followed the woman with the sad eyes and flaming hair?

No; I had heard the rustle of her dress as she moved towards me, had heard the clang of the door that shut her out from my sight, had seen her silence the old man who welcomed her coming so gladly, and had carried the image of her living beauty home to where her intangible 'Alter Ego', the creation of my brain, awaited me.

Then, in the silent hours of the night, my pen flew over the paper, inspired as it had never been before, till I knew that if only I could continue as I was doing, my work would be a masterpiece that must appeal to the great world I longed to stir.

And when, as morning dawned grey and chill, my stiffening fingers refused to transmit words and thoughts I could not bear to put aside, I started—through the sombre silence of the dawning twilight there floated a deep drawn sigh that might have been wrung from my Marian in the first great sorrow her life-story had entailed.

There was little repose for me that day; my anxious expectations of the evening made me nervous and unstrung, unable to settle to my work and yet strangely unwilling to leave it, even to seek the spot I longed to visit again—the spot where I had seen 'Ruth', the embodiment of 'Marian'. I wrote a little, but in a half-hearted manner, and, till I saw Ruth again, I knew this would be so.

It was raining heavily when I left the house and gained the Embankment. The lamps, like sentinels keeping their watch, were blurred and indistinct, but under the one near to my resting-place were two people—a man, a stranger, and a woman—Ruth. He was about to leave, and, as I approached, Ruth's lips were lifted and met his in a long, passionate kiss. Then, as he left her, she fixed her eyes on a glittering gem that sparkled on a finger of her ungloved hand, but raised her head almost immediately and followed his figure with a yearning, lingering look of love. Yes, it was the same beautiful face of the night before, but though the rapt, prophetic look of tragic intensity was still there, it was veiled by an expression of great happiness that gave an almost supernatural glow to her features. So absorbed was she in her own sweet thoughts that my presence passed unnoticed, and once more I saw her enter the house in Cecil Street that, with its shabby, gloomy frontage and dark windows, seemed unfit to contain such loveliness.

As Ruth vanished from my sight the clocks struck the hour, and I remembered an engagement for this evening, which, in spite of my longing to sit down to work, protruded itself so urgently on my mind that I was forced to give up all ideas of writing, and hurry home to don the conventional garb of evening civilization. The card said, 'Lady Charnase, at home, 10 o'clock', and when I stepped into a hansom at eleven a feeling of unusual excitement had taken possession of me.

Why was I, who rarely took the trouble to be sociable, turning out at night when I could have stayed happily for hours, bending over my table covering sheet after sheet of fair white paper with the regular black ups and downs that were my mental food and drink. I could not answer the question, and dubbed myself a fool for my pains, putting up my hand almost unconsciously to stop the cab, then hesitating and finally resigning myself to my fate. I could leave Lady Charnase's within the hour. I should have pleased her by putting in an appearance at her party, and as I entered her brilliantly lit rooms and saw her look of genuine pleasure, I was rewarded.

'How good of you, Mr Cranston,' she said, giving my hand a grateful pressure. 'I was almost writing to you to beg you to come this evening.'

I murmured a few words of thanks for the kind flattery, and she continued:

'Yes, I am most anxious to introduce you to a young friend of mine who is always talking of the pleasure your writings give her. She has not arrived yet; come to me when I beckon you.' And with a friendly little nod, she let me leave her and make my way amongst the numerous guests who thronged her beautiful rooms.

I found many there I knew, but tonight I was in touch with none; and secretly wondering why I had come, I leant against an arch leading into a conservatory and, silent myself heard the ceaseless chatter around as in a dream, my thoughts, for the most part, with the two women who had crept into my life so suddenly—the one, a breathing, living, beautiful creature, whose life was as apart from mine as the two poles are asunder; of whom I knew nothing but the fact that she was the magic mirror of the other; the other—that other, my own, *my* creation, filled with my association of ideas, into whom I was breathing my intelligence, my spirit, my whole soul—by whom I was dressing fiction with such a semblance of truth that I myself was astounded at its realism. I was glad I had come. I could look back on what I had done with pride. I saw the words before me, and nearly laughed aloud as I looked at all these triflers, who seemed to have not one serious thought amongst them, and heard them, in the future, with but one topic of conversation—my book! I was drunk with my self-conceit, and quite forgot, in the wreaths of triumph I was weaving, to watch for Lady Charnase's signal, until her voice brought me back to a sense of my discourtesy.

'Mr Cranston, I am ashamed of you,' she said, laughing lightly as she touched my arm.

'Not more so than I am of myself,' I answered, bowing before her.

'Come with me, then, and do penance for your wandering thoughts. Ah, no, I cannot call it that. To be introduced to Ruth Stapleton is an honour to be envied.'

Ruth! How the name rang in my ears as I followed my hostess to another room; there seemed to be nothing in the air but Ruth!—Ruth!—Ruth! And yet the name was common enough. Why connect it, as I did, with the exquisite face in my heart?

But suddenly Lady Charnase stopped. 'Miss Stapleton,' she said, 'may I introduce Mr Cranston to you?—Oswald Cranston, Ruth.'

And there in the soft-toned light of shaded lamps, apart from the crowd in soul as in body, sat Ruth—the Ruth who already, though I did not know it then, had taken entire possession of me. Dressed in some clinging soft silk, shaped in the fashion of the day and yet individually hers, that showed off her exquisite figure, her glorious hair crowning her most perfect face, she stirred my inmost being by the marvellous light of her eyes, even before she spoke in a low, rich voice that seemed the echo of some memory of what had gone before.

It was Ruth. And yet, could it be—could it be the same woman I had seen barely two hours ago?

What she said I could have told beforehand, for every word was *mine*, and sank into my heart. I listened, not only with my ears but with my eyes, watching each change in her mobile face; as miraculously a description and a scene I had written that very afternoon were carried out before me. Unintentionally I had made my rooms those we were in; my Marian speak Ruth's words to one who yet was not myself.

We spoke on many subjects, for Miss Stapleton's was no ordinary mind, and presently we were deep in a discussion as to the capabilities of men and women to endure. In every phase of life she maintained that women could suffer in silence what man could not bear alone; that women suffered slights, treachery, betrayal as their due, where men would proclaim their wrongs, and confer lifelong disgrace on those who dared to play havoc with their sensibilities.

'Then, Miss Stapleton, you think women feel they *ought* to endure in silence?' and as she spoke my lips framed her answer word for word.

'We are born to trouble, and must endure, even unto death—it is our birthright,' she said dreamily; then added brightly, 'Oh, how foolish you must think me, talking in this gloomy strain when I am, oh, so happy.'

I looked at her. Yes, there was the look I had seen under the gas lamp on the Embankment—the look I had left in Marian's face as reluctantly I had laid down my pen to follow the impulse I could not control. And there was a magic in her presence and in the mystery of her life that kept me chained to her side longer than strict etiquette would have thought allowable.

The evening was far advanced, and the rooms had thinned perceptibly, when suddenly I saw Miss Stapleton bend forward eagerly and look past me into the room beyond. I listened; a man was speaking, regretting his late arrival: and at the sound of his voice Ruth rose and moved as though to leave me, but at that moment Lady Charnase came into the second drawing-room we were in, on the arm of a tall, handsome man, and the girl sank back into her seat slowly, and, as though her thoughts were far away, asked me if it was not very late.

Lady Charnase and the stranger were standing in the centre of the room—she talking to some of her guests, his eyes wandering round the room; and as I watched the group it seemed to me that they rested on Ruth with a strange expression, as though he knew but would not recognize her. There was something familiar in his build, but I could not bring to mind that I had ever seen him before; and as Miss Stapleton asked me to take her to the cloakroom, I had no time to think, though it struck me curiously that as she shook hands with Lady Charnase, she carefully avoided looking at this man, who as studiously turned away from her. She leant rather heavily on my arm, and confessed a little wearily to being tired, then thanked me warmly as I put her into a four-wheeled cab, on the box of which the old manservant from Cecil Street took his place beside the driver.

The rooms seemed very empty when I re-entered them, but the latecomer still stood out prominently beside Lady Charnase, who introduced him to me as I came up—'Mr Cranston—Colonel Marchmont', and then she moved away, leaving us together. And as he bent his head slowly in answer to the words, I knew the man. It was Ruth's companion on the Embankment!

What could this mean? Thank heaven he had as yet no place in my book, for I saw his eyes were hard, and his mouth had cruel curves, even as he smiled with polite conventionality and said he was proud to make my acquaintance. But however courteous, I did not like him, and took an early opportunity of leaving the house.

After this evening I buckled to my work, the more seriously that a terrible yearning to see Ruth again seized upon me—a yearning that, if not controlled, might lead me to neglect everything for the sake of striving to bring about another meeting. Now that she knew me, I dared not haunt her steps as I had done before—what would she think of me? She, who was already mistress of my heart and soul, but who loved another and was happy in his love—had she not told me as much? And yet! and yet! If Colonel Marchmont was the man who made her happy, why the secrecy of their meetings? Why the pretended ignorance of each other's presence at Lady Charnase's 'At Home'? It was a mystery that made me sad, that made me live for Marian, and try with might and main to keep Ruth out of my thoughts, though Marian was Ruth, as Ruth was Marian, and I wove the story of their lives, they, one and the same, in my perplexed mind.

My poor Marian! I longed to make her happy! her life had begun so brightly, had promised everything beautiful that life could give—but alas! black shadows of treachery and betrayal had closed in upon her, and all was tending towards destruction, shame, and misery.

The crisis of her story was approaching and there came an hour when I could not write. I sat before my desk, with head bowed on my outstretched arms, the pen, guiltless of ink, dry and powerless by my side. The awful longing for the living creature had come to me, and imagery was helpless. Unnerved, exhausted with vain desires, I could not rest, and with irresistible impulse, rushed out to keep a solitary tryst.

As I neared my favourite spot, someone was leaning over the stonework, and I distinctly heard a sob of anguish, then Ruth turned and rushed past me, her beautiful face wild with unutterable despair. She did not see me, nor, in ulster and cap would she have recognized me, had she done so. Far from calming my restlessness, this momentary glimpse and the certain knowledge that all was not well with her, cast a deep gloom over me. Why was the gladness gone from her face? What had brought that look of shame and agony to my darling's features? Were Ruth and Marian one in suffering as in looks? What strange power was at work binding their lives in one network of unhappiness?

I stole home, sad at heart, and wrote again for many hours, striving to get Marian's story finished quickly, that I might not be haunted by this terrible feeling of influence over a fellow-creature's life; for though till now I had not seen Ruth since the night of our personal introduction, I seemed instinctively to know that the words I wrote applying to Marian portrayed Ruth's story word for word, and with love burning at my heart, the battle 'twixt art and inclination was too hard—must this girl fade and die like my poor little woman of fiction—fade away under the grief tearing at her heartstrings?

Next morning I received a note from Lady Charnase—could I call on her? She knew she was a nuisance, but would be so grateful for my advice.

I found that, like most idle women of the day, she had been dabbling in literature, but I was able to encourage her to persevere, and she was grateful accordingly. When we had finished talking business, she asked me if I had met Ruth Stapleton again, and I was able truthfully to answer 'No'.

'Ah! I had hoped you would be interested enough in my friend to follow up the introduction.'

'But, Lady Charnase,' I stammered out, 'how could I?'

'Oh! don't ask me that! Men can always find ways and means. I am anxious about Ruth. I have not seen her for many days, and I hear vague rumours——'

'Tell me about her,' I asked entreatingly.

Lady Charnase looked at me for a moment before she answered. 'So you are interested, after all?'

I nodded. 'Very much so,' I said calmly. 'Who is Miss Stapleton—she seems to be very lonely.'

'Ah! you know that, do you? Well, it is only too true. She lives with an old uncle in an out-of-the-way place off the Strand, a place that makes me shiver and my coachman swear, every time I go to see her. Old Lawrence Stapleton is very wealthy, but very eccentric, and though the dear girl is his only relation and heiress, he will not allow her a chaperon or even a companion, and she gets terribly depressed at times.'

'So she is an heiress?'

'Yes; and not only her uncle's, she has already a very nice little fortune of her own; but alas! her money does not bring her happiness.'

'I wonder so beautiful a woman has not married.'

'She might have married a dozen times, but she is difficult to please, and her uncle gives scant welcome to suitors—in his odd way he is fond of the girl. I had hoped that perhaps you——'

I started to my feet. 'Lady Charnase!' I exclaimed.

'There, don't be offended,' she cried; 'I was sure you would admire her, and she thinks so much of you; and then I have been hearing all sorts of rumours about some man who is always dangling after her, though no one seems to name him; and I am so fond of Ruth, I would do a great deal to make her happy.'

'I am not offended, Lady Charnase,' I answered gently; 'I will even confess that I ask nothing better than to become better acquainted with your beautiful friend.'

'No! really!' exclaimed she, pleased and triumphant. 'Then I wonder whether you would mind undertaking a little commission for me—are you very busy today?'

'Not if you want me,' I said, my heart beating at the prospect of being brought into contact with Ruth Stapleton once more.

'Will you go to her now, from me—say that I have a box for the "Haymarket" tonight, and want her to come with me.'

'With pleasure,' I said quietly, wondering how I could excuse myself as her messenger; her next words, however, put this matter at rest.

'I want you to come also,' said she; 'and I want you both to dine with me first. If Ruth cannot come, will you try and bring someone? it seems a pity the box should be wasted.'

'I will do what I can,' I answered; 'shall I go now?'

'Yes.'

'Au revoir, then.'

'Stay—do you know where she lives?'

'You told me—in Cecil Street.'

'I told you! no, you are mistaken!'

For a moment I was nonplussed—how could I explain my knowledge of Ruth's address, then recollection came to my aid: 'No, I remember, you did not tell me, but I put Miss Stapleton into a cab on the night of your party, and gave the address to the man.'

'Ah!'

I fancy that Lady Charnase was a little sceptical, but I paid no attention to her meaning look, and hastily saying goodbye, went on the errand that was only too pleasant to me. If I had tried my utmost, I could not have found a better introduction to the gloomy house with whose exterior I was so familiar, and I started off full of anticipations of the joy I had so long looked forward to.

It did not take me long to reach Cecil Street, nor to be deposited at No. 100, and though the afternoon was still early, the house struck me as even more gloomy than before. There seemed a shadow hanging over it, and I pitied my poor, beautiful love for her surroundings as I speculated on what Lady Charnase had told me of rumours concerning her life. The man whose presence with her had been remarked upon must be the same with whom I had seen her—Colonel

Marchmont; and if so, why were the rumours adverse to her? Perhaps he was not known—perhaps her uncle would not let him visit her openly? But if the man was really in love, why did he not marry her at once and take her away from such a life? Was he but one of the many fortune-hunters who throng an heiress's footsteps, and would he not risk the loss of her uncle's money, deeming it's insufficient for his rapacity?

These thoughts all passed rapidly through my mind as I was standing on the well-worn doorsteps waiting for my bell to be answered. The old servant was slower than when he came at his mistress's summons after night had fallen, and it was some time before I heard his heavy, almost faltering step on the other side.

'Is Miss Stapleton at home?' I asked, trembling at the near prospect of seeing her.

'Miss Stapleton, sir, is ill.'

'Ill!' I exclaimed in such horrified accents that the old man looked at me in surprise.

'Yes, sir; Miss Ruth has been ill for some time now.'

And yet, I had seen her with my own eyes, on the steps of Westminster Bridge only the night before! What was this mystery? 'I am sorry—I understood that Miss Stapleton had been out very lately, and I come with a message from Lady Charnase.'

The man hesitated and looked troubled, then, as if unwillingly, he said: 'I am sorry, sir—Miss Ruth can see no one.'

'Will you at least give her a message from me, and bring an answer?'

Again he paused, but for a very short time, then brightening up, said: 'That I will, sir; perhaps, who knows, it may do my mistress good; I think she do want rousing; what shall I tell her, sir?'

'Say that Mr Cranston is here, and that if possible he would like to see her—tell her I come with a message from Lady Charnase.'

'Step in, if you please, sir,' answered the old fellow, as he opened wide the door and let me enter into a room on the ground floor to the right.

The house was, if anything, more gloomy inside than out, and I felt depressed and uncomfortable at having forced an entrance, though I knew that under the circumstances I should be held blameless, even by Ruth herself. I was not left long in doubt, for very few moments had elapsed before Ruth Stapleton herself was before me. But how terribly changed from the brilliantly beautiful creature to whom I had been introduced so short a time before! I saw at once that theatre-going was out of the question, and marvelled how she had had strength to venture out into the night air on the previous evening. I must have looked my surprise, for before I had time to speak, she advanced with a slight, wan smile, and putting out a hand that felt cold, she said: 'I am so sorry my old servant was so loth to admit you, Mr Cranston, but the truth is, I am far from well, a fact you have noticed for yourself, I see, and he knows that I dislike seeing visitors when not quite up to the mark.'

'I assure you,' I said, confused, 'that if it had not been for Lady Charnase, I should not have dared to be so importunate.'

'Ah! she has sent me a message?'

'Yes—and a petition, but one which I see little chance of your granting.'

'Tell me, at any rate,' she said softly.

I told her of Lady Charnase's plan, but added that of course our mutual friend had no idea that Miss Stapleton was even ailing.

'No—I have seen so little of my friends lately,' said Ruth wearily.

'They miss you.' I answered, 'if you will forgive my saying so.'

'Lady Charnase is always so kind—I have felt ungrateful, but I have had no heart to see anyone.'

'Perhaps she could do you good,' I ventured to say; 'she is so bright and cheery.'

'Yes, she is; too bright for me just now—I could not bear it!' There was almost a sob in the voice that spoke so wearily, and my heart ached to hear it, but being such a stranger to her, I dared not show my sympathy openly and kept on the tack of coming simply as a messenger.

'I will tell her how suffering you are, and I am sure you will see her here tomorrow.'

'No—no! Beg her not to come; I cannot see her. I would not have seen her today; I don't know why I saw you—I am not fit to see any-one.' She spoke hurriedly, and as her voice broke down, I was intensely miserable at seeing large tears gather in the beautiful eyes, and fall slowly one by one, as if the effort to repress them was too great.

'Miss Stapleton,' I cried, 'you are in trouble—what can I do? Can I not help you? Oh, forgive me, I know I am a stranger, but if there is anything, please tell me; I would do anything to help you.'

She shook her head. 'No,' she said, 'you are very good, but no one can help me. Please tell Lady Charnase how kind I think it of her to have thought of me. Goodbye.' She put out her hand as she spoke, and I could do nothing but respond to the action, but I said: 'You will let me call again to enquire how you are?'

'Yes,' she said, 'do come again, perhaps I shall not be so foolish.'

The old manservant was waiting for me in the hall; he seemed to know I was interested, if nothing else, in his mistress, for he laid a hand restrainingly on my arm as I was about to leave the house. 'Oh, sir,' he said apologetically, 'please forgive me—but—will Miss Ruth go out? I heard you ask her, and it would do her so much good. She tells me she will see no one, that she is too ill, and sometimes, indeed, she seems to be dying right away. She needs a friend sadly, sir.'

'But Mr Stapleton—is he not at home—does he not see—not understand?'

'My master, sir, is no good at all where Miss Ruth is concerned; as long as she looks bright before him, and does not spend too much money, he is quite satisfied that all is well. My missus tried to tell him that Miss Ruth ought to have advice, and he laughed at her.'

'I will tell her friend—Lady Charnase.'

'Aye, do sir; only, if I may make so bold, they as says anything to my young mistress must be careful; she knows her own business, and there are those who think they can help her by warning her against——'

At this moment the door of the room on our right opened, and Ruth came out slowly. I was glad to see she did not notice I was still talking to her old servant, but passed on up the stairs as in a dream, only her advent had the effect of staying his garrulity, and though burning with baffled curiosity, I was forced to take my leave.

I went out with the old man's words ringing in my ears—'Sometimes she seems to be dying right away,' but with no clue to the mystery of her nocturnal visits to the waterside, except in my own imagination, which had written of the same wanderings as regarded Marian, my heroine. God forbid, that Ruth's and Marian's stories should be really alike, and yet, how they seemed to be shaping themselves on one and the same models. In my book Marian was wont to steal from her home, from under the vigilant supervision of an old aunt with but little sympathy for the young, and in the darkest evenings would meet her lover unknown to all except one faithful servant, who watched her outgoings and her return with dogged fidelity that would let no breath of slander touch his adored mistress if he could help it. Alas, already my reader would foreshadow the end. Could it be possible that, as I had already felt, I had an influence over Ruth Stapleton's life—if so, how easy to save her! I would go straight home and change the whole current of the novel! But no, I could not now. I had promised Lady Charnase to dine with her. But I could not invite anyone else to join us; she was a woman of the world, and on more than one occasion had allowed me to be her escort—I would be tonight—and in the course of a more intimate conversation than was possible in the presence of a third, might glean more facts about Ruth than she had chosen to tell me in the afternoon visit.

I hastened home, and resisting an almost irresistible impulse to sit at my desk dressed quickly and found my way to Berkeley Square. Lady Charnase was rather pleased than otherwise, that as Ruth could not be with us, I had taken the liberty of dining 'en tête-à-tête' with her, and we were quite merry over our meal, she putting forth all her charms to disperse what looked singularly like gloom on my brow.

The piece at the Haymarket was that most successful of plays, *The Dancing Girl*, which neither of us had seen: we were much interested, even from the curtain of the first act, and talked about the play before looking round the house.

'It is a wonderful idea,' said my companion. 'I am anxious to see the unravelling of the story.'

'Strange,' said I, 'that with so many hypocrites amongst us, this one method of falsehood has never yet been unmasked on the stage.'

'You think then that most men are—liars?' she asked, laughing a little sarcastically; 'you give yourselves away.'

'Lady Charnase,' I said earnestly, 'you know I am no pessimist as regards my fellow-creatures, but there is a great deal of this "hypocrisy", as I call it, which is very incomprehensible.'

'You talk as though you had some special case in your mind,' she said seriously.

'I have.'

'May one ask?'

'I was about to confide in you, for the "case", as you call it, has been brought very near to me today.'

'How strange! today?'

'Lady Charnase, what do you know of Colonel Marchmont?'

'What a singular question, Mr Cranston; of Colonel Marchmont?'

'Yes; why is it singular?'

'Because, if there is a man who is open and aboveboard, that man is Lucien Marchmont.'

'Indeed!'

'Yes; I have known him for some time, and know nothing but good of him.'

'Can you explain why, knowing Miss Stapleton well, he should, at your house the other evening, pass her by as a stranger?'

'Lucien know Ruth! Impossible! I must have known of it.'

'Notwithstanding, he does, and intimately too'.

'How do you know this. I thought you had never seen Ruth Stapleton till you met at my house, and never since, till this afternoon; are you one of these hypocrites also?'

'Quite unconsciously, though I confess to having misled you this afternoon, even after you saw that I was much interested in your friend. Tell me about Colonel Marchmont,' and Lady Charnase leant forward eagerly. 'Why, there he is!' She pointed down into the house, and sure enough, there in the stalls, faultlessly dressed and looking very bored, was the man we were discussing.

'Do not attract his attention, Lady Charnase, till I have told you.'

'I am all impatience.'

'Sometime before you issued your invitations for your last "At Home", I had commenced a novel for Mr Kerr.'

'No, really!' she exclaimed; 'how delightful! Tell me about it.'

'That is what I am about to do,' I said, smiling at her impetuosity. 'One evening I had been writing for a long time and went out, as I often do, to try and get fresh ideas from the outer world; that night I first saw Ruth Stapleton—she was alone.'

'How does this concern Colonel Marchmont?'

'Listen. I was immensely struck and astonished to find in your beautiful friend, the very counterpart of my heroine, and could not rest until I had seen her again. The next day I went to the same spot, a lonely one near to Westminster Bridge.'

'Do you mean to say you saw Ruth alone near to Westminster Bridge? You must have been mistaken, surely!'

'No—and on the second day I saw her again, but this time Colonel Marchmont was just taking leave of her, in such a way as to leave little doubt in my mind but that they were affianced lovers. When, not three hours afterwards I saw Miss Stapleton at your house, I knew her immediately, and was not more slow to recognize her companion, when, to my surprise, you introduced me to Marchmont.'

Lady Charnase had turned very pale, and looked at me horror-struck.

'What is the matter?' I asked.

'I—I don't know—I hardly like to tell you. Oh, poor Ruth! poor girl!'

I leant forward. 'Tell me,' I said; 'I am intensely interested in the matter.'

'Colonel Marchmont is—married,' came from Lady Charnase's lips, as she looked at me steadfastly. 'What shall we do?'

I pondered; the mystery was thickening. So they were not lovers after all! But why did my companion look so horrified? 'Ah,' I said; 'then is he a relation of Miss Stapleton's?'

'No.'

'What could they meet in secret for? Surely Miss Stapleton knows——?'

'I do not think she can. I have heard rumours; and now I see how they have arisen; he is a villain!'

'Oh! I thought he was everything that was open and aboveboard!' I could not help this little touch of sarcasm. 'You women are so easily deceived.'

'We are indeed. See, he is coming; he has seen us; try and conceal our thoughts from him. I will unmask him to my own satisfaction and at my own time, but not here.'

In another moment the handsome Colonel was bowing over her

hand, and had even offered me his cordially. I could not take it, and, stooping, made an excuse of picking up the glasses which I had knocked over purposely.

'You like the play?' asked our visitor suavely.

'Hum. I think it always a pity to put the dark side of things before us so very plainly. Do you think the world is as wicked as we try to make it out, Colonel Marchmont?' asked Lady Charnase, as if perfectly unconcerned in what his answer might be.

'No—by Jove! I think it's a very nice world. Lots of clever people; lots of beautiful women: What more can a man want?'

'Ah, talking of beautiful women, have you seen my friend Miss Stapleton lately?'

He changed colour visibly, but managed to say calmly, 'No, I have not had that pleasure.'

'You think her very beautiful?'

'She is rich, which comes to the same thing,' he said with a slight sneer. 'But is she not, just a trifle—how shall I put it—dull?'

I could have struck the man. 'No one who knows Miss Stapleton could accuse her of that defect,' I said warmly.

'Ah, you do; I don't. Perhaps I may alter my opinion on closer acquaintance.'

I could not stand the man's cool assurance, and making some excuse, I left the box for awhile. When I returned the Colonel was gone, and Lady Charnase was leaning back in her seat, thinking deeply.

'Tomorrow,' she said, 'I must go and see Ruth, and try to get at the bottom of this.'

'Do,' I answered; 'her old servant said she needed a friend.'

'He denied again knowing her better than as a mere acquaintance.'

'What do *you* think about it?'

'I cannot tell; I am perplexed. Mrs Marchmont is in America, with her own people; her mother has been very ill. He would not go, which, as he professes to be very devoted, is, to say the least of it, strange.'

'He cannot be such a villain; there must be some explanation.'

'I hope so,' she said gravely. 'I don't think we will stay for the fourth act. I hear it is the weakest, and I will write to Ruth tonight, asking her to see me.'

We spoke no more on the subject nearest to our hearts, and, after the third act, I put Lady Charnase into her carriage, refusing her offer of dropping me in Jermyn Street. I, too, wanted to think.

When I reached home the spirit of work was upon me, and I sat down to my desk. Hour after hour passed, and so absorbed was I, that I hardly noticed the grey dawn creeping in at the window, putting my lamplight to shame. I was happier than I had been for some time. I thought I saw a way of saving my heroine from the misery in store for her and wrote on and on, weaving her web of fate with each stroke of my pen. Yes, even such an influence as Colonel Marchmont's might be in Ruth's life, could be counteracted and made to work for Marian's ultimate good. It was not till the servant entered the room to dust and sweep, that I realized how I had spent the night; but as she appeared I had just made up my mind that for the time I must leave off writing, and I did so, quite satisfied.

Towards the middle of the morning I went to Cecil Street. I had determined that now I had a sort of entrée to Mr Stapleton's house, I would call from time to time, if not for the purpose of seeing his niece, to interview her affectionate old retainer, and glean what information he could conscientiously give me. I knew it was of no use to try and corrupt him with money. If I could serve his mistress he would willingly talk; if not, of what use was it to try and bribe him?

The sun was shining brightly, and I fancied that my heroine's happiness had something to do with the sunshine! How silly we are when our spirits rise; how childish to think that God takes thought and feeling for each of those foolish souls He has created beyond providing for their path in life to be according to His will. I thought that my heroine's happiness, arising from a wish to do Ruth good, might have found favour in his sight!

Old Barton opened the door much sooner than on the previous occasion on which I called, and his face reflected the brightness of mine. He was jubilant. 'Miss Ruth,' he announced, 'is much better. I think, sir, your visit did her good.'

'Or,' I ventured to feel the ground, 'the walk she took after I left her!'

Poor Barton! I laughed to see the astonishment depicted on his wrinkled features.

'Oh, sir,' he cried, 'how could you know?'

I smiled enigmatically, and he continued. 'No one, except myself, knows that Miss Ruth went out, and I am sure I never told a soul. But, as you know the fact, sir, I may tell you that it *was* the walk that did her good. She came home a different creature from what you saw her in the afternoon, and now, I do believe, she'll soon be quite well again.'

I was intensely glad to hear the old man's news, but my brain was in a whirl. My pen was ruling Ruth's life! It was more horrible than I had thought at first; for though I myself was delighted at the way in which I had brought Marian out of her difficulties, I had no idea how Mr Kerr would take the change. When I had sketched out my novel to him, he had thought the plot must be strengthened by a tragic ending, from which I had now deviated; would he object? I should not dare tell him my motives. He would laugh in my face, and think my brain was turned with too much work, or, with self-conceit! Then, again, if I brought my story to an absolutely happy ending, as a work of art it would be valueless! How terribly different things seem viewed in the glaring light of day, to the aspect they assume in the silent watches of the night; then, all wickedness seems powerless, all good triumphant! Why can this not last? Today Ruth and her story had possession of me, and I longed to know whether Lady Charnase would see her, and, if so, whether she would arrive at any conclusion about the Colonel.

It was about four o'clock, when I thought I might venture to call in Berkeley Square, and I went there on foot, up St James's Street, down Piccadilly. It was a lovely day and the streets were very full. I could not resist the temptation to enter the Green Park, and I lingered there for some time. When I get thinking I am soon lost in my thoughts; and I was seated under a thick, bushy tree for some minutes before I realized that on its other side the two chairs that had been unoccupied when I took mine, were now in possession of a lady and gentleman in earnest conversation. I caught a few words that aroused my attention.

'You say you saw Lady Charnase at the door?' asked the woman's voice.

'Yes,' was said in a man's deep tones, which I immediately recognized as Colonel Marchmont's, for though I had only heard him speak twice, there was a slight lisp in his speech which made it the more noticeable—'and she was admitted.'

'What can this mean! You made Ruth promise to see no one.'

'I told you so; but, of course, I dared not say too much; it does no good to strain the bonds; and the poor little soul was so happy yesterday that I had not the heart to scold.'

'Bah! you men are so soft-hearted; you should let me deal with her!'

'I don't think there would be much of Ruth left if you took her in hand for a week.'

'What do you mean?'

'My dear Emilie, you frighten the very life out of her; she was ill for days at the thought even of having to live under your roof!'

'Little simpleton! Did she understand she could not be married without?'

'Oh, yes; she understood; but when she comes to you it seems that old Barton will come too.'

'No chance of gaining old Stapleton's consent?'

'Do you think I am such a fool as to seek it? Stapleton is wide awake, if he is a miser; he would soon know too much. No, Ruth's money must be enough for me, at present.'

'When——.' The next words were whispered and I heard no more. But I had overheard more than enough; what vile plot was concocting? Who was this woman whose presence terrified Ruth? Why was she to leave home to be under her roof?'

I hastened to Lady Charnase's and found her at home.

'What news?' I cried, almost before I had shaken hands.

'I have seen our friend; but, my dear friend, you were mistaken; Ruth was wonderfully well and explained her depression of yesterday—a headache and a fit of the blues! Poor, romantic novelist, you must not try and get copy out of your friends!'

'Don't laugh, Lady Charnase; the matter is very serious.'

She was sobered in a moment at the sight of my face. 'You, then, have heard something?'

'I have.' And I told her all that the pair had said in the park.

'I cannot understand it; Ruth assured me she did not know Colonel Marchmont.'

'Most likely not—under that name.'

'What a fool I am,' she exclaimed; 'I ought to have guessed he would not pass as himself if concerned in any plan against her peace.'

'I wonder who the woman was.'

'Someone in his power, whom he has got to help him.'

'But he cannot be such a wretch as to propose to marry Miss Stapleton, with his own wife only away for a short while!'

'I have learnt something else about the gentleman; his wife has left him—means to sue for a divorce once she can leave her mother.'

'Phew! This is dreadful, to think that Ruth can believe in such a fellow! What can we do to enlighten her?'

'Girls are easily deceived, and very difficult to persuade, where love is concerned, that the hero they adore is not all their fancy pictures him. Perhaps she knows the truth.'

'Lady Charnase!' I exclaimed, 'how can you——'

'I am only supposing! Why should she not declare her love openly?'

'Because he will not allow her to do so.' I knew the whole story—had I not written it before I knew any of these people, on the tablets of my mind? 'His plan is to get her into his power, take what money he can get, and then—poor Ruth! poor, poor Ruth!'

'Mr Cranston,' said Lady Charnase angrily, 'you are not writing a novel; don't be absurd.'

She would not listen to another word—was firmly persuaded that all that could be done was to let Mr Stapleton know what was in the wind, and then let events take their course. I pointed out that even if this was the proper and only way out of the difficulty, it was no business of ours, and that we should get no thanks for our pains; and before I left her she promised not to move in the matter till I had seen her again.

I had not the vaguest notion of what I was going to do at present. I could not go to Cecil Street again for a day or two, when most likely things would have shaped themselves to better purpose, and perhaps show me how to act. Well, I always had my book, and to this I sat down as soon as I reached my rooms, working away with as much zest as yesterday, but alas! with such utterly different results. Ruth and her wrongs faded from my mind in the intense excitement of guiding my Marian through the most difficult part of her life, and I soon found myself undoing all I had done on the previous evening, and going back to the old plans laid down, which I now saw were the only possible ones if I wished not to throw away the whole thing.

And as I worked in the fast falling twilight, I seemed to hear the air sobbing and sighing round me, and later on, the lamp, lighted silently by a well-trained maid, seemed agitated and flickered strangely, as it had never done before; one moment burning low, so that I could hardly see; another, flaring up with unusual brightness. But I never stopped to think over these phenomena, I went on and on, from night to morning, and to night again. They brought me food—I could not eat; they brought me drink, which I took feverishly, the wine mounting to my head, but only serving to stimulate me to fresh efforts. No need to seek thoughts outside; my brain was teeming with the multitude of ideas that crowded on me. I gave no thought to the hideous horror that had come upon me only the day before; that I held a supernatural power over the life of this girl, who was so much to me, whom I had fallen in love with at first sight, because I had already fallen in love with my own creation—now, I was only Marian's—Ruth was far away, I had forgotten her. And Marian I did not want to save—I wanted to make her a perfect heroine, not a happy woman! That was when human nature was at rest! when I had forgotten Ruth!

Two days passed, how I hardly knew. I was no longer the lover; I was the author, living only for the work in hand. And I had not been near Lady Charnase.

On the morning of the third, a hurried note from her brought me to a sense of my neglect; had I not as good as promised to look into this question, and see what could be done, preventing Lady Charnase from moving in the matter by this tacit promise? I felt I had behaved very badly, and went straight to her on receipt of her letter.

'Well?' she asked.

I knew what she meant, though she was so curt, and could only apologize humbly.

'What!' she exclaimed, 'you have done nothing! Mr Cranston— Mr Cranston, and I imagined you hard at work!'

'I have been,' I said deprecatingly, 'but not at the work you mean.'

'And now we may be too late!'

I started. Could this be? If so how shameful my conduct was; I should never forgive myself. To think that while I had been scribbling at what might, after all, perhaps be wasted work. I had allowed time to get the better of me and play havoc with the beautiful girl, who once again filled my heart and soul with longing.

'Lady Charnase,' I said, 'what shall I do? I confess that I have been neglectful in the extreme. Can I repair my mistake?'

'Go to Cecil Street at once,' she said, 'find out what has been taking place—Stay,' as I made a movement, 'you had better have some credentials!' and she hastily wrote a few lines, not telling me their purport, but begging me to wait for an answer.

'Miss Stapleton is out of town,' was the answer to my enquiry, not given by Barton but by a maidservant I had not seen before.

'For long?' I asked.

'I believe, sir, indefinitely. Mr Stapleton is in, sir, if you would wish to see him.'

'No, thanks; I have not the pleasure of knowing Mr Stapleton. Could you give me Miss Stapleton's address; Lady Charnase will be anxious to write to her.'

'I will fetch it for you, sir.'

My mind was relieved; such alacrity betokened no secrecy, and if the household knew where their young mistress was, it meant that, at all events for the present, she was safe and Lady Charnase's fears groundless. But I was terribly disappointed at not seeing her, at learning that she was beyond reach. I could invent no possible excuse for following her wherever she might be, and yet, once more I was mad with longing to be with her.

The maid came back: Miss Stapleton was staying with an aunt by marriage, a widow, Lady Steuart, at Richmond.

And this was the only news I could take to Berkeley Square. It had an unexpected effect. 'I know Lady Steuart,' said Lady Charnase. 'Why should we not go down this afternoon and call?'

I supposed she meant *me* by *we*, and willingly acquiesced.

The way to Richmond was soon covered by the magnificent pair of roans that were the pride of their owner's heart, and we found Lady Steuart at home. There were no signs of Ruth, however; and, to my lover's thinking, if she had been there, I should have known it by instinct as soon as I entered the house.

'Ruth Stapleton!' exclaimed Lady Steuart, in answer to her visitor's question concerning her niece. 'I have not seen her for a long time. I was thinking of making an effort to reach Cecil Street one day, for I hear she has been far from well, and that house is enough to kill any-one outright. But you know I am not on the best of terms with my brother-in-law, and go there as rarely as possible. How is she? I dare say you have seen her more recently than I have.'

Lady Charnase and I looked at each other. Should we tell this old lady of the dreadful revelation her answer was to us; or for Ruth's sake, had we better hold our tongues? I made an almost imperceptible movement of negation which Lady Charnase understood, for she said quietly. 'Yes, I have seen her quite recently. She was not very well, but as you say, that house——' And an expressive shrug of the shoulders finished the sentence.

When we had drunk the tea Lady Steuart insisted on our taking and which nearly choked me, so anxious was I to find myself alone with Lady Charnase, we left Richmond and hurried back to town as fast as the horses could go. We were both in a terrible state—Lady Charnase because she really loved this girl who was being betrayed into we knew not what, and I because, not only did I love her with heart and soul, but because I had, through my culpable negligence, allowed this flight to come to pass. That it was flight we could not doubt.

Lady Charnase was very determined. She would go to Colonel Marchmont herself; no squeamishness on her side should prevent her from trying, at least, to save her friend. Would I go with her?

Would I? I would do anything, go anywhere, if only I could undo what I had done.

Before we reached Sloane Street she pulled the check-string. 'Drive to Cadogan Square,' she ordered, and the horses' heads were turned away from the Park, southwards.

Colonel Marchmont was out of town!

We looked at each other, despair and anguish in our hearts. What was to be done now?

His address? The Colonel had left his address at the club, from where all his letters were to be forwarded—would I leave a message?

'No,' said Lady Charnase in an undertone; 'it would put him on the alert.'

We drove away in silence, I too miserable for words. I would not enter the house with Lady Charnase, although she begged me to; she could think of nothing, and I might, perhaps, help her to come to some decision. But I felt too deeply—I must be alone. And alone I went back to Jermyn Street.

For a long time I sat with my head in my hands, too wretched even to think. Then an impulse came to me; I took up my pen once more and wrote. And once more, as I wrote of Marian, I forgot Ruth! It seems almost incredible, now that I think over it calmly, but at the time, of course, I was not conscious of the fact; though my tears fell more than once, I did not realize that my overstrung nerves were finding vent in sorrow for the living heroine I could not help. I thought it was only for the child of my brain whose story was fast nearing completion.

Tonight there was a great sense of unreality about me—I was myself and yet was someone else—I knew I was alone—and yet, at intervals I heard another breathing at my side, though when I raised my head no living presence was there. At times I was frightened at the solitude, and stretched out my hand to touch the bell—even a servant would be a relief from this unbearable loneliness—but no sooner did my fingers close round the handle than all my fears fled, and I called myself a fool for my pains, laughing aloud to think what fiction could do—how the imaginings of a brain could take shape and form, and even materialize themselves sufficiently to stir such nerves as mine!

The clocks were striking three—I was writing still—but now, there was but one sentence left, and as I penned it, the concluding words. . . . 'And thus she died!' there were borne in and round me two whispered words, that seemed breathed into the air, so gently did they reach my ear.

'I rest.'

Then came a sigh of deep thankfulness, and then. . . . a silence.

With a cry, I rose from my chair, passing my hands through my hair as I did so. Was I awake or dreaming? Floating in mid-air, carried as though on the waves of the wind that was softly wafted in through the open window, was the figure of a dead girl, with rich red hair flaming round her lovely, pallid face.

No need for me to read the papers—no need for me to hear from

Lady Charnase, as between her sobs she told me all. I knew before I rose from my knees in the early morning of that terrible day, that Ruth Stapleton was dead.

Was it an accident? Or had her betrayal so preyed upon her mind that death itself was the only relief possible? No one will ever know, and. . . . I shall never write again.

# 8

ARTHUR CONAN DOYLE

# The Story of the Man with the Watches

There are many who will still bear in mind the singular circumstances which, under the heading of the Rugby Mystery, filled many columns of the daily Press in the spring of the year 1892. Coming as it did at a period of exceptional dullness, it attracted perhaps rather more attention than it deserved, but it offered to the public that mixture of the whimsical and the tragic which is most stimulating to the popular imagination. Interest drooped, however, when, after weeks of fruitless investigation, it was found that no final explanation of the facts was forthcoming, and the tragedy seemed from that time to the present to have finally taken its place in the dark catalogue of inexplicable and unexpiated crimes. A recent communication (the authenticity of which appears to be above question) has, however, thrown some new and clear light upon the matter. Before laying it before the public it would be as well, perhaps, that I should refresh their memories as to the singular facts upon which this commentary is founded. These facts were briefly as follows:

At five o'clock upon the evening of the 18th of March in the year already mentioned a train left Euston Station for Manchester. It was a rainy, squally day, which grew wilder as it progressed, so it was by no means the weather in which anyone would travel who was not driven to do so by necessity. The train, however, is a favourite one among Manchester businessmen who are returning from town, for it does the journey in four hours and twenty minutes, with only three stoppages upon the way. In spite of the inclement evening it was, therefore, fairly well filled upon the occasion of which I speak. The guard of the train was a tried servant of the company—a man who had worked for twenty-two years without blemish or complaint. His name was John Palmer.

The station clock was upon the stroke of five, and the guard was about to give the customary signal to the engine-driver, when he observed two belated passengers hurrying down the platform. The one was an exceptionally tall man, dressed in a long black overcoat with an astrakhan collar and cuffs. I have already said that the evening was an inclement one, and the tall traveller had the high, warm collar turned up to protect his throat against the bitter March wind. He appeared, as far as the guard could judge by so hurried an inspection, to be a man between fifty and sixty years of age, who had retained a good deal of the vigour and activity of his youth. In one hand he carried a brown leather Gladstone bag. His companion was a lady, tall and erect, walking with a vigorous step which outpaced the gentleman beside her. She wore a long, fawn-coloured dust-cloak, a black, close-fitting toque, and a dark veil which concealed the greater part of her face. The two might very well have passed as father and daughter. They walked swiftly down the line of carriages, glancing in at the windows, until the guard, John Palmer, overtook them.

'Now, then, sir, look sharp, the train is going,' said he.

'First-class,' the man answered.

The guard turned the handle of the nearest door. In the carriage, which he had opened, there sat a small man with a cigar in his mouth. His appearance seems to have impressed itself upon the guard's memory, for he was prepared, afterwards, to describe or to identify him. He was a man of thirty-four or thirty-five years of age, dressed in some grey material, sharp nosed, alert, with a ruddy, weather-beaten face, and a small, closely cropped black beard. He glanced up as the door was opened. The tall man paused with his foot upon the step.

'This is a smoking compartment. The lady dislikes smoke,' said he, looking round at the guard.

'All right! Here you are, sir!' said John Palmer. He slammed the door of the smoking carriage, opened that of the next one, which was empty, and thrust the two travellers in. At the same moment he sounded his whistle, and the wheels of the train began to move.

The man with the cigar was at the window of his carriage, and said something to the guard as he rolled past him, but the words were lost in the bustle of the departure. Palmer stepped into the guard's van as it came up to him, and thought no more of the incident.

Twelve minutes after its departure the train reached Willesden Junction, where it stopped for a very short interval. An examination of the tickets has made it certain that no one either joined or left it at this time, and no passenger was seen to alight upon the platform. At 5.14 the journey to Manchester was resumed, and Rugby was reached at 6.50, the express being five minutes late.

At Rugby the attention of the station officials was drawn to the fact that the door of one of the first-class carriages was open. An examination of that compartment, and of its neighbour, disclosed a remarkable state of affairs.

The smoking carriage in which the short, red-faced man with the black beard had been seen was now empty. Save for a half-smoked cigar, there was no trace whatever of its recent occupant. The door of this carriage was fastened. In the next compartment, to which attention had been originally drawn, there was no sign either of the gentleman with the astrakhan collar or of the young lady who accompanied him. All three passengers had disappeared. On the other hand, there was found upon the floor of this carriage—the one in which the tall traveller and the lady had been—a young man, fashionably dressed and of elegant appearance. He lay with his knees drawn up, and his head resting against the further door, an elbow upon either seat. A bullet had penetrated his heart, and his death must have been instantaneous. No one had seen such a man enter the train, and no railway ticket was found in his pocket, nor were there any markings upon his linen, nor papers or personal property which might help to identify him. Who he was, whence he had come, and how he had met his end were each as great a mystery as what had occurred to the three people who had started an hour and a half before from Euston in those two compartments.

I have said that there was no personal property which might help to identify him, but it is true that there was one peculiarity about this unknown young man which was much commented upon at the time. In his pockets were found no fewer than six valuable gold watches, three in the various pockets of his waistcoat, one in his ticket-pocket, one in his breast-pocket, and one small one set in a leather strap and fastened round his left wrist. The obvious explanation that the man was a pickpocket, and that this was his plunder, was discounted by the fact that all six were of American make, and of a type which is rare in England. Three of them bore the mark of the Rochester Watch-making Company; one was by Mason, of Elmira; one was unmarked; and the small one, which was highly jewelled and ornamented, was from Tiffany, of New York. The other contents of his pocket consisted of an ivory knife with a corkscrew by Rodgers, of Sheffield; a small circular mirror, one inch in diameter; a readmission slip to the Lyceum theatre; a silver box full of vesta matches, and a brown leather cigar-case containing two cheroots—also two pounds, fourteen shillings in money. It was clear then that whatever motives may have led to his death, robbery was not among them. As already mentioned, there were no markings upon the man's linen, which appeared to be new, and no tailor's name upon his coat. In appearance he was young, short, smooth cheeked, and delicately featured. One of his front teeth was conspicuously stopped with gold.

On the discovery of the tragedy an examination was instantly made of the tickets of all passengers, and the number of the passengers themselves was counted. It was found that only three tickets were unaccounted for, corresponding to the three travellers who were missing. The express was then allowed to proceed, but a new guard was sent with it, and John Palmer was detained as a witness at Rugby. The carriage which included the two compartments in question was uncoupled and side-tracked. Then, on the arrival of Inspector Vane, of Scotland Yard, and of Mr Henderson, a detective in the service of the railway company, an exhaustive inquiry was made into all the circumstances.

That crime had been committed was certain. The bullet, which appeared to have come from a small pistol or revolver, had been fired from some little distance, as there was no scorching of the clothes. No weapon was found in the compartment (which finally disposed of the theory of suicide), nor was there any sign of the brown leather bag which the guard had seen in the hand of the tall gentleman. A lady's parasol was found upon the rack, but no other trace was to be seen of the travellers in either of the sections. Apart from the crime, the question of how or why three passengers (one of them a lady) could get out of the train, and one other get in during the unbroken run between Willesden and Rugby, was one which excited the utmost curiosity among the general public, and gave rise to much speculation in the London Press.

John Palmer, the guard, was able at the inquest to give some evidence which threw a little light upon the matter. There was a spot between Tring and Cheddington, according to his statement, where, on account of some repairs to the line, the train had for a few minutes slowed down to a pace not exceeding eight or ten miles an hour. At that place it might be possible for a man, or even for an exceptionally active woman, to have left the train without serious injury. It was true that a gang of platelayers was there, and that they had seen nothing, but it was their custom to stand in the middle between the metals, and the open carriage door was upon the far side, so that it was conceivable that someone might have alighted unseen, as the darkness would by that time be drawing in. A steep embankment would instantly screen anyone who sprang out from the observation of the navvies.

The guard also deposed that there was a good deal of movement upon the platform at Willesden Junction, and that though it was certain that no one had either joined or left the train there, it was still quite possible that some of the passengers might have changed unseen from one compartment to another. It was by no means uncommon for a gentleman to finish his cigar in a smoking carriage and then to change to a clearer atmosphere. Supposing that the man with the black beard had done so at Willesden (and the half-smoked cigar upon the floor seemed to favour the supposition), he would naturally go into the nearest section, which would bring him into the company of the two other actors in this drama. Thus the first stage of the affair might be surmised without any great breach of probability. But what the second stage had been, or how the final one had been arrived at, neither the guard nor the experienced detective officers could suggest.

A careful examination of the line between Willesden and Rugby resulted in one discovery which might or might not have a bearing upon the tragedy. Near Tring, at the very place where the train slowed down, there was found at the bottom of the embankment a small pocket Testament, very shabby and worn. It was printed by the Bible Society of London, and bore an inscription: 'From John to Alice. Jan. 13th, 1856', upon the fly-leaf. Underneath was written: 'James. July 4th, 1859', and beneath that again: 'Edward. Nov. 1st, 1869', all the entries being in the same handwriting. This was the only clue, if it could be called a clue, which the police obtained, and the coroner's verdict of 'Murder by a person or persons unknown' was the unsatisfactory ending of a singular case. Advertisement, rewards, and enquiries proved equally fruitless, and nothing could be found which was solid enough to form the basis for a profitable investigation.

It would be a mistake, however, to suppose that no theories were formed to account for the facts. On the contrary, the Press, both in England and in America, teemed with suggestions and suppositions, most of which were obviously absurd. The fact that the watches were of American make, and some peculiarities in connection with the gold stopping of his front tooth, appeared to indicate that the deceased was a citizen of the United States, though his linen, clothes, and boots were undoubtedly of British manufacture. It was surmised, by some, that he was concealed under the seat, and that, being discovered, he was for some reason, possibly because he had overheard their guilty secrets, put to death by his fellow-passengers. When coupled with generalities as to the ferocity and cunning of anarchical and other secret societies, this theory sounded as plausible as any.

The fact that he should be without a ticket would be consistent with the idea of concealment, and it was well known that women played a prominent part in the Nihilistic propaganda. On the other hand, it was clear, from the guard's statement, that the man must have been hidden there *before* the others arrived, and how unlikely the coincidence that conspirators should stray exactly into the very compartment in which a spy was already concealed! Besides, this explanation ignored the man in the smoking carriage, and gave no reason at all for his simultaneous disappearance. The police had little difficulty in showing that such a theory would not cover the facts, but they were unprepared in the absence of evidence to advance any alternative explanation.

There was a letter in the *Daily Gazette*, over the signature of a well-known criminal investigator, which gave rise to considerable discussion at the time. He had formed a hypothesis which had at least ingenuity to recommend it, and I cannot do better than append it in his own words.

'Whatever may be the truth,' said he, 'it must depend upon some bizarre and rare combination of events, so we need have no hesitation in postulating such events in our explanation. In the absence of data we must abandon the analytic or scientific method of investigation, and must approach it in the synthetic fashion. In a word, instead of taking known events and deducing from them what has occurred, we must build up a fanciful explanation if it will only be consistent with known events. We can then test this explanation by any fresh facts which may arise. If they all fit into their places, the probability is that we are upon the right track, and with each fresh fact this probability increases in a geometrical progression until the evidence becomes final and convincing.

'Now, there is one most remarkable and suggestive fact which has not met with the attention which it deserves. There is a local train running through Harrow and King's Langley, which is timed in such a way that the express must have overtaken it at or about the period when it eased down its speed to eight miles an hour on account of the repairs of the line. The two trains would at that time be travelling in the same direction at a similar rate of speed and upon parallel lines. It is within everyone's experience how, under such circumstances, the occupant of each carriage can see very plainly the passengers in the other carriages opposite to him. The lamps of the express had been lit at Willesden, so that each compartment was brightly illuminated, and most visible to an observer from outside.

'Now, the sequence of events as I reconstruct them would be after this fashion. This young man with the abnormal number of watches was alone in the carriage of the slow train. His ticket, with his papers and gloves and other things, was, we will suppose, on the seat beside him. He was probably an American, and also probably a man of weak intellect. The excessive wearing of jewellery is an early symptom in some forms of mania.

'As he sat watching the carriages of the express which were

(on account of the state of the line) going at the same pace as himself, he suddenly saw some people in it whom he knew. We will suppose for the sake of our theory that these people were a woman whom he loved and a man whom he hated—and who in return hated him. The young man was excitable and impulsive. He opened the door of his carriage, stepped from the footboard of the local train to the footboard of the express, opened the other door, and made his way into the presence of these two people. The feat (on the supposition that the trains were going at the same pace) is by no means so perilous as it might appear.

'Having now got our young man without his ticket into the carriage in which the elder man and the young woman are travelling, it is not difficult to imagine that a violent scene ensued. It is possible that the pair were also Americans, which is the more probable as the man carried a weapon—an unusual thing in England. If our supposition of incipient mania is correct, the young man is likely to have assaulted the other. As the upshot of the quarrel the elder man shot the intruder, and then made his escape from the carriage, taking the young lady with him. We will suppose that all this happened very rapidly, and that the train was still going at so slow a pace that it was not difficult for them to leave it. A woman might leave a train going at eight miles an hour. As a matter of fact, we know that this woman *did* do so.

'And now we have to fit in the man in the smoking carriage. Presuming that we have, up to this point, reconstructed the tragedy correctly, we shall find nothing in this other man to cause us to reconsider our conclusions. According to my theory, this man saw the young fellow cross from one train to the other, saw him open the door, heard the pistol-shot, saw the two fugitives spring out on to the line, realized that murder had been done, and sprang out himself in pursuit. Why he has never been heard of since—whether he met his own death in the pursuit, or whether, as is more likely, he was made to realize that it was not a case for his interference—is a detail which we have at present no means of explaining. I acknowledge that there are some difficulties in the way. At first sight, it might seem improbable that at such a moment a murderer would burden himself in his flight with a brown leather bag. My answer is that he was well aware that if the bag were found his identity would be established. It was absolutely necessary for him to take it with him. My theory stands or falls upon one point, and I call upon the railway company to make strict enquiry as to whether a ticket was found unclaimed in the local train through Harrow and King's Langley upon the 18th of March. If such a ticket were found my case is proved. If not, my theory may still be the correct one, for it is conceivable either that he travelled without a ticket or that his ticket was lost.'

To this elaborate and plausible hypothesis the answer of the police and of the company was, first, that no such ticket was found; secondly, that the slow train would never run parallel to the express; and, thirdly, that the local train had been stationary in King's Langley Station when the express, going at fifty miles an hour, had flashed past it. So perished the only satisfying explanation, and five years have elapsed without supplying a new one. Now, at last, there comes a statement which covers all the facts, and which must be regarded as authentic. It took the shape of a letter dated from New York, and addressed to the same criminal investigator whose theory I have quoted. It is given here in extenso, with the exception of the two opening paragraphs, which are personal in their nature:

'You'll excuse me if I am not very free with names. There's less reason now than there was five years ago when mother was still living. But for all that, I had rather cover up our tracks all I can. But I owe you an explanation, for if your idea of it was wrong, it was a mighty ingenious one all the same. I'll have to go back a little so as you may understand all about it.

'My people came from Bucks, England, and emigrated to the States in the early fifties. They settled in Rochester, in the State of New York, where my father ran a large dry goods store. There were only two sons: myself, James, and my brother, Edward. I was ten years older than my brother, and after my father died I sort of took the place of a father to him, as an elder brother would. He was a bright, spirited boy, and just one of the most beautiful creatures that ever lived. But there was always a soft spot in him, and it was like mold in cheese, for it spread and spread, and nothing that you could do would stop it. Mother saw it just as clearly as I did, but she went on spoiling him all the same, for he had such a way with him that you could refuse him nothing. I did all I could to hold him in, and he hated me for my pains.

'At last he fairly got his head, and nothing that we could do would stop him. He got off into New York, and went rapidly from bad to worse. At first he was only fast, and then he was criminal: and then, at the end of a year or two, he was one of the most notorious young crooks in the city. He had formed a friendship with Sparrow MacCoy, who was at the head of his profession as a bunco-steerer, green-goodsman, and general rascal. They took to card-sharping, and frequented some of the best hotels in New York. My brother was an excellent actor (he might have made an honest name for himself if he had chosen), and he would take the parts of a young Englishman of title, of a simple lad from the West, or of a college undergraduate, whichever suited Sparrow MacCoy's purpose. And then one day he dressed himself as a girl, and he carried it off so well, and made himself such a valuable decoy, that it was their favorite game afterwards. They had made it right with Tammany and with the police, so it seemed as if nothing could ever stop them, for those were in the days before the Lexow Commission, and if you only had a pull, you could do pretty nearly anything you wanted.

'And nothing would have stopped them if they had only stuck to cards and New York, but they must needs come up Rochester way, and forge a name upon a check. It was my brother that did it, though everyone knew that it was under the influence of Sparrow MacCoy. I bought up that check, and a pretty sum it cost me . Then I went to my brother, laid it before him on the table, and swore to him that I would prosecute if he did not clear out of the country. At first he simply laughed. I could not prosecute, he said, without breaking our mother's heart, and he knew that I would not do that. I made him understand, however, that our mother's heart was being broken in any case, and that I had set firm on the point that I would rather see him in a Rochester gaol than in a New York hotel. So at last he gave in, and he made me a solemn promise that he would see Sparrow MacCoy no more, that he would go to Europe, and that he would turn his hand to any honest trade that I helped him to get. I took him down right away to an old family friend, Joe Willson, who is an exporter of American watches and clocks, and I got him to give Edward an agency in London, with a small salary and a 5 per cent. commission on all business. His manner and appearance were so good that he won the old man over at once, and within a week he was sent off to London with a case full of samples.

'It seemed to me that this business of the check had really given my brother a fright, and that there was some chance of his settling down into an honest line of life. My mother had spoken with him, and what she said had touched him, for she had always been the best of mothers to him, and he had been the great sorrow of her life. But I knew that this man Sparrow MacCoy had a great influence over Edward, and my chance of keeping the lad straight lay in breaking the connection between them. I had a friend in the New York detective force, and through him I kept a watch upon MacCoy. When within a fortnight of my brother's sailing I heard that MacCoy had taken a berth in the *Etruria*, I was as certain as if he had told me that he was going over to England for the purpose of coaxing Edward back again into the ways that he had left. In an instant I had resolved to go also, and to put my influence against MacCoy's. I knew it was a losing fight, but I thought, and my mother thought, that it was my duty. We passed the last night together in prayer for my success, and she gave me her own Testament that my father had given her on the day of their marriage in the Old Country, so that I might always wear it next my heart.

'I was a fellow-traveller, on the steamship, with Sparrow MacCoy, and at least I had the satisfaction of spoiling his little game for the voyage. The very first night I went into the smoking-room, and found him at the head of a card table, with half a dozen young fellows who were carrying their full purses and their empty skulls over to Europe. He was settling down for his harvest, and a rich one it would have been. But I soon changed all that.

' "Gentlemen," said I, "are you aware whom you are playing with?"

' "What's that to you? You mind your own business!" said he, with an oath.

' "Who is it, anyway?" asked one of the dudes.

' "He's Sparrow MacCoy, the most notorious card-sharper in the States."

'Up he jumped with a bottle in his hand, but he remembered that he was under the flag of the effete Old Country, where law and order run, and Tammany has no pull. Gaol and the gallows wait for violence and murder, and there's no slipping out by the back door on board an ocean liner.

' "Prove your words, you——!" said he.

' "I will!" said I. "If you will turn up your right shirtsleeve to the shoulder, I will either prove my words or I will eat them."

'He turned white and said not a word. You see, I knew something of his ways, and I was aware that part of the mechanism which he and all such sharpers use consists of an elastic down the arm with a clip just above the wrist. Is is by means of this clip that they withdraw from their hands the cards which they do not want, while they substitute other cards from another hiding-place. I reckoned on it being there, and it was. He cursed me, slunk out of the saloon, and was hardly seen again during the voyage. For once, at any rate, I got level with Mister Sparrow MacCoy.

'But he soon had his revenge upon me, for when it came to influencing my brother he outweighed me every time. Edward had kept himself straight in London for the first few weeks, and had done some business with his American watches, until this villain came across his path once more. I did my best, but the best was little enough. The next thing I heard there had been a scandal at one of the Northumberland Avenue hotels: a traveller had been fleeced of a large sum by two confederate card-sharpers, and the matter was in the hands of Scotland Yard. The first I learned of it was in the evening paper, and I was at once certain that my brother and MacCoy were back at their old games. I hurried at once to Edward's lodgings. They told me that he and a tall gentleman (whom I recognized as MacCoy) had gone off together, and that he had left the lodgings and taken his things with him. The landlady had heard them give several directions to the cabman, ending with Euston Station, and she had accidentally overheard the tall gentleman saying something about Manchester. She believed that that was their destination.

'A glance at the timetable showed me that the most likely train was at five, though there was another at 4.35 which they might have caught. I had only time to get the later one, and found no sign of them either at the depot or in the train. They must have gone on by the earlier one, so I determined to follow them to Manchester and search for them in the hotels there. One last appeal to my brother by all that he owed to my mother might even now be the salvation of him. My nerves were over-strung, and I lit a cigar to steady them. At that moment, just as the train was moving off, the door of my compartment was flung open, and there were MacCoy and my brother on the platform.

'They were both disguised, and with good reason, for they knew that the London police were after them. MacCoy had a great astrakhan collar drawn up, so that only his eyes and nose were show-ing. My brother was dressed like a woman, with a black veil half down his face, but of course it did not deceive me for an instant, nor would it have done so even if I had not known that he had often used such a dress before. I started up, and as I did so MacCoy recognized me. He said something, the conductor slammed the door, and they were shown into the next compartment. I tried to stop the train so as to follow them, but the wheels were already moving, and it was too late.

'When we stopped at Willesden, I instantly changed my carriage. It appears that I was not seen to do so, which is not surprising, as the station was crowded with people. MacCoy, of course, was expecting me, and he had spent the time between Euston and Willesden in say-ing all he could to harden my brother's heart and set him against me. That is what I fancy, for I had never found him so impossible to soften or to move. I tried this way and I tried that; I pictured his future in an English gaol; I described the sorrow of his mother when I came back with the news; I said everything to touch his heart, but all to no pur-pose. He sat there with a fixed sneer upon his handsome face, while every now and then Sparrow MacCoy would throw in a taunt at me, or some word of encouragement to hold my brother to his resolutions.

' "Why don't you run a Sunday-school?" he would say to me, and then, in the same breath: "He thinks you have no will of your own. He thinks you are just the baby brother and that he can lead you where he likes. He's only just finding out that you are a man as well as he."

'It was those words of his which set me talking bitterly. We had left Willesden, you understand, for all this took some time. My temper got the better of me, and for the first time in my life I let my brother see the rough side of me. Perhaps it would have been better had I done so earlier and more often.

' "A man!" said I. "Well, I'm glad to have your friend's assurance of it, for no one would suspect it to see you like a boarding-school missy. I don't suppose in all this country there is a more contemptible-looking creature than you are as you sit there with that Dolly pinafore upon you." He coloured up at that, for he was a vain man, and he winced from ridicule.

' "It's only a dust-cloak," said he, and he slipped it off. "One has to throw the coppers off one's scent, and I had no other way to do it." He took his toque off with the veil attached, and he put both it and the cloak into his brown bag. "Anyway, I don't need to wear it until the conductor comes round," said he.

' "Nor then, either," said I, and taking the bag I slung it with all my force out of the window. "Now," said I, "you'll never make a Mary Jane of yourself while I can help it. If nothing but that disguise stands between you and a gaol, then to gaol you shall go."

'That was the way to manage him. I felt my advantage at once. His supple nature was one which yielded to roughness far more readily than to entreaty. He flushed with shame, and his eyes filled with tears. But MacCoy saw my advantage also, and was determined that I should not pursue it.

' "He's my pard, and you shall not bully him," he cried.

' "He's my brother, and you shall not ruin him," said I. "I believe a spell of prison is the very best way of keeping you apart, and you shall have it, or it will be no fault of mine."

' "Oh, you would squeal, would you?" he cried, and in an instant he whipped out his revolver. I sprang for his hand, but saw that I was too late, and jumped aside. At the same instant he fired, and the bullet which would have struck me passed through the heart of my unfortunate brother.

'He dropped without a groan upon the floor of the compartment, and MacCoy and I, equally horrified, knelt at each side of him, trying to bring back some signs of life. MacCoy still held the loaded revolver in his hand, but his anger against me and my resentment towards him had both for the moment been swallowed up in this sudden tragedy. It was he who first realized the situation. The train was for some reason going very slowly at the moment, and he saw his opportunity for escape. In an instant he had the door open, but I was as quick as he, and jumping upon him the two of us fell off the footboard and rolled in each other's arms down a steep embankment. At the bottom I struck my head against a stone, and I remembered nothing more. When I came to myself I was lying among some low bushes, not far from the railroad track, and somebody was bathing my head with a wet handkerchief. It was Sparrow MacCoy.

' "I guess I couldn't leave you," said he. "I didn't want to have the blood of two of you on my hands in one day. You loved your brother, I've no doubt; but you didn't love him a cent more than I loved him, though you'll say that I took a queer way to show it. Anyhow, it seems a mighty empty world now that he is gone, and I don't care a continental whether you give me over to the hangman or not."

'He had turned his ankle in the fall, and there we sat, he with his useless foot, and I with my throbbing head, and we talked and talked until gradually my bitterness began to soften and to turn into something like sympathy. What was the use of revenging his death upon a man who was as much stricken by that death as I was? And then, as my wits gradually returned, I began to realize also that I could do nothing against MacCoy which would not recoil upon my mother and myself. How could we convict him without a full account of my brother's career being made public—the very thing which of all others we had to avoid? It was really as much our interest as his to cover the matter up, and from being an avenger of crime I found myself changed to a conspirator against Justice. The place in which we found ourselves was one of those pheasant preserves which are so common in the Old Country, and as we groped our way through it I found myself consulting the slayer of my brother as to how far it would be possible to hush it up.

'I soon realized from what he said that unless there were some papers of which we knew nothing in my brother's pockets, there was really no possible means by which the police could identify him or learn how he had got there. His ticket was in MacCoy's pocket, and so was the ticket for some baggage which they had left at the depot. Like most Americans, he had found it cheaper and easier to buy an outfit in London than to bring one from New York, so that all his linen and clothes were new and unmarked. The bag, containing the dust-cloak, which I had thrown out of the window, may have fallen among some bramble patch where it is still concealed, or may have been carried off by some tramp, or may have come into the possession of the police, who kept the incident to themselves. Anyhow, I have seen nothing about it in the London papers. As to the watches, they were a selection from those which had been entrusted to him for business purposes. It may have been for the same business purposes that he was taking them to Manchester, but—well, it's too late to enter into that.

'I don't blame the police for being at fault. I don't see how it could have been otherwise. There was just one little clew that they might have followed up, but it was a small one. I mean that small circular mirror which was found in my brother's pocket. It isn't a very common thing for a young man to carry about with him, is it? But a gambler might have told you what such a mirror may mean to a card-sharper. If you sit back a little from the table, and lay the mirror, face upwards, upon your lap, you can see, as you deal, every card that you give to your adversary. It is not hard to say whether you see a man or raise him when you know his cards as well as your own. It was as much a part of a sharper's outfit as the elastic clip upon Sparrow MacCoy's arm. Taking that, in connection with the recent frauds at the hotels, the police might have got hold of one end of the string.

'I don't think there is much more for me to explain. We got to a village called Amersham that night in the character of two gentlemen upon a walking tour, and afterwards we made our way quietly to London, whence MacCoy went on to Cairo and I returned to New York. My mother died six months afterwards, and I am glad to say that to the day of her death she never knew what had happened. She was always under the delusion that Edward was earning an honest living in London, and I never had the heart to tell her the truth. He never wrote; but, then, he never did write at any time, so that made no difference. His name was the last upon her lips.

'There's just one other thing that I have to ask you, sir, and I should take it as a kind return for all this explanation, if you could do it for me. You remember that Testament that was picked up. I always carried it in my inside pocket, and it must have come out in my fall. I value it very highly, for it was the family book with my birth and my brother's marked by my father in the beginning of it. I wish you would apply at the proper place and have it sent to me. It can be of no possible value to anyone else. If you address it to X, Bassano's Library, Broadway, New York, it is sure to come to hand.'

FRANK AUBREY

# The Third Figure

'From life? N—no; scarcely that,' said Morland, musingly. 'Yet it represents a scene that actually occurred. It is very strange how I came to paint it; a strange business altogether, in fact.'

'It is exquisitely, wonderfully drawn,' I exclaimed, enthusiastically. 'Never do I remember to have seen anything that conveys to the mind so striking a combination of the gruesomely pathetic and the vividly tragical—if I may make use of a somewhat mixed expression. This figure of the woman bending over the dead man is perfect in its suggestion of hopeless anguish and stony horror. Is it really your work, Morland? If so——'

'It is my work—at least, I believe so; yet I could not well swear to it, for—I did it in my sleep. A sort of sleepwalking feat, you see.' Morland made this answer slowly, and, as it were, reluctantly, looking very puzzled and a little sheepish, I thought, the while.

'In your sleep!' I repeated, very much surprised. 'Really? You say it seriously? If so, then all I can say is the sooner you go to sleep again and do something else like it——'

'Oh, stop that!' he snapped, irritably; 'I might have known you wouldn't believe me, and would only turn it into chaff. If you talk in that way I won't tell you the story.'

At once I was all grave attention and sober earnestness. I was not going to miss a likely story for the sake of indulging in a little mild pleasantry. I humbly apologized, and, after some trouble, managed to so far mollify my friend that he presently proceeded to tell me the strange and curious narrative I have here set down.

Arthur Morland, in whose studio in Chelsea the foregoing

conversation took place, was a very old friend of mine, but I had not seen him for some years. He had been in Paris and Rome, studying; and by the time he returned to England I myself had gone abroad. This, therefore, was our first meeting after a very long separation.

As to the sketch of which we had been speaking, it was painted in oil and in bold colouring upon a small canvas about twelve inches by eight. It showed a stair-landing, upon which lay the figure of a man in evening dress, and apparently dead. Over him bent, in a kneeling position, the figure of a beautiful woman, gazing down at the prostrate man with such a terrible expression of horrified agony apparent, not in her face merely, but in the pose of the whole figure, as I scarcely believe could have been conveyed by the cleverest artist alive. Standing back from these two was a third figure—the murderer, as I guessed—holding in his hand a poniard. This figure was shown as though standing with his back to a light. The outline was clear and sharp enough, but all the rest was vague and shadowy and unfinished, and contrasted strangely, in its uncertain touch, with the drawing of the remainder of the picture, the details of which were portrayed with masterly firmness and decision.

All I could make out of this dim form was that it seemed to be that of a man in the dress of a Venetian or Florentine noble of three or four hundred years back. He was masked, and the cloak was open; beyond that one could make out little except the dagger which, held in the extended right hand, cut sharp lines against the background.

'Why,' I asked of Morland, as I continued to regard the sketch, quite fascinated by its weird, strange intensity, 'why is this figure at the back so vague and unfinished where all else is so vividly detailed?'

'Ah! thereby hangs the tale,' he replied. 'To explain that I must tell you the whole story.' And he thus began:

'The murdered man—he was not dead then, but died a few days afterwards—was named Ernest Milner. He was one of the few English friends I made while living in Paris. He was a cashier in the Paris branch of a well-known English banking house; and he was one of the nicest, and, at the last, one of the most unfortunate men I ever knew.

'Yet when I first became acquainted with him he was as happy and contented a being as you need wish to meet with. He married a charming and beautiful girl of English parentage—a Miss Edith Belton—who had been educated and had lived most of her life in France. I knew her before she married Milner; she was then living with her widowed mother a little way out of Paris.

'Another English clerk in the same bank was one Dorian Norman, a very old and intimate friend, as I understood, of Milner's, and he also fell desperately in love with Edith Belton; but she, in the end, chose Milner, and, as I have intimated, married him. Thus did the latter gain all that he then most desired in life; while Norman, though he continued to be on good terms with his old chum, had to bear, as he best could, what was to him, as I could see, a very bitter disappointment.

'Suddenly, one day, the news was brought to me by a fellow student that Milner had lost his post—had been suddenly discharged, in fact; and not only that, but under such circumstances that he might think himself lucky in not being prosecuted for theft and forgery.

'The facts, as I afterwards ascertained them, were these. Milner one day had gone out to his lunch in the middle of the day as usual, and when he came back declared someone had stolen a bank draft for a large amount out of his desk while he had been absent. The manager at once went across to the bank on which the draft was drawn, to stop payment, when he was met with the statement that he was too late; the draft had already been presented and paid, within the last hour or two. The thief had forged the necessary endorsement, drawn the money, and disappeared.

'But later on, when the cashier who paid the amount saw Milner, he recognized him as the person who had presented the cheque and received the proceeds; and he swore to this so positively that there seemed to be no room for reasonable doubt. Moreover, Milner was unable to account for his time while out in the middle of the day. He had not lunched at his usual restaurant; had not, indeed, lunched anywhere; according to his own account he had felt unwell and had gone for a sharp walk instead; but he could not produce anyone who had seen him out. In the end he was discharged, but was told that he must not leave the country; he was given a sort of time of grace to see if he could clear himself, the decision as to whether he would be prosecuted or not being, it was understood, held over meanwhile.

'Thereafter our little circle in Paris was broken up into two camps—those who believed in Milner's innocence, and those who thought him guilty. Amongst those who stood by him, and unceasingly declared his unshaken belief in his old friend, was Dorian Norman, and the two were much together, devising plans, as we heard, to trace and bring to punishment the real culprit. For myself, I fully sympathized with them, and, so far as I could, tried to aid them; for I never for a moment believed the accusation.

'Thus matters stood when, one morning, we—all Paris indeed—were startled with the news that poor Milner had been struck down and mortally wounded by an unknown hand, just outside his own apartments in the Rue Maubenge, where he now lay dying. It seems that he had gone in plain evening dress to the *bal masque* (it was the Micarême ball) at the Opera, having been invited thereto by an English friend who was over from London for a day or two, and had secured a private box. Returning, alone, he had reached his home, and ascended the stairs to his flat, when he was set upon and stabbed by someone who had evidently been waiting for him.

'His wife, who was sitting up for him, hearing a cry and the sound of a fall, ran out and found her husband lying unconscious, and beside him a masked figure, of whom she caught but a hurried glimpse, and who at once hurried off down the stairs. The assassin got clear away before any outcry could be raised, and with little fear of subsequent recognition by the concierge or anyone else; for, as I suppose you know, on such a night, people in fancy dress are so common in the streets that they attract scarcely any particular notice.

'The police failed to trace the murderer; and after poor Milner's death, which occurred within two days, the matter remained an unexplained mystery, and gradually faded from the public mind. Just about that time I went on to Rome, where I stayed a year, and then returned to London and settled down where you now see me.

'I had not been here long when Dorian Norman somehow found me out. He had been transferred, it appeared, from the Paris to the London branch of his bank, and was now permanently residing in town. He was terribly altered, so much so that I hardly knew him. He was thin, haggard, and careworn, and seemed like a man haunted by some secret, overmastering trouble. After a while he took me somewhat into his confidence, and proceeded to tell me what had passed between poor Milner and himself before the former died.

' "He left me," he said, "two legacies."

'Norman spoke thus in a broken voice, and then paused. To encourage him to go on I asked what they were.

' "Ah! You could never guess, I think," was the reply. "First, he left me his wife."

' "His wife!" I repeated the words in some astonishment.

' "Yes, my friend, his wife. He said, 'Dorian, I know you always loved Edith, and next to me I know there is no one she likes and respects more than yourself. I leave her to you—to your care. I leave you in her the most precious treasure this world contains, and in so doing I give you the most solemn proof of my affection for you and unabated trust and confidence. I need not say be ever kind to her, for that I know you will always be. And if she knows and understands that it is my wish that—after a while—she should become your wife, I do not think she will refuse. But it must be so only on the condition of the other legacy or trust I bequeath to you—it is that you first clear my good name. You cannot, Dorian, marry the widow of a disgraced man; remove that foul stain from my memory, and I and God shall bless you, and she will prove to you the greatest comfort, the greatest blessing, that ever one friend left to another.' "

' "And Mrs Milner?" I asked, curiously.

' "She keeps to that," he returned, sorrowfully. "She is living with her mother in Paris; we correspond and are very good friends. But she insists upon my remaining no more than a friend until that other condition is fulfilled. But how can I fulfil it?," he went on, gloomily. "Time is going on, and it becomes less and less likely every day that the mystery will ever be cleared up."

'I felt genuinely sorry for him. I saw that his old love was asserting itself more than ever, and, in the circumstances in which he was now placed, had become a canker that was eating into his very heart.

'After that he often came to pass a quiet evening with me, and one afternoon brought with him two ladies—Mrs Milner and her mother, Mrs Belton. They had come over to London for a few days.

'I had not seen Mrs Milner since just before the attack upon her husband, for while he lay dying none but very intimate friends had been admitted. I saw that suffering had left its marks upon her, too; but it could not destroy her natural grace of manner nor steal from her the sweet smile that had so charmed all those who had once been admitted to her friendship.

'Naturally, we spoke after a while of her husband's sad death, and I then heard, for the first time, from her own lips, exactly her own part in the tragedy; and she told it with such a depth of agonized feeling as made a deep and lasting impression on me. Long after the three had left me, I sat thinking over all she had told me, half-wondering, while I did so, at the strength of the emotion she had called up in my mind.

'When they had come in I had been about to start a sketch on that same canvas you hold in your hand. The blank canvas stood on the easel, and I had put out on my palette a selection of colours I intended to use, and had picked out a few clean brushes and so on, when I had to put them hastily down on a side-table, as my visitors were announced. Now, instead of going on with my work, I sat staring idly at the fire—it was in March, and the east winds were cold and biting—going over and over again in my thoughts all that Mrs Milner had told me with so much vivid description and in such glowing words.

'I lighted the lamp, and still sat thinking, making up the fire now and again in a listless sort of way, till at last I dozed off to sleep upon the couch; and then I had a strange dream.

'The door opened and someone entered very quietly—so quietly that I heard no footfall. A figure advanced into the middle of the studio, and then, as the light of the lamp fell on the face, I saw it was Ernest Milner. Strange to say, at that I felt no sort of surprise; it seemed to me the most natural thing in the world—just as though I had been expecting him.

'He was in evening dress, and I seemed to feel, or expect, that it was Micarême, and that he was going to the *bal masque* at the Grand Opera House. Instead, however, he beckoned to me to get up, and pointed to the easel; and in a mechanical fashion I rose, went to the easel, sat down in front of it and took up the palette and brushes I had laid down in the afternoon. Milner seated himself in a chair at a little distance, and, extending one hand, appeared to breathe the word "paint!"

'Then the room seemed to become lighter—with a strange brightness—so that I could see all the colours as by daylight, and I worked and painted rapidly like one under some strange spell. I put in quickly a bare staircase landing; the panellings, the balusters, the boards, all were there, but the place was empty. And when I had done that, and not till then, I looked up at Milner, and——'

Here Morland paused and visibly shivered.

'And what?' I asked in a low tone. His manner had gradually worked up my interest until I had become almost as much excited as I could see he now was.

'I can scarcely tell you,' he answered, looking at me with what seemed a half-frightened expression. 'You will never believe it! When I had turned my eyes away before, he had been the old Ernest Milner that I had known, always grave, but kindly looking; now, when I glanced at him again, he was——'

Once more Morland hesitated and seemed to gasp. I remained silent.

'His face was like that of a corpse,' he presently got out, 'and from his breast was flowing a thin stream of blood. He had his hand pressed to the wound, but the blood ran out between the fingers, and down over his shirt front and white waistcoat. Then, with a smothered cry that sounded like "My Edith, oh, my poor Edith!" he sank down, and lay full length upon the floor!'

'What did you do?' I asked breathlessly, so carried away by his realistic manner that I quite forgot he was not describing an actual scene.

'I—I—went on painting,' he returned solemnly; 'I had to; I was impelled to do so by some power that seemed to dominate and control every nerve of my body. Snatching up a piece of rag, I wiped out in the wet paint his outline as I saw it before me on the floor, and then rapidly put in the details, looking ever and anon at the figure before me; the while, as it seemed to me, the stream of blood trickled down and ran out along the floor, just as you see it depicted there.'

I looked at the canvas and shuddered. A strange feeling of repulsion seized me.

'You could go on painting!' I cried, 'whilst——'

Morland turned to me with a half smile.

'You forget,' he said quietly, 'that it was only a dream, and in a dream one has to do what the dream makes one do. You have——'

'Yes, yes, of course,' I interrupted, feeling somewhat foolish. 'I forgot you were only relating a dream. Go on.'

'When I had finished the figure of Milner,' Morland continued, picking up the canvas which had fallen near him, 'I thought I heard another cry, and turning, I saw Mrs Milner kneeling beside him. She was quite still; neither moved nor spoke, only gazed down with a dreadful, fixed, stony stare. Then I seized the rag again, and wiped out another outline, and very soon had painted in the details of her figure, too.'

'Ah!'

'When I had finished it and looked again she had gone; but now I saw a third figure standing over the one on the floor. It was clear enough for an instant—just for one moment, and no more. For that brief space I saw it clearly, distinctly—the colour of the dress, the mock jewels upon it, the shape of the mouth and chin, and the gleaming savage eyes that looked out through the mask. Then it faded into deep shadow, as though a strong light had been first thrown on it in front and then suddenly moved behind it. But against this light it was clearly silhouetted; and again I caught up the piece of rag and wiped out the outline.

'Then I peered into the shadow and tried to make out all that I had so clearly seen just before; but, strange to say, I could see nothing but shadow; and, stranger still, I could not recollect what I had seen. A voice seemed to say to me in a tone of indescribable agonized entreaty, "Try—try—oh, try to remember! Paint it—paint it—paint it!" But, try as I would, I could not recall it.'

'What did you do then?' I asked as he paused, as though lost in thought.

'I could do nothing; but sat and stared, first at the canvas with its empty space and then at the shadowed figure. But at last'—here Morland shivered again and spoke hesitatingly—'at last the figure on the floor—Milner—rose slowly and stood swaying backward and forward, as if in deadly pain, between us, pointing at me with one hand and at the shadow with the other. It seemed to me as though he exercised some great effort of will or other force to compel the shadow to disclose itself, for gradually I began to see the figure become less dim, and I could vaguely make out a few particulars, and these I had perforce to paint in as vaguely as I saw them. And just as I got one part thus done, the shadow would grow dense again; but once more Milner seemed, as by a great effort, to compel it, as at first.

'This happened several times, but each time the details were fainter; and then, glancing at Milner, I saw that he, too, seemed to be growing shadowy. But each time I looked at him he gazed back with an awful expression, such as I can scarcely convey the meaning of. It seemed to say with agony, "Do not look at me, but paint—paint—paint! Do you not see the time is growing short?"

'Finally he—the whole scene—faded slowly from my sight; and never shall I forget the last expression I saw on his face. Utter despair at having failed to convey to me what he wished was the language of the last look I had from that ghastly phantom, and it will haunt me to the day of my death.' And Morland wiped his face with his handkerchief as though in a violent sweat.

'Was that the end of it?' I asked him.

'Yes; except that as these figures faded, I was seized with a great, a terrible, an overwhelming feeling of horror. I tumbled off the stool I was on with a loud cry—as they tell me, for Norman came back just then—and fell to the floor. I was ill, delirious more or less, for more than a week.'

I took the canvas again, and began to examine it with a new interest.

'It's a strange story,' I presently said, 'I hope that's not the end of it. Is there no sequel?'

'Why, yes there was; but not for some little time. Mrs Milner stayed in town till I was better and able to talk to her. Very astonished she was at the painting, tearfully declaring that it truthfully depicted the actual scene. Therefore we hoped it might lead at once to some solution of the mystery; but time passed on and nothing came of it.

'At Norman's request I made him an exact copy of the sketch on a bit of millboard; and he carried it about with him, and we would sit gazing at it by the hour together, trying to read the message that, as we believed, must underlie the picture. But still nothing came of it.

'One evening he came to me even more upset than usual. He told me that Mrs Milner was bent upon retiring into a convent—they were

Roman Catholics—and would certainly do so if he failed within a short time to achieve the task that had been bequeathed to him. "And if she does that," said Norman, distractedly, "I shall—well, you know—go under."

'His morbid, despairing words and manner very much upset me; I thought of them all night, and when, next day, I started off to go down to Richmond, I found myself in very gloomy—not to say grumpy—mood. I do a little in scene-painting at times, you must know, and I was going down to Richmond to see some scenery I had painted, and to touch it up in a few places on the spot. It was at the old theatre, not the present one; a great barn of a place that stood in one corner of the old Green.

'It was, I remember, a cold, dull depressing November day; one that did not at all assist to raise my spirits; and when I got to the theatre there was no one there, and I had to go hunting for the doorkeeper—which did not improve my temper. I found him, got the key from him, and went to the theatre alone; the man saying he would be round shortly and that I was to leave the door unlocked for him. I lighted the burners of the gas-light used for rehearsals—it had been left ready—and, having found my pots and brushes and a stool, sat down to work on one of the corners.

'I had not been long thus engaged when someone came upon the stage and stood watching me. Thinking it was Davis, the doorkeeper, I at first took no notice, but went on with my work. Presently, however, I looked round, and then seeing the newcomer was not Davis I went on again with my painting; but it seemed that he had recognized me.

' "Why," said he, "it's Arthur Morland!"

'Upon that I turned again and regarded him more carefully. Still I could not recall him, though something about him seemed familiar.

' "Don't you remember me?" he went on, "my name is Farley—Stephen Farley. Used to know you in Paris, you know. You remember now?"

'Yes, I did remember now; but it did not make me any more pleased to see him, especially just then. He had been, I recollected, a fellow clerk or cashier of Milner's in Paris, but he had been one of a fast set. I had never liked him, and was not at all anxious to renew the acquaintance. So I merely said:

' "Ah, yes; I remember now. And what brings you here?" And I went stolidly on with my task, to avoid getting up and shaking hands with him.

' "Why, I've left the banking business, and turned actor, some time since," said he. "Don't you remember I used to be mad on private theatricals?"

'I grunted that I did recollect something of the kind.

' "I'm here now," he went on, "to attend rehearsal. I am playing in a company here next week. We play *Romeo and Juliet*, and I take Romeo. The company will be here in half an hour or so for a dress rehearsal."

'At that I turned and faced him. I said I had come down specially to do a day's work, having been told I could have the theatre all to myself; and now, if there was going to be a rehearsal, I should have had my journey for nothing. I might just as well go back to town. But he went away, saying something about its being no business of his, and I once more settled down to work.

'Presently, he came back again—this time, as I could see out of the corner of my eye, dressed as Romeo, with a cloak. He held his part in his hand, and read aloud from it, strutting up and down the stage as he did so. Gradually, his voice rose and his steps became heavier; he shouted, raved, and ranted, stamped his feet, and altogether made such a noise that I turned round to see what on earth was going on, and how many there were in it; for I thought surely others must have come and joined in.

'He was, however, still alone, and at the moment I turned had temporarily ceased his antics and struck an attitude. He was standing with his back to the flaring gas jets, to get the light on the part he was reading from, and holding in his right hand a naked dagger which I saw clearly against the light. As I looked I started, threw down what I had in my hands, and rose and stood staring at him; for in that moment a terrible thought darted into my mind. I strode up to him, and catching him by the shoulder I, with no very tender grasp, pulled him round to face the light.

' "Let me have a good look at you, my friend," I exclaimed, and, as he complied wonderingly, I looked him up and down from head to foot. And then it all came back to me in a flash! Yes! There it was, the

168

same dress I had seen for one brief moment in that terrible dream, and which had ever since eluded my memory. But I remembered it now clearly enough. Everything was there—the same colours, the same tawdry mock jewels—everything except the mask!

' "You villain!" I cried, shaking him. "I know you now; for you are the Third Figure!"

' "The what?" he demanded, but turning pale.

' "Where is your mask?" I almost shouted.

' "Mask! What mask?"

' "The mask you wore when you murdered Ernest Milner!" I said, sternly.

'He started and stepped back.

' "I—that is—how could you know?—you were not there," he stammered.

' "Ha, ha, you've admitted it—confessed!" I cried, seizing him again. "Come with me. I mean to——"

'Then he tried to get away, and finding he could not do that, raised his hand with a vicious oath, and would have stabbed me with the naked dagger he still held. For it was a real dagger; no toy stage weapon. But I caught his wrist, and then we closed, and it became a wrestling match.

'We grappled, and swayed backwards and forwards, then caught our feet in something and fell on the stage together. And there we fought and rolled over and over, one time crashing into the footlights and smashing a lot of the glasses, at another rolling against one of the "wings" and bringing it down amid clouds of dust. Then we knocked over some of my paint pots and rolled in the mess. Still I would not let go. But he had the devil's own strength in his fear, and made the most frantic efforts either to get away or to stab me. And at last I really thought it was all up with me, for he had managed to get his wrist loose at the very moment when he was on the top as we rolled about. He raised the dagger, I saw it flash in the air, I heard the hissing oath of fierce exultation that already rose to his lips, when there came a loud shout close at hand. My antagonist paused an instant to glance in the direction of the sound, and in that instant I seized his wrist again and forced it down to his side, at the same moment, by a great effort, turning him off me. In another second we rolled over, I being uppermost this time; but his grasp relaxed, and he gave a half-sobbing, half-choking cry, and then lay still.

'I sprang to my feet to find several people looking on in amazement. They were members of the company who had come to rehearsal, and at first they had stood watching us under the impression, I believe, that it was only a very clever and lifelike bit of stageplay. However they were soon undeceived as I got up and we all saw a dark stream of blood flowing from under the motionless form on the floor. In rolling over, the dagger had been pressed against his own side, and our united weights had forced it well home!

'A few minutes later he was carried in a dying state to the Richmond Infirmary.'

'Farley lived long enough and revived sufficiently,' Morland continued, after a pause, 'to make a full confession. He admitted that it was he who stole the draft which poor Milner had lost. And the way he managed to cash it so as to throw suspicion on the latter was by going home and putting on a wig and "making up" his face to resemble Milner's. He had practised all this at private theatricals, and had had his plans laid in readiness for the first opportunity chance might throw in his way. Then he went boldly and cashed the cheque at the bank, rushed back home, and shortly after coolly returned to his duties as though he had merely been out to lunch.

'As to the murder, it seems he became alarmed at hearing that Milner had boasted that he was on the track of the real thief, and would shortly catch him. As we know, this was but an idle, or too sanguine, declaration on Milner's part. But it frightened Farley, and when he saw him with a stranger at the *bal masque*, the alarmed villain thought the stranger was an English detective, and that the two had come there to look for or watch him. In his fear and anger he madly resolved to kill Milner before matters became more threatening; so he went away before Milner did, managed to pass the concierge at his place unseen, slipped up the stairs, and there lay in wait.

'Dorian Norman and Mrs Milner are married, and living very happily together, and I shall be pleased to take you round one evening to see them.

'And that, old friend,' Morland continued, 'is all I can tell you about the mystery of that sketch and its dimly painted Third Figure.'

# 10

J. B. HARRIS-BURLAND

# The Yellow Box

' "And to my nephew, James Frederick Carlton, I leave my house and the sum of ten thousand pounds." '

The old lawyer stopped, and they all glared at me, while I tried hard to look unconscious of my unexpected good fortune. Mr Simes peered at the will again, as if it were just possible that he had made a mistake. But, as he had drawn it up himself, it was quite an unnecessary piece of legal precaution.

' "Ten thousand pounds," ' he continued, wiping his glasses, ' "together with the care of my soul, which lies within a small yellow box in the Chinese bureau." '

I regret to say that at this point the conduct of the assembly was not at all suited to the solemnity of the occasion. I only smiled inwardly; but my two cousins, boys from Marlborough, made no efforts to restrain their mirth; while my Aunt Jane, who had been left nothing, sniffed audibly and whispered to her neighbour, 'Poor soul! I was always afraid that it was so. Of course, we shall not say anything, but——,' and the rustling of her black silk dress was more eloquent than anything she could have said. Mr Simes alone preserved an unmoved demeanour, and frowned.

' "In the Chinese bureau," ' he repeated, looking sternly round, as though someone was going to deny the fact. ' "The said ten thousand pounds to remain in trust for ten years [naming the trustees, of which Mr Simes was one], and the interest thereon to be paid to him only so long as he shall preserve the said yellow box and its contents in safety, and in accordance with the conditions set forth in a document attached to this will. If at any time he shall lose or destroy the box or its

171

contents, or shall break any of the conditions aforementioned, the said sum of ten thousand pounds is to pass with the residue of the estate. At the end of ten years the money is to become absolutely his." '

He laid down the will, and took another paper from the table. It contained the conditions. They were only three in number: that I was not to sleep out of the house more than twenty nights in any one year; that the box was to remain in the house, and remain unopened; that once a year, the anniversary of my uncle's death, the trustees should satisfy themselves of its existence.

There were various other legacies, of no interest to the reader. The residue was left to a Learned Society.

At the conclusion of the reading there was an ominous silence. My uncle had been fairly well off, but not a man of great wealth, and ten thousand pounds represented more than half the estate. They all felt that this was not as it should be. Aunt Jane rose stiffly, and said she must go, and that the lawyer would hear from her later on. The others followed, and each said something to Mr Simes, the general drift of which was that he would also hear from them later on. The two boys went out whispering something about a Jack-in-the-box, and I heard their laughter in the passage.

At last I and Mr Simes were left alone. I gave a sigh of relief, and no longer tried to appear melancholy. Indeed, there was no reason for my doing so. I had never set eyes on my uncle in my life, and could feel no real sorrow at his death. The old lawyer saw my look of pleasure, and stopped turning over a pile of papers which he was examining.

'They will not be able to upset the will,' he said quietly; 'your uncle was perfectly sane.'

'It sounds a bit odd, though, doesn't it?' I said with a laugh.

'Only an idea of his. You cannot upset a will because a man has a single strange idea. Besides, he was a clever man—a noted scientist and philosopher. We are none of us in a position to laugh at him.'

I was silent for a few moments, and then I asked to see the box.

'I will show it you,' the lawyer replied, cramming all the papers into a shabby black bag. 'The bureau is upstairs in the room where your uncle died.'

He led the way, and, entering the room first, drew up the blinds, which were still down. The funeral had only taken place that day. As I followed him, my lightness of heart died away, for there is always something indescribably solemn about a room from which the dead have just been taken.

The bureau stood in one corner. It was covered with hideous carved heads, and profusely decorated with Chinese lacquer-work. The old lawyer took out a little brass key with an ivory tab hanging from it, and unlocked the top left-hand drawer. Then he groped about at the back of the drawer, which seemed to be filled with odds-and-ends, and, taking out the box, handed it to me. It was about eight inches square and six inches deep, and was painted a bright yellow.

I looked at it curiously. It was not particularly heavy, and made apparently of wood. The hinges and lock were of thick brass, engraved with what I took to be Chinese characters. I tapped it with one finger; it did not sound hollow, and I gathered that it was filled with something. Then I put it to my ear, and shook it; there was, I thought, a faint rustle inside, but there was no clue to what it contained, and I handed it back to the lawyer. He had not said a word while I was examining it, and when I gave it back he silently replaced it, and, locking the drawer, handed me the key. I put it in my waistcoat pocket.

'Well,' Mr Simes said, 'that is all. If you can keep that box for ten years, the money becomes yours absolutely.'

'It will not be difficult,' I replied with a smile, 'provided no one steals it.'

'And your house is not destroyed by fire,' he added, as we left the room. 'If I were you, I should get a fireproof safe; you will have nothing to fear then.'

'I will do so at once.'

'I suppose you will sleep here tonight?' he said, as we reached the dining-room, 'or, at latest, tomorrow night. You must remember that your nights of absence are limited in number.'

'I have to arrange my affairs. I will come down tomorrow.'

He took up his hat and umbrella, and held out his hand. 'I must go, Mr Carlton—4.45 the train. I suppose you will come up later. Good afternoon. You have my address? Oh yes; thank you—my gloves. Well, good-day.'

The door clanged behind him, and I was left alone. I rang the bell for the housekeeper. She was an old woman, and had, I knew, been with my uncle for a very long time.

'I am going to live here in future, Mrs—Mrs——'

'Jones, Sir,' she said, with a curtsey.

'If you would stay on I should be very glad. If you can't manage it, perhaps you could recommend me a responsible person.'

'I should like to stay, Sir,' she said. 'The old house is like a home to me—I have lived in it for thirty years.'

'Very well. I shall have to return to town tonight; but please get my bedroom ready for tomorrow.'

'The—the master's room, Sir?'

'No, the one opposite. Expect me to dinner at seven tomorrow.'

I returned to town, gave up my business, and came back the next day, with the prospect of residing at Belchester for ten years all but two hundred days. It seemed to be a sleepy, old-fashioned place, and I began to think at dinner that those twenty days a year would be very welcome indeed. Afterwards, when I lit my pipe and thought things over, I was not quite sure if the legacy was such a godsend, after all. Ten thousand pounds was a lot of money—at least, it seemed a lot to a man who had been a bank-clerk at a hundred-and-twenty a year. But there was no doubt that Belchester was a wretched hole after London. It had rained while I was coming up from the station, and the dull little streets were peculiarly damp and dismal. It looked, too, like the sort of place where it always rained. And supposing, after all my sacrifices and care, I lost the box. Supposing I lost it in the ninth or even in the tenth year. It would not be pleasant to lose everything just at the end of my time, with ten years wasted.

I resolved two things that night before I went to bed; one, to get some occupation in the town, both for the sake of something to do and as a provision for the future, in case of accidents; and the other to purchase the strongest steel safe that could be made.

The latter of these resolves was easily accomplished, and the thing came down in a few days—a great six-foot cube of steel with sides nearly a foot in thickness. As it was borne through the streets on a trolley drawn by six horses, it was the wonder and admiration of the whole town, and for two days most of the population whiled away their spare time outside my house. I could not help smiling as I watched the place being wrecked to accommodate this huge lump of metal. The wall had to be broken down, and the floor strengthened with iron girders. It seemed such a gigantic undertaking for the safety of a little yellow box.

The former was not so easily obtained. Belchester was one of those places where men spun but little, and toiled not at all. However, in a month's time, when the 'best families'—this is a Belchester phrase—had called, and I had made a few acquaintances, I managed to obtain a post in the Bank I dealt with. People sniggered a little at what they were pleased to call my 'eccentricity', but I professed a mania for work, and settled down to the joint position of bank-clerk and owner of Helicon House, as my uncle had chosen to christen the old, rambling mansion he had lived and died in.

I took the yellow box out of the bureau and placed it in the safe, where it looked ridiculously small and unimportant. I amused myself for a little while with examining the complicated machinery of the locks, and wondered if anything but the crack of doom could burst it open. Then, I am ashamed to say, I felt a little curiosity, and, picking the box up again, I looked at it hard, as if it were possible by so doing to see inside it. I shook it, and again heard a faint rustle. I laughed at my childishness, and, remembering how Fatima's curiosity met with its reward, I put it back in the safe. It may have been fancy, but as I was closing the great door, I thought I still heard the rustling. I paused a moment, and, stooping down, listened carefully. There was perfect silence. I rose up, and, clanging the door to with all my strength, shot the triple bolts one after the other with three separate keys. One of these I kept, and one I sent to each of the trustees.

The first year passed placidly enough. I was terribly dull, but I made each of my twenty days into a wild orgy, the effects of which lasted for quite a week afterwards. So I really got a week's dissipation at the expense of one night's absence.

As for the safe, it stood facing me as I lay in bed, and looked like a small steel cottage. No local burglar had been fool enough to try his hand on it, though all the neighbourhood knew of its existence, and hazarded wild guesses at the value of its contents. When the day came for opening it, the box would be found to be still there, unless it had been spirited away. I began to idly wonder if any supernatural agencies had been at work, and when the day actually arrived I felt more curiosity than I should have cared to acknowledge. I had a sort of idea that we should find the safe empty. My uncle, if all accounts were true, was a strange man, and had spent many years of his life among strange people. Only a few months before his death he had returned from a scientific expedition into the wildest regions of Northern China, and I imagined that a man might learn almost anything in that part of the world. He was besides a great scientist, and might have discovered natural means for working effects that to other men would appear supernatural. Perhaps the box was only an illusion, a tangible illusion; for why should it not be possible to cheat the sense of touch as well as the sense of sight? Perhaps it was made of some material that would vanish into thin air after a certain lapse of time and leave no trace of its existence. One could never tell. There was something peculiar about it, of that I was certain, or why should a sum of money be left to preserve it in safety? Anyone could keep an ordinary yellow box; it would be a senseless condition to attach to a will. Therefore, with some show of reason, I argued that it was not an ordinary yellow box.

The two trustees arrived: Mr Simes and a younger man, Mr Willing, a member of a banking firm, I believe. They had lunch, and we all three went up to my bedroom. The banker laughed when he saw the safe, but Mr Simes nodded approvingly.

'Can't be too careful in a matter like this,' he said, and, drawing out his key, he shot back one section of the bolts. Then the other trustee did the same, and my turn came. I must confess I put my key in the lock with rather trembling fingers. The last section of the bolts gave a click, and the door swung automatically open. The box was still there.

I took it out, and they each looked at it in turn. Mr Simes identified it as being the same box, and handed it back to me.

'The box is all right,' I said with a laugh. 'Of course, we assume the contents.' I started. The box was lying quite still in my hands, but I could have sworn I heard something rustle inside it as I spoke. I put it to my ear, and shook it.

'Papers,' I said, though I felt quite sure that papers would not rustle if held perfectly still.

'Perhaps,' Mr Simes replied. I put the thing back in the safe, for I felt a growing repugnance to it, and was glad to get it out of my hands. I closed the door, and we all three locked it and pocketed our keys.

The second year I was more uneasy than I had been in the first. The charge of the box began to prey upon my mind, and I was in constant dread lest it should be stolen. I got the idea into my head that those who would profit by its disappearance would take some steps to remove it. Perhaps they would employ trickery of some sort; perhaps they would even resort to personal violence. The safe was strong enough, but there were a good many ingenious devices nowadays in the hands of dishonest men. I began to employ a manservant, and he slept in the adjoining room. Then I bought a revolver, and kept it loaded by my bedside, a practice which I discontinued after firing it off in my sleep one night and breaking the looking-glass. But I placed it in a drawer where it would be easily available. I also had fresh bolts and locks put on my own door, and a patent fastener screwed on to every window.

But I was more afraid of other schemes than robbery for depriving me of the money. Perhaps, when I went up to town, I should be forcibly detained and made to break one of the conditions of the will—namely, that I was not to sleep more than twenty nights in the year away from Belchester; and this thought so grew upon me that every day I spent away from Helicon House became a perfect misery to me. I fancied I was being followed everywhere, and avoided all the side streets. I eyed strangers in the train suspiciously, and if left alone with a man in a compartment, got out of the carriage as soon as possible. I rarely went about unaccompanied by a friend, however short a distance I had to walk. The consequence was, I only took fourteen days of absence that year. The other six I kept in case of an emergency. The emergency never came, and they were wasted.

However, nothing happened in that year, and on the second anniversary of my uncle's death, when we opened the safe, the box was still there, and there was still something inside that rustled.

During the third year I gave but little thought to designs upon the safe or plots against my liberty. This was not because I had no longer any reason for fearing them, but because a new and greater terror began to creep into my mind.

It came to me one night as I lay awake watching the huge safe in the corner, where it loomed like a great black shadow in the faint glow of the night-light I always burned in the room.

Supposing the soul were really there, I thought to myself. Supposing that by some means it were actually caged in that narrow yellow cell. There was something in the box that moved, for I had heard it; and as I recalled the faint rustle, I started up in my bed and leaned forward, listening attentively. There it was again, a faint, almost imperceptible sound coming from the corner. Then it seemed to cross the room with a sort of scratching noise, like tiny legs would make on a rough carpet. Now and then it stopped, and then went on again, sometimes slowly, sometimes quickly, brushing and rustling round the room. There was no possibility of locating the sound, and I stared in vain, with parted lips and wide-open eyes, to discover anything in the dim light.

I jumped out of bed, and, lighting a candle, went over to the safe. There was nothing to be seen. I looked carefully all over the floor, but found no trace of any insect or animal whatever. The noise had ceased. I clapped my hands sharply, to startle the thing, but still there was silence, and, blowing out the candle, I got back into bed, trembling violently. I did not sleep any more that night, for every few minutes I heard the same noise, and, lighting the candle, looked again and again, and still found nothing.

As the days went on, this new idea began to grow in strength and clearness. The noise continued, and I became quite certain that not only was my uncle's soul in the place where he had bequeathed it, but that, night after night, it moved about the room. I never saw anything, but that faint, scratching sound went on for hours, and my nerves became so overwrought with listening for it that any sound whatever was a terror to me.

I tried sleeping in another room, and for a few nights I got some rest. Then it began again, outside, on the landing. I opened the door and listened. It stopped. Then, as I stood there, candle in hand, it seemed to come faintly from my old room. I got back into bed, and left the candle burning on the chest of drawers. In about a quarter of an hour the noise returned, and this time it was close to me, under the bed. I again got up and looked everywhere, but saw nothing.

I realized that little was to be gained by changing rooms, and returned to the one with the safe in it. There, at any rate, I could keep guard over the box and protect it from physical dangers.

As the year drew to a close, I suffered acutely from mental terror and loss of sleep. I think I should have gone mad if it had not been for the few nights I was allowed to pass away from Helicon House. I missed none of them that year.

And yet I felt through it all that I was really only the victim of my own imagination, and found it easy enough in the daytime to laugh at my own fears. When I reasoned quietly with myself, I came to the sound conclusion that I was a nervous idiot. My ideas, I argued, were, of course, utter rubbish. My uncle had got a bit crazed in his scientific researches, and had put a clause in his will which every sensible person treated as a joke, and to take it seriously was to prove oneself madder than the man who made it. I would go to a doctor and get a tonic. I would dismiss the whole thing from my mind, and go on living my life just as if there were no little yellow box in existence. I was taking too much care of it, that's what it was. One cannot be always thinking of a thing without conjuring up all sorts of wild ideas about it.

So I reasoned in the sunny daytime, when everything seemed bright and cheerful. But when the night came on, all my resolutions and arguments grew shadowy and incomplete. I still trembled and lay awake; as for the tonic, it did nothing but sharpen my powers of hearing—I still heard noises, and looked for explanations of them, and found none. I still felt that there was all around me an atmosphere of darkness and terror that nothing could dissipate.

At last the third anniversary of my uncle's death came round. I must confess that when the trustees arrived there was a secret hope lurking within me that we might open the safe and find the wretched thing gone. But when the door swung back, it was still there. I walked a few steps away while they were handling it, for I wished to see as little of it as possible. I did not shake it this time to see if anything moved inside, but stood at the window, whistling softly, to drown any sound that might come from it. They replaced it, and we locked the safe again.

'Not very well?' said Mr Simes, looking at me keenly.

'No,' I replied sharply; 'I want a change. I can't get a thorough holiday anywhere under the present conditions.'

'Only seven years more,' he said.

'Is that all?' I queried sarcastically.

I had resolved to go away that very evening, and take one of my nights of absence, for I had got the idea into my head that the third anniversary of my uncle's death might be attended with some unusual manifestation of his presence, and that, if I stayed in the house, it would not be altogether pleasant for a man in my present state of nervousness. So I went up to town with the trustees.

However, I left instructions with the manservant to sleep in my room and see that no one tampered with the safe. I had no fear that anything would frighten him, for he was a rustic of particularly stolid demeanour, and slept like a top.

We spent a most delightful evening. We all three dined together, then Mr Simes left us, and we went to a music-hall, and finished up with a Covent Garden Ball. I did not think it worth while going to bed, as I had to be at the bank early; so I left town at 5.30 in the morning, and reached Belchester about 6.15.

It was still dark as I walked up from the station, but a bar of faint grey light on the horizon showed the coming dawn. Not wishing to disturb James or the housekeeper, I let myself in with my latchkey, and closed the door quietly behind me. As I did so, something brushed against my legs and scuttled up the stairs in the grey dawn. My heart gave a jump, and I stepped back close against the wall. Then I laughed, for I remembered that Mrs Jones always let her cat sleep in the kitchen. The door had evidently been opened, and it was roaming about the house.

I made my way to the dining-room to get a drink, for I was beginning to feel the effects of my dissipation. As I entered it, an indistinct figure seemed to cross the room to meet me. I passed my hands across my eyes, and, standing still, looked again. Yes, there was certainly someone there. It was motionless, and I felt the sweat pouring from all over my body. I seized a chair to strike it with, and, to my surprise, the creature did the same. Then it all broke upon me, and I cursed my cowardice. There was a looking-glass opposite me, and it was only my own reflection, after all.

'Confound this dawn,' I muttered, 'with its cold, ghostly light! One can see everything, and yet nothing as it really is.'

I went over to the spirit-stand on the sideboard, and then remembered that the key was in my bedroom. I was too thirsty to respect James's slumbers any more, and went upstairs to get it. The boards seemed to creak a good deal more than usual, and the whole place appeared to be full of blurred shadows. They were only hat-racks and other pieces of furniture, but they looked strange enough to be anything.

I turned the handle of the door of my room, but found it locked. I was not surprised, as I always fastened it myself when I slept there. I knocked; there was no answer. I knocked again, more loudly. There was still no answer. I heard a door open overhead, and a voice cry out, 'Is that you, Sir?'

'Yes, Mrs Jones,' I replied; 'James has locked himself in, and I can't wake him. I want the key of the spirit-stand.'

She came down, half-dressed, and we both hammered.

'He sleeps very sound, Sir,' she said, beating the panels vigorously.

'He always did,' I replied with a laugh; but at the same time I shuddered, for a sudden fear had gripped my heart. I stepped back, and threw my whole weight against the door. The lock was one of the new ones I had placed in the house, but the woodwork was old, and I heard it break away from the screws. I put my shoulder to it again, and it gave way. I went in, and Mrs Jones stood on the threshold.

'James!' I shouted, going close up to the bed. Then I stamped on the floor and repeated his name. Somehow, I did not like to shake him. He did not move, but I could see him lying there. I went to the window and drew up the blinds.

It was getting much lighter now, and, as I crossed back to the bed, I could see his face quite plainly. His eyes were wide open, staring at something which was not there, and his hands were clutching the counterpane, which was drawn up quite eight inches towards his chin. He was dead.

The doctor said at the inquest that the man had died of heart-disease, and evidence was given to show that he had been suffering from the complaint for a very long time. The incident caused but little sensation in Belchester. It was talked of for a few days, and then the matter was thought no more about except by his relations and myself.

181

But I am almost ashamed to admit the extent to which my own thoughts and feelings were affected. For two weeks afterwards I lay absolutely prostrate with weakness and terror. I kept to my bed in a room as far away as possible from that in which my servant had died, and could not bear to be left alone even for five minutes. At this period I can never be sufficiently grateful to a friend of mine, who left his work in town to be with me day and night until I became stronger and more composed. He does not know to this day that I owe my life to him. For I am quite positive that a single night of solitude at that time would have resulted in my death; perhaps I, too, should have been found with open, staring eyes, and fingers twisted rigidly in the counterpane. For every shadow and every noise conveyed some terrible meaning to me, and I would start and get out in the middle of the night, and almost whimper, until dear old Frank got up and held my hand, and then gave me some medicine that sent me off to sleep again.

Nothing on earth could persuade me that James Thomson's death was due to purely natural causes. I was sure that he had seen something—something I should have seen if I had not chanced to be in town that night—and that he had died from the effects of terror on a weak heart. While I was drinking and dancing, and forgetting all about Helicon House, he was lying there facing the unknown and powerless with terror. When he was found, his eyes were fixed in the direction of the safe. The drawer by the side of the bed where I kept the revolver was not quite closed, as if someone had tried to open it and get the weapon, and then his strength had failed him and he had sunk back to die. Over and over again I tried to remember if I had left it like that. It would have been a comfort to think that I had; but I could not honestly remember anything about it, and my mind refused to accept anything but the most absolute certainty. Hour after hour, as I lay in bed, I tried to conjure up what had happened, and when I was well enough we both went into the room and examined it carefully, as detectives examine the scene of a murder. Everything was just as usual. We paid particular attention to the safe; there were no marks or scratches on it, and no sign of it having been tampered with in any way. We discovered nothing, and if the secret of the little yellow box had been divulged, it had died with the man, and I was still left to guard it—for seven years. In two months I had sufficiently recovered my health and strength to return to my old room. But I engaged another manservant, whose sole duty was to sleep during the day, and watch all night in the next room to mine. He had instructions to keep a lamp burning through all the hours of darkness, and to leave his door open. I kept the door of my own room ajar, and, in the feeling of security which this arrangement gave me, I had some good nights of rest. I certainly woke every night, but whenever I did so, I could catch the reflection of his light in the landing through the chink in my door, and could hear him moving softly about and turning over the leaves of a book or a newspaper. Then I turned over and went to sleep again with an easy mind. I also still kept a night-light burning on the washing-stand in a saucer of water.

In this way everything went on quietly until one night in May, the 15th, I think it was. I woke up, as usual, in the middle of the night, and, looking at the clock, which I always placed just behind the night-light, I saw that it was half-past two. Then I heard a slight cough in the other room, and the clink of a plate; the man was having his dinner—he had to take it in the middle of the night, which, for all practical purposes, was the middle of his day. I turned over, and tried to go to sleep again; but after a few minutes I felt so wide awake and restless that I lay on my back, and began to count. I fancy this ancient remedy for sleeplessness is of more mathematical than physical value; but I counted up to five thousand, by a peculiarly long and tedious process, which entailed the repetition of the thousands and hundreds for each separate number. At the end, I was still wide awake, and seemed likely to remain so. I thought it odd, for I had slept very well the last few weeks. Certainly, I invariably woke up, the result of my old habit of sleeplessness and terror, but I never stayed awake for more than a quarter of an hour.

I did not feel inclined to do any more mental arithmetic, and, my eyes wandering to the safe, I began to amuse myself by counting the rivet-heads round the edge. They were about an inch square, and were, I suppose, to bolt the two steel plates together, back and front, the intervening space being filled up with cement. They were painted a rather deeper grey than the rest of the surface, and it was easy enough to see them, but not so easy to count them, as anyone knows who has tried to count a number of things placed in a continuous line;

one keeps on losing one's position on the line, and having to start again.

However, I counted them three times, and made the number to be forty-two each time. Having attained this satisfactory result, I turned over on my left side, and had another attempt at sleep. I shut my eyes, but found my ears were beginning once more to pay too much attention to details. I could hear the rustling of a newspaper in the next room, and could almost tell when the man had reached the end of a line by the faint movement of his fingers. I could imagine exactly the position in which he was sitting, and could tell if he shifted that position by a quarter of an inch. Then I heard a soft thud, as if a lump of butter had been dropped on the floor, and I started up, for I was positive the noise had come from some part of my own room. I got out of bed and looked carefully round, but saw nothing.

'Pooh!' I said to myself. 'It's only the old nervousness coming on again.' Yet, in my heart of hearts, I knew that, if it were so, a worse thing than any material or spiritual enemy had come back to me.

I laughed uneasily, and, getting into bed, began to count the rivets again, simply for something to think about. I made them forty-three this time, which irritated me. It is astonishing what trifles will irritate a man who is lying awake. I counted them again, almost savagely. There were still forty-three; again, and yet again, with the same result. 'I was wrong before,' I said to myself; 'there are forty-three.' But I counted them six more times, to make sure, and then, just as I was turning my eyes away, I stopped and uttered an exclamation. One of the rivets had moved about four inches nearer the centre of the plate. I rubbed my eyes, and looked again. Yes, it certainly had moved, and, what was more, was still moving. Moreover, its shape was larger and more indistinct about the edge.

I jumped out of bed, and, lighting a candle, went up to the safe. As I approached, the dark-grey spot ran along a few inches, and stopped. It was an enormous spider, with a body quite covered with a mouse-coloured fur, and eyes glittering like jewels. Its legs must have been about three inches long, but when I came near with the light it drew them up under its body, and was perfectly motionless. Then I recalled the thud I had heard, and shuddered. Supposing I had stepped on the thing when I had got out of bed. I have all the human dislike of fat-bodied things that squash, and could never kill even a fair-sized moth. As for killing the spider with a boot, which, I suppose, would have been the right thing to have done, I would rather have faced a lion with the same weapon. I called the servant.

'Kill this thing for me, Evans,' I said; 'and mind it doesn't bite you; some of them are poisonous.' Before he could reply, the spider took the matter into its own hands, and swiftly disappeared round the corner of the safe.

We could not find it anywhere, and as I refused to sleep in the room whilst it was still about, I dressed, shaking every article of clothing thoroughly, lest it should have concealed itself in them, and spent the rest of the night smoking in Evans's room.

The next morning, we both made a thorough search of the whole house, but beyond finding a few thick silky threads spun across a corner in the room where my uncle had died, we discovered no trace of the insect whatever. It had vanished as mysteriously as it had appeared. I could not imagine where it could have come from; it must have escaped from some collection and hidden itself in the house. Those sort of things can lie concealed in almost any crack or crevice, attracting no more notice than a lump of accumulated dust. And it had probably returned to its hiding-place. In that case, I should see it again, and I did not altogether relish the prospect.

'Perhaps her crept into the iron chest,' said Evans, after our useless search. 'I'd never seen her afore, and I'll scrunch her if I see her again.' It did not strike him that there was any danger in having the creature about the house. Spiders were to him only things to be 'scrunched'. The possibility of their being at all venomous was, of course, unknown to him.

I was not so easy in my own mind. The mere thought of that loathsome, hairy lump crawling about the house was enough to keep anyone awake at night. The fact of its being possibly poisonous was a secondary consideration. The light, creepy touch of those long, thin legs was quite a sufficient horror for me to look forward to. I examined the room carefully and minutely every night just before I went to bed. Then I closed the door. It was a choice of evils; but I preferred to face solitude rather than give the spider a chance of creeping into the room.

After a few days, my old nervous state gradually returned upon me. This time it was a fear of something material. But it kept me awake, just the same, and once more I began to wish Helicon House and all its contents at the bottom of the sea. Every little noise in the night startled me, and I thought I heard the insect creeping about, and waited for the soft thud of a small body dropping to the floor. I lay well in the centre of the bed, and looked fixedly at the white counterpane, expecting to see a dark patch come slowly over the edge of the bed and crawl towards me. I almost forgot about the yellow box, until one day I was reminded of its existence, and, putting two and two together, arrived at the last and worst terror of all.

It was in this way: I particularly wished to discover if the spider was of any known species, and if its bite was at all venomous or not. So, one day when I was up in town, I spent several hours at the British Museum, examining works on Natural History. After a long search, I came upon a coloured plate which closely resembled the creature I had seen. The letterpress confirmed the likeness. I read it eagerly. After a technical description containing a good deal of imaginary Latin, it said: 'These spiders are natives of Northern China, and amongst certain tribes are held in great reverence, even if they are not actually worshipped. It is believed by these people that their bodies are tenanted by the souls of the departed.'

I laid the book down and stared slowly round the reading-room. I can remember to this day the exact position of everyone who was there, and can recall their clothes and features as well as if I had photographed them. Separate thoughts came rushing into my brain, and whirling round and round it, until they settled down into a consecutive order. The rustling in the yellow box—a rustling that did not cease when I stopped shaking it—the sounds I had heard in the night all last year! That extract from the book, 'The souls of the departed'! My uncle's sojourn in Northern China! The sudden appearance of the loathsome creature on the safe! Its sudden disappearance; our inability to discover any trace of it. Even rustic Evans's apparently senseless words, 'Perhaps her crept into the iron chest'; and, more vividly than all, the memory of Thomson's face.

This, then, was the thing he had seen on that night. Perhaps the truth had been made known to him in some way as, half-insect, half-human, it came crawling slowly and steadily up the counterpane towards his terror-stricken face. He had watched the dark, soft body, with its fringe of hairy legs and its glittering eyes, come closer and closer; he had reached for the revolver, and then, powerless with terror, he had sunk back to die.

I returned the book, and, faint and giddy, reeled into the street and called a hansom. As I drove along, the cool air swished in my face, and I felt better; but, before I reached the place where I intended to dine, I had made up my mind—I would never sleep at Helicon House again.

After dinner I wired to the Bank at Belchester that I should not be able to return for two or three days. I thought a good deal during those days, weighing everything in my mind—my income, my future prospects, the possibilities of my living down terror and sticking to my post for more than six years. I was still hesitating, for one does not throw away ten thousand pounds without proper consideration, when a letter came from the Bank which helped me to a decision—

DEAR SIR,—We are sorry to hear of your illness. [I had said I was ill to account for my absence.] By all means stay away till you are fit for work. We may mention we have received a communication from the Directors asking us if we can recommend a suitable person to take charge of a new branch of our Bank at Pickford. We should like to see you before returning an answer.

I laughed. They had thought to pay me the empty compliment of an offer that they knew I could not accept. I promptly returned to Belchester, and accepted it.

Then I wrote to the trustees, and announced my intention of leaving the house. They both came down, and expostulated with me. I would give no reason for my action, except that I could not stand Belchester any longer, and if the amount at stake was a hundred thousand pounds, I would not stay there.

Mr Simes looked keenly at me. 'You are concealing something,' he said.

'Perhaps,' I replied coldly. 'It is enough for you that I never intend to pass another night in this house.'

He bowed, and the other trustee suggested we should open the safe for the last time.

Mr Simes assented, and we all three went upstairs. I looked sharply round the room as we entered, and was particularly careful to see where I stepped. We unlocked the three bolts, and the door of the safe swung back. The yellow box was there.

I picked it up, and turned to the others. 'You see, I have been faithful to the last,' I said with a grim smile. Then I walked to the door. 'Evans,' I shouted, 'bring me up a chisel and hammer!'

'Are you going to open it?' Mr Simes said. 'I am not sure if you are entitled to do so.'

'Certainly,' I replied; 'it still belongs to me, for I have as yet broken none of the conditions of the will. I am going to break one of them now—with a chisel and hammer.'

Evans brought the tools, and I forced the lid off, rather savagely and roughly, I'm afraid, for I was not particularly well-disposed towards the thing or its contents. The others peered over my shoulders. But there was nothing very startling to be seen. The box was full of small, withered leaves.

Mr Simes gave a grunt, and the other man laughed. 'A precious thing to guard in a hundred-guinea safe!' he said, and began to poke about among the leaves with his finger. I drew the box sharply away from him, and he looked at me in surprise.

'You don't know what may be in there,' I said half-jestingly, and, taking a pencil from my pocket, I slowly stirred about among the contents on the surface. It may have been my fancy, but I thought the surface heaved a little after I had stopped stirring it.

'What do you expect to find there?' Mr Simes said, looking at me closely.

'I know what is there,' I said quite quietly.

'You have opened the box before, then?' he queried sharply.

'I have never opened the box before, Mr Simes,' I replied; 'but I am quite aware of its contents. You shall see them for yourself,' and I quickly turned the box over. The dry leaves fluttered to the floor; but I saw some heavier substance strike the ground first and dart away almost before the eye could take in its form and colour. I looked at the others. The bedroom was rather dark, and it was a dull day.

'Well,' I said, 'did you see it?'

'See what?' said the younger man, looking up from the floor. 'I saw a lot of old leaves,' and he stirred them with his foot.

'No, the other thing; the thing that scuttered away.'

Mr Simes looked at me compassionately, and interchanged meaning glances with his companion. He thought, good man, he had solved the mystery of my departure—I was in the habit of seeing things that did not exist. I did not care to argue the matter, and we went downstairs to lunch.

I went up to town with them, and, as I said 'goodbye' to Mr Simes in Piccadilly, he said gravely to me: 'Did you really think there was anything in the box but dried leaves?'

'I know there was,' I replied.

'Hum! Well, goodbye. You are not looking very well; I should see a doctor if I were you. Goodbye.'

I did not think it necessary to see a doctor, and there the matter ended. For I never wish to discover more of the truth than I already know.

# 11

## WARD MUIR

# The Man with the Ebony Crutches

Amongst the mixed and somewhat tawdry throng that clustered round the *trente-et-quarante* table like flies hovering over some luscious decayed thing, this man alone was remarkable. He stood a little to the rear of the other players, as though he watched them rather than the game; and only hobbled nearer—for he was lame—to lean forward and gather up his winnings or replace his losses at the intervals between the dealing of the cards. During the tense minutes while the croupier dealt, he never so much as glanced at the green cloth; but kept his small dark eyes flitting perpetually from point to point in the crowd, as though furtively seeking an enemy or a friend.

His was a figure which even at Monte Carlo could not fail to be noticeable. Had he been able to stand upright I guessed that he would have exceeded every other man in the rooms in stature; but his back was humped, and his head sunken between contracted shoulders. He leant heavily upon a black crutch; and, as I afterwards learnt, used a pair of them for walking out of doors, though now he had left one in the cloakroom at the entrance. His nationality it was impossible to guess, but the high cheekbones, long, narrow slits of eyes, and sallow complexion, suggested a Slavonic origin. His hands were encased in black gloves, so I could gain no clue from the shape of the nails. Blackness was, indeed, the predominant note of the man's whole personality. His garb was black, his hair and waxed moustache were black, his very crutch was of ebony; and I would have pronounced his soul to be black too. Seldom have I beheld a countenance from which

190

Evil looked out more unmistakably than that of the hunchback in the *trente-et-quarante* saloon.

In the act of making a note upon the scoring-card I had caught this man's fleeting glance, and cards and cloth all vanished. In a flash, for the hundredth part of a second, I had peered through an uncurtained pane of this fellow-creature's mind, and what I saw there struck me into a sort of paralysis. My brain had no room in it for any other impression save just this one. It refused to take up again its previous train of reflections. The hunchback filled it completely. All I could do was to follow him with my eyes, and try my best to overcome an unreasoning nausea which rose in me unbidden each time I looked him in the face.

When presently he moved with a shuffle of feet and a tap-tap of the crutch to the hither side of the table, some instinct whispered that his object was to be near me. So I was neither startled nor surprised when I heard his oddly silken voice at my ear, and saw one of the black-gloved hands laid upon my arm.

'You will, I trust, pardon me if I ask whether I have the honour to address Mr Bevan Floyd?' His English was that of a cosmopolitan, not that of an Englishman.

I bowed.

'At present staying in the Hotel d'Or at Mentone?'

Again I bowed.

He smiled, and drew me aside, and we sat down together on one of the sofas at the wall of the apartment. He leant his crutch against his knee, and folding his hands on the top of it, turned to me and spoke again.

'Permit on old *habitué* of Monte Carlo to offer his greetings to one who is, I judge, a newcomer.' He drew a gold card-case from his pocket and, with a touch of the 'grand manner', which sat grotesquely on one so deformed, handed me a card.

'Graf Holzstein Borla', was the name inscribed upon the paste-board; and, except for the use of the word 'Graf' to indicate his title, it gave no further clue to his origin.

'I am always interested to meet the inventors of systems,' he went on; 'and you must lay the blame of my forwardness upon your own fame in that respect. Bevan Floyd, author of *The Algebraic Significance of Roulette*, is a personage whom my curiosity and admiration would not allow me to miss. When I learnt that you were here, I followed immediately. It did not take me long to identify you, once I had entered the rooms. I flatter myself that with my experience of physiognomies I could have picked you out in a crowd of far greater dimensions than this.'

His words were courtly and a trifle pedantic, but the compliment he had paid to my slight celebrity in the mathematical world conveyed rather irony than genuineness. The feeling of discomfort which I had felt ever since our eyes had first met, increased instead of diminishing. I longed to escape from his presence, yet was incapable of doing so without unpardonable rudeness. I looked round in the hope of attracting the attention of Van Leon, with whom I had come to the Casino; and in the remote corner of the main saloon I caught a glimpse of him—surrounded, as usual, by a bevy of overdressed lady friends—recklessly flinging down rolls of notes upon the roulette table. It was evident that relief from that quarter was hopeless.

'Senhor Van Leon is a friend of yours?' The smooth voice was speaking again. Apparently the Count had followed my glance and possibly guessed its object. My face burned at the thought of having been detected in the discourtesy I had meditated.

'I should hardly describe Van Leon as a friend,' I stammered; 'but——'

'Precisely,' he interrupted; 'Senhor Van Leon is—shall we say?—your partner. Brains on the one side of the firm and money on the other.'

How this man had obtained his information I could not imagine, but he had expressed the position of affairs with scathing accuracy. I had cultivated the vapid young Brazilian millionaire solely for his money. He was to act as my supporter in my new system of play.

'Mr Floyd,' Count Borla continued, laying a gloved hand upon my knee, 'if I were you I would not be in such a hurry to become rich. Believe me, you will regret this friendship. Already I can see from your expression that you are dissatisfied. Van Leon's follies are revolting to a man of your temperament. Be warned in time. Drop him, and go your own way.'

Was it imagination on my part, or had those piercing eyes really softened? For a fraction of a second I fancied they had.

'I thank you,' I said, 'for your kindness, which is, however, uncalled for. Mr Van Leon and myself are on very good terms. I do not deny that the vast capital he has at his command is of use to me, but I venture to hope that I shall be able to reward him for its loan.'

The cruel lines came on his face again, and by the twitching of his thin lips I saw that he was furious at my rejection of his proffered advice. But his outward control was perfect. He took no notice whatever of the rebuff.

'I hear that Van Leon insists on playing maximums,' he observed, 'and that consequently you have had to devise a system of flat stakes to suit the fad.'

'Your informant was correct,' I replied hotly; 'though why you should care to pry into my affairs I fail to see. I will therefore wish you good-day.'

I rose from the sofa, angry at myself for my hastiness, yet full of unreasoning anxiety to be quit of my strange companion. He rose with me.

'Tut-tut,' he laughed. 'Why this urgency? I was merely reflecting that it is a pity I shall be unable to witness your battle with the bank. I should dearly love to be present when Van Leon's dollars, guided by Floyd's learning, are pitted against M. Blanc's wheel. *Hélas!* I leave Monte Carlo today.'

'You leave Monte Carlo today?'

He chuckled horribly, and linked his arm in mine. 'Good news, you think? Your face betrays you. Englishmen are all like that. They do not cultivate the art of concealing the feelings. It is refreshing, but sometimes—awkward. Never mind, I am not offended.'

I had tried to draw away from him, but he held me tight. Again he had read my thoughts with embarrassing ease. The news that he was on the eve of departure had occasioned me a quite inexplicable sensation of relief, and my face, or the inflection of my voice, had revealed my feelings.

'You will at least give yourself the satisfaction—and me the pleasure—of walking as far as the station,' he added gleefully. 'My train is due in ten minutes.'

There was nothing for it but to acquiesce. Together we left the Casino. At the door the Count received from an attendant his hat, a long coat, and his second crutch.

*Ward Muir*

Aided by the two crutches, which he used with a skill little short of marvellous, he moved at so rapid a pace that I had no small difficulty in keeping at his side. We arrived almost immediately at the door of the *ascenseur*, and it quickly deposited us by the station platform.

Count Borla chatted incessantly of trivial matters. His talk was deliberately meaningless; and it was with relief that I observed a *train de luxe* approach round the curve in the cutting, and the Count making preparations to enter it.

'This is the Genoa express,' he remarked. 'I have booked a place in it. My servants, of course, proceed in front. That is one of the conveniences of modern travel: however far one goes, one does not need to change trains or worry about frontier *douanes*.'

'Are you going to Italy?' I asked.

'Yes, I shall be well out of the way, you see. You need not fear to be bothered with me again. Adieu!'

With the aid of the brown-liveried conductor, he clambered into one of the coaches. Through the bevelled plate-glass window I saw him limp to a *fauteuil* and place his cloak on it. Then he came forward and, lifting the window a few inches, spoke to me again.

'Do you know,' he said, 'I really think I'd drop Van Leon if I were you, Mr Floyd.' His queer, cruel smile came and went momentarily. 'If you don't', he added, 'I have a premonition that you will regret it.'

The locomotive hooted, and the line of parlour cars and *wagons-lit* drew slowly out of the station. He waved his crutch in farewell; and was gone.

I stood motionless till long after the train had disappeared. My nerves were jangled, and I upbraided myself for my childishness. Why should this interview have made so deep an impression upon my mind? What had a senior wrangler to do with emotions and loathings such as I had felt in the presence of Count Borla?

I returned to the rooms and joined Van Leon and his party.

We adjourned to Ciro's; and the young Brazilian, who was already slightly intoxicated, insisted on treating us to a costly meal. I laughed and jested with the rest, and hailed with acclamation his stupid jokes and ridiculous extravagances. Yet all the time a question haunted me, and repeated its dread whisper through the merriment. Why had Count Holzstein Borla spoken to me? What had he gained by doing so? Why had he been so earnest in his warning or threat to one whom he had never seen before?

Glasses clinked and voices babbled a myriad inanities; but above the din I fancied I heard the tap-tap of the ebony crutches as I had heard them in the Casino, bringing the hunchback into some future episode of my life; and with him came—I knew not what.

How Van Leon had contrived to make the acquaintance of Prince Fernand of Ilmenheim I never precisely learnt; but the young Brazilian—like all *nouveaux riches* of his breed—was inordinately proud of the occasional notice taken of him by his noble fellow-guest at the Hotel d'Or. The Prince, who had retired into exile upon the absorption of his country by the Austro-Hungarian Empire, was a well-known and honoured figure at Mentone. With his clean-shaven, almost ascetic face, and unmistakable dislike of fashionable society, he presented a charming, if somewhat sad, individuality. Notwithstanding that he was profoundly grieved at the annexation of his territory, he still seemed to take a keen interest in its welfare, for he spent many hours of each day in the study of European contemporary politics. It was all the more astonishing to me, therefore, that he could spare attention for the foolishly ostentatious entertainments of Van Leon.

Amongst other tributes of the Prince's friendship for the young Brazilian was the loan of the royal automobile. It appeared that Prince Fernand never used it at night, and would esteem it a favour on our part if we would ride in it upon our now regular trips to Monte Carlo.

Van Leon eagerly accepted the offer. Apart from the glory of spinning up to the Casino entrance in a coroneted car, the arrangement possessed this advantage—that we were able not merely to cover the few miles between Mentone and Monte Carlo in quicker time than the average train, but could depart and return at our own hours, instead of being pinned down to those of the timetable. Each evening after dinner beheld us, then, rushing along the lower Corniche road upon the perfect springs and tyres of Prince Fernand's car towards our play; and, a few hours later, returning with equal speed and luxury after the closing of the rooms. Those glorious spins along the peaceful moonlit Côte d'Azur formed a strange interlude to the unhealthy strain and excitement of the gambling tables.

The Prince's own chauffeur invariably accompanied us. He was a somewhat morose individual named Karl, who, while excellent as a *mecanicien*, could hardly be described as an ideal manservant. I conceived an intense dislike for him, which was added to by the fact that on more than one occasion I fancied I caught sight of his face in the *Salles de Jeu* while we were playing. If so, he was always at his post by the car when we left off play, and drove us along the winding coast road with a celerity and caution which were irreproachable.

For the last week, Van Leon and I had been devoting the whole of each evening to a system of flat stakes devised by myself for use at roulette. It was in vain that I had endeavoured to persuade the youth to experiment with comparatively small sums of money, and likewise to do so only at those periods of the day when the tables were least crowded. His insane love of display made him insist on staking nothing less than maximums, and doing so at night when the rooms were fullest. The consequence was that we repeatedly handled prodigious sums of money, and did so under the gaze of hundreds of curious and greedy eyes. I confess our notoriety made me anxious. That thieves or sharpers would soon be attracted to our vicinity seemed inevitable. What precautions to take I hardly knew. At length I went so far as to purchase a revolver, which I kept permanently in the pocket of my evening clothes.

At length there came a night when fate was all in our favour. Again and again we raked in winnings of a size which even my system could not explain. The magnitude of each of Van Leon's individual stakes was so great that every favourable turn of the wheel saw us several hundred pounds to the good. More than once the bank was depleted almost to breaking point, and attendants had to be sent for fresh supplies of cash from the Administration. The pile of money which lay on the table in front of Van Leon had assumed gigantic proportions, though it was all in notes. When at length the table closed, we rose with little less than a fortune in our pockets.

I urged Van Leon to obtain the services of one of the Casino detectives to accompany us home, but he scouted the notion. He was flushed and excited more with his own new-found fame than with the extent of his monetary gains.

'Let's have supper first,' he said; and no protests of mine could turn him from the project. It was thus long after midnight before we were seated in the Prince's automobile, and even then some delay was occasioned by the refusal of one of our three acetylene lamps to light. Eventually we did without it.

Whether it was the supper of which he had partaken so freely, or whether it was the sudden cessation of the high nervous tension at which we had been kept all the evening, I do not know; but Van Leon fell into a deep slumber almost as soon as we had started. I cannot say I was sorry. My own fatigue was great, and I felt in no mood for talking. The motion of the car soothed me, and the beauty of the night acted as an agreeable soporific upon my mind. There was no moon, but the stars shone in the calm blackness overhead; and in front of the car the lamp-lit patch of snow-white, dusty road was constantly devoured by our whirring wheels. Soon we passed out of the zone of suburbia, and began to thread our way along a more lonely strip of route. Great rocks lifted their heads on one side of the track, and far below, on the other, one could catch a glimpse of shifting purple sea.

I had almost succumbed to the peacefulness of the scene, and followed Van Leon's example by falling into a doze, when there was a sudden jar, followed by a series of unpleasant but not very violent bumps. Karl instantly put on the brake and stopped the mechanism. We came to a halt.

'What's wrong?' queried Van Leon, yawning.

'A tyre punctured, sir,' answered Karl, descending from his seat.

'Tyre punctured on a road like this? Oh, nonsense!' Van Leon sleepily stumbled out on to the road after the chauffeur.

I followed. A glance showed me that Karl was right. One of our front tyres had softened, and where it came in contact with the road was perfectly flat.

'Nothing for it but to try a repair, I suppose,' remarked Van Leon, grumblingly seating himself at the roadside. 'Karl will manage it all right in a few minutes.'

Karl removed the cushion from one of the seats and fumbled below it for his tools. For a moment or two silence fell upon our little party. Not a breath moved the air. We seemed utterly alone on the road. No sound was to be heard save the plash of the gentle Mediterranean on the invisible beach.

And then, through the solemn stillness of the southern night there arose a noise which made my heart throb with unspeakable dread.

'*Tap—tap—tap—tap*': it came from a point in front of us along the road: '*Tap—tap—tap—tap*', in an odd half-shuffle that struck my ear with sinister familiarity.

It was the sound of crutches. Somewhere in the darkness a lame man was approaching us.

There are many hundreds of lame persons in the world, and I suppose the majority use crutches. But I could have sworn to that especial pair of them anywhere. The agility with which they were being used, for one thing, would have singled out their owner as amazingly active for one so deformed. And—and—well, I could not have explained the sensation, but all the same I felt a conviction that the individual who was approaching was no other than my acquaintance of the Genoa express.

'*Tap—tap.*' Nearer and nearer it drew, till at length the figure of the newcomer resolved itself out of the darkness. Already I had recognized him, but as he hobbled into the vivid glare of our pair of Bleriots my fears were confirmed. I beheld once more the black-cloaked, black-gloved Count Borla.

He paused on his crutches, and took a leisurely and smiling survey of the car. Then his gaze fell on me, and he lifted his hat with a flourish.

'Aha, so it is Mr Bevan Floyd who is in difficulties?' he observed. 'And—if my eyes do not deceive me—I think I see his partner, Mr Van Leon, sitting there by the roadside. This is an unexpected pleasure. You have punctured a tyre, *hein!* But that will not take long to put right.'

He limped towards Van Leon, and coolly entered into conversation with him. For my part, I was glad to take no notice of his mysterious return from Italy, but busied myself with the tyre. Karl had, it appeared to me, taken needlessly long over his preparations, and I spoke to him sharply, ordering him to be as quick as possible. As I did so, and he was bringing his tools, I bent down to examine the puncture.

'Why,' I cried, a stab of fear flashing across my mind, 'the puncture is a bullet hole! Someone must have fired at us with a rifle! We were stopped on purpose, and——'

A hand was pressed over my mouth, and I was pitched face down upon the road. With a totally unexpected treachery, Karl, the chauffeur, had leapt on me and pinned me to the earth. Almost at the same instant I heard a cry from Van Leon.

'What's that, Floyd——?'

The words were cut off short by a horrid gasp and a stumble.

I was dazed by my fall, but managed to make a struggle for freedom. In vain I turned and twisted in the dust of the roadway, and made frantic efforts to reach the pocket in which reposed my revolver. Karl's strength was enormous, and I was shortly aware that he was being assisted by the hunchback. With startling speed they managed to bind me hand and foot with a cord. I lay like a log, and could not even cry out, for they had forced a gag into my mouth. Bitter indeed were my reflections as I felt the stealthy gloved hands of Count Borla explore my jacket and remove thence my share of our night's colossal winnings. The humiliation, not unmixed with fear (for I had no hope of being left alive to serve as a witness against the criminals), was almost more than I could bear.

But an unexpected interruption came to my rescue. While the pair of villains were apparently treating Van Leon as they had treated me, a welcome sound arose in the distance. It was that of horses' hoofs and wheels. A carriage was approaching.

I heard an annoyed exclamation from Karl, and then, by the sound, I judged that he and Borla had entered the car. The mechanism was started, and, jarring unpleasantly on the punctured tyre, they moved off in the Mentone direction.

A few minutes of agonized anxiety passed, and then the carriage was upon us. It was brought to a standstill, and a moment later kindly French voices were sounding in my ears and swift hands were unfastening the knots which held me.

The newcomers were a party returning from a ball at Cap Martin. Many were the expressions of sympathy which they poured out upon me, and eager were their enquiries as to the appearance of the thieves. I made no attempt to reply. Staggering to my feet, I strode across to the side of the road, for I was sick with fear for Van Leon.

My worst apprehensions were only too true. There lay the lad, his weak face turned mutely to the stars, his coat flying wide open, revealing the white expanse of shirtfront within. Not a movement did he make when I bent over him and called his name, although neither gag nor cords bound him. A glance told me the truth. He was dead; and the restless wavelets seemed to be singing his dirge on the shore below.

Upon his corpse there was no sign of violence. Not a vestige of blood stained his clothing. His face was not contorted with pain, but looked pathetically placid and innocent, notwithstanding the unmistakable traces of excess which showed in the blotchy skin and puffy cheeks. He had neither been stabbed nor garrotted; and I knew he had not been shot, inasmuch as I had heard no detonation. However death had come to him, it was not foreseen. It had brought neither pain nor terror.

Yet poor Van Leon had been murdered, of that I had no shadow of doubt. And his slayer was Count Holzstein Borla.

We brought a lamp from the carriage, and tenderly lifted him up. As we did so his hat—which had been knocked rather far forward upon his temples—rolled off.

In the middle of his brow was a shrivelled brown spot.

A year later saw me settled in London. I had completely abandoned all thoughts of exploiting the mathematical side of Monte Carlo. Van Leon's horrible death had given me a severe shock. The place and its atmosphere were disgusting. I turned my attention to a quiet existence of writing and research.

Already the incidents of that strange night had sunk out of the public memory, but in my own they were as distinct as ever. Indeed, I was determined not to forget them. Van Leon had never been a great favourite of mine; but the youth's blood cried to heaven to be avenged, and I was determined to bring his murderer to justice if I could.

How it came about that I abandoned this resolve I now propose to relate.

It was a cold night of early autumn. Fog drifted sluggishly along the streets. The roadways flowed with mud, and occasionally a few drops of rain fell to add to the dirt and slime of the pavements.

I had been working late, and, as it was close on midnight, it behoved me to hurry if, as I purposed, I was to obtain a meal before closing-hour. I swiftly threaded the well-known maze of Soho in the direction of my favourite restaurant. But just as I reached it a face drifted by me which made me pause.

Where had I seen that man before; and why should he have set my heart pulsating at such a pace? Ah! I had it! The face was that of Karl, the chauffeur.

I turned and pursued him. Without pausing to reflect, I seized him by the collar and shook him with fury.

The wretch's skin blanched as he recognized me; but immediately afterwards a look of cunning crept into his frightened eyes.

'All right, sir,' he gasped, with an oily politeness which made me scorn him more heartily than ever. 'All right. I will not try to get away; but would you not rather catch Count Borla than me?'

I saw his meaning.

'You know where he is?' I queried. 'Then if you tell me aright, so that I can have him arrested, I shall let you go. But do not try to deceive me, or——'

'No, no; I will not deceive you, sir,' he cringed. 'I hate him as much as you do yourself. I should love to see him swing for his crimes.'

'Do you live with him?' I asked.

'Live with him! *Ach Gott!* I would not do so for worlds. But pardon, sir, might I ask you to treat me to a drink and some food? I have not eaten all day.'

I noticed now that he was shabbily attired and very emaciated. Without a word I led him into the eating-house towards which I had originally been directing my steps. We sat down at a table, and I ordered supper.

A small orchestra was thumping out cakewalk tunes and waltzes in a corner of the restaurant, so there was no danger of our conversation being overheard. I let him finish his meal, however, before attempting to question him. By the time our plates were removed his tongue began to wag of its own accord.

'I have been on Count Borla's track for many months,' he observed, rolling and lighting a cigarette; 'but it is only within the last few days that I have found his whereabouts. It is lucky that you met me when you did.'

I passed over the effrontery of the remark without comment.

'Then you have not kept in touch with him since leaving Mentone?' I asked.

'Indeed, no. We parted that same night, as soon as he had paid me the price we had agreed upon. Till this week I had not seen him since.'

'Who was he, and where did he come from?'

He shrugged his shoulders.

'I know as little as you do. He met me in a café once, shortly after I entered the Prince's service, and told me that he had reason to think that—as Van Leon persisted in playing maximums—one of these nights you would be certain to come back to the hotel with a large sum of money in your pockets. I was to spy upon you until a time came when you made a big gain. Afterwards I was to leave one of the car's lamps unlit as a signal. Count Borla said he would conceal himself at the loneliest part of the road, armed with a compressed-air rifle with which to puncture the tyre, and thus cause us to halt. The plan worked beautifully, though we were interrupted by the approach of that carriage. We drove in the car as far as the outskirts of Mentone, and there parted. He gave me a paltry couple of thousand francs. Bah! I was a fool. I might have shared the profits of that transaction properly, half and half, if I'd had the sense to stand up for my rights. However, I took the notes and fled with them by the next north-bound train. I made sure that the Count's peculiar appearance would result in his immediate arrest wherever he went, and that, having captured him, they would not bother about me.'

'But—but——' I cried, perplexed, 'Van Leon was killed, you know. How did he do it?'

The chauffeur crossed himself. 'I cannot tell,' he responded with superstitious awe. 'It was all over in a moment. Who can say what a person like Borla might not do? He is like no one else.'

Karl was evidently bent on Borla's downfall, and from his somewhat indefinite narrative I gathered that he had squandered his ill-gotten two thousand francs in an orgy of drunkenness in Paris, and then crossed to London to seek employment, which he was unable to obtain owing to his lack of references. He had then hit on the idea of blackmailing Borla, and it was in pursuance of this scheme that I now found him.

'But where are we to catch Count Borla?' I enquired. 'Remember I shall not allow you out of my sight until you have guided me to his hiding place.'

'I have found out that every night he traverses a certain street in the West End. Three times I have followed him, and three times he has eluded me. Where he goes I do not know, nor what can be his reason for wandering about at so unusual an hour. I warrant he is employed on some fresh villainy; otherwise, why should he pass by my lodgings—as he always does—at three in the morning? If you will accompany me tonight we can await his coming, and follow him to see where he goes. When we have found out where he lives or, at least, what he is doing, we can perfect our plans. But, sir, I must beg of you to let me proceed some paces in front of you. I dare not think of the consequences if Count Borla were to see us together.'

I considered his proposal with care. There seemed no alternative but to agree. I thought I read in his trembling hands and fearful glances not so keen a wish to blackmail Count Borla as to sweep him off the face of the earth by delivering him into the hands of the police. The truth was, Karl went in fear of his own life as long as that of the Count continued.

That his terror was not unfounded I was soon to discover for myself.

We sat for more than an hour silently smoking, until at length (the musicians having packed up their instruments and straggled out into the night) we were the last customers left in the eating-house.

Then we passed out through its swing doors and trended steadily in a south-westerly direction until I guessed we must be somewhere in the Fulham district, though I had long since lost my bearings. The chauffeur never hesitated, and seemed to be thoroughly acquainted with the route which he was pursuing. He walked without hesitation or enquiry.

At length he drew up.

'Here is the street,' he said. 'He always passes this way. We must simply wait until he comes. As soon as he has passed I shall follow at a distance of about fifty yards. I dare not go any closer. You in your turn will maintain about that space behind me.'

We withdrew into a sheltered corner, and prepared for our vigil. The wind whistled dolefully and stirred some wet rags of paper which lay in the roadway. Looking at my watch, I could just see that the hands pointed to half-past two.

How long we stood thus I hardly knew. It must have been an hour at least. I was already petrified with cold, and almost deciding that our quest was to be a futile one, when out of the waning night there arose a sound which sent the blood racing afresh through every vein in my body.

'Tap—tap—tap—tap.'

It was the unmistakable, unforgettable beat of Count Holzstein Borla's ebony crutches.

'Tap—tap.' Closer and closer it drew. He was approaching at his habitual hurrying pace along the thoroughfare at whose corner we stood, so that for the time being he was invisible.

As the tapping grew more and more imminent I heard Karl draw in a hissing breath of suspense.

And then, in the faint yellow light of the street lamps I beheld the hunched figure limp swiftly into view from behind the angle of the wall.

He crossed the road not a stone's throw away from us. For a terrible fraction of a second I fancied that he was going to turn and plunge into our arms. But he kept right on, and disappeared again down the vista of street. The *tap—tap* diminished in intensity.

'Quick! After him!' I whispered, and was amazed on the instant at the strange sound of my own voice.

Once more Karl drew in his breath, and though I could not see his face, I knew he was trying to screw up his courage to obey me and carry out our plan. For an instant I think he wavered; then, with an agonized gesture enjoining at once silence and caution, stepped out in Borla's wake.

I gave him about a minute, and followed.

I found myself in a long road of tall and unlit mansions, stretching away into the distance, its length surmisable alone by the thread of twinkling gas-lamps which lay in front. Far down the deserted thoroughfare I could descry momentary glimpses of the hunchback, and the tapping of his crutches was borne to me gustily upon the wind. Sneaking in the shadow of the wall at an interval between us moved the chauffeur.

By degrees I found myself tiptoeing nearer Karl, whether owing to my own eagerness or his dilatoriness I cannot now say. Thus, when

Borla at length rounded a corner and disappeared from sight, and Karl did likewise, I was not more than a dozen or so paces behind.

I did not notice that the tap-tap of the crutches had ceased, and, presumably, Karl failed to realize it likewise, or he might have paused and been saved. As it was, I was already rounding the corner when his cry reached my ears.

The sight that met my view made me stop with amazement.

In the wavering circle of light thrown by a lamp stood Count Borla and the chauffeur, face to face.

Count Borla's long black cloak was wrapped round his body by the wind, and he leant heavily on his crutches. He was looking his former accomplice full in the eyes, and his white teeth were bared in a smile of ironical greeting.

Karl seemed petrified with fear. He stood transfixed, making no attempt either to speak or to move.

For an instant the pair stood thus, motionless.

Then Borla slowly lifted one of his crutches and pointed it at the chauffeur's face.

There was a staccato crackling, hissing noise. A blue flame leapt from the point of the crutch. Without a moan Karl fell with a crash on the ground.

The Count swiftly turned on his heel and hobbled up the steps of a house opposite which we had paused. Whipping a latchkey from his pocket, he inserted it in the lock. An instant later he had disappeared.

The profound emotion, which had held me as a passive spectator to the crime, ebbed, and I sprang forward.

Upon the forehead of my late companion was imprinted the same scorched brown circle which had marked that of Van Leon.

I did not pause to bend over him, for I knew well that no aid of mine could avail him now.

Fury boiled in my breast. I leapt up the steps of the house into which the Count had retreated and beat madly upon the portal with my fists.

To my astonishment it gave way before my blows. It had not been latched.

I entered the gas-lit hall of a large but barely furnished dwelling. Above me I heard a shuffling sound, and, looking up, saw that the

Count had reached the head of the staircase, which was of the type known, I believe, as a 'well'. I instantly gave chase.

As I surmounted the last steps I found myself at the end of a long passage. At its other terminus I beheld Borla enter a room and, with a furtive glance back, close its door behind him.

I ran along the passage and laid my hand on the door. Then I paused—why, I hardly knew. Something made me hesitate and, with a cold-bloodedness which was extraordinary at such a moment, consider my own position.

By opening that door might I not walk straight into a similar trap as that by which Karl had met his death? Might I not be struck into eternity, too, with a touch from one of those dread crutches? Would it not be more prudent to sally forth and summon the nearest constable to my aid?

My knees trembled beneath me, but an inward voice forced me to proceed. Meanwhile, the murderer might be quietly escaping by some back passage, and here was I lingering like a child afraid of bogies! I chided myself, and, with the reproachful faces of Van Leon and Karl urging me on, threw my weight against the door and immediately burst it open.

The room in which I found myself was cheerless and dusty. Its sole furniture was a deal table, a chair, and a huge mirror. It was lit by a single gas-jet, caged in wire gauze. There was a second door in one of the whitewashed walls.

These details I hardly noticed. My attention was riveted by the familiar figure who sat at the table.

It was Prince Fernand of Ilmenheim.

The Prince rose and held out his hand.

'I was expecting you,' he said.

I paid no attention to the greeting. My anger had redoubled. I could hardly control myself.

'So Count Borla was in league with you all the time!' I gasped. 'It was your plot from the very beginning. You lent us your car so that your accomplice might rob us the more conveniently. You hypocrite! Oh, you hypocrite!'

'Do not be so hasty, my young friend,' said Prince Fernand; and there was a singularly sad note in his voice. 'It is true that Count

Holzstein Borla is my servant. It is true that at my orders he killed and robbed Mr Van Leon. It is true that—also at my orders—he has tonight put an end to another useless and wicked life. I have many servants, good and bad. Borla is (as the world judges things) a bad man. But what would you? Would it be seemly for me to perform these menial deeds of justice myself? Surely not. Wherefore I use Borla. And he is not so evil as he seems, though sometimes I confess I have difficulty in restraining him. Do you know why I sent him to speak to you that day in the Casino? Simply to learn what sort of person you were, for I foresaw that as poor Van Leon's partner it might be necessary to mete out to you the same fate we gave him.

'Borla did his best to warn you, when he found that you were a person of different calibre to the weak and silly Van Leon. As a precaution, he thought it best to throw you off the scent of his whereabouts by pretending to take the Genoa train—a manoeuvre designed, also, to lessen the probability of your mentioning him to your partner. Was all this the work of a wholly depraved man? I think not. Borla might have spared himself the trouble by killing you as he killed Van Leon. Instead of that he chose to endanger his own liberty and my reputation by leaving you alive.'

'But—but—what do you mean?'

He smiled at my bewilderment.

'I can understand your anger, Monsieur Floyd,' he replied quietly. 'It is righteous anger, and I admire you for it, and for the bravery with which you followed Borla when—at my orders—he left the street door of this house open behind him. Some explanation is due to you, I admit.'

He paused, and commenced to pace up and down the apartment with measured strides.

'We in our position have different ideas to you in yours,' he began reflectively; and I understood that he alluded to his royal birth. 'We look at life through different eyes. In our veins the habit of ruling and commanding flows as surely as does the blood. Although I am now only a pawn on the chessboard of European politics, you must remember that I am still Prince of Ilmenheim. I am an exile, and I dare say that in the opinion of politicians my responsibility towards my country has ceased. I cannot look at it in that light. My subjects are still my deepest care. Their cries against the misrule of the new government reach me wherever I go, and I make it my business to alleviate their suffering as best I can.'

He stopped, and rounded on me with unwonted excitement. 'I wonder if you can imagine even remotely what it feels like to see one's country groaning, and be fettered hand and foot,' he cried. 'Do you know that in the mountains of Ilmenheim there are half a million people starving at this moment? *My* people, too; and I cannot lift a finger to help them! My poor people, my poor people!'

The moment of intense feeling passed.

'Do you recollect the exact amount Van Leon won that night in the Casino?' he asked abruptly.

'It was about twenty-five thousand pounds.'

'Correct. That was the precise figure of the donation which I was able to dispatch immediately afterwards by a confidential messenger to be distributed amongst the peasants of my native land. How many mothers and babes it fed, I cannot tell you; but money goes far in poverty-stricken Ilmenheim, so there must have been nearly as many human beings saved as there were pounds taken from the Casino table. Do you blame me for using Count Borla's cunning to effect such an end? Do you blame me for sacrificing one useless life to benefit those thousands—I, who at a nod could order the execution of any of my subjects, were I in my rightful position on the throne?'

I stood abashed. I remembered Van Leon's expensive dinners and the sycophantic guests. And then I thought of the barren hills of Ilmenheim and the peasantry dying like sheep in the cold winter.

'Admit that Van Leon's life was an unworthy one,' urged the Prince; 'and that Karl was a rogue too. Do you not think that I was justified in sacrificing the former; and ordering the destruction of the latter when I found that he had scented Borla's whereabouts, and might at any moment discover his link with me, and thus ruin at a touch the plans of my whole life? Oh, I assure you, I do not enter upon a course of action such as you have witnessed without due thought. Had it been possible to spare either Van Leon or Karl I would have done so; but I had to make sure of the money first and foremost, and I gave Borla his orders accordingly. It was against his judgement that you survived the interview on the Corniche road. He does not approve of leaving any witnesses.

'He is a little too fond of using that crutch of his,' he went on. 'It was his own idea to provide its interior with an accumulator in which an enormously powerful charge of electricity can be stored, and whence it is released at the touch of a button in the handle. I will not deny that Borla's fiendish ingenuity has been of use to me. An individual in my position has to use tools of all tempers, Monsieur Floyd. Borla and his cunning and treachery are tools which I dislike; and they have to be held in a steady hand. But I do not respect them any the less.'

I could find no argument in reply. 'But is it wise on your part to select as your messenger such a conspicuous figure as the deformed Borla?' I temporized.

'I chose him on purpose,' responded the Prince. 'To you it may sound cruel to say so, but the truth is that his hunched back, his lameness, his evil face, all aid in drawing off attention from his master and director—myself. He does what you English call my dirty work, however; I cannot forget that. My poor misgoverned Ilmenheimers have often had cause to be thankful for Borla's existence, though they little guess it.'

Outside in the street there arose a shrill whistle, followed by a sound of hurrying feet. Prince Fernand moved to the window and gazed out.

'A policeman has found Karl's body,' he said, 'and it is being removed.'

'Count Borla is a murderer,' I cried, 'and as his accomplice and shielder you are a murderer too!'

'Put it that way if it pleases you,' he responded wearily. 'My philosophy may be right; it may be wrong. I do not ask you to judge me. But you have penetrated too far now into my secret to withdraw, without being convinced one way or the other. When you leave this house you must make up your mind either to remain silent, or else to betray me to the world, and destroy all my projects. It is not a matter of giving up Borla to the gallows; it is destroying the power for good or ill of the Prince of Ilmenheim. Do not mistake me. I plead not for myself, but for what I honestly believe to be the welfare of my subjects.'

He stood with his back to me moodily gazing out of the window. The East was grey with dawn, and across the street I could see a wilderness of chimneys stretching far into the distance. Already wisps of new smoke rose from a few of them. The mighty city was awakening to a new day.

My eye wandered round the room, and fell upon the second door. Was Count Borla concealed in the room behind it? Or did it only cover another exit, through which he had escaped?

'Borla is hidden here!' I blurted out accusingly.

He continued to stand with his back to me, and I heard him sigh.

'You still think me wrong in my methods?' he asked at length.

I looked again at the door, and a horror of it filled me. As I gazed, that strange nausea which had arisen within me at Monte Carlo when speaking to the Count came back again. Behind that door I felt sure crouched the hunchback: the murderer, the thief, the inventor of the death-dealing crutches.

'Monsieur Floyd,' said the Prince, 'are you going to withdraw, and leave me to pursue my way as I choose? Will you let me succour the mountaineers of Ilmenheim after my own fashion, answering to no earthly tribunal for my deeds or those of my servants?'

But I could not move. I seemed drawn to the door with invisible bonds. The Prince sighed again. He spoke over his shoulder.

'You insist?' he said. 'Then you have my permission to open the door.' He looked out of the window once more.

I stepped across the room to the door, and laid my fingers on its handle. It rattled, for I was trembling like a leaf. With a mighty effort of will, I pulled it. . . .

The door swung easily open, revealing—a cupboard.

There was a loud crash.

The pair of ebony crutches had fallen down at my feet.

Within the cupboard hung the hunchback's cloak. On a shelf were paints, some pieces of skin-coloured plaster, false hair, eyebrows, and moustache.

Count Holzstein Borla and Prince Fernand of Ilmenheim had been one and the same person.

I looked at the crutches lying at my feet and the disguise in the cupboard. Then I drew back and gazed long at the tall, melancholy figure silhouetted at the window.

I turned and very softly stole down the staircase, and into the street.

# 12

GUY THORNE

# The Horror of the Automaton

Off Fleet Street, though quite unknown to those who pass down that busy and celebrated thoroughfare, there still remain many quaint old courts and alleys, relics of the time when Dr Johnson, Goldsmith, and the famous literary men of the past lived in this quarter of London.

One of the best of these places is known as Gough Square, and in one corner of it is the house where Dr Johnson and his assistants compiled the greater portion of the famous dictionary.

In a room high up in one of the old houses in this square a lean, shabby-looking, and elderly man was sitting.

The room was large, and lighted with three square windows, all of them grimy and with the glass much in need of polishing. A threadbare carpet, which had once been a handsome enough affair, covered the floor.

It was about four o'clock in the afternoon of a winter's day, and the curious-looking man sitting by the fireside was reading by the light of a cheap lamp, reading one of the sixpenny illustrated weeklies with strained attention.

He was dressed in a shabby frock coat and an old-fashioned black cravat edged by a thin strip of somewhat dingy collar. His hair, which was long and grey, fell almost to his shoulders. His face was parchment yellow, the mouth set in one firm, bloodless line, the nose hawk-like and predatory, the eyes, under bushy black brows, singularly steadfast and fixed.

Despite his shabby surroundings and the general air of poverty surrounding him—a poverty which was perfectly real and not in any way assumed—the man by the fire was a European celebrity. He was

Ivan Paczensky, generally spoken of as the greatest chess player in the world.

In spite of this fact, however, he found it a hard struggle to live, and it was a fortunate year for him when he made more than three hundred pounds. Chess, the most intellectual game—if, indeed, game it can be called—of all has no hold upon the general public of today.

Of course, Paczensky's name was known to the world at large in a vague sort of way. The men in the street, if asked who were the greatest chess players of the day, would vaguely have mentioned Paczensky, and perhaps Levenstein, of Berlin, but there their knowledge would have stopped.

Paczensky pulled the lamp a little nearer to him, and gazed with a knitted brow at a photograph in half-tone which occupied a full page of the sixpenny weekly.

It was an extraordinary picture, and one which was calculated to arrest the hand of anyone who turned over the leaves of the journal.

Sitting before a chess table of solid mahogany, upon which were the pieces of a set for a game, was a curious figure. It was in evening dress. One arm was stretched out and the hand seemed to be about to move a piece on the board. The face of the figure represented a clean-shaved man with fixed, glassy eyes and a curious, not quite human, smirk and leer upon the lips. It was sitting in a high-backed chair, and the whole pose and attitude suggested an image of wood or wax rather than a human being.

Underneath the picture were two or three lines of the letterpress, which ran as follows:

'It', the marvellous Automaton at the Italian Hall. An illusion which has puzzled all London. Mr Durante, the famous magician, offers a prize of five hundred pounds to anyone who can discover the mystery.—See page 6.

Paczensky, his face fixed in a frown, turned over the leaves of the journal until he came to the indicated page. There he read the following paragraphs:

### THE MYSTERY OF THE MOMENT

By the kindness of Mr Durante, of the Italian Hall, we are now able to give this week a full-page photograph of 'It', the extraordinary and mysterious figure which is puzzling the whole of London at this moment. There have

been automata before, and very astonishing things these weird creations—
these modern Frankensteins of latter-day magicians—have shown themselves capable of performing, but sooner or later the mystery ceased to
interest; the mystery has been discovered or exposed.

In the case of 'It', the greatest mechanical and other experts have entirely
failed to earn the reward of five hundred pounds offered by Mr Durante to
those who can see how the astonishing feats of 'It' are performed. It can
hardly be known to many of our readers what occurs daily at the Italian Hall.
A large sheet of glass several yards square is placed upon the stage. Upon this
is a chess table, and sitting at the table in a high-backed chair is the strange,
uncanny-looking figure, appropriately named 'It' by its creator. Members of
the audience are allowed to walk round the stage and make a thorough
inspection of the Automaton at the table. Then any member of the audience
is invited to play a game of chess with the figure. An ordinary cane chair is put
at the other side of the table, in which the human player sits. The game is
begun, the Automaton moving the pieces with its flexible and prehensile
hand with almost the freedom and exactitude of human movement.
The game invariably results in one way—'It' is the victor. No one who has
watched this contest but can fail to come away with a sense of bewilderment
which almost amounts to awe, and when the harsh 'Checkmate' comes in a
sepulchral voice from the figure a thrill is experienced by the audience unlike
anything else one can imagine. But more than this. During the last month
some of the most famous chess players of the world have been challenged by
'It' in the advertisement columns of the daily press. Four or five of them have
responded, and some games of extraordinary interest to chess players have
resulted. Whoever or whatever may be the animating spirit which controls
the waxen figure at the Italian Hall, the result has been that O'Grady, of
Dublin; Simpkins, the champion of London Chess Club; Jules Toché, of
Paris, and one or two lesser lights, have been absolutely vanquished by the
Automaton.

This journal has always devoted a considerable space weekly to the great
game of chess, and our chess editor reports that the extraordinary feats of
Mr Durante's figure have stimulated interest in the great game to a remarkable degree during the last few weeks, as abundant letters upon his table from
chess players testify. He makes a very pertinent suggestion in his column,
and one which we heartily endorse here: 'Why,' he asks, 'don't one of the
two acknowledged masters of the world enter into competition with the
figure? What are Paczensky and Levenstein doing?' We have made enquiries,
and we find that Mr Levenstein is in Berlin, on a visit to some friends,
though there are hopes that he will accept the challenge later in the year.

Mr Paczensky, however, Levenstein's great rival and the only other man in Europe of the German master's form, is in London, and all chess players are hoping he will respond, and vanquish the mysterious figure which bids fair to become the inanimate and anonymous champion of European chess. We shall see.

Paczensky put down the paper, rose from his seat, and began to stride up and down the room.

Seen thus in the large, sombrely lit room, striding noiselessly up and down like some great, ill-omened bird, the famous chess player suggested something quite alien and remote from ordinary life, some monomaniac, as it were, a soul animated by one consuming passion, one single life motive, and unable to conceive that the world held anything else.

And it was with Paczensky. The world was ruled for him in squares of black and white, his castles in the air were of polished boxwood and two inches high. Men and women were less to him than the pawns upon the board.

A new gambit was more important than a European war.

He had ceased long ago to be human; he was nothing more nor less than a spirit and embodiment of chess.

He was thinking deeply now with a fierce and smouldering anger.

This sinister figure of wax, that sat motionless in its chair and defeated the chess masters of the world, rode his imagination like Black Care itself. Nobody knew better than he what consummate skill was necessary to defeat men like O'Grady, Toché, and Simpkins. They were not in the same class as he himself or his hated antagonist, the German Jew Levenstein, but nevertheless they were masters. The mechanical part of the figure did not trouble the detached student of chess. By what cunning arrangement of electricity or wires or what not the figure was animated did not in the least interest him. He knew very well that somehow, by some extraordinarily ingenious means, there was a controlling brain behind it. It was this brain upon which all his interest was set. What was it? Who was it? Why was it?

As he walked up and down—and his promenade went on unceasingly for more than an hour—he began to come to one conclusion. By a process of careful elimination, rejecting this idea and that in turn, he saw no other solution of the mystery than this.

The animating mind behind the machine could by no possibility be any other than that of Ernst Levenstein, his own rival and a man he hated with the bitter hatred of a monomaniac who realizes his only equal, if not his master.

It must be so! Nothing else could possibly account for these continued triumphs. It was Levenstein without doubt! The man with whom he divided the chess honours of the world! They had played four games together during the last two years, and each game had resulted in a draw. No one knew which was the better of the two men, though in his heart of hearts Paczensky felt with a fierce revolt that when—as was inevitable in the future—he once more met his opponent the Jew would prove the conqueror.

About seven o'clock the thin, odd-looking man left his rooms and walked to a small restaurant in the Strand where he was accustomed to dine. He sat down in his usual place and the waiter brought him his simple meal, together with an evening paper.

He opened the paper and began to read it mechanically, though his thoughts were very far away, when suddenly his eyes glowed as his attention was caught by an announcement in large type upon the front page.

It said that Mr Durante's marvellous Automaton, having conquered most of the great chess players of the day, now offered a prize of two hundred and fifty pounds to anyone who could beat it.

The paragraph went on to say that it was understood that Mr Ernst Levenstein, the famous German player, would, in the course of a month or so, be returning to England, when there was every possibility of his accepting the challenge. It concluded by expressing wonder that Paczensky, who was known to be in England, had not seen fit to play a game with the mystery.

The great chess player sipped his glass of thin claret and smiled sardonically to himself. The paragraph was obviously a blind in so far as it concerned Levenstein. Paczensky was absolutely convinced in his own mind that Levenstein was in league with the well-known conjurer Durante, and nothing by now would have altered his opinion. The challenge, however, made thus publicly, was obviously genuine enough, and the sum to Paczensky was a very large one. Should he or should he not send in his name for the contest in the following week? He debated the question within himself during the whole of his dinner, and finally, when it was over, strolled westwards to the Italian Hall, where the evening performance, with its various attractions, culminating in the doings of 'It', was now in full swing. During the interval he asked for and was conducted to the presence of Mr Durante, a big, burly, bearded man, who did not in the least suggest the marvellously clever illusionist that he was. From him he heard the full details of the competition. If Paczensky won the game with the Automaton he would receive two hundred and fifty pounds at the conclusion of the play. If he lost he would forfeit nothing. The game would begin at nine o'clock in the evening and would finish at eleven, this being more or less arranged for by the limited time given for each move. The one stringent rule, so as not to disappoint a large and interested public, which would be certain to be attracted by an event of this importance was as follows: If Paczensky did not turn up at the appointed hour ready to begin the game, then he must pay a penalty of one hundred pounds.

'You see, Mr Paczensky,' said the conjurer in his bland, silken voice, 'I must guard myself in this way to avoid disappointing the public and the whole thing becoming a fiasco.'

The stipulation was reasonable enough, and Paczensky said so.

'But on the other hand, Mr Durante,' he remarked, 'supposing that for some reason or other your Automaton went wrong and was unable to play with me? It would be I who would look foolish then.'

'Quite so, quite so,' Durante answered, 'though you need have no fear of that, Mr Paczensky. It is not troubled with any little human failings, ha, ha! Well, if you are going to enter into an agreement with me to appear next week I shall be most pleased to insert a clause to the effect that if for any reason "It" does not play with you, you shall be paid the two hundred and fifty pounds at once.'

Paczensky expressed himself perfectly satisfied, and stayed for the remainder of the performance, going in front to witness it. Afterwards, two brief but binding agreements were written out and duly signed over a bottle of champagne, and by midnight the great chessplayer was once more in his lonely rooms off Fleet Street.

He slept but little that night, his whole being strung up into an intensity of excitement. He saw clearly that this occasion would attract an enormous number of people to whom chess was but a name. The daily papers would be full of it: If he won he would be the hero of the hour, the acknowledged champion of the whole world. Feeling certain that somehow or other Levenstein was behind the whole business, he knew that if he beat him then his whole life would be complete.

Within two days the hoardings of London were covered with announcements of the forthcoming contest. The newspapers took it up—it was a slack season for news—there were columns of conjecturing and surmise, and reporters were knocking all day long at Paczensky's door. From a vague name he became a real and living entity to thousands upon thousands of people.

Haggard and worn, for three days before the contest Paczensky began to haunt the neighbourhood of the Italian Hall. He could not keep away from it. Some lurid attraction drew him there as if it were some powerful magnet. There was a little dingy corner public house not far from the stage door of the hall, a place much frequented by conjurers of a low class. These dingy ministers of pleasure grew quite accustomed to seeing the shabby, elderly man sitting in the corner by the window with a glass of gin and water before him, gazing fixedly out at the door with the red lamp over it which led to the stage of the popular place of entertainment. He spoke to nobody, and after a few attempts to draw him into conversation the habitués of the place left him alone. He was another piece of London's jetsam, a failure like themselves! Nobody recognized him, nobody had the slightest idea who he was. But there was a purpose in the great chess player's strange behaviour. Although a letter dated Berlin and signed 'Levenstein' had appeared in one of the daily papers, saying that, if Paczensky beat the Automaton, the Jew would at once come to England and challenge 'It' himself, the certainty that this was a blind and that Levenstein was really the controlling influence never left Paczensky. He watched the stage door with grim persistence. Durante, in his fur coat, would come out after the afternoon and evening performances, jump into a cab, and drive away. Then his assistants would follow, but there was never a sign of the man Paczensky sought.

The day of the contest itself arrived, and shortly after lunch Paczensky slunk through the fog of a dull December afternoon and took up his post as usual in the dingy parlour of the public house.

'Now or never,' he thought to himself, 'if what I suspect is true, Levenstein will show himself. I must satisfy myself as to the truth of whom I am going to play with tonight. Surely there must be arrangements to be made before this evening! Surely my patience will be rewarded at last!'

The excitement, which was quite general in London, had penetrated to the dingy resort where Paczensky sat waiting. He overheard one drunken fellow—obviously a professor of legerdemain by his conversation—talking to a friend with bitter envy and disdain.

'Lord love a duck!' said this individual, 'it passes my comprehension how the public can be such fools. Durante and his "It"!' He spat on the floor in envious disgust. 'If I'd the money,' he said, drinking off his glass of bitter with a flourish, 'I could get up a show every bit as good. There isn't a man in the conjuring profession who doesn't know how it is done.'

'Then why don't you expose it and get the reward, Billy?' asked his friend.

'Who's to prove it?' said the other bitterly. 'Durante is far too cunning for that, though the method is obvious enough. Wireless telegraphy, that's what it is. That there blooming figure is full of electric works. Placing it on the sheet of glass is only a blind, and because the silly jugginses of the public don't see any wires connecting the bloke what really plays the game with the figure they can't imagine how it's done. It's a little private installation of wireless telegraphy, that's all. But it can't last. They'll get tired of it soon, and small blame to 'em.'

He strode out of the room, followed by his friend.

Paczensky heard this with some interest. It seemed very likely that this was the true solution of how the Automaton was controlled, but that, after all, to him was but a minor consideration.

It was about five o'clock. With a feeling of deep disappointment and anger he was about to leave his post of observation to go back to his rooms and dress for the evening, when he suddenly saw a figure come out of the stage door—a figure which made him start and stiffen into fierce attention.

The man who came out on the quiet pavement of the bystreet was short and thickset. He wore a heavy Inverness overcoat and a soft felt hat. His face was clean shaved.

Paczensky knew in a flash of realization that his long vigil had been rewarded at last. Levenstein was a man with a long black beard and whiskers, but there was no possibility of mistaking this clean-shaved man for any other but the famous Jew. Walk, pose, the upper part of the face, all were the same. Levenstein was not in Berlin at all. He had disguised himself by shaving all the hair from his face, and he was the secret confederate of Durante!

At the sight of his rival the hatred within Paczensky's breast welled up like molten fire. Hardly knowing what he did, he slipped out of the bar and followed the other man, who walked briskly towards Piccadilly in the fog.

As he came on to the pavement of the great street two taxicabs slowly rolled along.

The man in the Inverness hailed the first, and was driven rapidly away towards the Circus.

Paczensky leaped into the second, with the direction to the driver to keep the other cab in sight, and in a moment more was being driven rapidly up Shaftesbury Avenue and in the direction of Bloomsbury.

He had no definite purpose in his mind. He did not know why he was following his enemy. There was, indeed, no room in his disordered intellect for anything but an almost maniacal fury. 'He'll beat me, will he! He'll beat me, will he!' He kept repeating to himself in a hoarse mutter. 'We'll see! We'll see!'

He was leaning back in the taxi, muttering to himself, when it came to a standstill. The driver got down and opened the door.

'He's gone in there, sir,' he said confidentially, pointing to the door of a block of flats only two or three yards away. Paczensky hurriedly thrust some coins into the man's hands and sprang into the doorway.

The flats were quite new. There was no hall porter nor lift. Stone stairs went up into the darkness, dimly lit here and there by a dull red electric bulb.

Paczensky heard footsteps echoing above him, and with the noise-lessness of a cat and with a feline rapidity of step he followed.

His feet made no sound whatever, so lightly did he walk, and he was gaining on the ascending figure rapidly, when he heard the click of a latch key in a door. He had come to the third landing, and, peeping cautiously round the corner, he saw the back of a short thickset man, who was letting himself in at a door marked twenty-four.

Paczensky withdrew his head cautiously, and in a second more heard the door close.

He stole along the passage until he came to it. His face was working with a hideous merriment, his long, bony hands clutching the air; he pirouetted with a mad and horrid glee.

Then, his yellow face one grin of malice, he tapped smartly upon the panels.

For a moment or two he heard nothing. He rapped again, this time more loudly.

Then he heard footsteps. There was a catch of the lock, and the door opened.

Levenstein had taken off his hat and overcoat, and stood there confronting the other. His keen Jewish face, strangely altered by the removal of the beard, but still unmistakable, stared in surprise for a moment. Then it became a deep, brick red. He gave a gasp of dismay and endeavoured to close the door upon the thin, quivering figure.

But it was too late. Paczensky twisted in like an eel, closed the door with his foot, and stood confronting his enemy. His eyes shone like the sun upon wet glass. His mouth jibbered; he lolled out his tongue.

' "It"!' he said. 'How are you, Mr "It"? I've unearthed you at last. It's you, then! I knew it all along.'

The Jew stood looking at him, without a single word or movement of his body. There was fear in his eyes.

At last he spoke.

'Are you mad, Paczensky?' he said in a thick voice and with some difficulty. 'What do you mean?'

'I saw you coming out of the hall,' Paczensky answered, his voice now quite soft and quiet. 'I knew all along it was you. So you think you are going to beat me tonight, do you? As you beat O'Grady, Toché, and Simpkins. You think that, do you? You devil behind a waxen mask!'

The Jew took a step backwards and opened his mouth as if to speak. As he did so Paczensky was on him with a strangled snarl.

The madman buried his long, thin fingers in the fleshy throat of his enemy. He shook the sturdy figure this way and that, as if it had been a reed, and then, with a superhuman force, flung it, an inert mass, upon the carpet of the hall.

He looked round him. The quiet hall was comfortably furnished with a hat-stand and a table of dark oak. Upon the walls were some of those trophies of savage weapons which are imported wholesale from Africa by the big furniture houses. Paczensky's eyes fell upon a brass-bound Kerri. He seized it as a monkey seizes on a nut and leaped upon the prostrate Jew, chuckling as he did so. . . .

Five minutes afterwards a thin figure sidled down the empty stairs of the flat, passed out into the square, and was swallowed up by the fog.

At eight o'clock, when Mr Simpkins, the president of the London Chess Club, called at Mr Paczensky's room in Gough Square, to escort the famous player to the Italian Hall, he found the master standing before his fireplace smoking a cigar, wearing very correct evening dress.

The remains of a good dinner, fetched from an adjacent chop house, stood upon the table, and Mr Simpkins noticed that a bottle of brandy half full, flanked by a tumbler and a syphon of soda water, was close to Paczensky's hand upon the mantelpiece. The Englishman had never seen the famous player looking so well. His eyes were bright and cheerful. In some curious way he seemed younger. A certain courtliness, as of a prince addressing an inferior, had come into his manner. There was a contagious atmosphere of coming triumph about him, which impressed the worthy Mr Simpkins enormously.

'My dear master,' he said, as they were driven towards Piccadilly, 'I am sure that victory will be yours tonight. You radiate it, positively radiate it!'

Paczensky leant back. 'Well, my dear Mr Simpkins,' he said quietly, 'I think I may say I feel assured. How this machine of Durante's is worked I do not know, and do not care. Who is behind it, who controls it, in common with the rest of the public, I am quite unable to say. But I think that tonight—I do think tonight, Simpkins—that the prestige of the Automaton will be considerably lowered!'

He rubbed his hands together with a dry chuckle, in the highest spirits.

The Italian Hall was crammed from floor to ceiling as Paczensky and Mr Simpkins, escorted by Mr Durante, with a large diamond stud in his shirt front, came upon the stage.

There was a deafening roar of applause from all parts of the theatre, and a loud chord of welcome was played by the orchestra.

In a few brief, well-chosen words Mr Durante acquainted the audience with the terms of the contest, leading Paczensky forward to the edge of the stage, and then pointing with a superb sweep of the hand to where the mysterious figure was sitting upon its sheet of glass, sideways, and in profile to the audience.

Paczensky bowed and smiled. There was something courtier-like and debonair in his manner, and many ardent chess-players, who had seen the man before, whispered and wondered to each other at the curious change and rejuvenation in the master's appearance.

Applause continued for a minute or two, and then there was dead silence.

'And now, Mr Paczensky,' said Mr Durante, 'I will invite the committee, composed of the members of the London and Metropolitan Chess Club, to take their seats on these chairs at the back. That being done, if you will sit down opposite our friend here'—he pointed to the stiff figure at the table—'the game can commence.'

Half a dozen well-known players stepped up on to the stage and sat down.

'I myself,' said Mr Durante finally, 'will now go and sit among the audience, so that no interference on my part can be suspected.'

The orchestra played another chord. Mr Durante jumped nimbly down into the stalls, and Paczensky drew up his chair and faced the Automaton.

There it sat, rather larger than the ordinary man, within a yard of him—one waxen hand poised a little above the table, the rigid face confronting him with its slight leer.

The first move fell to the Polish master—it had been drawn for by Mr Simpkins and one of the committee.

Paczensky moved out his queen's pawn two squares. Without a moment's hesitation the mechanical arm of the figure gripped a pawn and made a corresponding move.

As it did so everyone upon the stage and all the nearer portion of the audience saw that Paczensky gave a violent start. It was most marked and curious, though everyone mentally put it down to the strangeness Paczensky must be feeling at playing with this dead and yet moving thing.

It was as if a black curtain had suddenly rolled up within Paczensky's brain—a black curtain which revealed unutterable and ghastly horrors.

The wave of madness which had passed over him had gone. The most grisly hands of fear were clutching at his heart.

Mechanically he made another move.

There was a pause of a moment or two, and then, with a slow, deliberate hand the figure made another move.

Paczensky, hardly knowing what he did, moved again, and as he did so there came a little gasp of surprise from the watching chess-players at the back.

A child would not have moved so.

There was a dead silence. Then, compelled by an irresistible and overmastering impulse, the chess-player looked up at his adversary. His face was like white marble, his eyes gleamed, like those of a man upon the point of death, from unutterable, nameless fear.

He stared straight into the waxen face before him, and as he did so the smirking lineaments seemed to dissolve and change. The eyes glowed with an unearthly light, the nose became large, pendulous, and pronounced, the lips wrinkled up into a stony grin.

The hand moved, and as it did so the murderer knew that no electric fluid gave it power; an awful, brooding, vengeful presence was hidden within the smiling doll—a sinister spirit from behind the veil, swift and relentless in its message of doom.

'Check!' The figure spoke in its well-known harsh cackle. That was all the surprised and breathless audience heard. But at the word, uttered in the dreadful and familiar voice of Ernst Levenstein, the tall Pole leapt from his chair with a horrid screech of fear, which no one of that great audience who heard it will ever forget. He spun round in the centre of the stage for a moment like a tee-to-tum and then fell against the Automaton, overturning it and the chess-table with a loud, resounding clang. Amid the shouting and tumult of the startled audience the curtain fell just as Durante leaped upon the stage and endeavoured to raise the body of the chess-player. When, with the united efforts of the committee, they lifted Paczensky he was quite dead, and his face was so horrible that the stoutest-hearted among them turned away their heads.

A quarter of an hour afterwards, when, after a doctor and the policeman had been summoned, Mr Durante slipped away to a room in the roof of the building and opened the door, he stopped and stared in amazement. The room was small, and there was a chess-table surrounded by wires in the middle of it.

Clamped to the walls were various pieces of electric apparatus.

But Ernst Levenstein was not there.

# BIOGRAPHICAL NOTES
# AND SOURCES

## 1

'A Night in an Old Castle' by G[eorge] P[ayne] R[ainsford] James (1799–1860). *Eva St Clair & Other Collected Tales* (1843). A torrential writer who, in his heyday, was certainly capable of turning out three novels or more a year, James was also a sharp businessman who hoodwinked the young George Smith (of publishers Smith, Elder) into contracting to pay him £600 for any new work he submitted. Thereafter he proceeded to deluge Smith with by no means first-rate three-deckers, until the aghast publisher (still only in his early 20s) had to break the contract. James's relationships with publishers were often fraught: on one occasion, infuriated at what he considered to be a publisher's high-handedness, he challenged him to a duel. James's early work has a good deal to recommend it, being spirited, pacy, and plot-led. *Richelieu* (1829) was praised by Scott. Later in the century, however, Robert Louis Stevenson had mixed feelings about James who, he considered, could write 'a good, dull interesting honest book with a genuine old-fashioned talent in the invention when not strained, (with) a genuine old-fashioned feeling for the English language'. James's chief problem was that he ground out too much too fast. In twenty years he published nearly seventy works, mainly historical romances; he was capable, if pressed, of dashing off twenty-four pages in a four- or five-hour spell (roughly, between seven and eight thousand words). This went straight to the publisher since James found 'more spirit and interest in the work when thus written'. The novelist and critic Alfred Tresidder Sheppard (no mean historical romancer himself, especially when utilizing the Regency period) thought him an 'entirely worthy man'. In the 1880s James entered government service as a mid-echelon diplomat. He died, in Venice, of an apoplexy.

## 2

'Sir Dominick's Bargain' by J[oseph Thomas] Sheridan Le Fanu (1814–73). *All the Year Round*, 6 July 1872; *Madam Crowl's Ghost and Other Tales of Mystery* (ed. M. R. James, 1923). Like Edgar Allan Poe, though by different paths, Sheridan Le Fanu successfully married the Gothic horror tale to the puzzle story. His early mysteries were by no means detective stories, but there were problems to be solved, and solvers who pondered rather than struck on the answer by sheer chance. Le Fanu—in his 1838 short story 'A Passage in the Secret History of an Irish Countess'—dreamed up the now much-used (and abused) motif of the hermetically sealed room, in which a murder is committed, but from which the murderer escapes so that it appears he was never there in the first place. This ingenious plot—the 'locked room murder', together with a myriad variations thereof—has proved an immensely useful milch-cow to nearly 1,000 authors over the past 150 or so years (at any rate, according to Robert Adey's 1991 bibliography of the sub-genre, *Locked Room Murders and Other Impossible Crimes*). Otherwise Le Fanu wrote historical novels, gruesome melodramas (e.g. *Guy Deverell*, 1865), and highly acclaimed terror tales such as *The House by the Churchyard* (1863), *Uncle Silas* (1864), and *In A Glass Darkly* (1872), a classic volume of stories that includes 'Mr Justice Harbottle', 'Green Tea', and the vampire tale with marked lesbian overtones 'Carmilla'. Le Fanu was devoted to his wife Susanna; when she died at the relatively early age of 34, he became a virtual recluse, at the same time creating some of his most chilling stories.

## 3

'The Knightsbridge Mystery' by Charles Reade (1814–84). *The Jilt and Other Stories* (1884). In his dealings with publishers, Charles Reade was disputatious, cross-grained, and convinced of their essential perfidy ('a Briton's literary property is less safe than his home, hovel, haystack and dunghill', he once said, probably through gritted teeth). However, unlike most authors, he could afford to be, since he had a fellowship at Magdalen College, Oxford, which brought him in a useful £500 per annum. His novels were good sellers too. All this meant that he was able to maintain a degree of independence from publishers—was able to slang them fiercely in letters—unusual in authors of the period, by and large a breed put-upon and hard-done-by. He had no time for critics, either, writing to one unfortunate: 'Sir, You have ventured to contradict me on a question with regard to which I am profoundly learned, where you are ignorant as dirt.' He had a Victorian fondness for sententious, sternly admonishing, or exhortatory titles, both in his novels (e.g. *It Is Never Too Late To Mend* and *Put Yourself In His Place*) and short stories (e.g. 'There's Many A Slip 'Twixt The Cup And The Lip' and 'What Has Become Of Lord Camelford's Body?'). Reade rarely told a less than compelling story, although on occasion his narratives could get lumpy with statistics and other extraneous matter that took his fancy while in the act of composition. *The Cloister and the Hearth* (1861), his sprawling medieval saga (so long it had to be accommodated in four instead of three volumes) is generally regarded as his masterwork ('to read it is like going through the Dark Ages with a dark lantern', declared Arthur Conan Doyle), although *It Is Never Too Late To Mend* (1856) is a gripping tale told with immense gusto, full of scenes and set-pieces of compelling drama (convicts, Australian goldfields, prison sadism, suicide, money). For such a contrary and quarrelsome man Reade had his champions: 'almost a man of genius', remarked Trollope; David Christie Murray reckoned him 'a giant'.

## 4

'Paul Vargas: A Mystery' by Hugh Conway [r.n. Frederick John Fargus] (1847–85). *The English Illustrated Magazine*, April 1884; *Paul Vargas, A Mystery, and Other Tales* (1885). Fargus was a man of consequence in his home city of Bristol, where he ran the family auctioneering business (one of his tasks was to value and catalogue the celebrated Strawberry Hill collection). For most of his tragically brief life literature was a sideline. He had a gloomy and morbid imagination and was much taken with the sensation novels of Wilkie Collins, whose dense plotting techniques he admired, and utilized. His novel *Called Back* (1884) hit a public nerve. The storyline is a bizarre stew of wildly sensational motifs: beautiful girl with total amnesia; murder stumbled upon by a blind man; drugs; nihilists; a trek across Siberia; a strange tune that triggers off total recall; paranormal perception. By the end of the century well over half a million copies had been sold. This extraordinary success not only launched Fargus, as 'Hugh Conway', into the literary empyrean, but also transformed the Bristol-based firm of Arrowsmith from little more than a jobbing printer into one of the most significant publishers of the late-Victorian era, specializing in bestselling adventure and sensation (e.g. Anthony Hope's *The Prisoner of Zenda*) and the 'New Humour' (chief exponent Jerome K. Jerome). Arrowsmith swiftly issued more of Fargus's sensation novels (*Dark Days*, *Slings And Arrows*), and the rather more mainstream Macmillan took an interest, issuing *Living Or Dead* and *A Family Affair*, both in 1885—by which time Fargus himself, now residing in Monte Carlo on his well-gotten gains, was dead (tuberculosis aggravated by typhoid). A memorial tablet, including a portrait in bas-relief, was erected in Bristol Cathedral in 1886. The verse (with perhaps a touch of the highfalutin) runs:

> Heedless of fame that was, or was to be,
> No word of ours may reach him where he lies
> Beneath the glittering vault of southern skies,
> In dreamless sleep, beside a tideless sea.

## 5

'Gerald' by Stanley J[ohn] Weyman (1855–1928). *The English Illustrated Magazine*, March, 1887; *Laid Up In Lavender* (1907). Stanley J. Weyman (the 'Wey' is pronounced 'Why') was the most successful and skilled exponent of the 'swashbuckler' school of historical fiction at the turn of the century, and reaped such huge rewards from the genre that he retired from writing for a decade (1908–18), only re-emerging into the literary round when not writing became irksome. He then put swashbuckling behind him and proceeded to toss off some of his finest novels, viz. *The Great House* (1919) and *Ovington's Bank* (1922, a masterly portrayal of small-town life in the post-Regency period). In an appreciative, and relatively unjaundiced, essay in his survey of genre fiction *Bestseller* (1972), the journalist and

critic Claud Cockburn acknowledged a good many of Weyman's superior quali-
ties, particularly as a painstaking painter of character and his liking, even in his
wilder romances, for a strong degree of realism. In his early years Weyman to an
extent played the field, writing all manner of non-historical material for (in particular) *The English Illustrated Magazine*, including a long series of articles on his
ramblings in France (during which he and a companion were thrown into a country jail as spies). Urged by friends to try his hand at a contemporary domestic
novel, *à la* Trollope, he wrote *The New Rector* (1891). This was a notorious publishing disaster—although it reads well enough today.

## 6

'My First Patient' by Mabel E. Wotton (*fl.* 1855–1912). *A Pretty Radical and Other
Stories* (1890). Mabel Wotton was a 'New Woman' journalist and writer who
seems to have followed the example set by Mrs Lynn Linton, friend of Dickens,
Landor, Swinburne, and a tireless novelist and journalist who proved that a
woman's 'opinion pieces' could be as acute, incisive, and valid as a man's
(although her opinions on women's suffrage were not to be borne). Wotton's
younger contemporaries were the kinds of young women who had discovered a
fluency, and thus liberation to an extent, with the pen (possibly even the type-
writer, so late in the century). These included Helen Black, whose *Notable Women
Authors of the Day* (1893) was a bestselling guide to its subject, and Flora Klick-
mann, whose early career, in the 1890s (long before she started tending her
'flower patch'), was spent pouring out articles for the new *Windsor Magazine*
(her first novel *The Ambitions of Jenny Ingram*, before it plunges into gruesome
religiosity, gives a good picture of sub-literary life in London, in the late-
1890s/early-1900s, as experienced by a young and wide-eyed hopeful, eager to
make her mark). Wotton's first book was *Word Portraits of Famous Writers*, which
Bentley issued in 1887. Thereafter her output was varied, including novels (e.g.
*The Girl Diplomatist*, 1892), children's books (e.g. *A Nursery Idyll*, 1892, and *A Man-
nerless Monkey*, 1892), even a volume of short-short stories which John Lane took
and published as one of the last of his famous 'Keynotes' series, *Day-Books* (1898).
She wrote short stories for most of the late-Victorian monthlies, including *Temple
Bar*, Dickens's *Household Words* and its successor *All The Year Round*, Cassell's *The
Quiver*, and *Chambers's Journal*. With her last book she returned to non-fiction:
*H. B. Irving, An Appreciation* (1912).

## 7

'A Fatal Affinity' by Roy Horniman (1874–1930) and C. E. Morland (*fl.* 1895–1905).
*The Ludgate Illustrated Magazine*, July 1894. Attracted to the stage at an early age
(he appears first to have trod the boards at 13), Roy Horniman poured out plays
and playlets for the medium, at one point leasing the old Criterion Theatre,
where he put on his own work as well as that of others. He was an early

scriptwriter for the Silents, although he seems not to have utilized his own novels—which were, perhaps, too epigrammatical to transfer successfully to the silent screen. Horniman's novels are droll, witty, clever, and, in the main, hopelessly amoral. The director and screenwriter Robert Hamer recognized Horniman's talents in this direction when, 40 years after the book was first published and nearly 20 years after its author's death, he stumbled across *Israel Rank: The Autobiography of a Criminal* (1907) and, with remarkably few alterations, turned it into the Ealing classic *Kind Hearts And Coronets* (the film's last few moments are a sop to what was perceived to be the morality of the day). *Bellamy the Magnificent* (1904) is a splendid tale of reckless upper-class adultery and cuckoldry, in which master tries conclusions with manservant, and loses. Fatally. There is a hard edge to Horniman which is a useful astringent to some of the clever froth. The Great War seems to have blunted his fiction-writing. His last book is the didactic *How To Make The Railways Pay For The War; or, The Transport Problem Solved* (1916), in which he advocated an even larger network with just about everything to go on it, solutions which would doubtless find much favour today. About Horniman's collaborator here, C. E. Morland, nothing has been discovered.

## 8

'The Story of the Man with the Watches' by Arthur Conan Doyle (1859–1930). *Strand Magazine*, July 1898; *Round the Fire Stories* (1908). Doyle, at a stroke, not only transformed the short-story form but presented to the world the 'continuing character'—in the formidable shape of the master-detective Sherlock Holmes—in a far more agreeable and reader-friendly manner than anything that had gone before (e.g. Poe's C. Auguste Dupin). Ironically, Doyle detested Holmes, even though the 'wretched fellow' had made him into a wealthy man. He lavished his enthusiasm on his historical novels—'my . . . better things'—rather than his mystery and detective stories, and could not understand a public who preferred matters the other way round. His Sherlock Holmes novels are far inferior to the often brilliant short stories, Doyle finding it difficult to maintain a detective interest in an extended work without setting lengthy passages in the story's past: e.g. the Mormon section in *A Study In Scarlet* (1888); Jonathan Small's narrative in *The Sign Of Four* (1890); virtually half the entire *Valley of Fear* (1915). His best Holmes novel, *The Hound of the Baskervilles* (1903), has a distinctly thin plot and is distinctly short (*c.*60,000 words rather than the more normal 'library' length of 70,000 to 90,000 words), but has atmosphere in abundance and a riveting storyline. Some of his finest non-Holmes work may be found in the various adventures of the blustering and braggadocioc Brigadier Gerard. A seemingly uncomplicated individual, Doyle's bluff exterior perhaps hid interesting and by no means entirely plumbed depths. His family has stubbornly refused to allow access to quantities of his private papers.

## 9

'The Third Figure' by Frank Aubrey [r.n. Francis Henry Atkins] (1840–1927). *The Queen*, 11 November 1899. The name 'Frank Aubrey' was just one of three (that are known about) that cloaked the identity of Francis Atkins, all bearing his own initials. As 'Fenton Ash' and 'Fred Ashley' Atkins wrote fantasy, science fiction (his most famous book as Ash is *A Trip To Mars*, 1909), and 'lost race' yarns for the Edwardian and Georgian juvenile markets. As 'Aubrey' he wrote mainly for adults: e.g. *King of the Dead* (1903), which featured corpse-revival, and the seminal *The Devil-Tree of El Dorado* (1897), which combined the Lost Race plot with that of sentient and voracious flora, and influenced what seems like a thousand 'man-eating plant' tales from 1900 through to 1940 (he himself may in turn have been inspired by Phil Robinson's 1881 short story 'The Man-Eating Tree'). Virtually nothing certain is known about Atkins's life. He was probably brought up in South Wales, beside the Bristol Channel. He almost certainly studied to be an engineer. At one stage, in the period 1900–10, he seems to have disappeared for a short while (there are hints of an engineering firm going bankrupt, shady dealings, a possible prison term). He ceased to use the name 'Aubrey' after this time. His son was Francis Howard Atkins, who also became a writer, hiding himself (with a tip of the hat towards his father's most celebrated work) under the soubriquet 'F. St Mars'. As 'St Mars' Atkins wrote quite superb nature sketches, much admired by, amongst many others, Theodore Roosevelt (and collected in such books as *On Nature's Trail*, 1912; *The Prowlers*, 1913; *Pinion And Paw*, 1919). He, too, wrote fantasy and 'Future War' stories, and may have contributed science fiction to the monthlies using his father's 'Fenton Ash' pseudonym. He was a close friend of the critic and whilom sensation-writer John Coulson Kernahan, who wrote a moving tribute in the *Quarterly Review* when Atkins junior (a martyr to debilitating ill-health, who wrote mainly at night) died, only 38, predeceasing by some years his rather more mysterious father.

## 10

'The Yellow Box' by J[ohn] B[urland] Harris-Burland (1870–1926). *The English Illustrated Magazine*, December 1899. A fine sensation-merchant with a vivid imagination and a fluent, compelling style, Harris-Burland was nearly in the army, then nearly a man of the cloth. At Oxford he won the Newdigate Prize for 1893 with his poem 'Amy Robsart'. He trod the boards for a short period, then joined the City rat-race, becoming secretary to a number of public companies. He began writing short stories for the illustrated monthlies in the late-1890s, demonstrating almost at once a talent for the off-beat and the bizarre. Many of his novels concern tough, hard-bitten adventurers who journey to the ends of the earth to discover civilizations cut off from the rest of the world for centuries. *The Princess Thora* (1904 in the USA; issued in the UK in 1905 as *Dr Silex*) features a 'lost race' of supermen located near the North Pole. *The Gold-Worshippers* (1906 in the

USA; 1907 in the UK) concerns magic, witchcraft, and modern-day alchemy. Much of Harris-Burland's early output was issued by Greening and Everett, two publishers who certainly liked their sensation hot, and as outré as possible. Towards the end of his career, Harris-Burland was taken up by the great Amalgamated Press popular magazine editor David Whitelaw, who commissioned him to write 'long completes' (i.e. 10,000- to 20,000-word 'novels'), with a bias towards the strange, the atmospheric, the outright weird, for the *Premier Magazine*. Harris-Burland fulfilled this task with enthusiasm for three or four years.

## 11

'The Man with the Ebony Crutches' by Ward Muir (1878–1927). *The Storyteller*, February 1908. An indefatigable journalist and 'short-piece' concocter, Ward Muir began writing for the Harmsworth brothers (i.e. what was later to become the vast general-interest and fiction factory the Amalgamated Press) in the early 1900s. He swiftly graduated from lower echelon weeklies such as the *Penny Pictorial* to the rather more prestigious monthlies, including the *London Magazine*, by which time he was also writing for Pearson's, Newnes, Cassell's, and other major publishers of the day. There is evidence to show that at some stage he had some kind of staff job with Harmsworth, although this seems not to have stopped him freelancing, or writing novels, some with a bias towards the fantastic (e.g. his first novel *The Amazing Mutes*, 1910; although his most celebrated fantasy was the 'Lost Race' adventure yarn *Further East Than Asia*, issued in 1919). During the Great War, Muir joined the RAMC, reaching the rank of corporal and still managing to keep up a steady flow of war stories and real-life sketches, mostly with a medical background. His *Observations of an Orderly* (1917), an entertaining mix of grim fact and amusing fiction, was well received even by reviewers pretty well jaded with 'war stuff'. His last two books—*A Camera For Company: Adventures and Observations of an Amateur Photographer* and the novel *The Bewildered Lover*—were both published in 1928, posthumously.

## 12

'The Horror of the Automaton' by Guy Thorne [r.n. Cyril Arthur Edward Ranger Gull] (1876–1923). *The Queen*, 11 January 1913. Gull (as it seems easiest to call him) was a clever journalist with a genius for gauging the public mood, then manipulating it. His xenophobic, and in particular anti-Semitic, novel *When It Was Dark* (1903) concerns a gigantic conspiracy to prove that 'the pale Nazarene' died on the cross but did not arise from the dead; thus Christianity is based on a lie. The villain of the piece is the multi-millionaire MP and newspaper magnate Constantine Schuabe, a truly Melmottian figure in full Zionist rig who, in the end, his schemes crashing spectacularly around him, becomes a drivelling lunatic. When the Bishop of London used the book as a text for a sermon in

Westminster Abbey sales took off. Gull lived off the book for the rest of his life. He was addicted to sensation, the bulk of his output featuring the most bizarre plots and situations, even the dullest-titled of his work concealing the extraordinary (e.g. *The Oven*, 1907, which features cannibalism in suburbia). His chief obsession was God: most of his heroes 'get religion', usually after the most searing experiences. In *The Greater Power* (1915), which Gull wrote for the military publishers Gale & Polden in two weeks flat, for a bet, Captain Knothe ends up crashing through the dome of St Peter's, Rome, where he strangles a treacherous Irish Monsignor who is radioing Allied secrets to the Austrians. In the final, somewhat crowded, chapter he kills the chief villain by snapping the man's spine across his knee (a method of delivering the quietus later pilfered by Sapper for the thuggish Bulldog Drummond), his dead brother appears as an apparition, he joins the Catholic priesthood, and the love of his life enters a convent. It could not be said that Gull did not give good value for the six shillings one paid over the counter for his thrillers.

# SOURCE ACKNOWLEDGEMENT

Sir Arthur Conan Doyle, *The Man with the Watches*, from *Round the Fire Stories*, 1908, © 1996 Sheldon Reynolds, Administrator of the Conan Doyle Copyrights. Reproduced by kind permission of Jonathan Clowes Ltd., London, on behalf of Sheldon Reynolds, Administrator of the Conan Doyle Copyrights.

OXFORD

# MORE OXFORD PAPERBACKS

This book is just one of nearly 1000 Oxford Paperbacks currently in print. If you would like details of other Oxford Paperbacks, including titles in the World's Classics, Oxford Reference, Oxford Books, OPUS, Past Masters, Oxford Authors, and Oxford Shakespeare series, please write to:

**UK and Europe:** Oxford Paperbacks Publicity Manager, Arts and Reference Publicity Department, Oxford University Press, Walton Street, Oxford OX2 6DP.

Customers in UK and Europe will find Oxford Paperbacks available in all good bookshops. But in case of difficulty please send orders to the Cash-with-Order Department, Oxford University Press Distribution Services, Saxon Way West, Corby, Northants NN18 9ES. Tel: 01536 741519; Fax: 01536 746337. Please send a cheque for the total cost of the books, plus £1.75 postage and packing for orders under £20; £2.75 for orders over £20. Customers outside the UK should add 10% of the cost of the books for postage and packing.

**USA:** Oxford Paperbacks Marketing Manager, Oxford University Press, Inc., 200 Madison Avenue, New York, N.Y. 10016.

**Canada:** Trade Department, Oxford University Press, 70 Wynford Drive, Don Mills, Ontario M3C 1J9.

**Australia:** Trade Marketing Manager, Oxford University Press, G.P.O. Box 2784Y, Melbourne 3001, Victoria.

**South Africa:** Oxford University Press, P.O. Box 1141, Cape Town 8000.

# OXFORD BOOKS

# THE OXFORD BOOK OF ENGLISH GHOST STORIES

*Chosen by Michael Cox and R. A. Gilbert*

This anthology includes some of the best and most frightening ghost stories ever written, including M. R. James's 'Oh Whistle, and I'll Come to You, My Lad', 'The Monkey's Paw' by W. W. Jacobs, and H. G. Wells's 'The Red Room'. The important contribution of women writers to the genre is represented by stories such as Amelia Edwards's 'The Phantom Coach', Edith Wharton's 'Mr Jones', and Elizabeth Bowen's 'Hand in Glove'.

As the editors stress in their informative introduction, a good ghost story, though it may raise many profound questions about life and death, entertains as much as it unsettles us, and the best writers are careful to satisfy what Virginia Woolf called 'the strange human craving for the pleasure of feeling afraid'. This anthology, the first to present the full range of classic English ghost fiction, similarly combines a serious literary purpose with the plain intention of arousing pleasing fear at the doings of the dead.

'an excellent cross-section of familiar and unfamiliar stories and guaranteed to delight' *New Statesman*

## ILLUSTRATED HISTORIES IN OXFORD PAPERBACKS

## THE OXFORD ILLUSTRATED HISTORY OF ENGLISH LITERATURE

### Edited by Pat Rogers

Britain possesses a literary heritage which is almost unrivalled in the Western world. In this volume, the richness, diversity, and continuity of that tradition are explored by a group of Britain's foremost literary scholars.

Chapter by chapter the authors trace the history of English literature, from its first stirrings in Anglo-Saxon poetry to the present day. At its heart towers the figure of Shakespeare, who is accorded a special chapter to himself. Other major figures such as Chaucer, Milton, Donne, Wordsworth, Dickens, Eliot, and Auden are treated in depth, and the story is brought up to date with discussion of living authors such as Seamus Heaney and Edward Bond.

'[a] lovely volume . . . put in your thumb and pull out plums' Michael Foot

'scholarly and enthusiastic people have written inspiring essays that induce an eagerness in their readers to return to the writers they admire' *Economist*

CLASSICS

*Mary Beard and John Henderson*

This *Very Short Introduction* to Classics links a haunting temple on a lonely mountainside to the glory of ancient Greece and the grandeur of Rome, and to Classics within modern culture—from Jefferson and Byron to Asterix and Ben-Hur.

'This little book should be in the hands of every student, and every tourist to the lands of the ancient world . . . a splendid piece of work'
Peter Wiseman
Author of *Talking to Virgil*

'an eminently readable and useful guide to many of the modern debates enlivening the field . . . the most up-to-date and accessible introduction available'
Edith Hall
Author of *Inventing the Barbarian*

'lively and up-to-date . . . it shows classics as a living enterprise, not a warehouse of relics'
*New Statesman and Society*

'nobody could fail to be informed and entertained—the accent of the book is provocative and stimulating'
*Times Literary Supplement*

# POLITICS

*Kenneth Minogue*

Since politics is both complex and controversial it is easy to miss the wood for the trees. In this Very Short Introduction Kenneth Minogue has brought the many dimensions of politics into a single focus: he discusses both the everyday grind of democracy and the attraction of grand ideals such as freedom and justice.

'Kenneth Minogue is a very lively stylist who does not distort difficult ideas.'
Maurice Cranston

'a dazzling but unpretentious display of great scholarship and humane reflection'
Professor Neil O'Sullivan, University of Hull

'Minogue is an admirable choice for showing us the nuts and bolts of the subject.'
Nicholas Lezard, *Guardian*

'This is a fascinating book which sketches, in a very short space, one view of the nature of politics . . . the reader is challenged, provoked and stimulated by Minogue's trenchant views.'
*Talking Politics*

# ARCHAEOLOGY

*Paul Bahn*

'Archaeology starts, really, at the point when the first recognizable 'artefacts' appear—on current evidence, that was in East Africa about 2.5 million years ago—and stretches right up to the present day. What you threw in the garbage yesterday, no matter how useless, disgusting, or potentially embarrassing, has now become part of the recent archaeological record.'

This Very Short Introduction reflects the enduring popularity of archaeology—a subject which appeals as a pastime, career, and academic discipline, encompasses the whole globe, and surveys 2.5 million years. From deserts to jungles, from deep caves to mountain-tops, from pebble tools to satellite photographs, from excavation to abstract theory, archaeology interacts with nearly every other discipline in its attempts to reconstruct the past.

'very lively indeed and remarkably perceptive . . . a quite brilliant and level-headed look at the curious world of archaeology'
Professor Barry Cunliffe,
University of Oxford

# A Very Short Introduction

## BUDDHISM

*Damien Keown*

'Karma can be either good or bad. Buddhists speak of good karma as "merit", and much effort is expended in acquiring it. Some picture it as a kind of spiritual capital—like money in a bank account—whereby credit is built up as the deposit on a heavenly rebirth.'

This Very Short Introduction introduces the reader both to the teachings of the Buddha and to the integration of Buddhism into daily life. What are the distinctive features of Buddhism? Who was the Buddha, and what are his teachings? How has Buddhist thought developed over the centuries, and how can contemporary dilemmas be faced from a Buddhist perspective?

'Damien Keown's book is a readable and wonderfully lucid introduction to one of mankind's most beautiful, profound, and compelling systems of wisdom. The rise of the East makes understanding and learning from Buddhism, a living doctrine, more urgent than ever before. Keown's impressive powers of explanation help us to come to terms with a vital contemporary reality.'
Bryan Appleyard

# JUDAISM

## *Norman Solomon*

**Oxford
Paperback
Reference**

## OXFORD PAPERBACK REFERENCE

From *Art and Artists* to *Zoology*, the Oxford Paperback Reference series offers the very best subject reference books at the most affordable prices.

Authoritative, accessible, and up to date, the series features dictionaries in key student areas, as well as a range of fascinating books for a general readership. Included are such well-established titles as Fowler's *Modern English Usage*, Margaret Drabble's *Concise Companion to English Literature*, and the bestselling science and medical dictionaries.

The series has now been relaunched in handsome new covers. Highlights include new editions of some of the most popular titles, as well as brand new paperback reference books on *Politics*, *Philosophy*, and *Twentieth-Century Poetry*.

With new titles being constantly added, and existing titles regularly updated, Oxford Paperback Reference is unrivalled in its breadth of coverage and expansive publishing programme. New dictionaries of *Film*, *Economics*, *Linguistics*, *Architecture*, *Archaeology*, *Astronomy*, and *The Bible* are just a few of those coming in the future.